D1736146

MESSALINA:
DEVOURER OF MEN
by Zetta Brown

ISBN: 978-1-905091-11-9

Published by Logical-Lust Publications www.logical-lust.com © 2008
Cover image by Helen E. H. Madden www.pixelarcana.com © 2008

ACKNOWLEDGEMENTS

Here's where I say a big THANK YOU to those people who put up with me during the process of writing this book:

Anne Drake (aka "The Goddess of All Things Computer"), Laura Parker Castoro for her mentoring and friendship; Melanie Eversley, Judi McCoy and Leslie Brown for their suggestions early on in the process; Cindy Passmore Malone, Krissy Guajardo, Suzy Koehler McMillan, J.C., and Ben Eden for reading the first *complete* draft, and finally, Rachel McIntyre for her editing and putting it all together.

Thanks to y'all—it's finally finished!

TO JIM

"YUM"

CHAPTER ONE

▲

"DARK PLACES"

My name is Evadne Cavell and I am a sex goddess.

At least that's what I keep telling myself.

For me, sex is a compulsion. Some want chocolate, I want sex, preferably anonymous sex, and I attempt to control myself by having rules. I can look and I can touch, but no names, no body fluids and no penetration. As a result, it's been over three years since I've had proper, hard-banging, toe-curling sex. That's when my fever comes because my sexual frustration is at a point where anything I see gets me aroused, but I act as if the word FRIGID is wrapped around my waist like a chastity belt.

As if I need one. I've been on enough blind dates, and placed and answered enough personal ads to realize when I'm being used as practice until something better comes along.

But let me say something else: There is a direct link between Denver's historic movie palaces and my sex life. For example, at the age of seventeen I saw *The Rocky Horror Picture Show* at The Ogden Theater as a "virgin" and was sacrificed on the altar of the Sweet Transvestite.

This led to my first act of defiance against my parents when I dyed my hair red, got tattooed, and every Friday for a year, I played the role of Columbia for the movie audience. I acted shamelessly with those people and lost a few friends when I began dating some of the white boys. Not only was I playing against type, I got a reputation as a black girl "playing in the snow."

I saw it as expanding my tastes.

Now, I'm thirty-five. The Ogden no longer shows movies, but my love for films still provides crucial access to my sexual nature.

Today, on this summer afternoon in early June, I sit in the second-floor lobby of The DeLuxe Theater waiting for the next showing of an animation festival. As usual, part of me is nervous at the thought of getting caught but this just makes another part of me wet with anticipation. I drum my fingers on the tabletop and look at my watch.

Twenty minutes to go.

I'm dressed in an outfit as liberating as it is confining that would scandalize anyone who knew me. Wearing a white linen shell with a red cashmere sweater and black ankle-strap shoes, I resemble one of those Parisian Apache dancers. My black cotton pencil-skirt is so tight and thin I suspect that I'll be leaving a damp spot on the red vinyl seat.

Thanks to my African heritage, I have no need for spray-painted tans or silicon implants. And although I give off signals as eye candy saying *Eat me*, I'm a size 20 in a size zero world with my full, rounded hips, the sharp dips at my waist and the paunch of my belly.

My size isn't the only reason why it's been three years since my last fuck. Family and work have made things difficult too. If I could live away from them both, I would be a poor, but happy, slut having sex whenever and with whomever I liked. But I can't turn my back on my responsibilities just to get laid. That's not how my parents raised me.

I'm the youngest child of the Cavell family, with its close ties in artistic and civic circles. I'm also an assistant professor at Bellingham College and one of the few African-American instructors there hoping for tenure. My behavior doesn't mesh with the College's increasingly conservative image. Any hint of "impropriety," to quote my boss, would not be welcomed.

It's nobody's business anyway. I'm just trying to get by living the life of a shy exhibitionist. I may dress plainly for the sake of my job and to cover my biker-babe-Betty Boop tattoo, but that's during the week.

I can look at anybody and see them naked—see them having sex, writhing and grunting and coming. Most of the time, the person I'm watching is the last person I'd want to see naked, but sometimes, I'll be spying on some man so intently that I get moist between my legs or cramp like I've come really hard. It's gotten to the point where I have to wear sunglasses so people can't see me observing them. I keep my expression bland and neutral. I am passion under ice. Except, once a week, on my day off, when I allow myself to thaw out.

I shudder despite myself. Enticing men in a theater for a bit of slap and tickle is not the way to conduct a happy, healthy sex life. But there's something thrilling about sitting in a dark room with other people all facing the same direction with our eyes, supposedly, focused on the screen. The darkness allows fingers to fumble with buttons, zippers, and other obstacles that prevent flesh-on-flesh contact. Darkness allows nimble digits to circle around a man's swollen pride or spread apart the vertical lips of a woman's secret. Suddenly, the room brightens because of a scene change and, depending on level of nerve, fingers recoil to their proper, prayer-clasped position on your lap or they probe deeper, squeeze harder . . . get wetter. I never wear panties to the theater. A quick rub adds more spice to an Italian film, or makes a French movie saucier.

I've been coming to the matinee at The DeLuxe for just over three years, and ever since I've started these anonymous encounters, there has been an increase in the number of single men coming to the same showing. Don't they have jobs? Where do they come from? Is it the warm weather, because in the winter, I can never get a hook up. It's a bit disconcerting because there's hardly a place less exotic to release my pent up sexual pressure, but at least it's an escape from mainstream movie dreck.

The DeLuxe is the sole, surviving business in a failed strip mall. Converted from a warehouse supermarket, it houses three screens, a split-level coffee shop, and a café. The décor is faux movie palace but *true* movie palaces, like The Mayan in Denver, have nothing to worry about. For a suburban theater, it's survived. But for how long? I'm too chicken to go to the porno arcade across town and terrified about running into someone I know here. What would I do if it happened at the porno theater? But I need some sense of closeness to let me know I'm still alive, if only from deep inside, and The DeLuxe makes me feel a little less cheap.

The following scenario happens almost every week with little variation—like clockwork.

Some man reads my signals in the lobby and suspects I'm looking for action, which is true, but on my terms. He follows me inside the theater and sits beside me despite the vast number of empty seats.

Mr. X will then put his arm around the back of my seat. I ignore him. His hand will rest on my knee. I keep my eyes looking forward. His fingers will push aside the material of my skirt and start exploring. Within twenty minutes of the movie starting, he knows I'm not going to resist. He tries to kiss me but I don't let him. Sometimes he'll whisper, asking if he can take me to a motel—or worse—he tries to mount me in my seat. I'll shake my head and push him away. So he ends up finger-fucking me. I'll feel an orgasm on the rise but it's over before it starts because that's when I realize how pathetic I am for doing this. I've become skilled at faking orgasms just to get things over with. But I'll give the guy a hand job, just to be polite, and he always comes.

When the film ends, I exit as quickly as possible. I have no idea what the man looks like, whether he's young or old, married or single and I don't care. I never look him in the face.

This is my problem and I need to stop before I find myself raped or my disguise as an upstanding citizen is blown.

The latter nearly happened a few weeks ago just before the movie started. My "partner" for the day had just sat down beside me when someone called my name.

"Dr. Cavell?"

Ice water filled my veins and I looked up to see the smiling face of a young woman with red hair, wire-rimmed glasses, and wearing a patchwork halter top that matched her patchwork jeans.

"I thought that was you! It's me, Meghan Cross. I was in your freshman seminar last semester."

"Ah, yes, Meghan. How are you?"

"I'm fine. I didn't know you came to the matinees here." She looked around the theater. "Great, isn't it?"

"Yes it is." I glanced at the man beside me and for the first time, I got a real look of my companion with his three-hair comb over, short-sleeved shirt and polyester, never-crease pants. He looked at us with wide, scared eyes. Considering I was dressed in a lightweight summer dress and a bra that boosted my assets, I'm surprised people didn't mistake us for a hooker with her john. Meghan caught my glance and laughed.

"Oh! I'm sorry. I didn't mean to disturb you. I'd better go anyway," she indicated over her shoulder, "my friends are waiting for me down front."

"Well, it was nice seeing you again, Meghan."

"You, too, Dr. Cavell. See you on campus."

I cringed when she said my name again and watched her trot down the aisle; the patches on the back pockets of her threadbare jeans emphasized her youthful, firm bottom.

The whole incident rattled me so much that, instead of it taking twenty minutes for the man to get his hands on me, it took thirty. It was also the day I started to think more seriously about the effects of my little compulsions. I resolved to stop. Who needs a man when you have hands and batteries? When I get the urge, I could satisfy myself.

And it worked. For two weeks, it worked.

Fast forward to today and here I am, back at the theater.

This place has become part of my life. It lets me enjoy my love for dark places and my need for anonymous fun, because in the dark, no one has to know or get hurt.

It's just so *naughty*, as my friend Tony would say—if he knew—but I like hiding in plain sight. I'm addicted to it, and right now, I need a hit.

Unfortunately, it doesn't look like I picked the best day to get it. The lobby is empty, there's no one hanging around downstairs and I didn't see any stray men hanging about like I usually do. My finger drumming increases so I take in my surroundings to distract myself.

Twenty minutes to go.

The space around me is dark save for the table where I sit that's located under a skylight. But I can see the polished, black concession stand glowing under the neon lights and from the constant wiping of a bartender dressed in a white starched shirt. Watching him wipe a circular groove into the counter top, I sigh, mesmerized. Round and round his arm goes and his movements reflect my life. From work to theater and back again, this pattern composes the two halves of my world, and although they're part of the same design, they never intersect.

I continue to nurse my cup of cappuccino and try to figure out if I have batteries at home. Sometimes not even hard vibrating plastic can compensate when you're in the mood for flesh. Looks like I'm going to have settle for a date with "The Bruiser" and take him out of his box when I get home.

"Excuse me, ma'am?"

My arm jolts and upsets my coffee. I see a tall man approach from out of the shadows. Then he starts to mop up my drink.

"I'm sorry I frightened you. Let me buy you another."

"What? Another skirt?" I frown as I wipe myself. "No, that's quite all right."

He chuckles. "Now I would love to buy you things, but I meant another coffee."

I couldn't help but give a short laugh and allow a tiny smile at his comeback. Squinting my eyes against the sun, I shake my head. "There's plenty left."

"Yeah, but the thrill leaves once the cream's gone."

Turning aside to toss several used napkins onto a vacant table, when I look back, he's sitting across from me.

"Did you want something?" I ask through clenched teeth accompanied by an insincere smile. The sun slicing through the small skylight gives me a better look at him and I try to figure out if I've seen him on campus.

He wears jeans and a blue Oxford shirt with the sleeves rolled up. His body is athletic but not muscle-bound. His face is what I would call boyish. He has a sharp, angular jaw line, full, sensuous—dare I say "feminine"—lips, a straight nose, and a long neck that, despite my annoyance, begs me to bite into it. In fact, his doesn't look too masculine at all. I smirk. He's probably gay . . . or bi. Just what I friggin need.

But what takes my breath away are his eyes—two glowing amethysts fringed with long dark lashes. I never believed eyes like that were possible but something beneath those irises burns making them incandescent as I look into them. Suddenly I want to bend in all sorts of bizarre positions. My skin gets hot. I think I'm blushing.

A disarming smile creates twin dimples by the corners of his mouth and he leans closer. His auburn hair, violet eyes, and the direct sunlight intensify the contrasts of his appearance with startling effect.

"Please don't take this the wrong way," he says, "but I've been watching you for the last fifteen minutes."

I frown. This is not part of the plan. Erotic thoughts or not, I level a gaze on him like a government employee asked to work on a holiday. But his confident manner has an edge that his smooth, easygoing voice belies, and I think I detect a Southern accent in his voice.

"No, please, don't be angry." He smiles and places a sketchpad before me. "I want to show you something."

I crane my neck to look at the sketch and my guard eases. An annoying sunbeam has been blinding me as I sit here and I must've been looking straight at him without realizing it.

He's caught me from the front but at a slight angle. The drawing is in a film noir style but it's definitely me. He even put a sparkle in the pupils of my half-closed eyes and colored the brown of my skin and the blush of my mouth. The composition is divided diagonally as a result of the sunbeam making one side dark, with just a hint of my face, whereas the other side is light and contains most of the drawing. I look mysterious and coy as if poking my face out of the shadows to drink my coffee. My lips look so sensual making an "O" to blow the steam rising from my cup. Considering the atmosphere of the theatre and the main attraction, it's very appropriate. The only other drawing I've seen of myself was a caricature done when I was seven years old. I've come a long way. I glance up at him and his smile broadens. But when I laugh, he frowns.

"Have I done you an injustice, ma'am?" His tone is icy and formal. Not that I blame him. If I found fault with his talent, all of my taste is in my mouth.

"No, I'm just surprised, that's all." I glance up at him. "Is that how I look?"

He nods and his smile is back again. His gaze on me intensifies, pinning me to my seat.

"You are a very attractive woman. Your features are symmetrical, balanced. More people than you can imagine have something out of proportion or off-center."

I blink. I've never heard myself described as "symmetrical" before. And that is a southern accent. Sort of Matthew McConaughey-ish with a slight twang, subtle but it's there. Jared makes a sound too guttural for a sigh and my PC muscles clench.

"Your skin glows. It reminds me of a chamois . . . all pale brown and soft."

His lips curve into a crooked smile that's almost too smug for my tastes, and I smirk. Yeah, this man knows he's got it going on.

"Well, that's very nice . . . the sketch." I push the notebook back across the table to him.

"Jared Delaney." He extends his hand. I look at it first with suspicion, then with scrutiny. I don't want conversation, just a hand up my skirt. His fingers are not too thick and not too thin. Three or four would fill me nicely. I smile.

"Evadne Cavell." Accepting the gesture and ignoring the charcoal smudges on his fingers, his hand encircles mine like a warm glove.

"Are you here for the show or have you been?" he asks.

"Both. This is my second time."

"You're an animation buff?"

"Yes." I say, slightly embarrassed. "Animation is art."

"I agree. It's what I do, actually."

"Really?" I grin. "Any of your . . . work . . . ?"

Laughing, he shakes his head. His laugh is rich, velvety, with a slight huskiness to it that tells of a history of smoking—recent or past—and the sound has me curling my toes in my shoes with desire.

"I haven't attempted film on my own, yet." He leans back in his seat to make himself comfortable. When he crosses his legs I see cowboy boots coming from beneath faded blue jeans. Not the flashy kind you may expect a country western singer to wear, but boots that are worn and comfortable from use. "You know a bit about art, then?"

"I was an art history major—briefly—until I decided that the best way for me to keep my appreciation is from an amateur's view." Smiling, I reach for the sugar dispenser and sense his eyes watching my every move. "I teach at Bellingham College."

"Ah . . . the land of the Bellingham Bucks."

"Yes," I sigh dramatically. Bellingham is a private college of about 2,800 students where the financial aid office is only there for students to get money out of their trust funds or from their parents in amounts too big for an ATM. Our mascot is the mule deer.

"Listen, Evadne, I can't sit and watch you try and drink that coffee anymore. I'll be back."

He is heading for the concession stand before I can put down the sugar dispenser leaving me to enjoy the presentation of his ass in his jeans as he walks. He moves with a fluidity of motion that reminds me of something.

A cat. Not the domestic kind, but one of the big cats walking in long strides. He may call me symmetrical but his features are easy on the eyes too.

He returns and shifts his chair closer to mine to get out of the sun. He smiles as he presents me with my drink. He's bought one for himself too. I'm about to blow the steam away and he's watching me again. I have to close my eyes to drink.

When I open them, he's still looking at me. Using a tactic I haven't felt compelled to use in years, I lick my lips while maintaining his gaze. His eyes follow every movement as the tip of my tongue slides from right to left over my upper lip. My breathing quickens. His vibes are far from subtle, but from the way he sits straight in his chair, he is holding back. Slowly, he raises his eyes to meet mine.

"I've seen you here before, you know."

I freeze for a moment, but soon recover then put down my cup. "I beg your pardon?"

"I've seen you—here—before. Several times." He takes a sip of his coffee not minding that he's just uncovered my greatest fear: the fear of discovery. "Frankly, I'm surprised you're alone."

I look at him again, hard, my brain cycling through all the faculty, departmental, and staff meetings to try and place his face. I can't.

"Who are you?"

He laughs but not in a derisive way and turns in his seat to face me. Once again his mouth turns up in a smile making me wonder if his lips are as soft as they look. His knee brushes against my thigh sending a spark of electricity up my spine.

"Don't look so scared, Evadne. Your secret is safe with me."

"And what secret would that be?"

"Do you really have to ask?"

"I think I do." Even I couldn't resist smiling as he gives me a knowing look. I twist my upper body in his direction and rest my arm on the back of my chair. As expected, Jared takes in the presentation of my cleavage but only for a moment. "I'm not used to conversation."

"Well that's a shame. A pretty thing like you is bound to have something to say." He winks and turns away to take another sip of coffee. His lower lip looks full and succulent as it supports the rim of his cup. The muscles in his neck flex as he swallows. I would love to bite that neck. Mark him.

"Do you think?"

"Come on, Evadne." Smiling, he faces me. "Don't sell yourself short. You may try to look easy, but you're not. You have taste. I can tell from the films you see—viewing companions not included." He winks at me again and I get butterflies in my stomach. "You carry yourself like a queen. And girl," he says, shaking his head, "there are some things you can't learn off the street."

This time it's my turn to laugh. "You're very observant."

"It's what I do, darlin'."

This time there's no hint of playfulness in his tone and we sit, taking each other in. For the first time I notice something else about Jared's gaze. Although clear and open, his eyes are still dark enough as not to give everything away.

In the silence, we hear the downstairs lobby fill with patrons. He looks back over his shoulder, once again giving me a view of his neck. "The film's letting out." He smiles and stands. "Shall we go?"

"It depends," I say while taking a napkin to wipe the corner of my mouth. I raise my head to look up at him and give a playful smile. "What do you think of my viewing companion now?"

In response I am treated to a flash of his white, even teeth in a grin that would melt the resolve of the coldest virgin.

"I also said you had taste."

And with that, he pulls my chair out, places his hand on the small of my back and escorts me downstairs. Maybe it's a measure of my excitement, but his touch burns through my sweater and beads of sweat form on my skin beneath his touch.

Inside the theater I estimate about thirty other people have decided to catch this matinee. We take our seats in the center section, four rows from the back. A few minutes later, the lights go out.

During the film I try to concentrate but can't help glancing at my watch. It's been nearly an hour and he hasn't tried anything. Apart from pushing up the armrest to remove any barrier between us, he hasn't touched me. We're just two people enjoying a movie together. But watching a movie with a man who's not feeling me up is a new experience for me and I can't help stealing side-glances at him.

He's different from other men, that's for damn sure. He had the balls to come up and start a real conversation, and what a pick-up too. I'll give him an A+ for that. My palms are sweating and, between my legs, I feel hot and empty—and wet.

He turns his head and catches me spying. He grins like I just sprang his trap. I turn away. His right arm goes around the back of my seat and he leans over to whisper.

"Evadne, it's OK if you look."

When I turn in his direction, his face is so close to mine I can feel it when he exhales. The scent of his cologne mixing with the coffee he just drank makes my mouth water. I close the distance. Our kiss is gentle, unhurried and tastes of chocolate and coffee. He gently takes hold of my chin to deepen our kiss.

"I knew those lips had to be delicious," he says when we part to take a breath. His hand goes up the back of my neck and into my hair. I lean into the caress, exposing my throat, letting his lips linger on my neck. His tongue tickles along the surging throb of my pulse. I sigh and my hand falls to the side split of my skirt. Pushing the thin material over, I slide my fingers up between my legs.

His long eyelashes flutter against my throat as he opens his eyes to see what I'm doing. Then I feel his hand, warm and soft, reach over to cup under my knee. He crooks my leg over his and I moan softly when he places his hand on mine. What sounds like my voice growls "yes" loud enough for him to take his cue and gently press our fingers inside me.

My head lolls back against his arm as my private entrance admits us, hand in hand, with my small forefinger next to his long, thick, middle and forefingers. We work together to build a rhythm and his thumb gently rubs the top of my clitoris. My hips jerk up and I gasp. He increases his hold on me while clamping his mouth onto my neck, just like the big cats do to restrain their prey.

His lips open to suck in the flesh of my neck into his mouth before biting down. His teeth dig in and hold before releasing and repeating the process. He's found my weak spot. I have a thing for necks and, although they may look trashy, I love hickies. These malignant bruises serve as the calling cards of heavy petting. I love giving and receiving them. But despite his amorous assault on my neck, I get caught up with the feel of his two, three—four—fingers pumping inside me.

Aww—*fuck*! He's about to get a real orgasm out of me! It's evident by the moist, sucking sounds coming from me. I'm almost there.

"God damn, Evadne, you're so wet," he says with such awe it only thrills me more and this time my groan is louder than expected.

My eyelids pop open and I remember we are not alone. Focusing my eyes, I count less than six people sitting in the rows behind us but they're on the opposite side of the theater. From what I can tell, they're all watching the screen. Then I see one man sitting in the row directly behind us but several seats to the left.

He wears a white T-shirt and stares directly at us, unashamed. Hearing a muted, squelching sound, I glance down and see his lightweight jacket lying across his lap, bobbing up and down.

Catching my breath, I don't know whether to stop Jared and bring the man to his attention. But he's about to rip a climax from me and I'll be damned if I'm going to sacrifice it. I open my mouth slightly in expectation, so does Jerk-Off Man who mouths the words *I love you* as his hand pumps harder and faster.

Instead of moaning, I scowl at our voyeur and his face crumbles as he shoots his wad. I make sure he sees me take Jared's earlobe into my mouth to nibble on it and I think, Yeah, buddy you wish you could have some of this. Jared moans and licks at my throat in return.

"Touch me," he begs from against my neck and his strained voice startles me. I reach between his legs and encounter a sharp rise in his jeans. He moves back and I unzip his pants and fumble for the opening. Once inside, I give his swollen cock a squeeze and he sighs as if I've done him a great favor.

"Oh, yes," he whispers and rests his forehead against my temple.

A slight tug gets his whole length out. His cock is getting thicker as blood rushes to swell it, making the skin tight. My God, it feels lovely, like a thick pipe wrapped in warm suede. Then, as to be expected, a scene change lights up the room, allowing me a better look.

During my theater adventures, I have encountered a lot of men of different races and have concluded that there is no accurate way to guess a man's penis size by looks alone. You have to experience him, literally, first hand.

And my chest heaves at the thought of getting fucked senseless by his cock. It's long and thick and the tip of its swollen head is moist. I lick my lips, wishing for a taste—but that goes against my rules.

His thumb presses my clitoris once again and I have to bury my face in the curve of his neck to keep from crying out. I grab his wrist and start guiding him, pumping his hand, making him fist fuck me harder, faster, and when he touches my clit again, I come, for the first time in ages, all over his creative, talented fingers.

The world falls out from under me and I'm on a roller coaster going down a bottomless pit. My orgasm goes on and on, overflowing and spilling onto the seat.

"Ah, lovely," he sighs. "That's it, sugar. Oh, *yes*, darlin'. . . give it to me."

And I do. I want to. But I'm not going to be alone in this. I pump my fist tighter and faster along his cock until his essence drips onto my hand providing me with just enough to lubricate my strokes. Jared thrusts, ever so slightly and I apply more pressure to increase the friction.

He turns my face to his and stabs his tongue far into my mouth, leaning into me, and I push back until I'm nearly climbing on top of him instead. He gives a moan of surprise against my mouth, driving his tongue deeper and I thrust my hips so his fingers can delve farther.

This man, whom I've met just over an hour ago, has gotten me more aroused than I have been in my life. But I'm not the only one excited. The skin of his penis is tight. He's going to explode.

"Mmm, that's right, baby." I smile against his lips before they crush mine again, taking my tongue deep inside his mouth. Sparks of purple, yellow, and green flash behind my eyelids. Suddenly, he thrusts his hips and thick, warm jet streams of cream erupt against my skirt and seeps through to my thighs. He shudders against me and releases his pent-up breath in a low, guttural moan and relaxes. My loins weep against his hand for being left out, but—after all—we've just met.

He collapses back into his seat, and holding his gaze, I remove his hand from my crotch. The wet, sucking sound lets us both know that he's plowed me deep and it was well received. I wipe his hand on the exposed flesh of my cleavage and daintily kiss the tip of each of his fingers to say thank you, tasting my spice on them.

"Good God," he rasps out, his eyes wide with surprise as he playfully twists his pinkie inside my mouth before I let it slip from my lips.

Grinning, I gently place his cock back inside his trousers. When I look up at the screen, the cartoon selection from Poland is ending. There's only one more film clip remaining. My heart is racing. I cross my legs and sit back in my seat, trembling, still feeling the sensation of Jared's fingers deep inside me along with the wake of my orgasm. That was not petting—that was sex. The best sex I've ever had. I look at him. He's leaning back, his face toward the ceiling, looking like he's either asleep or in desperate need of a cigarette.

By the time the house lights come on ten minutes later, we are composed and with our clothes in order. I've tied my sweater around my waist to hide the wet stain on my skirt.

Although the lights aren't harsh, they're strong enough to shatter the bubble we created around ourselves and I feel exposed. Keeping my eyes on the floor, I rush into the aisle. Jared doesn't touch my back like before. I'm not sure if he's even behind me.

Entering the lobby, I walk on shaky legs out the front doors. Standing on the sidewalk, I see that rush hour has started and the road in front of the strip mall is thick with traffic.

Leaving the dark, air-conditioned surroundings of The DeLuxe only to be slapped in the face by smog and dry heat is too much. My stomach churns and my head starts to throb. I start to walk away.

"Hey! Hold up!"

I turn and see Jared approaching with a smile on his lips. We can now finish our assessments of each other without the hindrance of shadow. I estimate him to stand about six-feet-four because I'm five-feet-ten. But in my three-inch heels, I'm almost eye level with him. His thick, dark, chestnut hair curls up as it touches his collar and stylishly frames his face. I can easily imagine how he'd look with his hair all wet after taking a shower or plastered with sweat after an afternoon of passionate sex.

Ooh, how I wanted to be the one to work up that sweat! But I can't. I've been naughty enough for one day. My fever has passed and now I must control myself until next week.

But what I assumed earlier about his not being masculine is wrong. His skin is slightly sun-tanned and, boyish face aside, Jared is all man. By the way he walks, with those long, smooth strides, he's more than sure of himself.

And those eyes.

Perhaps *those eyes* are still adjusting to the sunlight because his pupils are big despite our being outside. Could he be on drugs? Maybe. He is an artist after all. But I dismiss the thought as quickly as it comes. He simply likes what he sees and I probably look like a prostitute from the 1950s with my tousled hair and smeared lipstick. All that's missing is a Lucky Strike hanging from my mouth as I wait for him to press a $20 bill in my palm.

"Care to join me for dinner?"

My jaw drops open and, in a momentary lapse of cool, I must resemble a bug-eyed fish out of water. This isn't the first time I've gotten an invitation like this. Darkness makes it easy. I can usually change their mind with a withering stare, but this time, I'm truly speechless.

I go to the movies to abandon myself, content to leave my fantasies inside the building. The fantasy is not supposed to ask me to dinner. That's against the rules. My rules.

OK, so I've been selective with the rules today—but this isn't supposed to happen! I have reduced my appreciation for men into faceless gadgets requiring batteries, or faceless men in a dark theater.

Faceless. Why couldn't he just remain faceless, sit next to me in the dark, and leave without introducing himself? I could've beaten a quick retreat without remorse. We both could have. But Jared is all flesh and waits for my answer. He also knows my name . . . and where I work.

Shit.

If ever I needed a reason to stop doing this, I have found it.

I'm about to reply when Jerk-Off Man comes out of the theater. He sees me and walks in our direction. I frown but he keeps walking with a half smirk, half grimace on his face as he passes.

"Is something wrong?" Jared asks.

"What? Oh! No, I'm fine." I get my keys out of my purse and head towards my car.

"Well?" he asks again, his long strides easily matching mine.

"Sorry?" I'm playing for time. I really have no contingency for such a development. I've even lost my ability in telling a man to fuck off. We reach my car. I'm about to put my key in the lock when he grabs my arm.

"Are you free for dinner?"

I drop my keys. He immediately crouches down and picks the spiked jumble off my foot. His gaze burns through the sheer material of my skirt and seems to focus on the damp apex between my legs. I shiver.

Standing upright again, he places the keys in my hand and we touch. My body heat activates the lingering scent of the orgasm I used to perfume my chest and when he inhales deep and takes a step closer, my breath catches in my throat. I need to slow the man down.

"No," I lie. "Ahh—my cat got spayed today. I have to go pick her up."

I can only describe his look as stunned disbelief. A flicker of disappointment, or is that resentment, crosses his face. He purses his lips into a thin line, and, with a sweep of his hand in a gesture I suspect he's done since childhood, he combs back the hair that's falling over into his eyes and huffs through his nostrils.

"I see."

Suddenly it occurs to me that few people—or specifically, few women—have ever denied him anything. Then again, he's never met me.

And I'm in no condition to follow up what we just did with casual conversation.

"Seriously, Jared I do have to go."

"Well then tell me, Evadne, do you plan on coming here next week?" he asks, raising an eyebrow in doubt, but there's a touch of eagerness in his voice.

"Listen." I look around the parking lot to see if there's anyone watching. "Let me give you my number. Call me later."

I reach into my purse and find a pen and a piece of paper. For a split second I thought about giving him a fake number, but when I look up to see him watching me so intently with those damn eyes—I give him the real digits. He'd make an excellent lie detector with eyes like that. Besides, if I was good at denying myself what I want, I wouldn't be coming to this place to get my kicks . . . I'd probably be a size zero too.

"Borrow your pen?" he asks and takes my pen in such a way that he grasps my hand with moist, sticky fingers and leaves a smudge of charcoal on my flesh. He writes his number on the back of the sketch.

"Well, Jared." I smile, trying to act casual as I open my car door. "Hope to hear from you soon." Perhaps I sound trite, because his reply isn't convincing.

"Yeah. Sure."

CHAPTER TWO

"TGI THURSDAY"

With my hands behind my back, I take a step away from the desk, move away from the podium, and slowly walk to the front of the room. Before me are five rows with five desks each. Ten of them support the bodies of students who claim they want to take a summer seminar about cultural criticism.

For two hours a day, Monday through Thursday, over a period of six weeks, I get students who sit here during the best time of the year only to end up wasting my time.

Well, shit. We assistant professors have other things we'd rather be doing too.

Plus, it's been a week and still no call from Jared. I haven't been back to the theater since and my "fever" is back with a vengeance. I could call him, but why? I need to keep focused. I started at Bellingham College five years ago, and after a year as associate professor, I was made an assistant professor and have been on the tenure-track. I can't afford to let myself get distracted by trivial things like daydreaming about sex. I need to exploit my mind not my body.

A strand of hair escapes the confines of my French roll and tickles the base of my neck, as if scolding me for making it behave so primly. I tuck it in and return my attention to the classroom.

I take off my glasses, close my eyes, and repress a moan. The hum of the electric clock on the wall behind me and street sounds seeping in between the window panes are the only things breaking the silence. Putting my glasses back on, I look straight ahead and out of the windows at the back of the classroom. It offers me a picturesque view of the green lawns of Bellingham College. Outside, the tree branches bloom and dangle above the heads of my students, but the branches aren't the only things that appear to be above their heads. I sigh.

"Let's try a simpler approach. Those of you who've never seen *I Love Lucy*, hands up."

Six out of ten hands go up.

"I will repeat the question. Hands up for those of you who have not seen *I Love Lucy*—ever."

Three out of six.

"In your entire life."

All hands stay down.

"That's what I thought. See how important it is for you to think before you answer? Let alone listen."

Silence, except for the birds in the trees chirping like the nagging mothers these kids thought they left behind.

"Anyway, since you all love, or at least like, Lucy, you may or may not know that Lucille Ball was older than Desi Arnaz and slightly younger than Vivian Vance—that's Ethel Mertz."

I back up against the blackboard chalk tray and sit on my hands to prevent chalk from dusting my rump. Crossing my legs at the ankles, I get a sharp pinch at the top of my thigh telling me my garter strap is twisted.

"Since the A/V Department messed up my request to have a TV and DVD player set up, we're going to do this next exercise the old fashioned way. I want you all to close your eyes and visualize scenes with Lucy and Ethel together."

A few students look around anxiously, but most of them comply. Ah! The blind faith students place in their teachers. I wait a moment or two before proceeding.

"Now that you have images of Lucy and Ethel burning your frontal lobes, compare the two women while keeping in mind what I said about their real ages. What do you see?"

Several of them breathe deeply. If they mistook this exercise for naptime, they'll be sorry, but I can't help smiling. That's when I notice how all of my students wear retro 1970s fashion. I got my first pair of bell-bottoms from childhood hidden in a drawer, and if I ever have a daughter, one day they'll be hers—and probably back in style again.

When I see faces starting to twitch and eyebrows rise in wonder at their new perspective of the comedic duo, I know I have their attention.

"Note their clothing and how much makeup these women have on. Lucy is more stylish, isn't she?"

With their eyes closed, I take the opportunity to walk around the classroom. The slow heel-toe-heel-toe clap of my high heels on the tile floor is evocative of a Gestapo officer stalking while interrogating a prisoner and I enjoy the sense of power.

"Now compare images of Lucy from earlier episodes to those of her toward the end of the series. I don't care if it was shot in black and white, there's a definite increase in the amount of powder and make up on Lucy's face."

This prompts a few snorts of laughter and nodding heads. I'm now at the other end of the classroom. My teaching assistant, Neil Hollister, is sitting at a desk in the corner with a smirk on his face. He did this exercise last year. I smile at him before turning to look at the backs of my students.

"Don't get me wrong. Lucille Ball was one of the best comediennes in the world, in my opinion, but why the elaborate need to suspend the audience's disbelief? Had they bit off more than they could chew? Remember, not only do we have an interracial couple, but a wife who is older than her husband."

One student puts her head on her desk.

"It's the 1950s, people!" My sudden increase in volume makes Miss Sleepyhead sit up. "What they did took balls . . . Hey! I made a funny!"

Nothing—except a polite chuckle from Neil. He heard me say that last year too. Oh well. I give him a shrug and turn towards the head of the class. "You may open your eyes."

After navigating my way through an aisle of carelessly deposited backpacks, I reach my post at the front of the room.

"Now, before you ask, I don't teach entire courses about *I Love Lucy* like some people. These are simply observations I've made. I can't say for a fact that they did this on purpose, but what could Lucy and Desi do to draw attention away from their interracial marriage? To what lengths will people go to create an image acceptable for human consumption?" I search my students' faces for signs of life. "They can change their ages, of course, on the outside at least. In this case, present Lucy as a younger woman. The Ricardos are a young married couple in contrast to the Mertzes. But what also becomes an issue in conjunction with age?"

I scan the room again to see if I'm striking a chord with anyone.

"Hint, hint! In case you've forgotten, today's topic is *Aesthetic Manipulation*. What do people associate with age?"

Finally, a henna-painted hand slowly rises. The palm is covered in a paisley design so elaborate it could be mistaken for a Magic Eye 3-D image.

"Yes, Paula?"

She shrugs. "Maturity?"

"Yes! Thank you! What else?" I gesture with my hands urging gimme more, more, more.

"Image," says Henry McGuinness, one of the three boys in my class. He's the Harris Tweed type and would bring that up. The third boy is absent, again.

I nod. "Okay, Henry, but can you be more specific? What aspects of image do you mean?"

"Well . . . I dunno. Clothes?"

"Excellent. Many articles have been written about clothes and prejudice. If you saw me for the first time, what would you think?"

I model for them. Today I wear a grey lightweight skirt suit. The skirt is short, just barely above the knee, but professional. Little do they know that when I get home, I take off these monkey clothes and slip into my favorite batik sarong, put bracelets on my arms, anklets that create music when I walk, and change the scent of my body from magnolia to musk.

But Henry's shoulders slump. "I dunno. I guess you're a pro?"

"Henry, where I come from, 'pro' could mean 'prostitute.'"

"No! I mean you are a professional," he says, smoothing his shirtfront nervously.

"What? And prostitutes aren't?" Neil adds from the back of the room. Some of the girls turn in his direction and giggle.

"Thank you, Mr. Hollister. OK, so I'm a professional. That means I must be . . . ?"

Stereotypical answers, eventually, come forth: mature, responsible.

"Boring. Dull," quips Hollister to the delight of the class.

"D'you think?" I challenge, giving him a pointed look. He returns it with a mischievous gleam in his eyes. Chancellor's nephew or not, I'm going to have to have words with my esteemed TA after class. "Anything else?"

Nothing. Their euphoria is gone quicker than an acid flashback. An impatient hand goes up as if yanked by a puppeteer's string.

"Put your hand down, Thompson, I'm coming to my point." I rub my hands together. "When you write your next paper on either Morrison's *The Bluest Eye* or Woolf's *Three Guineas*, think of Lucy, think of Pecola, and think of Woolf." I smile. "Playing the race card is an option, but it's a no-trump. I want you to connect society's perception of feminine beauty and propriety and how it affects people's judgment. More specifically, how it affects your opinion, if at all."

I move behind the desk and grasp the sides of the podium. "This will end our section on the first half of the last century. Have feelings changed since then? Convince me, whatever you do."

A hand goes up again. I sigh.

"Yes, Thompson?"

"How long does it have to be?"

"Class?"

"Five to seven pages, one-inch margins, double spaced, three outside sources. Annotated bib for extra credit," they reply in unison and with less energy than a bulimic after a purge.

"Thank you, class." I grin. "See what happens, Mr. Thompson, when you choose to participate through borrowed notes alone?" I want to say, How do you like them apples, smart ass? but take a look at my watch instead. Only an hour and thirty minutes left. Resting my chin in my palm, I look at the sea . . . the puddle . . . of less-than-eager faces.

I have looked into the future—and was unimpressed. Trying to get these kids, these young adults, to understand the importance of digging beyond the surface, because that's where the gold lies, is hard to do when they're bombarded with airbrushed images of so-called perfection. Why should they waste time in here when they could be the next mega-idol and see themselves splashed over the tabloids? If the students of Bellingham College are dissatisfied with something, they can simply charge it on their—or their parent's—credit card. This is what I am up against. Time to give these kids a little incentive to get to work.

"You guys, I've never missed a day of teaching, but I'm not above dismissing class early once in a while."

Happy smiley faces brighten the room. Some of the really happy students have their books packed and ready to go.

"You have until the start of class on Tuesday to turn in this assignment. Any earlier, put it in my office mailbox. Any later—"

"And live to regret your GPA," they finish.

"You are so good! I *am* breaking through. Get out."

They bolt for the door.

Taking off my blazer, I reveal a shell blouse and my skin breathes a sigh of relief. I swear that steam rises off me. It is over eighty degrees outside and this Victorian building is resistant to 21st century cooling systems. Rummaging through my purse, I look for my eyeglass case. Talk about aesthetic manipulation. I don't need glasses. They just make me look more studious and professional while separating me from the students.

After meeting Jared, I'm in heat so frequently it threatens to soak through my clothes. The late June temperature doesn't help. It's making me cranky and making my sexual dry spell even more noticeable.

God, I need to get laid.

I rub my eyes. Damn. Jared Delaney will not get out of my mind. Not his face, his voice, his cock—none of it. It's probably for the best. But I Googled him out of curiosity, along with the words "Denver" and "artist," and got almost 1,700 matches. Apparently he is known for his work on several national ad campaigns, independent films, and book covers. He's had art shows at a few local galleries and in New York. One critic's review said his studio work "focused on abstracting the human form but is very intimate."

Unfortunately, I need to get more memory for my computer and faster Internet connection. I couldn't open or download any images of him or his work. But some of Denver's cultural elite who own or have commissioned his work. Apart from general praise, his official biography is a single line: Mr. Delaney currently resides in Denver.

"Excuse me, Dr. Cavell?"

I jump because I forgot I wasn't alone. Turning around, I find Neil Hollister standing inches behind me. Any closer and we'd risk breaking some archaic decency laws. He smiles as his eyes linger on the V-neck of my blouse. His claim to fame as the chancellor's favorite nephew makes him bold, but it didn't save him from getting a D in my Women in Fiction seminar last year. That was one elective course he should have taken more seriously.

Before he became my student assistant, I thought he had more nerve than a bad tooth, but he's changed and his other instructors have thanked me for it. Apparently, his grades have improved, justifying everyone's opinion that Hollister is very smart, but lazy. I may have played to his ego by introducing him as my personal "aide-de-camp" and my "right arm" after he braved me for two semesters. This made him smile and he's been indispensable helping me with my freshman survey courses.

Maybe that was too much because, more often than not, when students file out at the end of class, Neil gets more than a few inviting glances. I see him wink at the girls every so often. One time he looked up, saw me smiling, and grinned. Standing just over six feet tall with an athletic hard-body—in training—short curly hair the color of corn silk, and puppy-brown eyes, Neil Hollister is a cutie. But he's a frat brat with a gab so gifted, he'll end up as the perfect wife in prison while serving a sentence for bank fraud or something, until his family bails him out.

"Yes, Neil?"

"It's only 12:30." He smiles.

"What's the problem? Don't you like the idea of getting out early . . . on a Thursday . . . with no class on Friday? Do you have another class or something?"

"No, it's not that. I was going to ask if you'd join me for lunch. Buy you a beer."

"A beer, eh?" I sigh, making my chest heave and the top button of my blouse rub against his shirt. He doesn't move away and I hold my ground. He smiles and takes a half step back.

I give him the once-over and he reciprocates. Unashamed, his focus starts between my legs and travels up over my midriff, then lingers on the prominent overhang of my chest before meeting my gaze.

"You make a tempting offer." I say and his already-confident grin swells. If he thinks he can flirt with me, I'm willing to spar with him a little bit. "But I don't think so."

"Aw, teach," he chides. "There's nothing that says students can't buy their instructors a beer."

I lean back against the edge of my desk and look at him over the top of my glasses. He's waiting for me to accept his invite. I decide to throw him a bone.

"Tell you what. I'll take a rain check on your offer until the end of term. Then," and I give him a wink. "I'll drink you under the table. My treat."

"You got a date . . . teach." He smiles and walks out of the classroom.

My skin is hotter than before. Neil is only posing but he's tempting, which isn't good considering my state of mind.

This is Jared Delaney's fault for making me so hot and bothered. I don't like being attracted to someone. It's messy and it keeps me from thinking clearly. I'll probably never run into Jared again, but the thought of giving Neil Hollister private lessons has a risk I don't care to take.

* * * *

My best friend, Ana, and I sit on the patio in front of The Market in Larimer Square watching yuppies and college students compete to appear trendy. It's become an unwritten rule among my friends that we take advantage of restaurants with outdoor seating during the summertime. While I pride myself on never having called in sick to work, it wasn't hard to convince Ana to play hooky for the rest of the afternoon.

Friends since elementary school, Ana-Marie "The Scarlet Woman" Scarletti and I met while serving detention together. I was there after being told for the third time not to chew gum in class. Ana was there after being caught showing her panties to Donny Nichols during recess. My early act of defiance for not wanting to waste my last stick of Juicy Fruit got me into trouble at school and at home, while Ana became a legend on the playground.

We once shared the same dream of artistic scholarship. I said we should've been artist's models: her, Erté; me, Reubens. Now she's Dr. Ana Benedetto and a curator at the Denver Art Museum. "I'm one of the DAMned," she likes to say.

Fanning the heat away, Ana looks delicate and elegant. Her willowy figure and porcelain complexion complement anything she wears. Right now, it's a cream-colored Donna Karan suit. As usual, our conversation quickly drifts to the subject of men.

"Eva, men have been waiting for you to open up like junkies outside a crack house. Why are you playing so hard to get?"

I haven't told her about Jared. Even so, I make a sound of disgust.

"Most of those men waiting look like junkies outside a crack house, Ana. My track record with men isn't impressive. Besides, most of them are incredibly boring."

"What about David Reese, the art instructor? You and he got along well."

"That man had no clue about art. He doesn't know his Asselyn from a Holbein."

Ana crosses her legs and the movement sends a subtle hint of musk-tinged perfume into the air. "Marcus Scaggs?"

"Oh, Marcus was irresistible," I say and take a sip of cola. "Until he admitted his goal in life was to have a clitoris of his own."

"Oops! Sorry, I forgot."

"Listen, why are we—"

"Troy Collier?"

"Ha! As soon as I let slip to Troy I was attracted to him, he back peddled fast enough to win the Tour de France."

She throws up her hands in frustration. "Hell, shit, and damn, girl! I'm sorry, but I don't understand why you can't put it about more." She starts playing with her watch, a clear sign of her agitation.

"Put it about? Ana, you make it sound like a product, or something."

"It must be made of gold considering the way you guard it. Why so uptight?" She leans across the table and slugs me on the arm. For someone so trim, Ana is tough. She has a firm, direct approach that's probably the result of being raised with four brothers. "What happened to the girl I took to Trisha Steven's New Year's party?"

"Oh, please." I drop my head in shame. "Don't go there." But it's too late. The event Ana jerks to the surface of my mind happened over three years ago and is the reason I put restrictions on myself today.

Trisha's party had a Roman theme and when in Rome . . .

Suffice it to say, Tom Collins and togas make quite a mix. It was like cramming the sexual energy of a herd of teenagers into one night. I never would've guessed I'd participate in group sex or public sex. By the time the New Year arrived, it was togas-off-and-the-last -one-penetrated-loses. Trisha had plenty of guests and I started the New Year with a bang.

"Mmm, yes," Ana drawls in recollection. "We tied for first place that night." She giggles. "You were in fine form, girlie. They were calling you Messalina by the time the night was through."

"Shut up!" But I'm not mad. "As if you can talk, Scarlet Woman."

She's right, though. I had earned the name Messalina and played the part of the infamous, sex-driven Empress of Rome to the max. I even had my own Emperor Claudius by the name of Eddie Norton.

Years later, we still laugh over it, but I have to admit that was the last time I'd been laid good and proper. Three years is a long time.

That night, for the first time in my life, I experienced a rush of freedom and abandon. Apart from going to The DeLuxe every week for public, mutual masturbation, I don't know any other way to get that feeling back. Sure, I can stay at home and do this sort of thing in private, but I don't. Trisha Steven's New Year's Eve party awakened something in me.

Why should I accept the stigma of being sex-starved because I'm a woman who likes sex? I like the way sex makes me feel, the giving and receiving. I may not be catwalk material, but I like the touch, smell, taste—the *sound* of sex. My "wild" history has taught me to appreciate the whole experience and refine my technique.

Hell, I'm getting too old for sport fucking. I don't want just any dick invading my space, and if that means letting strangers feel me up until something better comes along, then so be it.

I think of Jared. Shit, I haven't felt anything so intense in my life, sexual or otherwise. Not even the New Year's Eve orgy or my list of miserable boyfriends compare to what I felt with Jared. He may be talented, handsome, and self-assured, but there's something about him I can't define that allowed him to get straight to the core of me.

If I ever see him again, maybe I'll discover what it is.

I look at Ana eating her ice cream cone. She's like a sister to me. Not long after that New Year's celebration, I introduced her to an acquaintance of mine who turned out to be her soul mate and future husband, Frankie Benedetto. They were married by the end of the year.

From that moment on, Ana's mission has been to hook me up. She wants to help me strike it big even if it means going through fool's gold before hitting the mother lode. Unfortunately, the men on her roll call were *her* choices for me—and they were the ones with potential. Those pairings always ended before sex came into it.

That's why I didn't accept Jared's offer after the movie. I don't think I can control myself in a private, sexual situation. In public, I'm forced to keep myself in check. What I'm doing is actually a public service, because the next man in my clutches is at risk of being worn down to a shadow.

Protect the body and exploit the mind, that's my mantra.

Ooh, that man . . . I replay our meeting over and over and keep his drawing in my purse inside a protective plastic sleeve. Thinking about him makes me hot and I put my glass to my forehead to cool down. Ana sees me and frowns.

"Are you all right?"

I nod. I haven't told her of my weekly excursions. They are mine and mine alone. But I have to say something. I pull the sketch from my purse, show it to her, and tell her the sanitized version of what happened. Her reaction hardly helps.

"Evadne Cavell, how can you sit for being so horny?"

Her sudden increase in volume has other patrons looking our way and I glance around.

"Lower your voice, for Christ's sake."

"And you're just telling me this now?" She clicks her tongue in annoyance. "What's he like?"

I blink as if trying to remember. "He's charming. Has to be to use that approach. I did my share of resisting."

"You give him the civil-servant look?"

I nod. She throws her hands up in despair.

"Little Miss Evasive rides again. And he stuck it out? I'm impressed."

"But—"

31

"What?"

"As we talked, I got this feeling, a warmth."

"You were blushing."

"As if he could notice."

"Nah, you're high yellow enough for anyone to tell." She licks her fingers and finishes her ice cream cone. "Eva, come off it. You take yourself too seriously. Brush the cobwebs from between your legs and join the living."

Oh, if she only knew. But I play along. "Why so mean, Ana? Retaining water?"

"Like a dam."

I push my half-eaten chocolate cheesecake in her direction. As she digs in, I tell her how I excused myself from the rest of the evening. She almost chokes.

"That cat's been dead for fifteen years! How could you drop a bullshit tale like that?"

Once again, her volume puts us center stage. She gives a frustrated sigh. "Has he called?"

"No."

She's annoyed and I can't blame her. I'm feeling sorry for myself for passing a chance to get screwed—in a good way.

"Have you called him?"

"No." I turn away, trying to play casual. But she's shaking her head because I hear her earrings jingle. I look back at her. "Don't worry, Ana. I'm not sweating it."

She arches an eyebrow and scans my face. "Aren't you?"

* * * *

When I get home my phone is ringing. I'm exhausted and debate whether or not to pick up, but I do just before the answering machine turns on.

"Hello? Evadne?"

"Jared? Hi, how are you?" I'm gushing. Fuck, I sound so stupid! It's been ages since a man called me at home, especially one who can blow any cobwebs straight to hell.

"Not bad. And yourself? You sound out of breath."

"I was just coming in the door." I collapse into the nearest chair. Out of breath or not, I'm about to pass out.

"That's good. Glad I didn't miss you."

His voice coats my body like honey and as I indulge, there's silence on the other end. "Evadne?"

"What? Oh! Yes, Jared?"

"Umm. Sorry I haven't called before now, but I've been working real hard on an assignment. Listen, I'm catching a redeye to Dallas tonight, but . . . "

He sighs and the telephone amplifies it into a growl, making me remember the orgasm he got out of me. I cross my legs.

"Are you free tonight?"

I hear the uncertainty in his voice and decide that Little Miss Evasive has run her course.

"Why don't you come over?" I say. "Let me make you dinner."

CHAPTER THREE

▲

"THE FIRST DATE"

From the balcony of my high-rise apartment in Golden, I can see across Denver or turn to face the foothills and mountains. I open the Venetian blinds so Jared can appreciate the view when he arrives and load the CD player with as many piano and saxophone jazz discs it will hold.

In the kitchen, I hide all evidence of takeout food cartons. Hell, I'm trying to impress, so I went to a bistro and bought chicken Alfredo and a wild-green salad. I even went to the best wine shop to pick the wines. There's a raspberry cheesecake for dessert, but hope I'll do instead. Tonight, I plan to use all my weapons of seduction.

My black velvet slip dress is designed to make grown men feel underage. I bought it months ago on a whim, but tonight will be its premiere. The dress hugs all my curves, while exposing just enough cleavage and leg. As far as panties are concerned—why bother?

Jared shows up right at seven o'clock. Taking several deep breaths, I wipe my sweaty palms on my dress and open the door.

He greets me with a dazzling smile and dimples that make him sinfully adorable. He wears black slacks and a navy-blue linen shirt. The lustrous sheen of his hair gleams like dark copper. This time, I can't keep myself from getting trapped by his gaze, which seems to turn a deeper shade of violet before my eyes.

He must know the power of his stare, because he holds a bouquet of deep purple irises on long green stems. I reach out and gently pull him inside by the arm.

"You look delicious, Evadne," he says as he crosses the threshold. I catch the scent of my favorite cologne which is, ironically enough, Obsession for Men. I smile.

"Please, call me Eva."

"Sorry. Am I mispronouncing it?"

"No, you're saying it perfectly. Everyone calls me Eva."

He inhales deeply and it expands his chest beneath the crisp linen of his shirt.

"Smells good." He leans forward to kiss me and wastes no time inserting his tongue for a quick taste. I moan in response. As he pulls away, he gently bites my lower lip and gives me a peck on the tip of my nose. "I've been thinking about you, girl."

I look down so he can't see my satisfied smirk. It's a struggle to keep myself from grabbing him and forcing him to the ground. We are going to have dinner first. We *are*, damn it! I step back and accept the bouquet. "These are lovely."

"You complement each other."

"Flirt." I spin on my heel to find something to put the flowers in. Using a vase from my china cabinet, I arrange the flowers and place them at the center of the coffee table in the den.

Jared follows me and makes a sound of approval. My home is an eclectic mix of family hand-me-downs and salvage pieces reupholstered with quality, jewel-toned fabrics. The beige color of the walls makes my home look warm and as plush as a sultan's den.

I motion for him to sit on an overstuffed couch that faces the balcony and the view. He's immediately drawn to my collection of art glass housed in a display cabinet. I see him study one of my prize pieces: a Blenko flower vase that was given to me by my great-aunt. In my best hostess voice, I ask, "You said you've been working hard. Tell me about it."

Reaching up, he smoothes his left eyebrow with his forefinger allowing me to catch a glimpse of a Rolex watch before he replies. "I freelance. Set my own hours, my own rates."

"You're that good, huh?"

"Yes."

No false modesty here, nor should there be from what I gleaned off the Internet. I go to pour us each a glass of wine and, when I bring it to him, I sit a discrete distance away on the couch. He frowns.

"Why so far away?"

I shrug. He reaches for my hand and gives it a squeeze. "Am I going to have to beg to get close to you?"

"Maybe."

"All right, I'll make a deal with you." He moves closer and with a conspiratorial gleam in his eyes, he says, "Whoever begs first has to submit to the other's wishes."

My lips curve into a wicked grin. "You're on, hot stuff."

"Oh, so you think I'm hot?"

My face flames with embarrassment. He laughs and his thumb caresses my knuckles, transferring heat to the hand he holds. I retract my hand from his before the sweat becomes noticeable. By his calm expression, he knows that if he plays his cards right, more than his gaze will be penetrating me before the night is through.

"Tell me about yourself, Jared."

He smiles. I think he knows I'm fencing.

"Let's see." He takes a sip of wine and looks out onto the balcony. "I'm forty-one, single, no kids. I've been told I have a quick temper, but really I just can't stand sloppy work and have no time for fools. I like animals and classic cars, but loathe squash and English peas."

Seeing my blank expression, he laughs. "I'm sorry, Eva, but you don't impress me as one who likes boring chit-chat." He reaches out to stroke my hand. "You seem the *60 Minutes* type to me."

"I don't know." I try to suppress a smile but fail. "*Washington Week in Review*, maybe."

He sets his wineglass on the table before turning to me, hands on his lap like an obedient schoolboy. "OK, Ms. Evadne . . ."

"Cavell."

"OK, Ms. Evadne Cavell of the *New York Times*, grill away."

"I'm not going to grill you. I'm sure you've had enough interviews to last you for a while."

He raises an eyebrow. "How would you know? You doing research on me or something?"

"I'm just curious, that's all." I pick at a cushion lying between us. "You're unlike anyone I've met before."

"That's because we haven't met before."

"You're a real smart-ass, aren't you?"

"I call it having a sense of humor."

"Hey, I'm just trying to get to know you because that six-word bio just doesn't cut it."

He picks up his drink and grins at me over the brim of his glass as he slowly finishes the contents. "You found my bio, eh? You *have* been doing research."

"There are no straight answers with you, are there?" I laugh and he puts up his hands in a gesture of defeat.

"OK, straight answers. What I said earlier is true and I've loved drawing since I was four. I got my degree in studio art from the University of Colorado in Boulder when I moved here but I was actually getting by doing design work but decided to go for it."

"So the art degree was just because you wanted it?"

"It was a challenge." He smiles.

"See, I figured you're not from around these parts. It took me a while to place your Texas twang."

He says nothing, but he's grinning and his eyes sparkle. Beads of sweat form at the back of my neck. My seduction skills are so rusty it's pathetic.

"A-any siblings?" I could kill myself for stuttering, but smile to play it off.

"Several, actually. I have an older brother in town. He's the one who got me up here when I was nineteen. I put myself through college by working in a restaurant."

"Oh, really? Which one?"

"DeGaulle's."

I blink. "Well, I'll be damned."

DeGaulle's is one of Denver's best restaurants serving classic and nouveau French cuisine, and my good friend, Tony Lobos, has a large stake in it. It's won international praise and recognition. A person needs to reserve a month in advance just to get on the waiting list. If it weren't for Tony, I would never see the inside of the place.

"Well, on that note," I say and stand up, "time to eat."

"Good." He rises to his feet and looks me in the eye. "I'm hungry."

Sitting at my small, round dining room table, the candle between us isn't the only thing burning. My body sizzles being this close to him. There's a force between us, like two magnets facing each other; it's strong but keeps us apart.

I suppose he's being a Southern gentleman, because apart from our kiss at the door and holding hands on the couch, he hasn't made any sudden moves or said anything crude. He doesn't have to. I feel his eyes on me, caressing and touching me all over. Resuming our conversation, I ask, "Out of your siblings, where do you fit in?"

"I've often asked myself the same question." He laughs. "Chronologically, I fall in the middle." He looks at me. "What about you? Any brothers and sisters?"

I nod. "One of each. They're older."

"That doesn't surprise me."

"Excuse me?"

"You seem a bit repressed, that's all." He shrugs.

I put down my fork. "Repressed is an interesting choice of word. How do you come by it?"

He leans back in his seat. The taper candles between us almost obscures my view of his face, but the candlelight enhances his features, softening their sharp edges. He places a forefinger to his lips, and scrutinizes me at his leisure.

"I say 'repressed' because there's something shy and innocent about you."

"Innocent?" I laugh then tell him of my *Rocky Horror* days and the fallout from it.

"Well, for someone with visible physical appeal, you don't seem too comfortable with yourself." He straightens up in his seat and resumes eating. "If you were, you wouldn't be such a cocktease."

He sees my stunned expression and nods the way when someone gets busted and caught on camera.

"That's why you go someplace where you can hide in the dark. You forget, Eva, I've seen you operate. I've seen the way you lure a man and leave him behind—almost like you left me." He winks. "I couldn't be sure until I saw you do it a few times but, yep, you're a cocktease. Sitting in the theater with your skirt all tight and your sweater barely containing your . . . abundance."

Now, my skin feels clammy. I've been outed. Jared has exposed me in more ways than one, but I can't let him think he's rattled me.

"Is that why you came over to me in the lobby?"

"Nah, girl, I just saw through you." He eats a few more bites before leaning back in his seat, crossing his legs, and casually turning the wineglass by its stem. "Now, I could sit here and feed you bullshit by saying I think you're different, blah, blah, blah. But honey, we're all different. Hell, even twins are different."

I frown, my appetite now gone.

"Nevertheless," he says, slowly drawing out each syllable.

I look at him expectantly, wondering what smart comeback he has.

"I could tell at the theater that the more we talked, your body was just a bonus. But then again, I knew it would be," he says and sips his wine, "because, Eva, you *are* different."

I shake my head and his smug grin makes me smile despite myself. He's a smooth-talking bastard, but a likeable one. OK, maybe I am a cocktease and my choice in men could definitely use a quality check. But now I've had both Ana and Jared tell me that my good-girl veneer is thinner than I thought. What am I trying to prove, anyway? That I'm *repressed*, as Jared so eloquently said?

"Touché," I say simply and resume eating. This sparks a chuckle out of him and I join in.

The rest of dinner goes smoothly despite his discovering an empty bistro carton on the kitchen counter when he helps me clear the dishes.

"Hey, time was tight."

"Don't be so hard on yourself." He puts an arm around my waist and kisses the top of my head. His lips brush my temple making me shiver as I feel the contrast of his soft lips, the firmness of his jaw, and the way his cologne mixes with the warmth of his body. All of this in combination with the wine makes me grip the countertop for balance.

"Go take a seat," I say with a smile and he leaves while I load the dishwasher. Then I open the bottle of Italian Asti set aside for desert and pour two tall, fluted glasses of the sparkling wine.

"I should apologize, Jared." I explain as I join him in the den. "If I really wanted to be rid of you the day we met, I would've been blunt." Like I was with Jerk-Off Man, I wanted to add.

"Glad to hear it." He takes the bottle from me and places it on the coffee table.

I dim the lights and turn up the saxophone jazz. Then we step onto the balcony to see the city lights. The sky glows orange and pink behind silhouetted mountains and the night comes in like a band of dark blue melting from above with only a few bright pinpoints for stars. Leaning against the railing, I want Jared's hands on me, his long fingers satisfying my fetish for them as they find their way into my center once again.

Instead, I sense his gaze on me, sliding down my exposed spine and lingering on my bottom before continuing down my thighs to the back of my knees. I'm riveted to the spot, pretending to look at the skyline. He finally comes close behind me.

"Cappuccino," he says as his cool fingers glide up the back of my neck and into my hair.

"Hmm?"

"The color of your skin. Definitely, cappuccino." His breath is warm against my ear. "I wonder if it tastes as good."

His kiss smolders on my collarbone and I wouldn't be surprised if a burn develops there. He traps me by wrapping his arms completely around my middle and I get to experience just how hard his body is for the first time.

"You're trembling," he whispers, pulling away. "Why?"

I stay focused on the view. "It's hard to let my guard down."

"Do you have to guard yourself?"

I shrug. "Once you start, it's hard to stop."

He laughs and I wonder if the man has a sensitive bone in his body. I turn to face him and encounter those eyes. For a moment, it's as if we stare into each other's core. He doesn't move and the warmth of his skin and the sweetness of the wine on his breath is turning me on.

"Let me guess." He smirks. "You have to keep in control to save from getting hurt?"

"So what if I do?" I reply, perhaps too defensively. "No one can handle me the way I can."

"Mmm, I don't know, Evadne. Seems to me as if your control is ready to snap." He traces my jaw with his finger. "What is it, girl? I hear that black women have a reputation for being lovers who take no shit." His eyelids narrow. "Or is it all myth?"

Excitement rushes through me, warming and moistening my flesh, melting the cobwebs away. I'm enjoying this sparring match, but all I say is, "Myths survive on a kernel of truth."

He grins. "Is that a challenge? I like a challenge."

My gaze carves into his and I put my hands on my hips. As I do, it forces him to back up, but only a few inches. "You try me. Are you man enough to handle this?" I indicate my body with a flourish of a hand.

He reaches out with his glass and lets the cool, wet rim trace along my exposed collarbone, making me tremble.

"Girl," he sighs, shaking his head, "don't you know that when you ice your passion, you just make it hotter when it's thawed?"

We stand, for what seems like hours, waiting for the first sign of weakness in the other. He tips his glass, letting a trickle of wine spill onto my shoulder.

"Oops." He smiles and bends forward to lick the wine away, trailing his tongue up the side of my neck. When his lips connect with mine they are wet and sweet and I let his kiss engulf me.

Taking me by the waist, he navigates us back inside with the grace of a ballroom dancer as we maintain our kiss. Soon I'm on my Victorian fainting couch in a position many Victorian women probably never had the luxury to experience as Jared's voyage of discovery takes him down between my thighs, his hair caressing me like silk.

As he pushes up my dress, I figure he'll just give me a cursory nibble and move on like other men, but he sighs with contentment, a crusader reaching his pilgrimage. Without hesitation, he places my legs over his shoulders and spreads my intimate lips so he can lick each inner fold. One moment he's soft, the next he's rough, and the contrast is exquisite. When he manipulates my little power switch with his expert tongue and she stands at attention. He blows on her gently and I'm dropped into an abyss of sensation making me release a trickle of my pleasure.

"Mmm," he moans. "Skin like cappuccino but tastes like mocha."

A squeal escapes my lips. Jesus Christ, I got me a connoisseur.

Jared seizes my hips in a vise-like grip while his mouth makes a seal to suction the hot liqueur seeping from me and I explode. My hands grip his head between my thighs while my pelvis thrusts against his face. Considering our first encounter, he is running true to form and is about to make me come again.

Tears come to my eyes in spite of my trying not to get carried away. This is a sweet release, and he's right. My iced passion is melting and it's hot, wet. He drinks from me and I gladly satisfy his thirst. When he finally rises, his expression is like one who has overindulged in a bacchanalian feast.

"Jared," I whisper and touch his face. He blinks and snaps out of his reverie. His eyes focus on me as he kisses the Betty Boop tattoo located above my left hipbone. He climbs between my legs, which reflexively encircle his waist. We're still dressed, but his cock is tenting his pants and is hard and swollen against me. I close my eyes, remembering how I saw it in the theater. Lacing my fingers behind his neck, I smile. "I was getting worried about you down there."

His kiss forces me deep into the cushions. I taste myself on his lips and strain to get more, leaving us both gasping for air. A high-pitched beep goes off. He raises his head and takes a look at the phone he's taken from his pocket.

"Fuck." He looks at me and strokes my cheek. "Eva, I gotta go. My plane."

My loins literally ache for him. I tighten my legs around his waist. His body trembles and he tries to calm his urge by pressing into me. Big mistake. Gasping, we shudder at the electric charge it provokes between us. He shakes his head rapidly, sucking air through his teeth.

"Sugar, please," he says, voice straining. "If I stay, I risk having an accident. I'm about to do myself an injury as it is." He makes a pointed glance to his crotch and I can see his distress.

"Here, allow me." In seconds I have him on his feet with his pants down and my hand cupping his crotch. He looks down at me in surprise. Looking him straight in the eyes, I lick my lips. I'm going to enjoy this. *He's* going to enjoy it. He swallows again, his breath expelling hard and fast from flared nostrils.

"Evadne," he groans, like a soul in torment as my lips make contact.

I hold his cock with both hands. He is rock hard. I won't be able to deep-throat him. That would take practice, lots and lots of practice. He plunges his fingers into the depths of my hair as I give his cock a gentle tug and trace the network of throbbing veins with my tongue.

Down, down, down the shaft I go and into the short curly hairs that tickle my nose at the base. I bury my face there, inhaling his spicy scent. The tip of his cock pushes between the plush pillows of my breasts, which I cup with my hands and squeeze, trapping his cock inside as I nuzzle.

Jared upgrades his caress to pawing. I continue licking his base before pulling my head back slightly.

"Don't leave me this way," I moan, close enough for my breath to feel cool against the moist skin of his erection. His cock twitches. I position myself and slowly enclose my lips around the head of it, relishing the girth as my mouth takes him in as far as it can. Again, he sucks his breath through his teeth and groans.

Tongue swirling, jaw pumping, I make sounds of contentment. He is my feast. I'm in heaven, and from the sounds he's making, I'm sure he feels closer too.

"Eva-ah-ahh—yes! God—*damn*, work your mouth, just like that."

I continue for as long as my jaw allows and his cock has grown to maximum capacity. He holds my head in place and thrusts forward, but I keep focused so as not to gag. Instead, I wrap my hands around his firm thighs urging for more. I want it all.

"Jesus, your mouth feels so good. So wet . . . so fucking wet."

He falls silent, gaining force. I look up and see his eyes are closed, his lips pressed into a thin line, and his face contorted. I've seen that look before at The DeLuxe. He's going to come.

He can't see my Cheshire grin as I continue. With his cock thoroughly lubricated, I move away as a pearly tear drops from its eye.

"Aw," I coo, rubbing his cock against my cheek. "Don't cry. You're breaking my heart. Eva's gonna make it better."

"Evadne," he growls. "You're killing me. Let me come. Please, I've got to."

"Not yet, you don't." I squeeze the base of his cock, making him grit his teeth. "You still have that plane to catch?"

He can't articulate a response.

Putting my forefinger in my mouth to get it wet, I prepare to make him come so hard that if I don't blow his mind, I'm wasting my time.

"I can't hear you, Jared. Do you still have to catch that flight?"

In an amazing show of self-control, he exhales slowly through clenched teeth. "Sugar, I have to." He shudders again. "Eva, darlin', please. Let me—"

With only seconds to spare, I take a swig of Asti from my glass. I release his cock and slowly slip my moistened forefinger through the slightly relaxed ring of his ass before enveloping his penis with a mouthful of liquid effervescence.

Never in all my life have I heard sounds from a man like the ones coming out of Jared as he explodes inside my mouth. It's part groan, part cry, part curse, but all orgasm. If I didn't know better, I'd swear he's in pain. Maybe he is.

Eyes closed, I concentrate on keeping my finger up his ass and my mouth around his cock drinking my cocktail and purring like the contented black pussy I am.

"Aw, *fuck*!"

Another spurt shoots to the back of my throat. Some of it dribbles past my lips and trickles down his shaft, but I'm quick to go after it. I want to swallow all of his excitement. I want everything he can give and more before I'll let him go. Finally, I take my mouth away.

"Gonna leave me, lover?" I push my finger even deeper inside his clenched ass, making him thrust.

His labored breathing sounds as if he just ran a marathon and I fear his legs may buckle. And although his cock is spent, I see enough life left in him that I'm smiling with expectation. He sighs, caressing my head, his thumbs glide down my cheekbones.

"Holy sweet mother of Jesus . . ."

He takes a step back and I look in his face; it's drained of color. His eyes are red, his hair is disheveled, and sweat beads on his brow. He shakes his head like a man who's just taken the ride of his life. He helps me to my feet. Grasping both sides of my face he lays a soul kiss on me and moans as I give him a taste of sperm-enhanced Spumante. When we part, he stares at me with amazement. But soon there's a desperate look in his eyes.

"Eva, listen to me. I have to go—now."

My longing turns to disbelief and he reads it in my face.

"Sugar, please understand," he pleads, a note of anxiety and concern in his voice.

Here I am, for the first time in three years, ready to get fucked and not just felt up. He has gotten me so hot my dress is plastered to me like a second skin.

Enough is enough. I'm not letting him get away again. I put my hands on his shoulders and shove him onto the couch. From the surprised look on his face, I think he has realized that my size belies my strength. I straddle him.

"Jared Delaney, you are exactly five seconds away from being date-raped. Any last words?"

CHAPTER FOUR

▲

"FLIGHT"

Jared stares at me, breathless and open-mouthed. The look in his eyes is unfathomable but his jaw is set in a firm line. I don't know this man, but I think I've gone too far.

"Get your purse," he says. "Now."

I don't know what startles me more, his tone or his request. I back off, letting him get up to pull his pants on.

"Get your purse," he repeats, raking his hands through his hair. "You're coming with me."

He zips his trousers and, before I can take a step, he grabs my wrist and drags me towards the foyer. Obviously, I'm not moving fast enough.

It's half past eleven and Jared is rushing me to his car. Parked under a streetlamp, I see a black 1966 Chevelle. As I climb in and inhale the scent of vinyl upholstery, something comes over me. Call it lust, but as I watch him slide behind the wheel, it's my turn to devour him with my eyes. He turns the key, revs the engine, and at that moment, both the car and me are alike: black, sleek, and our motors purring and ready to go. He turns to me.

"Evadne," he asks, surprise in his voice, "are you growling?"

He pulls me over for a kiss. It's deep, passionate, but cut painfully short when he moves away to take a breath. "Hold on, girl, because when I get you alone I'm …"

He doesn't finish but I can see it in his eyes.

I'm amazed we don't get ticketed or killed on our way to Denver International Airport. Once inside, he keeps his frantic pace, dragging me along like a barge in tow. He handles me and his luggage with ease. I can't wipe the stupid grin off my face as I allow myself to be hauled across state lines for the sake of sex.

The red-eye flight is nearly empty and I experience flying first class for the first time in my life. Despite his gracious offer of the window seat, I choose the aisle. Flying from Denver to Dallas is a fairly short trip, but I suspect it's going to be hard for us to keep from joining the Mile High Club.

Once we're in the air, we engage in another deep kiss when the captain turns off the seatbelt sign. Jared pushes up the armrest separating us so we can move closer. He grabs my wrist when I pat the rise in his trousers and he shakes his head. I groan and he makes me look at him.

"We have to do this right." His lips find mine and I smile as we kiss. "What is it?" he asks.

Crossing my legs allows the hem of my dress to slink up higher. He notices and I sigh to make my chest heave seductively.

"Jared, when we get to Dallas . . . what are you going to do to me?"

He leans forward and buries his face in my cleavage. His lips excite my exposed skin. I stroke the back of his neck and inhale the clean scent of his hair. He raises his head to look at me. The hand he has on top of my thigh is warm and smooth and inches higher up my leg. His lips barely touch mine.

"When I get you alone, Eva, I'm gonna claim every inch of your body."

My breathing quickens and he kisses the tip of my nose.

"Wherever my hands go, my lips, teeth, and tongue will follow." His tongue flicks against the corner of my mouth. "I'm going to taste you, bite you . . . I'm gonna eat you, girl."

He proceeds to give me a sample of each and it's a good thing my legs are crossed. I put my head on his shoulder as he continues.

"I'll spread your legs wide, and once again, drink my fill of you." His words burn against my earlobe and the side of my neck as his hand presses between my thighs. I allow my legs to part slightly before trapping his hand there. He smiles while his forefinger presses into me.

"You want it, don't you, sugar? But first, my tongue has to slip inside." His finger presses harder. "Deep inside to get you ready for me."

"Jared—"

"Hush, darlin,' let me finish." He smiles. "I'll wrap your juicy thighs around my waist and then, Eva," he adds, using his free hand to make me look at him. "I'm gonna ride you hard and put you away wet."

That does it. My legs clamp together tighter as a short cry escapes my lips. He chuckles and holds me close.

"Excuse me?" the cheery-but-husky voice of the flight attendant comes out of nowhere. I freeze with my back to her and hide my face in the curve of Jared's neck, too embarrassed to move.

"Can I offer you a drink, sir? Madam?"

I suppress a giggle at her choice of words. When Jared answers, the resonance of his voice vibrates through me, making me even more aroused.

"I think we have everything we need, thank you."

I hear the flight attendant continue down the aisle. When I get the nerve to look up at him, he's grinning like a fool and we laugh until he moves in for another kiss. After that, we call a truce for the rest of the flight. I can't bear to look at him without wanting to tear off his clothes, so I pretend to look out the window in the row across from me. But Jared keeps one hand between my legs, casually claiming his territory while holding my hand in the other. Occasionally he strokes my knuckles or pulls my hand to rest on the peak of his arousal.

"That's for you, sugar," he whispers.

I bite my thumb and whimper. He laughs softly and yet, despite my molten hormones, I'm getting sleepy. Very sleepy.

* * * *

I don't remember landing in Dallas, Jared's renting a car, or riding to the hotel. I must have been sleepwalking. Suffice it to say, the next thing I do remember is waking up on my stomach in a strange bed with sunlight coming through the window.

It takes me a few moments to get my bearings. When I do, my eyes focus to see a very comfortable looking room with two chairs and an ottoman, a desk and chair, and a tall wardrobe. This is the type of hotel room that company executives with a generous expense account would get. Fully rapt in my senses, I turn over to see crumpled sheets and pillows beside me, but no Jared.

"What the . . . shit."

Well, at least we slept together. I reach between my legs to touch myself, only to discover my garter belt and stockings are still on. This cheers me a little. At least I haven't wasted my time flying out of state for a fuck I couldn't feel the next day.

But where is he? And what am I supposed to do now? Hell! How am I going to get home? This time, listening to my body instead of my head is going to cost me plenty.

But something feels very odd. Every time I move, I hear a crackling sound. I turn to look over my shoulder and catch a glimpse of something white.

"Why, that little punk."

Jared has taped a note to my ass.

I peel the piece of paper from my bottom and realize it's not a note, it's another drawing—a quick sketch done in ink of me lying prone and nude from the waist up, exactly how I awoke.

Good. At least he didn't capture my face first thing in the morning. He drew my arm dangling off the side of the bed with my hand pointing to the floor where he wrote the message:

I'll be back by six.

As I reach to place the sketch on the nightstand, I see a pink sticky note with the words *Enjoy yourself* written on it. Beneath is $400 cash.

"God damn. Who does he think I am? Julia Roberts?"

The thought has me laughing. I can't. Can I? It's a generous offer. And I have nothing to wear. I look around, still trying to get an understanding of my surroundings and see that Jared put my dress on a hanger in the wardrobe.

I take a shower, using the complimentary toiletries to scrub the remains of my makeup off my face. Fortunately for me, my complexion is clear and makeup is used to enhance and not to disguise. Then I discover I have another problem. If I go to the lobby dressed in my most seductive dress and three-inch come-fuck-me pumps, I'm going to look like the call girl who overstayed her welcome.

I am in a foreign town. Hell, Texas is a foreign country as far as I'm concerned, and my knowledge of "Southern" is slim.

Fuck it. Needs must. Nobody knows me here. Besides, I wore this dress last night is because it makes me feel confident. Now it's time to walk the walk.

I go downstairs and approach the front desk with as much poise as possible and discover I'm at the Anatole Hotel. Looking at my watch, it's 10:30 and people are checking out. On my left is an older couple dressed as if ready to hit the links and on my right is a younger man in Dockers and a polo shirt. I stand a discrete distance away in the center, positioned to go to the next available counterperson. As the men take care of business, the older woman, who must be in her fifties or sixties, makes no secret that my attire is not suited for such an establishment.

Her blue eyes take their time going from the top of my head to the tips of my painted toenails. Her thin lips are pressed into an even thinner grim line. When she finally focuses on my face and gives me a look to say I'm not fit to clean her house, I decide she's gone too far.

I clasp my hands behind my back, effectively thrusting my bosom out, and relax my stance, putting my weight on one leg, and return her stare. Then I crane my head to get a glimpse of her husband's ass, notice his wallet sticking out of his back pocket, and smile. The woman follows my gaze and spins back around, her mouth open as if about to speak. I shift my weight to the other leg and arch my eyebrow, daring her to say one damn thing. She moves closer to her husband.

The young man on my right finishes his transaction at the desk, picks up his bag, and turns to leave. He sees me and cannot hide his surprise. I think he's more embarrassed at his reaction than my attire and he blushes.

"G-good morning," he stammers. Not a Southern accent, more Midwestern.

"Good morning." I smile brightly and step aside to let him pass. He smiles at me, grateful to escape out the door. I approach the counter and a tall, slim man with short, dark hair and a pencil-thin moustache. He gives me a friendly smile.

"How can I help you, ma'am?"

Oh, thank god, he's gay. I want to jump for joy and sing the Hallelujah Chorus. I'm going to have fun with this.

"Hello. I was wondering if you could tell me of a good place to buy some clothes?" I cast a sidelong glance to the woman next to me and then back to the man behind the counter. "I'm afraid I don't have any with me, you see."

The man, whose nametag identifies him as "Sidney," catches my glance and I detect a sparkle in his eyes. "Well, if it's shopping you're interested in, I recommend NorthPark Mall or the Galleria." He reaches beneath the counter and pulls out a few brochures.

Despite the normality of his words, Sidney puts enough inflection on them to tell Mrs. Nosey Parker that he and I are on the same page. As I study the brochures, Sidney steps back and puts his finger to his lips in appraisal.

"From what I can tell, you can definitely wear clothes, so I'm going to suggest you go to the Galleria. It has more selection and it's a bit younger." He tosses a look at the old biddy. "If you know what I mean?"

I did and so did she.

"James," the woman snaps at her husband. "Will you just pay the damn bill and let's go?" She picks up her Coach bag and scuttles out of the lobby, leaving her husband, Sidney, and me looking after her.

"Shall I call a cab for you, dearie?" Sidney asks.

"Would you? You're such a love."

He gives me a wink and picks up the phone. I give him a twenty and he is worth every penny.

Getting into the cab, I tell the driver to go to the Galleria Mall in North Dallas. He deposits me in front of the gigantic, glass atrium mall entrance. Inside, over two hundred stores wait for me and my cash allowance from Jared.

I create my first ensemble in Macy's out of a much more conservative combination of short-cut overalls and a T-shirt. I wear these clothes and put my evening dress in the bag. Then I get some canvas shoes, because the ones I have on are meant for perching, not walking. With those tasks complete, I feel more at ease and buy a pair of pants, a summer dress, a pair of espadrilles, and toiletries. I don't splurge, but I'm satisfied with my purchases.

I take another cab and ride from one end of Dallas to the other. I've never been here before and keep my face to the window while the cabby gives a running commentary. He drives me to the Deep Ellum area in downtown Dallas where the "cool cats hang out," he says.

All I see are a bunch of warehouses and shops that are eclectic in their merchandise, but empty of customers. I say as much.

"Hey, it's daylight," the driver says. "You can't expect action in this heat."

By now I'm hungry and he suggests I eat at Baker's Ribs on Commerce Street, which turns out to be another worthwhile suggestion. Satisfied with a full tummy, I have a third cabby cruise around town. At the intersection of Greenville Avenue and Lovers Lane, I see a shop I simply must visit: Condoms To Go.

"Driver, stop!"

When I return to the hotel it's nearly four o'clock. Just enough time to build up my energy in preparation for the evening's festivities. I take a long, cool bath, washing away the humid Texas heat and scenting myself with honeysuckle and rose.

I have got to relax. But the thought of having real sex—not just fingers, but cock—after such a long dry spell makes me giddy to the point of being sick. Thinking of Jared's imminent arrival, I tense. It's like I've waited a lifetime for him and now, the time is near. When I get out of the tub, it's 5:15. I call room service to order champagne and hors d'oeuvres.

"And please, if you can have them here before six, I'd be grateful."

"Certainly, ma'am. We'll send that up right away."

I smile. They really are friendly in the South. As I'm applying scented body lotion before putting on my garter-and-corset ensemble, a knock on the door stops me.

"Room service," a friendly male voice calls.

I open the door to see a young, dark-haired man who looks at me in a strange way.

"I, uh, good evening, ma'am."

His uncertainty makes me suspicious and then I notice the knot of my robe is loose and reveals practically the entire left side of my body and part of my sex. But instead of acting modest, I smile. This boy's never going to see me again. I might as well get warmed up and have some fun.

"Marvelous. Come in." I hold the door only slightly open to make him brush pass me. It's a cheap thrill, but I'm in a frisky sort of mood.

"Where would you like it, ma'am?"

My throaty laugh makes him turn. "In the bedroom, of course."

Squaring his shoulders as if preparing to meet his fate, the room attendant pushes the trolley into the bedroom.

"Close to the bed, if you don't mind."

He glances at me over his shoulder and smiles. As he positions the cart, I shake my head. He can't be been more than twenty years old. As far as I'm concerned, he's an adult-in-training, but I play La Coquette to the hilt as I sashay past him to get my purse. After getting a decent tip, I reach for his hand and press the folded bill into his surprisingly moist palm.

"Thank you." I say and lead him out of the room by the hand. "Be a dear and hang the 'Do not disturb' sign on the door on your way out."

He swallows hard. "Yes, ma'am. Anything else?"

I grin at the expectancy in his voice. He's only a starter, like the tray of hors d'oeuvres he just delivered. Jared is the main course.

"Yes. You have a good night."

His last image of me is my waving to him as my robe slips off my shoulder, exposing even more of my body. My last image of him is his blushing face and his wide eyes as he closes the door. I giggle and can only imagine what the staff will be saying about me, especially after the scene this morning. Moments later, the electronic key unlocks the door.

Jared has returned.

CHAPTER FIVE

ʌ

"CLIMAX"

My heart stops beating as Jared opens the door. He's wearing a casual suit with a cream-colored shirt and carries a soft-sided attaché case. His glossy auburn hair and bright eyes compete for dazzle effect. Yes. Here he is, my man, coming home to me after a hard day's work. Several other words: elegant, dashing—sex machine—flash inside my brain.

"Nice," he drawls. "I was hoping you'd have little on."

"Anything else you hoped for?" I put my hands on my hips.

He lays down his car keys and portfolio on the small lacquer table beside the door and in two long strides, Jared closes the distance between us to crush me in a hug. The knot of my robe slips even more, letting my damp, naked body press against his clothed one. My breasts compress against his firm chest and the sensation thrills me. It does wonders for him, too, because I feel his erection growing.

He inhales the floral scent from the curve of my neck and nibbles my jaw. I place my hands on his shoulders and tilt my face for a welcome kiss. He grabs my hips and jerks me forward to introduce me to the extent of his desire. I gasp, allowing his tongue deeper access to my mouth. He reaches between us to untie the belt of my robe and gives it some slack so it falls beneath the swell of my bottom. Then he lassoes me close once again.

"How was your day?" I murmur against his lips.

"Filled with thoughts of you," he replies and kisses me harder. I increase the force and loosen his tie.

"This is it," I say, pulling away. "No more stalling."

"So who's stalling?" He grins as two of his fingers dive deep inside me, making me jump at the suddenness of his attack. "Follow me, sugar."

With calm assertiveness, and using a method more effective than any choke chain, he leads me to the bedroom but stops short inside the threshold when he sees the trolley. He turns and gives me a heart-melting grin. "Good thinking."

As he guides me to the bed, my robe slips to the floor. Suppressed excitement bubbles from my mouth in the form of a giggle. He glances at me over his shoulder.

"What's so funny?" He gives me a sharp tug, stimulating me in the process.

"Ooh! Nothing," I gasp, taming my urge to come.

Taking the bottle of champagne from the ice bucket, he sits on the edge of the bed and pours it into twin glasses. He hands me one and as I take a sip, a wicked grin comes to his lips.

"Cootchie cootchie coo!" he teases, wiggling his fingers inside me.

My right hand shoots out and clasps his shoulder to balance myself, causing me to lean forward. He uses the opportunity to kiss between my breasts. Keeping my eyes closed, I stroke his hair, luxuriating in it as his fingers push further. My eyelids flutter as he licks the bud of my left nipple. Opening my eyes, I see him put down his glass and reach for a strawberry from the tray. He takes a bite of the giant berry.

"Nice and sweet." He nods. "But it needs something."

I look down at him with glazed eyes only to meet his amethyst stare. He takes the berry and strokes it against my slit. I bite my lip at the sensation of cool strawberry flesh dripping with its own juice as it mingles with mine. He gently taps the berry against my swollen clitoris, sending white-hot flashes up my spine and into my brain and I see stars before my eyes. Sighing, I coat the strawberry with my own cream.

"Whoa there, girl!" He reaches up and grabs my drink before the glass slips from my fingers. He removes the fruit from me and pops it into his mouth.

"Delicious. Much better." He swallows and lies back on his elbows. His eyes scan my face, noting my lack of composure, and his lips curve up with amusement. That little episode drained me and we haven't started yet.

"Do any shopping today?" he asks in a husbandly way and grins with the same self-confidence I noticed in my apartment.

"Yes, I did. And thank you for the loan."

"It wasn't a loan. A lady needs her things."

He says it in a way to leave no room for discussion and I don't want to spoil the moment. Luckily the nightstand is only a step away, because my legs are about to give. I open the top drawer and lift out a small bag. "I discovered a nice boutique that reminded me of you."

I toss it to him. He reads the receipt and laughs. Reaching inside, he takes out several small jars of body paint, two brushes—and several boxes of condoms.

"Since you're the artist," I say, kneeling beside him on the bed, "I figured I'll be your canvas tonight instead of your bulletin board."

He smiles up at me, making my heart race, and strokes my thigh with a hair-tipped brush while his other hand manipulates the small paint jars like Chinese worry balls. I let this action distract me and watch the way his fingers move. They are so agile. He lays the jars and a brush down on the bed.

"Paint me, Jared," I say in a voice I don't even recognize as my own, it's so thick and husky. His eyes seem to turn darker as he removes his jacket and takes off his shoes and socks.

"Lie down on your back," he orders gently and I obey. The little jars roll against me from where I lie on the mattress and the glass containers cool my fevered skin.

I watch him cross the room to lay his jacket neatly over the back of a chair. He removes his tie and sets it aside while keeping one brush in his mouth like a long filter cigarette. As he approaches, his mouth wiggles the brush contemplatively. Standing at the foot of the bed and unbuttoning his shirt, he isn't looking at me but at my body, his canvas.

I try not to get self-conscious under his scrutiny, but I invited it. I am allowing someone to analyze every inch of me when I would rather fade into the background.

He rolls his sleeves up to the elbow and climbs onto the bed, straddling my legs. He has the colors red, blue, orange, yellow, and black to work with. Situating the containers, he places them on top of my pussy mound. He removes the lids and swirls the brush end in his mouth to get it moist.

After dipping into the black, he starts painting just above the center of my breasts. He strokes down in a curve, stopping at my pubic hairline, then he does it again. With a few simple strokes he's created the silhouette of a woman, arms outstretched, as she dives between my breasts, her buttocks curve just above my navel, which doubles as her sex opening.

I try to regulate my breathing to facilitate his brush strokes and it's hard, very hard. I groan in spite of myself to prevent my passing out. Jared covers my breasts with kisses to moisten them before painting a sickle moon on my right breast and a fiery sun on the left.

Scooting down further, just enough for him to part my legs slightly, he paints a bonfire with its source coming from the center of my pussy. The satiny texture of the brush and the wet, stickiness of the paint assault my senses. I wiggle my toes, and the movement causes me to brush against his stiff cock. He sucks in his breath, and as sweet torture for my moving, he places more feathery strokes along the top of my thighs.

The small jars of paint precariously balanced on my pelvis make a tinkling sound as I tremble. He grabs them and holds them in his palm before moving away from me.

"Okay, darlin', spread 'em wide."

Never have I felt more exposed. But I do as I'm told. I want this. He situates himself over the end of the bed as I bend my knees and place my feet flat on the mattress. Just when I think he's viewing me in a strictly objective manner, he says.

"Evadne, if only you could see what I see."

A blush burns my face. What I do see is his devilish, grinning face from between my legs, just above the curls of my unshaved mound, and my inner muscles contract in expectation. He lets the paintbrush handle enter me just enough for me to get a sense of penetration. But it's not enough. I need the length, girth, and force of his cock slamming inside me.

"Jared—"

"Shh." His fingers rake through my neatly trimmed bush. "That's a good kitty."

Then I feel the second brush flick against the rim of the tight ring leading to my ass before he suddenly buries his face between my thighs. He nuzzles me, breathing warm streams of air into me along with a few random licks before poising his brush to paint once again. His face, now smeared with body paint, gives him a savage appearance and he goes about repainting the area. A line here, a dot there, he paints with one brush as he pushes the other further inside me.

"Jared," my voice quavers but he just chuckles.

A brush trails between my ass cheeks and I thrust my hips up, inadvertently driving the other paintbrush deeper.

"Oh, Jared, fuck me now . . ."

"Not yet," he says, patting my right thigh.

I exhale with a long hiss. How can he be so damn calm? If I didn't think it would ruin the mood, I'd mount him at this moment—or start without him.

Finally he removes the brush from my body. Good. Time to get fucked till I'm blue. But, instead of mounting me and riding me to glory, he hides his face between my thighs again and licks each succulent inch of my pussy before inserting his tongue to the hilt. I can't hold back and grind circles on his face as he sucks the sensitive flesh into his mouth.

"Now, now, now!" I cry, my hands clutching at the sheets to keep from clawing at him.

He reaches up and his hand does a quick inspection of my body and backs away.

"Good, you're dry."

He obviously means the paint. Before I can open my eyes, he grabs my waist and turns me onto my stomach and is straddling my thighs again, his strong legs clamping mine in place. He stretches out above me, pushing my hair aside to kiss my ear.

"Almost finished," he whispers. "These colors look gorgeous on you, sugar."

"Jared," I moan. "Please . . . fuck me . . ."

"Hard and deep, babe. Just give me a few more minutes."

His erection brushes the crest of my buttocks and I rear against him causing him to release a pent-up breath against my cheek. I do it again. His arm hooks around my waist to hold me against his swollen cock and he thrusts back. We dry-hump for a few minutes and I'm smothering my cries in the pillow and he's breathing harder than before.

"Do you want me now?" I moan.

He doesn't answer. I kick my legs and thrash my arms in frustration until a hard, resounding slap on the ass stuns me into stillness. A lump swells in my throat. That fucking hurt.

"Be still," he says angrily, "or there will be more."

I bite my lip and hide my face. That spank, hard as it was, only serves to get my juices boiling as I once again receive a sample of Jared's no-nonsense side. I am hundreds of miles away from home with a man I barely know. Part of me says I should be scared, but I'm not. My lust is the only thing that matters and I am so hot for Jared right now, my skin is burning. When the weight of his body lifts from my back, I know he's sat up, and when the paintbrush returns on my skin, it's at the top of my spine.

More bold, curving strokes go down my back and sides. Then, he brushes inside the spaces as if filling them in. I can't see and have no idea what he's doing. I don't care.

"Oh, Jared, use me."

"Almost there, love. Be patient."

Easy for him to say. My legs are sticking together from all the erotic syrup I've produced since his return.

"Okay, I'm done."

His declaration makes me jerk my head out of the pillows, completely alert, like a retriever at the sound of her master's gun. Jared gets off the bed and I roll onto my side to watch him strip out of his remaining clothes. For the first time, I see him in all his glory and I'm confronted with his long, sculpted body as his strong hands roll a condom onto his fully extended cock. After days of dreaming of this very moment, the time has finally come.

"You look heavenly," he smiles and advances towards the bed.

If I were strong enough to take my eyes off him, I would cast a glance over my body to view his handiwork.

He climbs onto the bed but doesn't let his body touch mine in order to suspend himself above me with his hands on either side of my shoulders. His eyes bore into mine like a hypnotizing serpent and I fall to the role of his prey. I close my eyes.

"What's wrong?" he says.

I swallow, trying to find my voice. "I need . . . I want you so bad, Jared."

My confession is met with silence. Slowly, I open my eyes to see him just staring at me for such a long time I wonder if he's having second thoughts. But his smile and kiss in reply are gentle as he nudges himself between my legs. When he lifts his head again, the same predatory gleam is in his eyes, only fiercer. He lowers himself and my body welcomes him like a soft pillow. My arms and legs wrap around him and he reciprocates by holding me tight. Soon, he's reaching between us to guide himself into me.

Inch by luscious inch, he infiltrates my yielding body until I envelop him to the hilt. For a moment, we're both still, relishing the fact that our bodies are finally joined, together at last. My inner muscles quiver and pulse around his firm penis, making him gasp, and I feel my heart thundering in my chest. This is what I've been waiting for, to have Jared's body inside mine, for him to possess me.

Maybe it's because our temples are so close with his head on my shoulder that allows him to read my mind, because he gives me a squeeze and raises his head to look at me. He's smiling.

"You got me where you want me, don't you?"

I return the smile. "The feeling's mutual, isn't it?"

"Oh, yes." And with a seductive leer in his eyes he thrusts his hips and we begin to move.

There's no more talking after that. And, despite my fears, I'm going to make up for lost time. From our tongues tasting, to our fingers stroking and probing, the sound of us gaining pleasure out of each other soon fills the room.

I have no idea as to Jared's sexual history, and perhaps I'm flattering myself, but it feels as if he's putting more than just his back into it, which he arches high before surging forward to stretch me. His loins slap my thighs as every ounce of his power goes into each thrust. He ploughs into me, making the bed springs quake, and we ride them for all they're worth. He paces himself like a prime athlete, breathing deep and exhaling hard, making me realize just how out of condition I am. All I can do is hold on and marvel at the man turning my insides into a trembling orgasmic sea. I spread my legs wide to accommodate him and he hooks his arms under my knees, anchoring me in place.

But I'm not passive. I rise to meet him and take each blow full-force, daring him to break me and my participation is appreciated. I look at him and his eyes are closed in concentration. Our breathing becomes strained from our workout and our kisses get deeper, our embraces tighter. He rises above me and I think his face is trying to convey multiple emotions—ecstasy, release, constraint. Then, he comes to a complete stop, opens his eyes to gaze down at my face, but he's not seeing me. I can feel him inside me, vibrating, on the verge of erupting. Pressing me deeper into the mattress, he pins my hands above my head. I can't look away from the violet pools of his eyes.

Suddenly, his eyes focus on mine and we hold each other within our sights, then something sparks, setting off an explosion. I rock my hips forward as he gives one final push, and together, we peak Mount Everest and shoot into the stratosphere.

In the past, for me, sex was just the act of building my arousal to such a peak I must jump off, only to crash and burn when I hit the earth. But with Jared, I'm not ashamed to say it's a religious experience. Tears come to my eyes, blinding me. I can only hear my blood coursing as my mind melts and the knot that slowly tied itself inside me starts unraveling, releasing my joy.

I gasp for breath only to have my mouth possessed by his moist, soft tongue. I hold onto his trembling body as the last of his essence flows and cradle him between my arms, between my legs, and return kisses between his sighs.

Slowly, my hearing and sight returns. His mouth lifts from mine and then, to my embarrassment, a sob escapes me. His lips take on the gentle task of kissing away my tears and a deep chuckle of satisfaction rumbles through his chest, making me laugh too. But this is nothing to laugh at. What we just did goes beyond physical fusion. The way he releases one of my hands to caress my cheek tells me he knows that was something special. He kisses my shoulder, still breathing hard.

"Evadne," he whispers, a smile on his lips. He tries to roll off me but I hold on.

"No, Jared, don't." I stroke his cheekbones with my thumbs. "Stay where you are . . . please?"

He looks down at me but says nothing. After all, we've gotten what we wanted. But his eyes still glow with the same fire that has warmed me since the day we met. It's a look that says he's comfortable and satisfied right where he is.

I pull him down for one last kiss and he relaxes on top of me. I nip at his left earlobe and whisper, "Jared?"

But he's asleep.

CHAPTER SIX

"THE NEXT DAY"

I wake up the next morning not knowing what time it is. When my eyes focus I see the window and sunlight, but still don't know where I am.

Déja vú? This has happened before, hasn't it? I decide to carry out the dream scenario and shift to touch myself.

Yes! I got it! The dull but telltale, "freshly fucked" ache between the legs. This is great!

Smiling smugly, I run a hand over the swell of my belly and rest it on top of my pussy only to meet Jared's hand already there. His leg lies over mine and I turn my head to the left to see him asleep on his back, one arm covering his eyes. Sleep makes his face look even paler in contrast to the dark stubble of his morning shadow.

His chest rises and falls in deep, even breaths and his nipples are two rosy pearls standing at attention, making me want to tease them with my tongue. But I resist and let my gaze continue its journey down, following the faint line of hair that divides his torso in two and creates a slight whorl around his navel. That's when I see it.

Lying dormant, but intimidating nonetheless, is the mighty organ that commands as much respect as the master who wielded it so easily. An active evening has not diminished its size much despite lying limp against Jared's thigh. At rest, his cock has a soft pink cast and sleeps like a baby, completely the opposite of the dusk-colored alter ego when preparing for battle.

His cock must've suspected my contemplating it, because it twitches and jerks in my direction. Jared sighs and shifts closer to me.

He flexes the fingers of his right hand, giving me an intimate squeeze. I prop myself up on my elbows to get a look at the man's handiwork. The colors are still bright, but the silhouetted woman diving between my breasts and the "flames of passion" emanating from between my thighs is smeared beyond recognition.

With another flex of his hand between my legs, his fingers start searching, snaking through the soft grass of hair until they find my entrance. I lie down, raising my right knee, and arch my back slightly to give him access. We both moan as his fingers reach their target. I place my hand on top of his, pressing it closer. Again, I look at Jared and see he no longer has his arm over his eyes, but they're still closed.

And he's smiling.

He strokes me, playing me better than a virtuoso. Soon he has me lifting my hips off the bed to let his fingers go deeper. For several minutes this continues until I can't take it anymore, but instead of letting him get a quick orgasm out of me, I roll onto my stomach making his hand fall away.

He reacts quickly by climbing on top of me and pushing my hair out of the way to kiss the back of my neck. His cock is awake, too, and I feel it press the base of my back. He lifts up slightly to push his penis down until the tip nudges my opening and starts to go in.

"Wait," I say, holding up a hand. "Before you go any further, what's my name?"

"Evadne!" He laughs incredulously.

"Just checking. You may proceed."

He can't see my grin with my face buried in the pillow. Still chuckling, he enters me smoothly and penetrates deep, making me catch my breath.

"Just checking," he mimics, kissing my neck again.

His arms encircle me, one going around my waist, the other just above my chest and around my shoulders. He squeezes me tight, as once again, he stretches me to my limit. He sets a less urgent pace this time and I'm grateful. I can't believe how sore I am. Even his steady, slow movements make me wince and he notices.

"You alright? You want me to stop?" He kisses my shoulder.

"Good God, no," I moan and he tightens his grip on me and I relish being crushed into something soft and yielding by the firmness of a man's body. My excitement builds as we slowly rock along. I grip my hidden mouth around Jared's cock and he growls like a prehistoric beast when he comes. He bites my earlobe and then whispers.

"Good morning, Eva."

* * * *

It's mid-morning when we finally roll out of bed and I take the opportunity to see what's left of the designs painted on my back in the bathroom mirror. Jared had created an ouroboros, a serpent eating its own tail, in black, red, and yellow. It reminds me of a Maori image. It's abstract, attractive, and when I remember how quickly he created it, I whistle.

"It's lovely. Shame I have to wash it off." I'm still looking over my shoulder at my reflection when he rises from where he sat on the edge of the bed to come near. His hands stroke down my back, his fingers tracing the snake in its coiled design.

"You'll never be able to reach." His eyes meet mine in the reflection and their soothing, hypnotic color engulfs me. I fancy I can see into him, way beyond the surface. I don't think I was meant to see that far, because he breaks our gaze to kiss the top of my head. When I try to hug him, he grabs my hands and steps away.

"Come on," he says. "Let me help you."

* * * *

There's no telling how much water we wasted showering together. After twenty minutes we decide to do some bathing. Later, standing in front of the vanity, Jared wipes the condensation off the mirror and I dry my hair. I've wrapped a towel around me. He doesn't bother with such modesty.

Standing beside each other at the double sink, we brush our teeth in tandem. It's a bit awkward because this is a new level of intimacy for me. When I get ready to spit, I look up to see him watching me. I stop. So does he.

"Considering how intimate we've been," he struggles to say, "Why feel shy about brushing your teeth?"

"Well," I say, smiling back, "It's the spitting that I find a bit rude."

"That's nothing." He turns on the faucet. "You should hear me being rude after eating refried beans."

I try not to laugh but my mouth is ready to burst with toothpaste, saliva, and all the other things that come with tooth brushing—and he's staring at me again.

"What's the matter, Eva?" He wriggles his eyebrows at me.

"I want to spit." My voice is garbled.

"So spit."

"No. You first, then look away."

"Embarrassed? C'mon, girl, spit!" Then he gives me an evil leer. "Or do you prefer to swallow?"

My mouth is burning and I want to laugh and cry. Instead I whimper. "Jared . . . "

"OK, we'll go together on three. One . . . two . . ." He bends over his sink and I copy him. "Three!"

I spit. He doesn't, so I remove the wet towel covering me and slap his bare, wet ass.

"I see *you* prefer to swallow."

* * * *

Once dressed, we go downstairs to The Terrace Restaurant. There aren't many people about. I give Sidney a wave as we go through the lobby and he gives me a smile and nod of approval.

"Making friends already, I see," Jared says and I smile.

Jared has the physique of a basketball player, tall but sort of beefy too. Today he wears a black blazer, white shirt, and jeans with cowboy boots. He's stylish and casual, but it's hard not to notice him as soon as he walks into a room. Right now is no exception, so I just stand beside him and bask in his glory, trying not to look self-satisfied.

The hostess leads us to a table and a few minutes later a waiter takes our order.

"I'm afraid I'm going to have to leave you again after we finish," Jared says halfway through our meal. "But don't worry. There's someone I want you to meet. In fact, she agreed to keep you entertained today."

"Is that so?" I say, cautiously. "That's mighty generous of her."

"She's that kind of gal," he says and winks.

I try to put my next question as casually as possible. "Is she an ex?"

He's putting marmalade on a buttered point of toast, but I see him trying to suppress a smile.

"Yes."

"Oh." I reach for the pepper mill. "Maybe I'll get an unbiased opinion of you out of her."

"I doubt it." He takes a bite of toast and chews slowly before leveling his eyes on me in the same predatory way that nailed me hours before. "I can guarantee excellent testimony."

* * * *

When Jared tells me the name of his friend, I couldn't believe it. Talley Monroe, mystery writer and *New York Times* bestseller, lives in the University Park area of Dallas. I've read and enjoyed her books.

And she is Jared's ex.

The street Talley lives on consists of old trees and a hodgepodge of homes representing various eras, starting with the Victorian. Most of them are genuine whereas others have the ersatz antiqueness of a 1890s house built in the 1990s.

But Talley's home is a genuine A-frame structure from the 1930s with dove-gray painted brick and white trim. A small, curved, gravel drive and grass so green it looks painted complete the picturesque setting. As soon as Jared pulls the rental car into the drive, the front door opens and Talley Monroe steps onto the porch. We get out of the car.

"Hey, Miss Firecracker!"

"J. D.! You bastard, c'mere!"

I will put Talley in the tall, blonde, Scandinavian goddess category. She wears flat shoes but stands nearly eye-to-eye with Jared. Her long, sand-colored hair is pinned into a loose roll. Two platinum-blonde highlights frame her face and complement her tanned skin.

The soft pink blush on her cheeks comes from a healthy complexion and not artificial means. Her eyes are pale blue, almost gray, but not icy, they exude warmth similar to the kind I get when Jared looks at me.

She wears a white scarf around her neck, loose white pants, and a pale yellow tank top showing off well-toned arms. I make it a point to appear confident in my navy-blue pedal pushers, pinafore top, and espadrilles, but I feel all that's missing is an all-day sucker stuffed in my mouth as I meet the darling of the country club set.

Jared and Talley make an attractive pair. They hug and kiss, but it's Talley who notices me first.

"This must be the poor girl who has to put up with you now."

She nudges away from Jared to reach out to me. Her large, soft hand envelops mine and it's cool despite the sticky weather.

"How do you do?" I smile.

"'How do you do?'" she teases. "You're just so proper, ain't you, girl?"

"I try to be."

"Yeah. In public, at least." Jared snorts. "Get her in a dark theater and she goes wild."

Talley grins. "Well, there's no need for all that. Here in the South we just say, 'hey.' Hey, Eva."

"Hey, Talley."

"The girl catches on quick. I like that."

"She's a doctor."

"You can't be a doc of psychology; otherwise you'd steer clear of him."

I give a small chuckle, not really sure whether to take her seriously or not.

"You two come inside before we all melt."

Jared shakes his head. "No, Talley, I can't. I got a meeting at the Prestonwood Country Club in about thirty minutes."

Talley's delicate lips turn into a frown. "For God's sake, Jared. It's Saturday. You bring this pretty lady all the way down here and you have the nerve to go do business?"

She gives my hand a squeeze and pulls me close to her so we present a united front against him.

"Yeah," I chime. "The nerve of him."

"Honey, you'll find Jared has more nerve than a bad tooth." She casts a disapproving glance at him. "But we'll forgive him this time." She wags a finger in his face. "I'm surprised you're not locked up in the hotel making this girl ride that monster of yours."

My heart stops and I feel the tops of my ears get warm with embarrassment. It's bad enough to have Jared's ex-girlfriend as my chaperone for the day without her referring to him and me in bed.

"Aw, c'mon, Talley. Leave me alone. It was she who begged me to stop." He winks at me.

I can't hide my disbelief, but he continues.

"You're right, though. If it was up to me," he says, pulling me to his side so unexpectedly I feel like a rag doll, "we'd still be joined at the hip." He looks at his watch. "I gotta leave."

He tilts my chin up and plants a kiss on my lips. His tongue takes possession of my mouth with such ease and command anyone would think we've been together for ages. When he pulls away to end the kiss, he snares me with those piercing violet eyes and says, "Take good care of her, Talley. Make sure she has a good time."

"Of course, J. D."

He reaches a hand down to squeeze my bottom and lowers his head for another kiss. When I kiss back, he makes a sound of approval.

"All right, you two. Break it up. The last thing I need is a visit from my holy-roller neighbors."

He kisses the tip of my nose. "I'll be back by four." He heads for the car. "Eva, you be good!"

"Yes, Daddy." I stick my tongue out for good measure. As he drives away, I turn to my hostess. I don't know what to say, but I'm determined not to act like some jealous female because of the awkward situation. I shrug. "Looks like you're stuck with me."

"Aw, now I wouldn't say stuck." She links arms with me and we walk indoors.

Stepping into Talley's home is like stepping into a Mediterranean dwelling with arched entryways and marble tile. A domed skylight in the entryway makes the space bright and cool, and relaxes as it illuminates the muted pastel colors of sand, coral, and azure.

Several objects are displayed on pedestals and pillars: Grecian amphoras, fragments of bas-relief, and parchment. The walls have frescoes depicting classical themes of feasts and festivals reminding me of what I always thought ancient imperial villas would resemble. An abundance of green plants and ivy, some with fragrant flowering blossoms, add splashes of color and a light, sweet scent to the air.

The sound of running water makes me take a few more steps inside until I see a sunroom with an indoor stream, complete with fish, housed by smooth, flat stones. In the center of some strategically piled rocks sits a Grecian temple serving as the source of the waterfall.

Talley, noting my interest, stands beside me, bends over, and explains, "If you get real close, you'll see I've rigged it with lights and an altar, complete with a statue of the goddess."

"Which goddess?"

"Whichever one I feel like worshiping at the moment." She smiles and stands straight. "At night, it serves as a nightlight and glows with altar fires."

The stream culminates in the center of the room but is rigged to go under a pair of double doors and into the backyard, where it meets another water garden with more fountains and waterfalls. And you needn't worry about missing the journey of the fish, because the tiles on the floor in front of the French doors are transparent.

I notice two cats, a calico and a gray longhair, watching the fish from their perch, a slab of sandstone jutting out alongside the stream at the base of the waterfall. Every now and then, a bit of water splashes up and the cats shake their heads with annoyance, but they don't move.

"That's Clio and Electra," informs my hostess. "Those two are crazy. They'll sit there for hours batting at the fish, sometimes catching a few. On a good day, I get the fish back in the water in time." She frowns. "Other times, I'll be walking along and step on something crunchy only to look down and see a half-eaten fish under my foot."

I laugh—until I see something small and pink scamper into the cracks between the stones. "What the hell was that?"

"What was what?"

"I thought I saw something beat a quick retreat down there." I move to the stream for a closer look. "Something with legs."

Talley shrugs. "Probably a gecko. Or a salamander."

I bite my lip. Obviously the woman doesn't mind having small reptiles running around her house. I decide to watch my step. Frankly, I'm surprised Talley would have all this water around her in a climate so humid and I tell her so.

"Hey, I'm from Louisiana," she says. "Near Lake Pontchartrain. This ain't nothin', girl." She looks at me. "Would you like something to drink?"

I follow Talley into her kitchen and sit at the island bar as she gets out the glasses. Her windowpane cabinets display all of her plateware, most of which are painted in bright, primary colors and geometric designs.

"I'll make us some adult lemonade."

She pours two tall glasses of lemonade and splashes in a shot or two of whiskey. Me and her are gonna get along just fine.

She cuts a few sprigs of mint from the window box before joining me with a plate of sugar cookies.

"Tell me something, Eva."

"What?"

"How did Jared really get you to come here with him?" She starts to laugh a deep chortle, the type that surrounds a joke told in bad taste. "He said it was for sex."

I bite my cookie and look away.

"Wait a minute . . . it's true?"

"So what if it is?"

She smiles and pats my hand. "No offense meant, girl. Jared can charm the sap from the trees. It's just that . . . never mind."

"No, tell me."

She sips her lemonade. "You're really smitten by him, aren't you?"

She's evading my question but I let her. "To tell you the truth, Talley, I don't know what I'm doing. Here I am in Texas, with no clothes, no money, as the last-minute traveling companion for a man I just met." I turn in my barstool to face her. "This is our first date!"

My saying this out loud makes me freeze. When I woke up the day before, if someone told me I'd be going to bed somewhere in Texas that evening, I would've made them take a sobriety test. But Jared has rekindled a spirit in me that I haven't felt since grade school. He makes me feel mischievous. Unpredictable. Naughty.

"Well, Eva, for your next date, may I suggest Cancun?"

I laugh. Ex-girlfriend or not, Talley reminds me of Ana with her attitude.

"Get your skates on, girl. You're not gonna be in our fair city long before you leave for the frozen tundra of the North." She takes my plate away. "Let's get you out and about. Show you a few stompin' grounds."

I hurry and finish my lemonade, forgetting about the alcohol until I stand and get a head-rush. I don't drink whiskey too often. Talley puts our dishes in the sink and then, linking arms, we head out of the kitchen.

* * * *

We ride in Talley's white 1970 Chevy Impala convertible with the top down. "This is one cherry I still have!" she laughs, with that short bark of hers: the kind that only a man or a woman of her stature can pull off. Seems both she and Jared have a love for classic muscle cars. I've never ridden in a convertible, but since meeting Jared, I've done many things I haven't done before.

I feel chic against the snowy interior with my eyes covered by opaque sunglasses and the wind whipping my hair about like a black cloud. The car's smooth suspension and Talley's breakneck driving create a lulling effect on me. She drives me around their old neighborhood in Oak Cliff and by their old high school.

"This is where we met," she says as we drive into the empty parking lot. She turns the car off. "Yes, ma'am," she says with a sigh. "Class of '85. Haven't set foot in the place since." She looks at me. "Neither has Jared, as far as I know."

"High school years suck."

"Yeah, but they suck more for some than for others."

I peer at her over my sunglasses. "What d'you mean?"

"I mean," she says, starting up the engine and driving out of the lot, "high school, more often than not, scars you for life. People just don't want to admit it." She looks me up and down. "I bet you were one of the popular ones, eh?"

"Hardly." I laugh. "But I wasn't lonely for company, if that's what you mean. We had two thousand students in my school."

"Shit, girl!" Her exclamation corresponds with her slamming on the breaks at a four-way stop. "If our school had a thousand kids in my day, we were pushing it."

"You and Jared were loners?"

She purses her lips together. "Not exactly. We were fringe-dwellers."

"Let's hear it for the fringe-dwellers! Woo hoo!"

Talley gives me a part-amused, part-confused glance. It's the Jack Daniel's talking.

"Hmm, I think it's time you had some lunch."

I prop my arm on the door and rest my head on my hand. "You probably think I'm pathetic, huh?"

"How are you pathetic?"

"Gee, let me guess. I come down here for sex. I get tipsy off one drink. And now, I'm being led around by my date's ex-girlfriend. Put it all together, that spells *pathetic* to me."

"If that's what you think, baby girl." She laughs and prepares to light a cigarette. "You are wrong."

"Oh, really?"

"Really."

I realize we are getting on an expressway and she has to yell over the rushing air.

"I haven't told you about me and Jared, yet!"

* * * *

"Are you sure you don't want any? It's good. Put hair on your chest."

I smile, but give a dubious glance at Talley's fork where a morsel with the appearance of fried shrimp dangles. I go ahead and take the piece, dip it in the special sauce, and pop it in my mouth. I immediately wish I hadn't. It tastes like deep fried gristle. My grimace says it all.

"Hmm." She frowns. "I guess alligator is an acquired taste." She takes another bite. "It's not as good as my Nana's, but it reminds me of home."

Smiling, I take another piece of my new-found favorite dish: fried pickles.

"You'll like the jambalaya, Eva, I promise."

Personally, I never understood the appeal of Cajun food, but my smile broadens. I can see why she and Jared got along. Talley may be louder than Jared, but they share the direct approach towards life. When our entrees arrive, she's right. I do like the jambalaya.

"If you can groove on this," she says between bites, "wait 'til tonight when we do Tex-Mex."

"Damn, Talley, what are you trying to do to me?"

She makes an impatient grunt. "Child, please. Look at you. You got curves saying you know what good food is all about."

If I hadn't grown to like Talley, I would've been insulted.

"Yes, ma'am. Jared likes women of substance."

I cast a glance over Talley's "substance." This athletic, blond, Nordic Amazon tucks into her meal like a marine and flirts with our waiter, and through him, the bartender—just enough to get our bar tab on the house.

"So, tell me about Jared." I wipe my mouth with a napkin. "You've known him since high school?"

She looks up at me and smiles. "I was wondering how long it would take for you to ask. Yes. We met as sophomores and have been together since."

I've barely put a dent in my meal, but Talley has finished hers and gets out a cigarette. Our table is outside and next to a window, and she leans against it so she can stretch her long legs on the bench seat.

"I know this is unfair, Eva. Jared's told me a little about you and how you met, but I'm sure he hasn't said squat about me." She takes a drag off her Winston.

"No," I confirm. "He hasn't said much of anything."

"He's like that. Don't let it get 'cha down." She gives me a sheepish glance. "I hope he hasn't scared you none."

My stomach lurches. "Scare?"

"Oh! Don't get me wrong. Jared's a gem."

"So I've heard."

Her eyes open wide. "Do I detect sarcasm? Good. He needs someone to spar with. Kick him in the ass every once in a while. It's hard with my being down here." Her voice trails off then picks up volume. "He's been burdened with some real lightweights. You're a breath of fresh air."

"Thanks. I think."

She points her cigarette at me. "No, Eva, I mean it. Don't lose that mouth of yours for nothing. My Jared gets bored with women. He gets stuck with a whiny, pampered type, but he's too much of a gentleman to take out the trash, if you know what I mean."

When she said "my Jared," I got a small pang. Is it jealousy or fear? Either way, it reminds me that I'm here with his ex-girlfriend, and she still has affectionate feelings for him.

Talley takes a long pull off her cigarette. It shrivels up, turning into a cylinder of ash dangling from her long fingers. With a well-manicured nail, she flicks the ash off into the tray and picks up her glass for a drink of beer.

"That's what keeps me and him so close, you see. We don't suffer fools for long. We need someone with whom to commiserate." Laughing, she brings the cigarette to her lips. "After all he's been through, he can be enough of a Southern gentleman to hook 'em when he wants 'em, but less than tactful when the time comes to tell these cunts to ride their rag somewhere else." Talley takes another drag and blows the smoke out of her nose, lending emphasis to her disgust.

I could only wonder about the "cunts" to whom she referred and if I would be relegated to one of their number, so I make a noncommittal sound. She laughs.

"One time, he dumped this girl by bringing the other girl with him on a date!" She wipes tears from her eyes. "It was cruel, but that's high school for you. I could've killed him, but he hates leaving anyone or anything behind."

My appetite is totally gone. I fold my napkin and rest it beside my plate. When I look up, Talley's blue-gray eyes are fixed intently on me. Is she trying to put me off him?

"What I'm trying to say, Eva, is that when Jared splits with a woman, they usually part friendly. But, depending on the woman, there have been some ugly breaks."

"And?"

"And Jared can be a USDA Prime Asshole when he wants to be. Let me tell you something," she says, leaning forward, "I noticed by the way he looked at you this morning that he wants you . . . if you know what I mean."

"Hmm, I think I do." I frown and can imagine a sign light up over my head advertising: *Have birth control. Will travel.*

"I don't think you do. Eva, the look he had in his eyes this morning is reserved for you and you alone. There is something in you that just clicks with him."

She snaps her fingers for emphasis, resumes her lounging position, and laughs. Cigarettes have given her voice a husky, low timbre. Throw in her back-bayou drawl and Talley Monroe has a voice that can bend steel to her will.

"Shit. Wish I had someone look at me that way. I tell you, Eva, for a moment I was jealous. Jared hasn't had a look like that for anybody in a *long* time. If ever. Now, I know we've just met, but you're what that boy needs in his life."

I swallow hard. Apparently, I have her blessing, but I can't allow myself to feel too secure. From the way he broke our gaze in the mirror this morning, Jared is playing his cards close to his chest.

"What you say is very flattering, Talley, but—"

"It's not meant to be flattering, Eva," she says firmly, her eyes suddenly turning cold as flint. "It's the truth. He knows you're no pushover."

"Except when it comes to sex."

She barks a short laugh. "Don't be so hard on yourself!" A huge grin slowly splits her face in half. "It was good, wasn't it?"

My shamed face can't deny it and she slaps her thigh.

"I thought so! Girl, you ain't fooling nobody. How you feeling? You looked a little stiff climbing out of the car this morning. He must've nailed you good."

When our laughter dies down, she takes another sip of beer. The smoke of her cigarette blends into the smoky quartz of eyes, adding to their devilish gaze. But there's a question I've been dying to ask and I can't stand it any longer.

"How long did you and Jared date?"

She puts her glass down and thinks for a moment.

"Just under two weeks."

I guess my face doesn't adequately hide my shock, because Talley's belly laugh gets people looking at us and assuming she's drunk. It takes a while, but finally she's able to sputter out a coherent reply.

"I had a crush on Jared when we first met," she says, wiping her eyes with the heel of her palm. "Other than that, we're best friends."

"You mean I've been walking on eggshells trying not to hurt your feelings for nothing?"

"Oh, bless your heart!" She takes my hands in hers. "You are so sweet. Most women would be doing their best to rub it in."

"Here I am thinking you were hot and sweaty lovers."

"Hold it. I didn't say we weren't lovers. In fact, I'm sure he's done nothing but improve in that department."

"Yeah, but you two seem so attached. Not just friends, not just lovers. I feel like a voyeur." I shrug it off. "It's my fault. I should've asked exactly what kind of 'friend' you were in the beginning."

"But instead you trusted Jared at his word," she says, squeezing my hands.

"Silly, huh?" I chuckle, but she doesn't join in. Instead, she stares at me with what looks like admiration and sighs.

"Eva, you've just made a whole bunch of anxiety go away." She leans back again, still holding my hands and causing me to lean forward.

"What do you mean? Earlier, you asked if I'd been scared of him. Should I be?"

Talley shrugs and releases one of my hands to push back a platinum-blonde lock behind her ear. "Well, he does have a temper that's on permanent simmer. But, like all volcanoes, he's pretty good about giving warning signals before he blows." She takes a sip of beer. "Then again, some people just can't handle change, and nothing in Jared's life has been static."

"Women included?"

"Women included." She shifts her position once again and gives my hand a squeeze. "Eva, I'm telling you this because I like you. You may look all shy and innocent, but I believe you're a party girl at heart."

"I like you, too, Talley." And I'm not giving her lip service. She reminds me a lot of Ana. They seem to know more about me than I do.

"Good. So trust me that although it may seem contrary, Jared craves stability, but he equates stability with total equilibrium. Get me?"

I nod. When the body's at total equilibrium, rigor mortis sets in. I'm glad for the advice, but it doesn't soothe me any. "You're saying Jared isn't looking for serious commitment?"

"What he needs is someone to show him that commitment means trust and permanence. It's a beginning and not an ending."

Suddenly, I get a flashback of the ouroboros he painted on my back and ask, "Do you know what causes him to feel this way?"

Nodding, Talley sighs and watches the pedestrians and traffic cruising by. I wait.

"Jared was placed in the system when he was four years old on the grounds of severe neglect by his parents."

Not expecting this, I blink. I thought his attitude would be attributed to something you hear on talk shows like: "My man won't commit to me because he's married," or "My man's a dog and won't give up his bitches."

But this is serious. I think of Jared, the day we met, and the few short hours we've spent together in Dallas. When I asked him to hold me last night and when our eyes locked in the mirror this morning—those two moments alone told me that he is vulnerable, whether he knows it or not.

"When the state took him in," Talley continues, "Jared didn't even know his name. Thought it was Boy." Talley frowns and grinds out her cigarette with such force, she probably wishes she could do the same to Jared's parents. "They had to wait until his mama sobered up enough so they could track down his birth certificate."

I sit back, stunned, reclaiming my other hand from hers. And I thought my parents were too nosy. It never occurred to me to think about the opposite. From the way Talley keeps her eyes on me, I wonder if she's sizing up my reaction.

"He went from foster home to foster home until he was sixteen, the same year we met." Talley smirks in recollection. "You should've seen him, girl. He was Goth before Goth was cool, and mind you, we're going to school down here in Tejas Cowboy Country."

"I can imagine doing something like that takes a lot of *cojones*."

"No shit. What is this crap they listen to nowadays?"

We high-five over the table and I'm secretly thankful that we get sidetracked into talking about some of our favorite bands.

"Eva, do you know how far we had to drive to get a Skinny Puppy single?" She finishes her beer. "Remind me to show you my photo album." She grins. "Jared looked so fine he could strut sittin' down. He had his hair cut all severe and dyed it this deep-ass purple that was almost black . . . God, did it make his eyes look divine." She lights a new cigarette and has me regretting missing the sight.

"But I think it was wearing the padlock and chain around his neck that finally got him kicked out of school."

"Permanently?"

"Oh, no. He just had to go home and take it off." She chuckles. "Jared was the shit in those days. I don't think he ever realized it, though. You know how those artistic types are. I mean, despite us being on the fringe, he had a way about him." Her smile turns sad. "Some of the jocks tried to kick his ass. Tried, mind you. And those damn cheerleaders wanted in his pants, and then called him a fag because he wasn't interested in them." She shakes her head. "People follow Jared; Jared doesn't follow people."

He can now add me to his list. I try not to frown but I'm not feeling too clever at the moment. I'm either a carefree spirit or a gullible little shit. Right now, I can't tell which. Suddenly, a sultry grin spreads across Talley's lips as our waiter appears at our side. He smiles.

"Get you ladies a refill?"

"You can fill me to the top, baby doll," Talley purrs with a voice so full of innuendo an alley cat would have to think twice before jumping on that proposition. "And get my friend here another Long Island iced tea."

As the waiter walks away, she licks her lips.

"Mmm, that boy's ass is tucked into those khakis *tight*. Give me a youngblood anytime. Where was I? Oh, yes. Anyway, Jared could always express himself through his art. You've seen his work, haven't you?"

"A little," I reply weakly.

"Have you seen his nudes? They will knock you on your ass."

"I bet they would." I look away, embarrassed. Our drinks arrive. "So, high school was a pain," I comment before sipping my tea.

"Was it ever. Like I said, Jared wasn't adopted permanently until he almost finished high school. Ma and Pa Petrie did that. They have five natural kids, but had more fosters coming and going than CPS." She shakes her head. "Talk about people with a whole lotta love. If I didn't think I was overstepping my place, I'd take you out to meet them. But I'll let Jared do that."

She winks and I purse my lips together. She's giving me too much information and too much credit. Although helpful, I'm not sure if all these inferences to my budding relationship with Jared make me feel better. She's counting her chickens before sperm and egg have collided, let alone hatched. But I guess it's to be expected since he did bring me all this way.

"Eva, I'm gonna give you my armchair, pop-psych analysis of Jared." Her hands look soft and elegant as she brandishes her cigarette, reminding me of a glamour queen from the 1940s.

"Jared's life in foster care has made him distrustful. He doesn't like being this way and he won't admit it, but he is. So, to protect himself, he works like a madman on crack and doesn't let anyone get too close. The man is never tired. I dare you or anyone to try to keep up with him. He is always working on several things at once."

I believe it. Jared must have had less than five hours sleep last night, and who knows when he last slept before that.

"He may look cool and collected on the outside, but he's very, *very* impatient. His philosophy is that you never know where you're going to be tomorrow—and he should know. My advice to you, baby girl, is that it's better to get to the point with him and cut the crap. And it better be the truth." She points her cigarette at me and its burning tip reminds me of a smoking gun. Her steel-blue eyes level on me and, for a moment, I wonder if she really does like me or is just being polite.

"It's all about trust with Jared." She adds and takes a drag on her cigarette. "It surprises me how he always ends up with these high-maintenance, phony bitches. I can't see how he stands it."

I smile but get more ill at ease. I haven't experienced Jared's distrust or temper in full flow and not sure if I want to. His impatience, yes, but I wonder how long I'll be around to see it all for myself.

"Why are you telling me this, Talley?"

"Because I like you. You don't seem to be the type of man-eater Jared saddles himself with. Don't get me wrong," she says, giving me the once-over, "I'm not saying that you couldn't attract a following." She grins.

I feel a blush rise to my cheeks.

"But then again, I don't sense that you're the type to use a man for what you can get."

I smile out of politeness. It's true, but my head is reeling. Jared and I are here on a whim driven by hormones. I shouldn't place more meaning in that, no matter what Talley infers or what I suspect. The major part of this equation, Jared, is missing—and I failed math.

She looks at her watch. "Hell! It's pushing two o'clock and he said he'd be back by four. Finish up, Eva. We have to hit the streets."

* * * *

Talley and I are loud as we drive the last hundred yards to her house. I even sit on the car door, holding onto the headrest while waving with my free arm. Jared is already there and leaning against the Chrysler Pacifica he rented.

She speeds into the drive and comes to a screeching halt inches from the Pacifica's rear fender and gives a holler. "Say, hey, chèr! Look here at baby girl!"

I swing my legs over the side and get out of the car. My fashion sense has changed considerably since the last time Jared laid eyes on me. I began the day with a nautical theme; now I wear a Dallas Stars home jersey. The black, white, gold, and green of the jersey clashes with my navy-blue pedal pushers and the red, white, and blue of my Texas Rangers ball cap. Grinning, Jared comes near and I model for him. He whistles.

"I see you girls had fun today."

"Yeah, we did," Talley answers getting out of the car.

"Aw, look at you," I say, reaching up to stroke his face. "Been working hard?"

He takes off my sunglasses and I blink at the sudden change in brightness. His soft lips against my eyelids muffle his laugh. "You're so cute," he says and his lips make their way to mine for a moment. He steps back. "I'm gonna have to take you back to the hotel to change for dinner."

"Nonsense!" Talley says. "Eva's just full of the Spirit of Texas."

Jared gives his pal an arched look, but I look at him with concern and wonder if Talley sees it like I do. Maybe she should rethink her theory about his stamina.

"You're tired. You haven't slept much since we've been here."

"See, I knew it."

I blow off Talley's remark with a brusque wave. Then, as if to play on my affections, Jared wraps his arms around my waist, lays his head on my shoulder, and sighs.

"Aw, poor baby. Talley, we'll catch you later." I lead him to the car. He tries to protest when I aim him towards the passenger seat.

"You don't have the keys," he says.

"Don't I?"

When I produce the keys I slipped out of his back pocket, both he and Talley whistle in unison.

"Damn, she is *good*. Go 'head on, girl. Take him back to the hotel and you minister to him."

Jared shakes his head in defeat as we get into the car. Talley calls after us as we drive away.

"Ya'll be back here by eight! I got reservations!"

CHAPTER SEVEN

▲

"WILD NIGHT"

We meet Talley at the appointed time feeling refreshed but hungry and go uptown to Javier's, a gourmet Mexican restaurant. Sitting in a booth towards the back, Talley tells Jared about our day, but I'm more interested in hearing about his.

"But Eva," she complains.

"Talley, I was there. He doesn't need to know how bad you trashed him or how many men got my phone number." I take a bite of my *Filete Cantinflas*. My flesh has gotten good at sensing Jared's penetrating gaze on me and this moment is no exception.

"Oh, all right. Jared, how did your precious little meeting go?"

He sighs. "I'm doing another gig for PsyTech."

Talley puts her fork down in disgust. "Hell, man, why don't you just take the plunge and sign on permanently? It'll get you back to Dallas where you belong."

"What's PsyTech?" I ask.

Jared chuckles and gives my knee a squeeze. "PsyTech specializes in some of the finest computer graphic work in the nation."

"If not the world," adds Talley.

"They've worked with the film studio out in Las Calinas on the other side of town and with studios in Hollywood."

"So what are they having you do?" I ask before Talley can.

"I've been commissioned to do some work on a full-length feature."

"Don't they have someone on their staff to do that?"

"You'd think," he says with a snort and takes a sip of scotch.

"Sure they have someone, but Jared's the best," Talley says. "They've been courting him for over a year. He won't give in."

"Let 'em court. My price keeps going up and they keep paying. If I was that important, they'd make me an offer allowing me to maintain the lifestyle and freedom to which I've become accustomed." He stretches languidly and laughs. "Even then I might not give in."

"A lifestyle that can afford a suite at the Anatole for a week?"

Jared toasts his friend. "Exactly."

"Well, you go, boy," I say, feeling like I need to contribute to the conversation. He smiles at me.

"Hey, you two, stop it. Don't be getting all hot and horny and leaving me to go clubbing alone."

"Talley, I only got Eva for one more night," he says, stroking my thigh. "I want to give her a night to remember."

"So do I."

"Yeah, I bet." He laughs. "I'm a bit nervous at how chummy ya'll have got after one day."

"Serves you right." I hit his arm. "Letting me believe you and Talley had this grand passion only to discover it lasted two weeks."

"I never said it was a grand passion."

"You never said it wasn't, either."

"Hear! Hear!" Talley raises her glass. "You've been giving the girl grief, Jared. I won't have it."

He shakes his head and sighs, not bothering to rise to the banter Talley and I present. Looking at him, I catch a flicker of an expression I can't quite identify. Weariness? Uneasiness? Whatever it is, he's not his usual charismatic self. If anything, he seems distracted. I give the hand he rests on my thigh a squeeze.

"Are you OK?" My words snap him out of his reverie and when he looks at me, it takes a moment for his eyes to focus. "Do you want to go back to the hotel? You seem out of it."

He shakes his head and leers. "We're gonna rip it up tonight, sugar—in more ways than one."

I push him away and they laugh at me.

"You're just so proper, aren't you?" Talley says.

* * * *

After dinner Talley drives us downtown. I sit in the front seat as Jared lounges in the back. The top is down allowing us to absorb the Dallas nightlife, humidity and all. When I recognize the pink and purple pig sign for Baker's Ribs, suddenly, the surroundings become familiar. We are in Deep Ellum.

"Hey, I was down here yesterday!"

Unlike my daytime visit, the night has brought out all the freaks despite the heat. I start looking around like a tourist on speed. I can't sit still. Most of them look young and barely legal. We come to an intersection and let a group of four kids, dressed in black with asymmetrical hairdos obscuring their eyes, skulk across the street.

"Now, I know they're out past curfew." I snicker. "Look at 'em. Thinking they're so original."

Talley continues cruising down the busy street at a worm's pace, pausing for pedestrians and other cars while I provide a running commentary.

"Ooh! I smell bacon, I see pork! Howdy, officer!" I wave at a bicycle cop and he returns the wave. Actually, he's signaling for a right turn.

I'm having a blast. I haven't experienced anything like it in Colorado in years. Not since they banned cruising down Colfax Avenue and stopped the Mall Crawl in Boulder. I feel like a kid again—immature, if not irresponsible.

Talley turns down a street appropriately named Crowdus. We inch along with bodies, cars, and music from various clubs pouring out into the street. It is a sensory overload.

And we garner attention gliding along in Talley's luminous Impala. Talley and I trade catcalls with pedestrians and have conversations with other motorists while waiting at stoplights. At the corner of Elm and Good-Latimer, we agree to hook up with another carload of people at one of the bars and Talley sets about the task of finding a parking place.   I turn around to see Jared stretched out all comfortable in the backseat. He's watching me with an amused look on his face.

"Having fun, baby doll?" he yells above the noise.

"Yes!" I twist around in my seat to get a better look from behind. He moves forward to rest his arms on the back of our headrests. I grin. "I know what you're thinking."

"I bet you don't," he drawls.

"You think I'm drunk." I look at Talley. "You both do."

"Nonsense!" "Perish the thought!" they scoff, but I know better.

"What will it take to prove to you that I need more than a few drinks to get drunk?"

Devilish cannot begin to describe the smile on Jared's lips. Suddenly, he puts his arms around me and leans back, pulling me over the seats and on top of him.

Our actions cause the car behind us to honk their horn and flash their headlights in approval. This encourages him to give my bottom a squeeze while simultaneously pressing me against his crotch.

"Hey!"

Talley's booming voice makes us stop.

"What?" Jared says.

"Cool it, you two. Pigs at twelve o'clock."

Jared and I straighten up, buckle up, and I nestle in the crook of his arm. This is the third time Talley has scolded us for being affectionate making me wonder if she's jealous and just putting on a brave face. I hope not, because I like her.

"Drive on," he orders and Talley flips him the bird.

The sidewalks glow with neon and I begin to see a pattern in the types of shops in the neighborhood. "Damn, how many tattoo parlors do they have here?"

"Hey, maybe it's time for you to get a companion for your Betty Boop tattoo," Jared says.

"I didn't know you had a tattoo, Eva."

"That's because you can't see it," I say.

Talley makes a knowing sound. "I can't speak for Jared, but I've always wanted to get a tattoo—on my inner thigh."

"Of what?" he laughs. "A sign saying 'one way'?"

"You better watch it, little man! I ain't afraid of whippin' your ass!"

If I couldn't see the amused gleam in Talley's eyes reflected in the rearview mirror, I would've taken the edge in her voice as genuine.

"Eva, you want to get tattooed?"

"Well, I . . . "

"Aw, c'mon, girl! Jared's getting one!"

"I'm what?" he bellows.

"Take it like a man, J. D. If Eva can, you can too. Frankly, I can't see why you haven't already with your fascination of the human body as art blah-de-blah-de-blah."

I look up at him. "Yeah, you know you want to."

"You're not gonna let this go, are you?" he says to her.

She shakes her head.

"Oh, alright," he says with a sigh. "Jesus fucking Christ, Talley! We've been driving for a half-hour! Just park the damn car!"

Then it hits me. Brother and sister: that's how they act, and for the first time since coming here, *my* anxiety goes away.

* * * *

No professional tattoo artist would work on somebody who's drunk, so the three of us decide to take the plunge before we hit the bars. We go inside the first parlor we come to and that's where Talley comes up with the idea that we should all get the same thing to symbolize our solidarity—and that Jared should design it. He bums a piece of paper and a pen from the woman behind the counter who wears a green tank top and is covered in tats. Her stringy blonde hair is pulled into a rattail on top of her head.

"Shit, I can't think of anything." Jared frowns then grabs my arm to pull me to him. "Eva, inspire me, darlin'."

I shrug, but after some thought, I do come up with something and Jared is able to translate it beautifully. Talley comes and leans over my shoulder.

"Seems like Jared's found a critic he'll listen to."

He raises his head. "Leave the woman alone. We're working here."

Our "gang" symbol is a black kitten, a la Tex Avery, and dressed like a hooligan wearing baggy pants with his front paws in his pockets, his cap down over one eye, and a cigarette butt hanging out his mouth. Curved beneath in gothic letters are our initials, J. E. T.

In all, it takes up about two inches of space.

"I like that," Talley says, nodding. "I approve."

"My life is now complete." Jared rolls his eyes and takes the drawing to one of the artists, leaving me and his ex-girlfriend looking at walls covered with tattoo art. He comes back a few minutes later.

"They got two chairs ready. Who wants to go first?"

"Lovebirds first," Talley decrees, pushing us in the direction.

"You're full of chicken shit, aren't you, Talley?"

She turns her nose up at him. "I'm just helping create a bonding experience between you two." She winks at me. "To keep you from getting jealous."

The chairs are in a small room with a curtain sliding on a rod to cover the entrance. Jared takes my hand and sits me in the second chair farthest from the curtain.

"Where do you want it, sugar?" he asks suggestively.

I slide back into the chair and sigh. "Unlike you artistic free sprits, I can't afford to have it anywhere conspicuous. The hip worked for me last time, it'll have to do again."

"Why not on your back?" asks Talley.

"Because I want to be able to reach it so I can treat it."

Jared opts to have his done on his bicep and stoically takes the jibes from Talley and me for being unoriginal.

"I guess it's up to us girls to be the kinky ones," she says and I put my arm around her waist in support. We look at Jared who arches an eyebrow.

"Fuck you, Talley. Eva, I'll get you later."

The curtain is pulled aside and a big barrel of a man with long, frizzy red hair and a beard to match comes in. His skin, if it isn't covered in clothes, is covered in tattoos.

"Alrighty, folks. Are we ready?" His soft, delicate voice totally contradicts his biker image. "My name's Boscoe, and this here is Arnie."

Boscoe indicates a tall willowy youth, who can't be more than twenty, and dressed in faded fatigues with the top dyed red. He has piercings in his eyebrow and nose and wears several silver rings on both hands, one of them being the head of a howling wolf.

"Howdy," Arnie greets in a voice lower than his testicles.

"Arnie, you take care of Sweet Miss, and I'll handle mister." Boscoe puts a hand on Jared's shoulder and it's my opinion that, if given the chance, Boscoe would rather Jared handle him.

Arnie grins. "OK, miss, show me where it hurts."

As I begin to raise my thin summer dress, I suddenly realize I'm about to flash my wherewithal to the crowd. The fact that we are behind a partition with Talley's giant frame blocking the entry barely comforts me. Thank God for bikini waxes.

Nevertheless, I reveal my G-string, stockings, garter belt, and a plump, fleshy hip. I look at Jared, who grins at me and my embarrassment.

"Stop it," I pout. When I push down the top of my garter belt Jared whistles. Even Arnie's eyes light up a little as his thin, pink lips turn up in a smile. "If you don't quit it . . ." I growl but they all laugh.

Boscoe continues to prep Jared's arm, unperturbed.

Arnie pats my shoulder. "Don't worry. You're in safe hands."

"Yeah, well you watch where you put those hands, buddy," Jared teases.

I close my eyes and try to relax as Arnie traces in pen, but my ears burn from the acid rock seeping out of the stereo speakers. Finally, I feel the cold damp of cotton drenched in alcohol. The bitter, antiseptic smell is reassuring. Soon I hear the high-pitched whirl of electric needles coming to life.

Boscoe and Arnie start at the same time. With the first touch of the pen onto my ample flesh, my breath catches in my throat as the needles etch away to permanently embed the image Jared and I created together. We are being branded.

I open my eyes and level a gaze on Jared. He's watching Boscoe, but soon enough, he turns to see me. The acid rock has melted away everything else and there is only us. Any discomfort on Jared's part he expresses only by flaring his nostrils. I, on the other hand, am not above biting my lip and whimpering. After holding my breath for what seems an eternity, I exhale, but it could be mistaken for a groan of pleasure.

"Arnie, what did I say about those hands?" Jared smiles but never takes his eyes off mine.

His stare is getting me drowsy, relaxed, and I smile. His eyes seem glazed too. Suddenly, he focuses on me sharply, just as Arnie adjusts his grip on my hip, giving me a slight squeeze. I'm so caught up in Jared's gaze, a sigh that is rarely heard outside of the bedroom escapes my lips. I'm two seconds away from an orgasm by way of an eye fuck.

"Goddamn, Eva, that boy must be good." Talley chuckles. "Hang in there, baby girl."

Her soft hand strokes a tendril of my hair behind my ear. I nod and my hands slide up the front of my dress to clasp the shoulder straps. She continues stroking my hair, comforting me. A lazy grin spreads across Jared's mouth and he blows me a kiss, but when he blinks, it breaks our connection and I gasp.

"Hurt much, babe?" His words are barely above a whisper but are like a soothing balm when they reach me.

"I'm use to pain, Jared. You should know."

His grin tells me he gets my point. In an effort to control myself, I thought it better to concentrate on the pain, rather than get caught up in the rapture of Jared's eyes. Talley's long, cool fingers caress my temple, taking the sting of the needles away along with a few drops of perspiration.

"Ooh, Eva," Talley murmurs. "This is looking gorgeous."

"Good, because you're next," I say and focus, once again, on Jared. He's looking at Talley with a soft smile on his lips making me wonder if he's remembering their brief affair.

A half-hour later, Jared and I are finished.

"There you go, Sweet Miss." Arnie smiles "It's been a pleasure."

"I'll say." Talley grins. "The way he had you moaning, Eva, are you sure you don't want a cigarette?"

"Quit stalling, Talley," Jared says. "It's your turn."

Arnie gives me a hand mirror to examine his work before applying ointment and a bandage. Despite the red irritation of my skin, our little mascot, full of bad-manners attitude, peeks just above my garter belt.

Jared gently maneuvers me out of the way. He leans against the wall and I lean back against him. Meanwhile, Talley, true to her word, is getting her tattoo placed on her inner thigh.

When she drops her pants, she puts all my modesty to shame.

"It doesn't take much for her to get out of her clothes," Jared says with a snicker.

Talley wears only the slightest suggestion of a thong which matches her complexion so well, for a moment, we all think she's nude.

Young Arnie is visibly taken aback then smiles appreciatively. Boscoe, in all his masculinity, is totally uninterested.

"Arnie, I'm going back into the shop."

Talley hops onto the chair as if hopping onto a saddle. Her athlete's body and outdoor tan has turned her legs into twin pillars of sculpted beauty.

"Tell me, Arnie," she says and spreads her legs wide. "Which thigh? Left or right?"

My jaw drops. From where Jared and I stand, the presentation she makes is like looking up Heaven's Highway for the Terminally Horny. I wonder how many men Talley has sent to their blissful final reward by way of her loins. I look up at Jared to gauge his reaction. After all, this is his former lover; she's beautiful, and still single. He is nonchalant, in fact, he nuzzles my neck. I look back at Talley.

"My God!" She laughs. "Eva, are you blushing? Shit, now I've seen everything."

"Is she really?" Jared cranes his neck to look at me. "I do believe you're right."

I jab him in the bandage and anyone would've thought I kneed him in the groin. Talley, totally casual in her pose, continues.

"Apparently Arnie's never seen a woman's crotch before, because he hasn't answered my question. So I'll leave it to you, Eva." Her mouth curves in a lopsided smile. "Left or right?

It doesn't matter to me. It's a shame to mar such a lovely sight. Finally, I reply. "Right."

"OK, Arnie. You heard the little lady. Right thigh, chop chop!"

I don't know if it's because of her commandeering tone or her dig at Arnie's sexual experience, but either way, Arnie's excitement wanes until Talley takes her right hand, and with one long, elegant finger points to a spot just inches away from going inside.

As Arnie works, Jared cradles me in his arms and we sway. Not to the music, that's far from danceable, but in our little world.

He whispers in my ear, "Let's make it an early night."

Before I can answer, Arnie is lifting his head and wiping the sweat from his brow as a result of his toil. Talley whistles as she gazes at her crotch reflected in the mirror she holds.

"Aw-*right*," she growls, swinging her body until both feet hit the floor. Not the slightest sign of discomfort suggested in her movements. Within seconds, she's dressed and mussing Arnie's mop-topped head like he's some rascally schoolboy, much to his chagrin. She turns to us.

"OK, you two. Let's go rip it up!"

* * * *

We get to a bar and it's packed with bodies dressed in sweat but the music jams. We don't bother stopping for drinks but push our way onto the dance floor.

I'm surprised to find the group of people we met cruising down Elm Street: three guys and five ladies, all in their twenties. They look the same age as my students back home, but this "small" gathering of new friends doesn't stay small for long. Other people gravitate to us, well, Talley and Jared really, getting caught up in their orbit.

As to be expected, the women outnumber the men and soon the women attaching to Jared's sphere threaten to turn me into a far distant satellite. A pair of buxom blondes work their way on either side of him on the dance floor.

OK, fine. I switch into "Dance Ho" mode and make myself available to what's left, dancing with several men. I'm not bothered. Actually, I prefer going to clubs with a group of girlfriends and then breaking off to circulate on my own. The fact that Jared's only a foot away is no problem.

I'm having a good time and on the verge of forgetting that I'm in a foreign state, in a foreign setting, and with complete strangers, when an arm goes around my waist and drags me off the floor. I'm about to do a roundhouse upside the person's head until I realize it's Jared. He's built up a sweat and his face is pale and flushed. He looks hot, and not just in temperature.

"I've been missing you, sugar."

"Could've fooled me," I say with a smirk.

"Jealous?" He grins, pulling me close, and his breath on my neck thrills me as he exhales onto my damp skin. His hands slide down my sweat-slicked back to clutch proprietarily at my ass. A drop of perspiration trails from behind my ear to meet his tongue and his lips suction it away. I gyrate, groove, and freak my body against his until I feel the telltale jutting of his arousal.

He takes my left leg, hooks it around his waist, and I am up against a part of his body swollen plump from the heat. He grinds against me and I cup his face in my hands to cover his mouth with mine. Other bodies brush and bump against us, keeping us vertical.

He breaks away from our soul kiss and when he raises his head, the strobe lighting makes his features alternate between hard and soft, light and dark. Jared looks like a god waiting to take possession of his virgin sacrifice. He's had enough playacting.

"Let's say good night, Eva."

Who am I to argue? When we find Talley at the bar with her new acquaintances *she* tries to argue, but Jared's having none of it.

"Forget it, Talley. Eva and I only have a few hours left and those hours are mine."

I notice some of the ladies around Talley are the same ones who got between Jared and me earlier when we arrived. I smile at them, they throw daggers with their eyes back at me.

While the guys I met start saying and kissing me goodbye, out of the corner of my eye I catch a lady with long red hair dressed in a leather halter top and matching hot pants and sitting next to Talley, slip something into Jared's hand. I turn my attention to them just as he looks at it.

He smiles at the note and at the woman, then leans against the bar, putting his arm between her and Talley. I see the lady's face light up. Time for me to close in. I tap his arm firmly, on his sore spot.

"Ouch!" He turns around with a murderous scowl on his face, ready to smear the bastard who touched him, but when he sees me, he grins.

"Ready to go?"

Smiling, I nod. I also smile at the woman, who smiles back but can't work up the sincerity. Jared moves his arm to put it around my shoulder and that's when I notice the slip of paper on the bar.

"What's that?" I ask, pointing to it.

When he, and she, sees what I'm referring to, he pulls me away. "It's nothing."

He turns away and doesn't see the redhead stand up, murder me with her eyes, and then move away from the bar. Her outfit gives away too much information from the way her ass cheeks spill out of her hot pants. Meanwhile, Talley breaks away from the conversation with her neighbor.

"Let me finish this drink and I'll take ya'll to the hotel."

Jared shakes his head. "We're getting a cab. And I suggest you get one too."

Talley and I look at each other. Her eyes are sad, as if she's losing her best friend.

"I guess this is it, Eva." She puts down her drink and gives me a big hug before planting a vodka-soaked kiss on my lips.

Despite my recent wild behavior, I've never been big on public displays of affection, even between women, but I allow it this time even though it's a bit much. Besides, I'm going to miss her.

"Don't forget about me now that you know where I am."

"As if I could."

"And if J. D. gets on your nerves and needs sorting out, let me know."

I grin at Jared, but he rolls his eyes and pulls us apart. We slowly make our way out of the bar. Stepping outside, even the air of lower downtown Dallas smells crisp and clean after being inside a funk-filled bar. He drags me to the nearest cab.

Luckily, the cab's air conditioning is on full blast. We ride with the windows up and cruise out of Deep Ellum in relative quiet.

"Did you have a good time?"

I look at him; his face is half obscured by the darkness of the cab and the streetlights.

"Jared," I say with a smile, "you have no idea."

He takes my hand in both of his and kisses each of my knuckles. With his head bent down, it's impossible for me to resist running my fingers through his hair.

"You kids callin' it a night so early?"

What the fuck? Oh, it's the cab driver talking. I haven't noticed him or anyone else since my arrival in Dallas, but it's easy for the world to be eclipsed with Jared or Talley around.

Jared says something back to the cabbie, but damned if I know what it is. When he told Talley these are our last few hours together, the word "last" had more than a ring of finality to it. A vise clutches around my throat and threatens to squeeze the life out of me. I look at his silhouette as he leans close to talk to the cabbie and it's hazy and blurred as if I'm looking at him from underwater. I can touch him, but soon he'll be leagues away, miles apart.

A lump rises in my throat. I force myself to swallow and it hurts. When I try to take a deep breath, it sounds more like a sniffle. I can't believe I'm about to cry over this man. Why am I being affected this way? Is it because this amazing weekend is ending and Jared has treated me better than any man has in my entire life? Or maybe I pity myself as an incredible idiot for being seduced? I know nothing about him. He could have a fat fetish or a subconscious superiority complex, and making love to a black woman is a subliminal power play. Maybe he's emotionally scarred from being in foster care and has stalker tendencies? He has issues—then again, who doesn't? But none of these reasons jibe with a man who's shown me nothing but kindness, generosity, and romance at a level I never thought possible and I'm ashamed of my cynicism.

Jared turns his head to me and I see his lips move, but can't hear. He moves again and this time the shadow cuts his face down the middle, much like the shadow he drew across my face at the theater. His face holds no expression but his eyes say it all. He's not playing, he's not being coy. His gaze locks me in place.

He pulls me in for a kiss and the tip of his tongue gently taps on the barrier of my teeth, unassuming, asking to be let in. I allow him complete access and he moans. Our kiss lasts the distance from Deep Ellum to the hotel, but it feels like seconds because soon the cabbie tells us our journey is at an end.

We make out all the way back to the suite, holding hands like young lovers, which is appropriate, I guess, but this feels different. We're not pawing and clawing each other in a frenzy to get our clothes off. We don't speak at all. In the elevator, I steal a glance at him. He's looking at the floor.

"Jared?"

"Hmm?"

"Tired?"

His embrace tells me he has enough energy to do what he wants to do. I inhale his scent of cologne, smoke, sweat, bodies, and heat that records our evening out and as I exhale, his arms constrict around me, molding my body to his. The elevator doors open and he quickly kisses my forehead before stepping out.

Inside the suite, our bed has been turned down and the little lamp on the bedside table is lit, casting a nice, cozy circle of light on and around the bed. He positions me just inside of that warm ring. He peels my dress straps off my shoulder and lets the dress float down into a sheer mass at my feet. The strapless bra is no obstacle as he removes it with finesse and with one hand.

My eyes never leave his as he slowly strips away layer after layer until I stand completely nude. He steps back. Being nude before him doesn't make me uncomfortable anymore, but it's the way he looks at me, as if in appraisal that's unnerving and I force myself to keep from trembling.

He walks around me, his eyes stroking here, caressing there, and raising little goose bumps along the way. I hold my breath and finally, after circling me three times, he stands in front of me again.

"I want to remember you as you are now. Silent." He moves near. "Vulnerable." His hand reaches out and his palm brushes against my right nipple, coaxing it to attention. "Mine."

Blood rushes from my head, making me lightheaded, but he turns and walks into the bathroom. I hear water running. When he returns, I can't see what he holds and I'm afraid to ask, fearing that speaking will break the spell. He gently—almost reverently—kisses me on the shoulder and gets behind me.

I feel it before I see it. A cool, damp washcloth slides down my back from my shoulders to the base of my spine and I sigh. Not stopping there, he kneels and strokes down the side of my thighs. Turning my head, I see him get down on his knees, holding a tiny bottle in his mouth. Then he fills his palm with a liquid and I smell the light scent of baby oil. His hands smooth up from my ankles and between my legs. Up my left leg and down my left leg, then up my right leg and down again. He does this once, twice, each time getting closer and closer to my narrow passages, front and rear.

The third time is the charm.

Jared's fingers slip inside me as another gently caresses the sensitive door to my other secret entrance.

"Oh . . . my . . . God."

My legs start to buckle but I force myself to keep balanced. He grasps my hip with his free hand and clamps his mouth just above my left buttock.

"Mmm," he groans, giving me another hard nip before moving around to the front. He gently kisses my bandaged hip before he buries his face between my legs. I stroke the top of his head as he uses both hands to help make access for his tongue. For several minutes, muffled sounds of contentment come from below my waist until he rips himself away, picks up the bottle of oil, and resumes slicking me up. Over my stomach and up my chest his hands go until they reach my breasts. By the time he stands on his feet, his breathing is quick and ragged compared to me trying to breathe again. He strips, quickly, his eyes lock onto mine, his nostrils flared as if preparing himself for his greatest battle. This is our grand finale.

We fall onto the bed. I straddle him, guide him into me, and apply some hip movements a dancer friend of mine taught me.

"Ah! That's m'girl! Ride it!"

I'm working to make the Rough Riders proud in an effort to burn off a fraction of the heat and passion I have for this man. It doesn't take long for his body to get as oil-slicked as mine. To keep from slipping out of each other's grasp, we cling to each other. Fingernails and bandages be damned, we'll both be mauled come morning.

I can only imagine how the back of my hips will look with four, small, half-moon indents from where Jared insures I stay clamped onto him, or the couple dozen tracks running the length and breadth of his back. As I ride on toward my next orgasm, I see it before me, the Road to Nirvana.

I've been on this path before because of this man, but this time I am closer than ever before. I hold onto the headboard as the kaleidoscope colors of Nirvana's gates come into view. The first time we had sex was intense, but this time is very different. This time, the gates are starting to open.

We're not having sex; we're making love. And the realization that this could very well be the last time I travel this road with him makes it hard for me to keep my emotion in check. My orgasm has me throwing my head back, crying out a loud, bellowing sound that leaves no room for passers-by to speculate about what we're doing. Tears well up in my eyes and spill onto my cheeks, but I don't care.

Jared catches me unaware and soon has me on my back with my ankles pinned on either side of my head. His strength amazes me with the way he can toss me about like a rag doll as I'm sure my flexibility surprises him. From the strained look on his face, I suspect that he's saving himself for one big climax. But when he stares down at me, that semblance of frenzy turns into one of barely constrained helplessness.

"Eva . . . look what you've done to me." He sighs as he comes, filling me to the brim, and I act like a sponge wanting to absorb it all. I press my lips to his and swallow the guttural moans from his mouth. There's a ringing in my ears and my body starts to unwind and ease into the mattress.

But my vision of Nirvana is gone, and I want it back.

Our energy is spent. He rolls off me and we lie catching our breath. I turn my head to see the clock on the mantelpiece. It chimes once. My flight leaves in exactly seven hours.

I sigh and close my eyes. I'm sore, bone weary, and emotionally drained. We lie in silence for a long time.

"You scare me, Eva."

The flat, dispassionate tone of his voice jolts me and gets me more than a little worried. Perhaps he thinks I'm asleep, because I don't believe I was meant to hear his words, but when he reaches out and pulls me to him, I lay my arm across his chest and snuggle into his side. He sighs.

"God, I don't want this weekend to end."

I'm surprised, and relieved, that he's put into words what I've felt all evening. I lift my head, but his eyes are closed and he's breathing deep. He's asleep.

"I wish we had more time together," he says suddenly, startling me. He opens his eyes, smiles at my reaction, and chuckles. "I could show you that I'm more than just a pretty face."

Our laughter helps alleviate the mood. We roll over and he's on top of me again, but not to make a move.

"Just making myself comfortable," he says and sighs when I open my arms wide to receive him. "Eva, what am I to do with you?" He kisses my breast and looks at me. "I know what I want to do *to* you."

I grin.

"But I want—I need—to do something *with* you."

"What do you mean?"

"If I told you, you'd think I was a freak."

"Too late." I'm trying to keep our banter going, but when he doesn't respond, I can tell he's really struggling with something and my smart-ass remarks should take a rest. I touch his cheek.

"Jared, tell me. What is it?"

He shakes his head. "Don't think that I get women to come with me on long weekends and subject them to nonstop sex and entertainment." A soft smile creases his full lips. "You are the only woman to move me to such lengths." He kisses me. "Only you."

He doesn't see my look of surprise in response because he rests against me, head on my breast like one big baby, and I think of what Talley said about his past.

Jared is vulnerable, and he does a great job keeping it inside. Perhaps yesterday, when we stood together in the mirror, or that last climax when he seemed at a loss, was a glitch in his sophisticated system of masculinity. Maybe I'm being too cynical again, but closing my eyes, I swallow and finally speak.

"Jared?"

"Yes?"

"Will I see you again?"

Silence.

My pulse stops and I'm sure that he can hear my heart skip a beat. His lips are softer than a feather when they brush against my skin.

"That may be a bit difficult, sugar."

I take a deep breath and it takes me an eternity to speak again. "I see."

"No, I don't think you do." He raises himself to look at me. "Evadne . . . I was wrong to bring you here"

CHAPTER EIGHT

"DISH"

I will never do that again.

What the hell was I thinking? That's just it. I wasn't thinking—my crotch was.

After spending the most exciting, adventurous, sex-filled weekend of my life, I have to start the week in a faculty meeting. I may be one of the few black instructors on campus, but that doesn't stop my colleagues from calling me Black Monday. I hate Mondays, but today, I'm more murderously annoyed than usual.

Let me back up and say that Jared and I acted like a pair of honeymooners when he saw me to my plane last night. Yes, *night*. We missed my scheduled flight because he wouldn't let me out of bed.

He avoided conversation for most of the day, preferring to keep me occupied with fucking, eating, and sleeping. Not bad as far as days go and I didn't attempt to ask for clarification to what he said the night before until we were on our way to the airport.

"Before you ask, Eva, the answer is yes."

"What was the question?"

"Do I want to see you again? Do I care about you? Is this more than sex?"

"So why—"

"Eva, please," he said and reached for my hand. "Let's not get into it now."

Well, when? Should I take that as a clue that we'll really get together again, or assume that he preferred we end on a positive note? But nothing else was said, and the gnawing in my stomach that started the night before as we left the club, and never really went away, came back. This time I thought I would really get sick and vomit all over the rental car, but I closed my eyes and pretended to enjoy the ride. He held my hand all the way. It's amazing how much can be said by holding hands; the occasional squeeze, the stroking of a thumb, it conveys volumes. The only time we broke physical contact was when we got out of the car.

I was just in time and my gate was just beyond the security check. People were boarding, but I was in no hurry. Despite admitting he wanted to see me again, Jared's reticence was little consolation. I watched people board the plane and then I looked at him. He pinned me once more with his gaze, but his eyes were red and tired, and the lips I've fallen in love with were set in a frown. He reached up and tucked a strand of hair behind my ear and tilted up my face. Once again, he sighed one of those sighs that sounded more like a growl, but it was tinged with regret. He pulled me close and nuzzled my neck.

"Take care."

I nodded.

"I'll be back Thursday."

I nodded again and he stepped back, smiling. "Don't you have anything to say?"

I shook my head. I was sulking. I had a lot to say but couldn't find the strength or the words. An omniscient voice announced my flight and once again he tugged me near, cupped my face in his hands, and kissed me. I felt my resolve give way by the constricting in my throat, but I wasn't going to cry.

"I'll call you," he whispered. "I promise."

I moved away and gave him a skeptical look, but he was serious.

"Eva," he whispered as if urging me to believe him. I gave him a little smile.

"Jared, call me if you want to."

His grin said it all. He was gloating and I'd just made the biggest jackass of myself by giving him an easy out. We looked at each other, and goddamn if I didn't wish I could read what those eyes were telling me: Stay here. Go away. This was fun, but it'll never last. You're too big, too poor, too smart.

I looked to the floor and Jared slung the duffel bag containing my "lost weekend" attire onto my shoulder, but the bag hit the sore spot on my hip. I winced in pain and the knowledge that I had a permanent reminder of a four-night stand. Jared gave my hand a squeeze of support and let go. I rushed through security without a problem and at the gate I turned to look back.

But he was gone.

Now it's Monday morning and I'm fidgeting in my seat as I sit in the faculty meeting. I'm not my usual laid-back, friendly self, and although I'm an assistant professor and not tenured, today I have the same jaded look and attitude of the lifers in the department.

I hardly pay attention, and it's not often that Dean J. Paul Mathis floats down from his office on high to tell us anything, so it must be important. I really should listen, but I have a crisis of my own, damn it. I have replayed and analyzed every action and every nuance of what was said last weekend. I have broken it into a million pieces in an attempt to make it easier for me to digest. Now, I may be able to swallow it, but I can never put those million pieces back together again.

"C'mon, Eva, let's go."

I blink and I'm back in the present with my friend, Glynnis Johns, poking me in the arm.

"What do you want?" I snarl.

"The meeting is over. What's wrong with you?"

I see faculty members filing out of the conference room, then focus on Glynnis. She's an attractive, plump, and buxom redhead in her late forties, sort of a cross between a grandmother and a saucy barmaid.

She was the first person I met when I came to Bellingham but it was her goofy sense of humor that made us friends. Her American Literature students love her—that and the costumes she sometimes wears to class, especially the ones she uses while covering the Jazz Age. I know for a fact there are students who have her on a Mothers-I'd-Love-to-Fuck list, only because some people haven't learned the art of discretion and that voices carry. But it amazes me how innocent and optimistic she can be, and although I'm years younger, I think I'm more worldly.

"Sorry, Glyn. I'm not here."

"That's obvious."

We exit the room and walk down the hall. She links her arm with mine and I wonder why.

"So . . . is that why you were so quiet during the meeting? Do you think you'll cope now that Hyde's gone?"

"What did you say?" I stop abruptly. This is news to me.

Glynnis gapes at me. "You really are gone, aren't you? Evadne, the whole reason for the dean coming to speak is to tell us, officially, that Hyde did get busted."

"Well, duh." I scoff. "Any professor stupid enough to get caught fucking his student *inside* the classroom deserves everything he gets."

She gives me a wide-eyed stare in return.

"Yes, Glyn, I said 'fuck.' Big deal."

"It's not that. I thought you liked Terry."

"I do like him, Glyn! He is—was—my faculty mentor." I stop to look out of the windows and at the crepe myrtles blooming outside.

"Oh." She is quiet for a moment. "Is that why you're upset?"

"Hmm?"

"I never felt it my place to discuss this sort of thing with you, you know? The whole sex thing and all, but . . ."

I turn to face my friend. "What are you talking about?"

"Terry liked you, Evadne. Didn't you ever notice the way he acted around you?"

I shrug. "He was like that with everybody."

She crosses her arms over her chest and looks at me the same way she would a student trying to feed her a line of bullshit.

"Oh, give me a break." I'm starting to get mad. Terry Hyde is the Ancient Lit professor. He's attractive and in great shape for a man pushing sixty. But, despite his Sean Connery good looks, his smug attitude kept me from being totally enamoured, unlike other faculty members and, apparently, other students.

"I think it was the day you stood up to him in the faculty meeting that really won him over," she says. "From that moment on, he didn't treat you like a mediocrity, but almost as an equal." She chuckles. "As equal as a female could hope to be in his book."

"That's because I'm not scared of him, Glyn. Besides, if Terry Hyde liked me in that way, why didn't I notice? And why did he get caught screwing a student? The man is married."

"You refused to notice him, that's all," she replies and we start walking again. "Hell, I wish we could all be so blind. We made bets in the department on how long you'd last."

This stops me dead and I look at her in total disbelief. I had no idea I was the subject of a bet, and a stupid one, at that. She shrugs.

"Terry would've slept with the student regardless. He's done it before. This time, he got careless."

"No shit. And thanks, Glyn, for telling me the entire department thinks I lack in morals so much that I'd go for a married co-worker. Glad you got my back." I shake my head. "Just because I like him and he was my mentor doesn't mean I don't think he fucked up big."

We're outside now and the street is getting loud with morning traffic. Glynnis makes a sound and I look at her.

"You're not as innocent and demure as you look, Evadne Cavell. And speaking of getting fucked, I'd say it's about time that you *were*."

My belly laugh is not what she expects to hear and the stunned look on her face makes me laugh harder. I take her by the arm. "Come on, woman. I'll buy us a coffee." We walk across the street.

"But this situation with Terry Hyde goes deeper than his yo-yo pants, you know that don't you, Eva?"

"It's a show of political force, you mean?"

"Exactly," she says as she opens the coffee shop doors. Inside, the line is short and there are empty tables since we are ten minutes into the next class period. We place our order and I convince her to split an apple danish with me. We get a table in a corner by a window.

"Terry Hyde is old school, Eva, and that doesn't help him right now."

I purse my lips together. It's something I don't like to admit to friends and family, but Bellingham College is tilting more into right-wing fanaticism that's been sweeping the nation for the last few decades. Three years ago, when Chancellor Justin McGivern retired after twenty-five years in the position, it was the end of an era. Since then, Bellingham College has been trying like crazy to catch up to the reactionary bandwagon—similar to the U.S. Supreme Court after it lost Thurgood Marshall and gained Clarence Thomas.

Under the new auspices of Chancellor Howard Gaylord (Neil Hollister's great-uncle), professors, tenured or not, who were left- of-center started feeling the squeeze of upper admin. Some retired, or opted for early retirement, because they could see the writing on the wall and couldn't face the pending battle over intellectual freedom. Others were cut off in other ways: they were overlooked for promotion or had their budgets cut. Others were just told their services were no longer needed. In their place, Bellingham College retained and acquired those whose thinking was more in line with the new regime.

For the past few years there has been a witch-hunt atmosphere on campus. When one of the grand dames of the "old school," Professor Agnetha Saunders, who headed the History department had developed a cross-discipline program between the History and Sociology departments, a plan on the verge of being blessed by Chancellor McGivern, the program was dismissed by Chancellor Gaylord without a backward glance. Professor Saunders resigned, causing a mass protest by students, faculty, and staff.

The New Order has succeeded in shaking the liberal tree and the rot's set in. Now with Terry Hyde getting caught with his pants down, it's another reason to rattle things up again and see what other fruit is ready to fall.

"Hyde may be old school," I say, "but there's a thing called privacy, Glyn. There are co-eds in this place that I wouldn't mind pumping." The look of horror on her face almost makes me do a spit take, it's that comical.

"Seriously?" she asks once she can speak again.

"Hell, yeah. Take Neil Hollister, for example." I'm being a smart ass for even suggesting it, but I just want to get a bigger reaction out of her. I succeed.

"Please tell me you're joking, Evadne . . . please?"

I give her my best poker face for about five seconds before grinning.

"Eva, don't you scare me like that!"

"Why does that scare you? Hollister is a hottie."

She looks around to check for anyone listening. "That kid is trouble."

"Because the only reason he could even register at BC is because of dear Uncle Howie?"

"Don't play around with that one, Eva, that's all I'm saying." She leans forward conspiratorially. "There's a group of snot-nosed brats who have devised a little game." She tears a piece out of the Danish. "A kind of blackmail to menace or to get their way, and these little players are sharp. I don't know if you've noticed, Eva, but some of our esteemed faculty can get a bit careless." She rolls her eyes and takes a sip of coffee.

"Anyway," she continues, "if they feel they have something on you and they target you, they give you a nickname like Oscar, or Emmy, or something, because you are now their prize booby. Get it?"

I fall back against my seat and laugh. "Glynnis, do you really think I'd be so stupid?"

"No, I'm just saying that sometimes it's the lame dog that has the biggest teeth."

I stare at her. Glynnis has a talent for coming up with colorful, if not poetic, statements. But I'm not even going to ask her to explain that last one.

* * * *

Jared returns today at five o'clock. He called on Monday afternoon, but I missed it because of another damn staff meeting. Although I was thrilled to hear his voice, his message was far from romantic.

"Hello, Eva. Just thought I'd call. Take care."

And that was it. Bastard.

I don't want to seem like a clingy female, but on Tuesday, I couldn't resist mailing a card to his house of a black and white photo showing a nude couple spooning on a bed with white sheets wrapped around their lower bodies. The photo is shot from directly above. His hair is short and blonde, but hers is long and dark and fans out over the pillows. They are asleep and obviously spent after an active session in bed. Inside, the blank card I wrote:

When you get lonely—call.
E.

Subtle enough, I thought. I'll give him a few days' breathing room, but he won't need it. He'll call me within twenty-four hours. I've been tempted to call him in Dallas, but I refuse to look that desperate.

Now it's Thursday and I've had trouble concentrating all day. It's exactly one week since Jared "kidnapped" me to Texas. I have to pace myself. I can't go rushing home and call him like some schoolgirl. No. I'll give him time to get home, unpack, find my card—then I'll call.

To keep my mind occupied, I arrange to meet Ana and our friend Tony Lobos at Marlowe's on the 16th Street Mall for dinner.

Tony Lobos is a Renaissance man when it comes to business. He's a bisexual Latin lover, and, in my opinion, a poor man's version of Chayanne, as far as his looks is concerned. After working for fifteen years in public relations and advertising, he and his cousin, Encarnaçion "Carnie" DeLuna, bought the small company Tony worked for when the owners retired. Now, Howling Moon Publications produces and promotes periodicals focusing on the Latin community. He also has real estate investments and interests in several businesses, like DeGaulle's Restaurant and the Te Amo Café. All these connections make him a social maven. Carnie, on the other hand, is a big "Mama Cass slash Mother Earth"-figure and absorbs everyone into her sphere, Tony included. She's also the kindest woman I know.

While we may not resemble a likely group of friends, the three of us met years ago at the University of Colorado in Boulder while Ana and I studied for our bachelor's degrees and Tony was a grad student.

Tonight we sit upstairs looking down at the sidewalk and commenting on the pedestrians.

"Will you look at this one coming up," Ana says. "Why must women wear white sneakers and white socks for their power walks?"

"That's my number one fashion pet peeve," Tony says before taking a sip of his rum and Coke.

"Aw, it doesn't bother me," I say and steal a piece of calamari off his plate. "But I think how some offices that mandate hosiery is sexist."

Ana and Tony stare at me.

"Evie," Ana says, "you've never classified anything as *sexist* before. You must be serious."

"Damn straight."

"Don't say 'straight', darling, say 'forward.'"

"Sorry, Tony."

Ana gives me a sidelong glance as she prepares to sip her martini. "Tony, has Eva told you whom she's been seeing?"

"No, she hasn't." He gives me a hurt look, and his hazel eyes take on a puppy-dog sadness, but I'm not buying it.

"Hey, I've tried! Why don't you clear out your voice mailbox sometime?"

Tony turns a deaf ear on me and faces our mutual friend. "Who's she messing with, Ana?"

"Jared Delaney."

Tony stares at me agape and I know I've done something big because he is speechless. Finally, he gains his composure. "No way. Our Little Eva's seeing *Mr. Libido*? Girl, I salute you."

"Uh, hold up. What's this 'Mr. Libido' shit?"

"Have you fucked him yet?"

"Why must you know?" I arch an eyebrow at him.

Tony grins. "I'll take that as a 'yes.' Don't be getting testy, girlfriend." He pats my hand. "It's just that he's well known in circles."

This doesn't relieve my apprehension and I think my face registers it.

"Does he swish, Tony?" Ana asks, once again making up for my lack of speed.

"Oh, no. He's strictly hetero as far as I know, damn it." He smiles wickedly. "But one hears stories."

"I hope they're amusing." I say, trying to sound casual.

"All I'm going to say is that he's been active."

I look down at my plate. My appetite is gone but I cut into my chicken anyway.

"So what do you know?" Ana's inquiring mind wanted to know. I would've asked but I've crammed my mouth full.

"I don't mean to say he's a dog, but talk about a small world." Tony makes himself comfortable in his seat, preparing to dish the dirt. "I have reliable sources. You womenfolk will tell a gay or bi man anything."

"Such as?" Ana squeals and her eagerness makes me look at her. This is how she reacts when she's ready to hear normal gossip, but this is about *me*—and I'm sitting inches away! I may as well be invisible as they carry on the conversation without me.

"I know Sarah Radcliff." Tony crosses his legs and shoots his cuffs.

"Who's that?" she asks.

"Jared's girlfriend."

Another forkful of chicken gets crammed into my mouth to keep me from screaming, but it doesn't prevent me from choking. Tony slaps my back and when I think I can do so, I speak.

"And who is Sarah Radcliff when she's not busy being Jared's girlfriend?"

Tony gives my shoulder a squeeze then takes my hand.

"She's an actress here in town."

"Oh, really? What has she done lately?"

"She's playing Nora in *A Doll's House*. Don't you remember? I introduced you."

I let my mind take me back several weeks to the opening night of the play. For once, a majority of the Denver critics agreed at the caliber of the production. I remember how the woman playing Nora captured the essence of the character: coquettish, naive, childish, but finally showing strength in the end. Then I get the vision of Sarah in my mind. She's a lithe, pale creature with long blonde hair.

Sarah is what you'd call a "twirler." A man could pick her up, impale her on his prick, and spin her around if he wanted—she's that tiny. The man playing the husband, Lars, could sweep her up into the air effortlessly.

Yes, Sarah Radcliff has talent and beauty to spare.

When Tony introduced us at the cast party, Sarah responded the way I expect a big fish in a small pond would. For being shorter than me, she still managed to look down her nose at me.

I frown and Tony strokes my hand lovingly. "I'm sorry, darling. I didn't mean to sound like a catty gossip." He shoots a pointed look at Ana and they giggle. "But seriously, chica, don't be upset. I can put two and two together."

I give him a questioning look but he laughs.

"Listen, dearie, the director told me that all during rehearsal, Sarah griped how she and Jared had been at odds. Then suddenly," he says and snaps his fingers, "it stopped. She stopped talking about him altogether and was decidedly less bitchy. More pleasant to work with too."

Tony releases my hand to digs into his meal. "I assumed they patched things up, but if you're seeing him, hats off!"

My lips turn up in a weak smile. I remember the greeting card and my heart skips a beat. But I continue to eat, hoping maybe it will keep me from being sick all over the table.

"So how's old Jared these days?" Tony asks.

I shrug. "I haven't had a chance to speak to him since last weekend." But I quickly add, "He did call and leave a message on Monday."

"After he took her to Dallas," Ana supplies. Tony's jaw hits the floor again.

"Stop it, Tony." I point my fork at him. "You'll be catching flies in a minute."

"I thought you just met," he says.

"They did," Ana says, "last week."

"Yes, thank you, Ana-Marie. Tony, I'll let our friend give you the details, but he comes home tonight. I'll talk to him later."

I look up to see Ana and Tony watching me in that knowing, but extremely indelicate way, as if I'm the new girl in the bordello.

"What?" I ask, impatiently and they only smile. "Oh, shut up."

* * * *

I get home at eight o'clock and, despite their behavior, Ana and Tony are always a good time.

After parking in my reserved space, I wave to Hank, the security guard, and rush to the elevators. The journey to the fifth floor seems slower than usual and by the way I shift from foot to foot, anyone would think I had to go pee.

The only thing I want is to hear Jared's voice. My self-restraint can take a vacation along with my sense of decorum. I close my eyes, wrapping my arms around myself, remembering the way Jared's body covered mine, blocking any means of escape.

The bell signaling my floor wakes me from my dream and I rush to my apartment. Grabbing the wireless extension, I make myself comfortable on the couch, grinning like an imp. I'm about to talk to my man. Someone who can make me act out the Divinyl's song "I Touch Myself" without shame. I press the button—already programmed with Jared's home number—and wait to reconnect with him.

On the fourth ring, I panic, but I let it ring two more times.

"Hello?"

The drowsy, yet curt female voice on the other end makes my insides churn. I swallow. Maybe I programmed the wrong number. Or the man *gave* me wrong number. The fucking bastard! I take a deep breath before saying, "Ahh . . . hello? Is Jared home?"

"He is asleep right now. May I take a message?"

Asleep? At eight o'clock at night? Texas time is only an hour ahead of Colorado. His reaction to jet lag must be strong—and contagious. This is a woman who was not expecting a wake-up call and certainly not from another female. Meanwhile, I can feel the ice travel through the phone line and I hope I sound composed in return.

"Sure. Could you please tell him Evadne called? And you are?"

"I'm Sarah. His girlfriend," she says and there's no mistaking her agitation. "Anything else?"

"Nope. I think that's all I have to say."

Immediately, the connection ends and a dial tone fills my ear.

Coldness washes over me. It starts in my fingers, travels up my arms, spreads down my torso and to my legs until it finally envelops my feet, freezing me in place. The dial tone is now that obnoxious siren sound. I turn off the phone and let it drop on the sofa.

"He played you, Eva. Played you like the stupid, gullible— *cunt*— you are!"

I feel a stitch in my side and looking down, I catch a glimpse of the bandage covering my tattoo.

"Fuck!"

At least I didn't tell Tony and Ana about the tattoo. I don't think I could ever live down the shame right now. If humiliation were a physical feeling, it would be deep, like a knife carving inside the gut.

Or a multitude of sharp, painful pinpricks from a tattoo gun.

I can even taste the blood coming up from the wound—but it's really just from me biting my lip to keep from crying, screaming, or throwing up. I look down and see the newspaper lying on the coffee table

I wonder what's playing at The DeLuxe.

* * * *

"Plan to live the lush life, Eva?"

Ana stands in my doorway with the requisite bottles of Jack Daniel's and Absolut.

"I would've gone to the movies, but I'm too late for the last showing. Where's Tony?"

"He had a date, remember?" She steps through the door and closes it behind her. "Went to it after dinner."

"What about Frankie?"

"Hell, he can fend for himself. He's not helpless." She brushes past me and goes to the kitchen to deposit the bottles. "It's a good thing I'm off tomorrow or we'd have to cut this party short." She gives me a hard look. "Damn, woman, you look horrible."

"Thanks, pal."

"I'm sorry, honey, but really." She takes me by the arm and we go to the den. "I haven't seen you this upset since you had Minette put to sleep." Ana steers me to the sofa and sits me down. "I'll pour you a double." She looks me over. "Even though you don't really need it."

"Oh, yes, I do."

Ana's methods are circumspect. She's not going to press the issue. We make ourselves comfortable and I turn on the stereo that I've already loaded with CDs to reflect my mood. When I'm ready to talk, she'll listen and by the fifth whiskey sour, the grizzly details flow as easy as the alcohol. She gasps.

"Sarah answered?"

"I don't need this, Ana." I shake my head. "I should've known when he started acting funny in Dallas."

"But what about this Talley Monroe woman? You and she got along. She said you were perfect for him."

"Yeah, but that's just her opinion, isn't it? Dating briefly in high school over twenty years ago doesn't mean she knows everything about him. Plus, she's his ex." I sit up. "Anyway, I'm sure she's a lesbian . . . or bi. Hell, I maybe I should be, too, so I wouldn't get so worked up about some man." I rub my hands vigorously over my face. "God, I've been so fucking stupid." I look at my best friend. "We've known each other most of our lives. You're like my sister. Would you ever guess I'd let a man take me out of state on our first date?"

Ana purses her lips together. "No. I must say you shocked the shit out of me when you told me. But Eva, control yourself. You could go out tonight and get any man."

I shudder at the thought. Ooh, little does she know.

"I don't want any man," I whine.

"You just want Jared," she finishes, mocking me. "Well go get him."

"Ha! Easy for you to say."

"Eva, please." She moves beside me from the opposite sofa. "What have you to lose? Your virginity?"

"You think maybe I should ice this Sarah bitch?" I take a swig of vodka.

"No, you're not listening." She puts her hands on my cheeks and makes me look at her. "Go . . . get . . . him."

I try to focus on her mouth and what she's saying. It finally clicks. "Oh, hell, no!"

The music stops as the last track on the CD has played out. Ana does the honors, Jack Daniel's bottle in hand, and rummages through my collection for more discs to load. She takes a swig.

I don't like simpering, Lilith Fair, vagina rock and won't give it space in my home let alone my stereo. I need something with an edge. I need to hear something by someone who is angrier than me at the moment. "Put in Rollin's Band," I tell her. "I'm still in a don't-fuck-with-me mood."

Ana starts putting away the CDs when she spots something on top of the player. Standing, on shaky legs, she opens the sheets of paper. "Holy shit!"

When I realize what she holds, I sober up quick.

"Gimme those!" Unfortunately, my legs refuse to support me and I slide off the couch.

Ana is now studying the drawings Jared did of me in various stages of sleep and recovery. She whistles. "This man has talent. When'd he do these?" She returns to sit by me.

I rub my face and groan. Then looking through my fingers, I reply. "That first one was the morning we got to Dallas. The other three were done the day I left."

"And you posed for him?"

"You could say that." I grimace. "I'm not gonna lie. He wore me out. It was all I could do to sit up." My laugh dissolves into a sob and Ana puts her arm around me. I wave her off.

"Throw those things away."

"Fuck no. You look beautiful in these, Evie. I'm jealous."

"But I can't stand it, Ana! They're just gonna remind me of the jackass I've made of myself."

"Will you cool it," she says, looking at me. "Has it ever occurred to you that Sarah's being at his place is more fire than flame?" She blinks.

106

"Or is that more chains than clank? Whatever. You know what I mean. Damn, come on now. The man takes you away, spends *hundreds* of dollars on your crazy ass, and fucks you 'til you're disabled. That must add up to something in the 'I'm interested' ledger."

"Oh sure, and Sarah was just there for convenience because Jared didn't want to tell me to piss off. Talley told me he was like that. Shit! Why didn't I think of that before? She could've been setting me up too."

Ana frowns and strokes my hand. "This isn't like you, girl, but I know what is."

"What?"

"Revenge."

" . . . I'm listening. Such as?"

"Oh, I don't know." She leans back into the sofa and takes another drink. I copy her and put my personal bottle of Absolut to my lips. "What say we go wake those lovebirds up and tell 'em about it?"

"Yeah." I giggle. "Grab 'em by the short and curlies."

"Show 'em we mean business," she says, then finishes the last of the whiskey.

"I'll change their definition of the word 'pussywhipped.'" I take another drink. "No one screws me over without getting some part of his anatomy put in a sling."

"From what you describe, that'd be a mighty big sling."

Vodka fountains from my mouth as I do a spit take and we howl with laughter. After a few minutes, we settle down. We look at each other, both of us knowing that to carry out our plans would require movement and eye-hand coordination.

"In the morning," Ana says. "We'll get 'im in the morning."

CHAPTER NINE

▲

"AFTERMATH"

It's almost noon when I roll onto my side and slide face first off the couch. My injured groan makes Ana stir from where she sleeps on the opposite sofa under a chenille throw.

"Oh, Jesus." I breathe slowly to prevent my belly from making any sudden moves. This is my first deadly hangover in years. Not even my night of debauchery at Trish Stevens's New Year's party compares to what I feel now. Something has to give—but not before I get to the bathroom.

I make it just in time. Fortunately, I don't end up worshiping the Porcelain God, but I do sit and think for a while.

It will take some doing, but I will do it. I will banish Jared from my thoughts and leave this part of my life to pass without remark. I have to. I'll even save up for tattoo removal. I'm not cut out for relationships and high drama. I just need to focus on my career and get tenure.

When I emerge from the bathroom, I'm totally prepared never to let the name "Jared" pass my lips again. Ana's in the kitchen making coffee.

"You have messages on your phone."

Sure enough, the red light is blinking on the handset. I press the button for the loudspeaker.

"Evie, it's your mother. Don't forget to be at the store at seven. I'm making Mexican cornbread for dinner."

Normally, the thought of Mama's Mexican cornbread has me licking my lips. Not today. The next message is from Tony.

"Hey, girl. I just got your message. I'm sorry, hon," he coos sympathetically. "I'll talk to you later. Ivor says hello."

"Nice to know one of us got laid last night," I say with a smirk. Ana smiles and places a mug of strong brew before me.

"Hello, Eva? It's Jared."

I choke on my coffee and the burning sensation brings tears to my sore eyes. Ana, on the other hand, leans closer to hear.

"Um, it's a quarter to twelve and I thought you'd be at home."

I click my tongue in disgust. He has the nerve to sound disappointed, the motherfucker.

"I'd like to see you, if possible, at about one o'clock. Call me if you can, otherwise, I'll just stop by and hope to run into you . . . 'bye."

"Shit, fuck, and damn." I put my coffee down.

"Mmm, nice voice." Ana grins. "Definitely a son of the South. What 'cha gonna do?"

"I ain't doing squat," I say and sit on a barstool for emphasis. "I have a deadly hangover, I'm supposed to help set up for the gallery exhibit at Daddy's store—and now this."

"Welcome to the wonderful world of relationships, Eva! Speaking of which, I have a husband waiting for me at home."

"Oh, no. You're not leaving me now, Ana-Marie Benedetto."

But she has her purse and one hand on the doorknob. She looks so fresh and moves so fast, no one would guess she helped kill two bottles of Chablis and a bottle of Jack. She gives me a warm, big-sisterly smile.

"And you, Evadne Louise Cavell, are a big girl."

She's out the door before I can protest.

"Coward!" But I'm the only one to hear my reply as it reverberates in my head.

I need a bath. Taking my coffee and grabbing a bag of saltines, I go to the bathroom and prepare for a long soak. I must've dozed off, because the security buzzer going off beside my front door wakes me. I glance at the bathroom clock. He's punctual, once again. Wrapping a towel around me, I go to answer the buzzer.

"What!" I bark.

"Eva?" There's a pause before he says, "It's Jared. Did you get my message?"

"Yes. Did you get *my* message?"

"What message?"

"The one I left with Sarah."

Silence. Then, softly, he asks, "Can I come in?"

"Listen, I have a headache and I'm in no mood to—shit!" Instead of pressing the "talk" button, I pressed "open" and can hear Jared opening the security door through the speaker.

"God *damn* it!" I rush to the bathroom to let the water out of the tub. The doorbell rings as I tie a knot in my purple silk robe. Taking a deep breath, I answer the door.

He stands in faded blue jeans and a black polo shirt emphasizing his athletic frame, looking very handsome and together. I want to slap the white off him, but cross my arms over my chest.

"Hello, Eva."

"What? No flowers?"

"May I?" He smiles and takes a step forward.

"If you must."

His eyes turn cold for a moment, but I don't care. He enters the living room where the remains of last night greet him.

"Wild party last night?"

"Yes. Too bad you and Sarah couldn't make it."

"You have a way with sarcasm."

"What do you want, Jared?"

"To see you." He takes a seat on the barstool I had occupied not too long before. "Thanks for the card," he says with a smile. "It was the first thing I read."

I glare at him. "You're welcome."

He takes me in with those damn violet eyes. I fear my determination may give, but I brace myself. He's nonchalant and looks around as if killing time, not offering any information about Sarah.

"Who's Sarah?"

"My girlfriend."

Case closed. In that instant, my blood pressure spikes and a rosy pink haze clouds my vision. It really is possible to see red when you're enraged..

"Why the hell are you here, Jared? I have no intention of being your spare."

"You're not my spare," he says, the sharpness in his voice matching mine.

"So Sarah's your spare, whatever. I hate to tell you this, but I *am* the jealous type." And I bet I made a fierce-looking sight, too, with my mussed, slightly damp hair, smudged eye makeup, and deathbed pallor. I walk the few steps from the door and into the kitchen. I'm aware that the front of my robe flashes a bit of flesh and fans the light, lavender scent of my bath soap. It gains his attention and I see him inhale deeply.

I refill my coffee mug, then the hostess in me gestures, offering him a cup. He accepts. When I push the mug his way and look at him, his face is soft with amusement.

"What's so funny?"

"You. You're cute when you sulk."

"Why, you son of a—get the fuck out of my house! If you think you can come here after balling your girlfriend and expect me to fall all over you, you're fishing up the wrong tree."

He laughs. "There'd be something wrong with me if I'm looking for fish up a tree. Some English prof you are, butchering metaphors like that."

"Well you can take your conceited smart ass and get the hell out of my face."

Instead, he sips his coffee as if I hadn't spoke. "Listen, Eva. I know I'm about as welcome as an outhouse breeze at the moment, but I'm not as bad as you think."

I raise an eyebrow. Outhouse breeze? I shake my head, not wanting his creative Tex-speak to distract me. "Oh, really? I'll reserve judgement on that." Taking my cup, I exit the kitchen. "I must make my own assessment of Mr. Libido."

He turns in his seat. "What did you call me?"

"Mr. Libido. Don't you know your *nom de guerre*? Seems your reputation precedes you."

"Who calls me that?"

I shrug and carefully step over empty bottles to go sit on the couch. Thankfully, the blinds are down over the balcony doors, because I can't deal with sunlight now. "My friend Tony Lobos told me that the other day. Apparently he knows of your prowess through a few of your conquests."

"I'll be damned."

He's beside me now. Close. I can smell his coffee and his aftershave—Perry Ellis, this time.

"Be flattered," I say with a scowl. "Obviously, the crowd you hang with gave you your title."

"Our crowds must mingle." He looks at me. "Tony Lobos. Didn't he host that theatre benefit and cast party for *A Doll's House* not long ago?"

I nod. "I was there." Now it's my turn to look at him. "Met Sarah too."

He grins. "We could've met that night, Eva."

"No, I would've remembered." I turn away to drink my coffee, cursing myself for letting him think he's so special. His gaze burns into my profile. I know I shouldn't, but I try to make polite conversation. "How was the rest of your trip?"

"Very boring. Eva, why are we talking like this? Will you look at me, please?"

He takes my coffee away and makes me face him.

"I have a hangover, Jared."

"Let me cure it."

"Don't touch me."

Maybe it's the tone of my voice, my choice of words, or a combination, but for the first time since his arrival, he loses his composure—briefly. For a split second, his self-assured attitude disappears and his shoulders slump as if my words hurt him. For a moment, I'm sorry, too, but he recovers and so does my defense. Does he really expect pity?

"Evadne, what can I do? What can I say to make you understand how I feel about you?"

"Talk is cheap. I am not a harem member here for your convenience."

"Should've thought of that before coming with me to Dallas."

I turn on him like a viper about to strike and his face registers his surprise. "Hold it, asshole. I wouldn't have if I knew you were taken."

"I was joking."

"Don't."

He lowers his head and sighs. When he raises it again, his expression is serious. "I don't find your disappointment out of place or unreasonable. Would I be here if I thought they might? Eva," he says, taking my hand in both of his. "Eva?"

I let my head fall back into the cushions and close my eyes. I can't deal with this right now. Correction: I don't want to deal with this now. I want to wait until I'm collected and strong with no chance of his breaking my will.

"Evadne?" his voice is soft and smooth and he raises my hand until my fingertips encounter the softness of his lips. He moves his head from side to side, making my fingers stroke the outline of his mouth. I turn my head away and the shape of his lips burn inside my mind's eye.

"Eva, after you left I could not believe the void it created." His arm goes around my shoulders and he pulls me close. "I know it's selfish, but when you're near me . . ." He sighs and his breath warm against my ear. "It's like I feed on your spirit. You open me. You inspire me."

Still, I won't look at him. He presses his lips to the side of my neck. "Jared, don't," I say, but he knows my plea is a weak bluff. His mouth is beside my ear.

"I want to learn everything about you." He squeezes me tighter. "I need to know every inch and curve of you. Please. I am sorry, Evadne. Will you look at me?"

I keep my eyes closed tight, not wanting to face the dilemma he has put me in: whether or not to forgive a man who cheated on me.

But did he cheat? Whirlwind trip aside, not once did Jared "claim" me to be his. Then again, I never bothered to ask if he were free for me to take.

"Evadne?" He gives me a squeeze, pressing me harder against him. His skin is warm. I reach up with my free hand and feel his throat. His pulse is racing. He moans at my first responsive touch and holds my head as his lips crush mine. We slide back. As he covers my face with kisses, I have to spread my legs to accommodate us on the couch, forgetting I'm nude and damp beneath my robe. When I feel the rough denim of his pants and the way his cock tents them, I moan. He presses his hips into me and sighs.

My mind races back to how we were exactly one week ago.

"Oh, Eva," his voice strains, "before we go any further, please say you forgive me." He lifts his head to look at me. "But I'm not going to force you."

I open my eyes and see his grim expression, his lips pressed in a thin line. His nostrils are flared as he tries to control both his breathing and his excitement. I could be a real bitch and push him off me, leaving him to deal with a painful erection, as well as rejection. But, if I'm really honest, it's not entirely his fault. I focus on his eyes and I see—what? Passion? Definitely. Love? Possibly. Sincerity?

I sit up making him move off me. He falls back on the sofa, stretches his arms out, and sighs. I look at him staring blankly at the ceiling.

"I don't blame you, girl. I just wish I could—"

"Jared," I interrupt and when I touch his hand he immediately sits up and faces me. Before he can speak I say, "We need to talk, but not now." His quizzical look makes me add, "I have to be somewhere tonight."

He nods, but I'm sure he thinks I'm blowing him off. He takes both of my hands in his and looks me in the eyes. "Just tell me when."

"Tomorrow?" I shrug.

Jared reaches up and strokes my hair. "Be ready at six o'clock."

* * * *

My father, Preston Cavell, after twenty years of being a successful CPA, cashed it all in and renovated a two-storey, four-thousand square-foot warehouse into a combination bookstore, coffeehouse, music hall, and community theatre. Officially, it's called "Preston's Place," but to the literati and the terminally hip, it's simply "Preston's" and it's located on the outskirts of lower downtown Denver, not far from the Platte River.

Dad's bookstore is the quickest way to understand the "spring from whence I sprang."

My parents, Preston and Ivory, met in 1960 at a sit-in in Montgomery, Alabama. They witnessed the civil rights turmoil firsthand and used to get the occasional personal greeting from "Miss Coretta." But despite everything, my parents' love has prevailed. I'm jealous, really. Considering my track record with men, will I ever be so lucky?

Then there's us—the siblings.

Brother Theo was born the day after Malcolm X was assassinated, and Sister Beverly was born the day MLK was shot. I, however, was born a few years after The Beatles split. Sometimes I think the events surrounding our births had some kind of cosmic effect on our lives. Theo, although not militant, is definitely opinionated. "You'd think the dashiki was invented especially for him," his wife, LaRue, would tease.

Beverly, on the other hand, is the peacemaker in the family, which comes in handy while teaching art in elementary school and dealing with her twin boys, Delius and Darien.

Then, you get to me. I was born with a general sense of confusion and left to wonder: What happens now? Probably similar to what Beatles fans felt after their break up. I dabbled in art and music and literature, only to discover I'm more competent studying their intrinsic value rather than creating them.

Among the three of us, you have in stair-step fashion, Theo the idealist, Beverly the artist, and me—the realist. Personally, I would've opted for one of the other two, but my parents tracked me and picked my course. They already have a son who can charm and do business, an artistic, beautiful elder daughter, so why not have the baby grow up to be a bookworm?

Tonight, I've promised to help set up for an exhibit featuring work of several young artists from the local after-school program designed to keep teens off the street. When I get to the store and park across the street, I see the caliber of the work already sampled in the front windows. I'm awestruck. These kids have talent. Some show a preference for classical conventions of form, subject, and technique, while others are inspired by modern influences and being totally different.

A large truck is parked in the alley between Preston's and the neighboring paint store. Some teenage boys are unloading chairs and pedestals. The young artists are here to help direct how they want their paintings and sculptures exhibited.

Then I see my brother Theo come out wearing faded jeans and a Colorado State sweatshirt with the arms and collar cut out. And although the Afro is back in style, my brother could really use a trim. He sees me and waves, but doesn't stop.

Stepping inside Preston's, you're greeted with the aroma of spice and old books—the spice comes from either incense or my mother, Ivory, whipping up some exotic dish in the back kitchen. When she's not teaching modern dance at her studio, Mom is on her quest to create the perfect curry, the best chili, or the most delicious soup in the world. Since it's summertime, 'tis the season for Mom to invent the world's best barbecue sauce. As a result, today the store smells of things being grilled and smoked to fork-tender perfection.

I walk through the front door and the little brass bell tinkles over my head. On the ground floor, bookshelves are stocked with hard-to-find titles any freethinking liberal would desire. If Dad doesn't have it—he can get it. Upstairs is a multi-purpose area where local talent exhibit their work under track lighting, be it art, literature, music, or theatre, with the help of an archaic, but reliable, stereo system.

At the moment, Dad is behind the counter checking out a customer and hands the woman her book with the receipt hanging out as a bookmark.

"Now, you come back tomorrow and see these kids' work. It'll blow your mind. Here, take these flyers and tell your friends."

I grin at the way my dad gives his customer about fifty handbills and the customer takes them as if getting change. But the amazing thing is that this customer will probably tell all her friends.

One of the reasons Preston's is so successful is because Dad and Theo have an eye for talent and enough personality that would have made Johnnie Cochran look reticent. Dad's CPA background helped finance the business, but Theo's MBA helped them expand. Together, they make the perfect team.

"Hey, Li'l Bit," Dad says with a smile when he sees me and comes around the counter with his arms open wide for a bear hug.

"Hi, Daddy," I say and kiss his cheek.

"How's my little girl?"

"Fine." I blush. If he knew what his "little girl" has been doing, even with his open mind, he'd change his pet name for me—to one that rhymes with "slut," I should guess.

"The set up is going well," he says. "Theo and our young artists are getting things in order upstairs. Bev's trying to get even more reporters to come." He pulls me closer and whispers, "There's a good chance the mayor will attend."

I'm not surprised. Beverly, can organize volunteers or form a coalition in her sleep. I sniff the air. Dad smiles.

"That'll be your mother grilling tuna to go with the Mexican cornbread."

"What's on the menu tomorrow?"

Dad shrugs. "It could be kabobs or quesadillas."

"What do you want me to do?" I ask, taking a look around. The store has its share of patrons browsing the aisles despite preparations for tomorrow's event.

"Go help LaRue with the book displays. She's in the art section."

I leave in time for him to serve another customer and I hear Beverly before I see her.

"Yes. I need your staff photographer here by 6pm tomorrow for the reception."

Her words trail away after her. She's a vision wrapped in blue with a scarf around her long, slender neck leaving the scent of *Escape* in her wake.

I saunter toward the art section, taking time to browse. Even though the store is less than twenty minutes from my apartment, I hardly ever get the time—or take the time—to visit. For a "small" bookstore, the selection is huge. The last time I asked, Theo said their inventory had nearly ten thousand titles. "And we're going into print-on-demand," he informed. Theo always looks to the future.

When I was a child, all I had to do was grab a book and go off to what my parents dubbed "Eva's Corner" at the rear of the store. That's where my late grandfather's overstuffed armchair and a Tiffany-style lamp waited for me. In the wintertime, the corner is warm and cozy because of a nearby radiator, and in the summer, diffused light comes through the window, but not enough to make the area too warm.

The walls that aren't hidden by bookshelves hold artwork, some of which are tagged for sale. The other pieces come from my parents' collection. In the children's section, there is a wall with the words "The Refrigerator" painted in black letters. Beneath, the wall supports a bulletin board that resembles a giant refrigerator door, and on the floor is a work area where small children can color and draw while the adults shop. When they're finished, the kids can put their work "on the fridge."

As I near the art section, I automatically steal a glance down one of the fiction aisles. At the end is a giant, solid-wood door with a brass knob and handplate. On one of the panels words are carved and stand out in gold lettering. I can't read it from where I stand, but I know what it says.

Adult Interests Section. Must be 18 to enter.

Yes. My dad's store has an "adult" section where one man's porn is another man's erotica. Years ago, when I was a child, the door was painted lime green, evocative of the song and the movie. Now, the door is highly polished dark oak and more refined to correspond with the changing attitudes of people to sexually explicit material. But does it show the change my own family has towards the subject? They never stop reminding me of my status as "the baby."

When I was five years old, I got caught behind the green door and my butt caught fire afterwards. The whole experience told me never to open that door because what's in there is something I need not concern myself with. I think the tears that followed blurred away most of my memories of the room, but I vaguely remember the yellow glow coming from the Spanish-style hanging lamp and a nude woman painted on black velvet. One of my dad's eight-track stereos was there along with a stack of tapes by Isaac Hayes, Marvin Gaye, Barry White, and Miles Davis.

I remember tobacco smoke mingling with incense and hushed, muffled footsteps on the burnt-orange shag carpet. As I stared open-mouthed at the issues of *Playboy*, *Penthouse*, and *Hustler*, I didn't notice my dad coming up behind me ready to tan my hide.

"Evadne!"

I jump at the sound of my name and spin around to see my sister-in-law, LaRue.

"Girl, you look spooked. What's the matter?"

"Nothing."

She glances over my shoulder to see if she can spot what intrigued me, but she can't. "Dad says you're here to help me with the displays."

"Yeah. Give me a minute to holler at Mom."

I choose another aisle to go down to reach the kitchen where I find my mom, Ivory, cutting vegetables for a salad. She's with her granddaughters, Maia and Tess—also twins. This scares me. Theo has twin daughters, Beverly has twin sons, and now everyone looks at me to make it a trifecta. When we researched our family tree, we discovered twins come from *both* sides of my family. However, the odds of two-out-of-three siblings having twins are not common, so Theo, Bev, and their families participate in genetic studies.

My mother lives up to her name. She's not what you'd call "high yellow," she's paler than that. She has "good hair" and hazel eyes that skipped a generation only to manifest in all of her grandchildren.

"Hi, Mama."

"Auntie Evie!" the girls chime and jump off their stools to charge at me. I put my arms around their shoulders. Each have their long, black hair brushed to a gloss and caught in two braided ponytails. They are eight and their cousins are fourteen, but they all act like brothers and sisters; and when they clash, it's amusing to see the girls forming a united front against the boys.

"Hi, Eva," Mama says, slicing some carrots. "Do you want to chop these cucumbers for me?"

"Nah. I'm supposed to help LaRue."

Mama presses her lips together. "You just don't want to cook."

I give the girls a nudge and they go back to their workstations on either side of their grandmother. "You have two helpers right here."

She gives me a quick glance up and down, appraising me.

"That scoop neck makes you look too full up top, Evadne. You should stick to a square neck."

"Really, Ma? I hadn't noticed." She's too concentrated on her task to see me roll my eyes. I drop off my purse and hurry out of the scullery before she can nit-pick about something else. I was never slim or athletic like her or Bev and she has always made sure to point it out. She's never accepted the fact I have hips, boobs, and a bottom, and the more I try to hide it, the more attention I attract.

Finally I join LaRue as she forms a pyramid of books by Henry Louis Gates, Jr., Sister Wendy, and Michael Wood, to name a few. I roll up my sleeves and get to work.

"This here is our theory pyramid," she explains without looking up. "Our coffee table pyramid will go over there." She jerks her head over her right shoulder.

LaRue comes from Mississippi. She's about six feet tall and has hair going nearly to her waist and it's natural—a tribute to her Choctaw blood, along with her suede-colored skin. She met Theo on a flight to Chicago when she was a flight attendant. I smile to myself, secretly thankful she didn't work on the flight Jared and I took to Dallas.

"You look like the cat that swallowed the canary." LaRue gives me a conspiratorial look. "What's his name?"

"What makes you think it's a *he*?"

LaRue puts her hands on her narrow hips. "Child, please. You look as if someone greased you up and tossed you naked into the Broncos' locker room."

Warmth rushes to my cheeks and LaRue's dark gaze notices.

"So I repeat: Evadne Cavell, what is his name?"

"Never mind his name." I frown.

I've kept the "men" in my life away from my family out of shame because how can I introduce someone whose name I don't even know? The one time that I have a man whose name I can divulge, I still can't. After learning about Sarah, why waste their time getting to know someone who may not be around long? But my sister-in-law grins.

"See! I knew it. You should know better than try to keep something like that secret."

"Why do women insist they have radar to detect this sort of thing?"

"It's not radar," LaRue says, picking up an armful of books. "It's a God-given talent." She looks me over again. "Just by standing next to you I can tell you've been making up for lost time."

I step away from her and her deep-throated laughter is like a knowing slap on the back, as if to say: you've been up to the Devil's business. Women *can* tell. I think men can, too, but won't admit it. Jesus Christ, did Dad sense it too? My stomach lurches at the thought.

"Calm down, girl." LaRue giggles. "Your secret's safe with me."

"What secret?" Beverly says as she comes from around the corner.

"Eva's got a beau."

I cut out LaRue's tongue with a glare, but she just laughs.

"Ooh, Eva," Beverly squeals. "Is he coming to the show tomorrow?"

I shrug and stack more books.

"What's his name? What does he do?"

I sigh in defeat. "His name is Jared Delaney and yes, he'll be here tomorrow. Maybe."

"Hey, I think I've heard of him." Bev says.

"You probably have. He's a graphic artist."

"Bank?" LaRue smiles knowingly.

"He's not a starving artist, if that's what you mean."

I get back to work. My "secret" is now shared and I don't feel any less relieved. I'm sick of living in a shell for my family's sake of propriety, but I haven't decided how I feel about this whole situation between me and Jared. One thing I do know is that I can either play to the status quo or break the mould.

But how?

CHAPTER TEN

ʌ

"MEANT TO BE"

Jared picks me up at six o'clock, which is early for a dinner date, but late for a Sunday. I meet him at the door wearing a deep-purple satin slip dress, strap-up heels, and with my hair piled loosely on my head. I'm dressed to look hot while keeping cool and his smile says mission accomplished.

"That color really suits you." He wears black slacks and an aubergine-colored linen shirt that complements both my dress and his eyes. He reaches for my hand and draws me near. His lips brush mine softly before kissing my neck and bare shoulder.

"Are you sure you wouldn't rather stay in?"

"I'm sure." I step out of his embrace and he looks concerned until I give him a smile. "This way, we'll talk . . . and nothing else."

I decide to let him interpret the "nothing else" part of my statement as I walk ahead of him to the elevator, knowing he will appreciate the presentation my rump makes in my lightweight dress. When I see a quarter on the floor and kneel to get it, the thin material of my dress flitters up, exposing stocking tops and a bit of garter. Jared sucks in his breath and jabs the elevator button with more force than necessary.

* * * *

The car ride is silent except for the music playing on the radio. DeGaulle's Restaurant is located in a converted warehouse. A red awning and red runner stretches from the door to the curb where a valet waits to park your car. The valet opens my door and, taking his hand, I step out. The night air is crisp and a little breeze from across the river helps alleviate the heat. The valet escorts me to Jared's side.

"Enjoy your meal," he says, more to me than to Jared, and gives a slight bow. As we walk to the front door, Jared takes my hands and turns my palms out.

"What are you doing?"

"Checking if he slipped you his number."

I allow myself a giggle. Even though he smiles, he's not being entirely flippant. Inside, the lobby is crowded and people sit or stand out of the way of the door. The maître d', dressed monochromatically in a fine silver-grey suit, shirt, and tie, spots us and comes from around his little podium.

"It's always a pleasure to see you, Mr. Delaney." His voice hints at some Iberian coast connection, as does his dark features.

"Hello, Baptiste. May I introduce, Dr. Cavell?"

Baptiste smiles and gives a bow similar to the valet. He turns to consult his book and gives Jared a knowing look that makes me suspicious. Tony said Jared is known "in circles" and now I'm wondering how tight these circles are.

"I see you have salon number three reserved. Excellent choice." Baptiste raises his hand to summon a willowy brunette straight from the pages of Paris *Vogue*, who traipses towards us in that bouncy, model-on-a-catwalk way. She wears black linen Capri pants and an elegant but simple white silk blouse, but on her, these simple items look exquisite and rich.

"Celeste, salon number three."

The woman smiles warmly at us, exposing glossy white teeth between slick red lips. "Will you follow me?" She leads us with Jared bringing up the rear.

DeGaulle's interior looks like an outdoor Parisian street café. The highly polished concrete floor reflects the soft string lights and paper lanterns, making it look like pavement after the rain. In the center, a row of belle époque townhouses, balconies included, hide the kitchens and you can see the wait staff enter and exit from various doors. At one end of the massive space is a bandstand with a live combo playing jazz.

The three of us squeeze into a small, gilded cage elevator that takes us slowly to the second floor. Although open to the ground floor, there are several doors going around the perimeter. These are private dining rooms, the "salons," of various sizes and each with a different theme. He whispers over my shoulder.

"I think you'll enjoy the one I picked."

Celeste pushes open the elevator door and takes us to the third door on the right. I'm excited because, even as friend to the owner, this is only my second time here and I have never been inside the salons before. Jared opens the door and I step across the threshold.

"Like it?"

He knew I would. The room is straight out of the 1920s, decorated with inlaid wood and chrome polished to a fierce gleam and plush furniture with rounded arms and backs.

"Enjoy your meal." Celeste's husky voice comes from nowhere but is heavy with innuendo as she closes the door behind her. For a second I'm apprehensive. Is this a restaurant or has Tony created a front for a cathouse? No, I'm being paranoid. The whole idea is romantic in the extreme.

At one end of the small room sits a round table and two chairs. White china with gold trim, tulip wine classes, and linen napkins folded into swans complete the elegant table setting. A cozy sitting area consisting of end tables with small shade lamps, a sofa, and a coffee table is arranged on an oriental rug before a gas fireplace and hearth providing atmosphere if not heat on this June evening. A panel of buttons and a digital display marks a wall stereo unit.

He goes to the stereo and asks, "What would you like to hear?"

I shrug, still trying to take this all in. "Jazz, of course."

"Classical, modern, fusion, or acid?"

He smiles at my blank stare and soon I hear Charlie Parker's saxophone surrounding us. Jared motions for me to sit on the camel-colored sofa. The suede cushions are so soft; this must be what it feels like to sit in butter. I can barely resist melting away. A red leather menu lies on the coffee table. He sits beside me, picks up the princess phone on the opposite end table, and orders a bottle of wine. Then, he makes himself comfortable by putting his arm on the back of the sofa and twisting towards me, but he says nothing. I can sense his thoughts in the dim light and tug the hem of my dress over my knees.

"This is lovely." I look around the room. "Thank you for bringing me here."

He remains silent, his face a mask in the dim light. Did he bring me here just to stare at me like a specimen under glass? His stillness makes it hard for me to be anything but cordial because what happens over the next few minutes will have lasting consequences. Time to get this over with.

"Tell me about Sarah."

He lowers his head and sighs. "Sarah and I go back several years," he says eventually, then settles deeper into the sofa as if preparing for a long ride. He looks at me with a plea in his eyes. "Can I order dinner first?"

I nod and allow him a few minutes to stall, silently enjoying the way his hands grasp the telephone and how his long, solid fingers punch at the tiny buttons. The crispness of his shirt stretches to accommodate the subtle flexing of his biceps. Then it occurs to me that I haven't told him what I want. I can't hear what he says, but he is confident enough to order for both of us. I wonder if I'll like his choice. But Jared oozes with so much carnality and control that, despite my peevishness, I'm getting moist and have to cross my legs. With the ordering done, he's ready to begin and I, too, nestle into the sofa, waiting for a tale.

"Sarah and I have known each other for about eight years but dated for the last three. When I first came to Denver, I worked in print shops and did design and art tech at community theatres around town. We met during a production of *What the Butler Saw*."

There's a soft knock on the door and a waiter enters with a bottle of wine and glasses. He pours and offers Jared a sample. He approves and waves for the server to fill my glass. Alone once again, Jared gives me my glass and I watch him over the rim as I sip. He twirls the glass stem and stares at the pale rose liquid inside.

"She was dating someone else at the time. Another actor, I think." He gives a hollow laugh and shakes his head. "Even then I knew I wanted to get next to her but that wouldn't happen for years. I wasn't making enough money, yet." He takes a swallow of wine. From the lack of emotion in his voice, he could've been asking for forgiveness in a confessional. "Sarah has a reputation for being an ice queen."

"Deservedly so," I quip, remembering our phone conversation, but he cuts me a glare. In fact, he looks insulted, making me speculate about his true feelings for her.

"Sorry," I mumble.

"No, don't be." He grabs my hand and squeezes. "I'm the one who needs to apologize."

"Why didn't you tell me about her?"

"Woman," he says, looking me straight in the eye, "I fell for you hard and fast. Sure, I'd seen you in the theater before, was intrigued by you. But it wasn't until we actually talked that I knew I wanted to know more. Sarah never entered my mind."

I stare back at him not entirely sure how to react and my dubious look must reflect this.

"Eva, judge me if you want, but it's the truth. You really should be careful what you wish for, because for all her beauty and talent, Sarah

124

is conceited and conventional. Butter won't melt in her mouth. She's boring, Evadne. Stale. I curbed some of my more . . . interesting personality traits to please her. But you . . . "

He squeezes my hand again. "I've only known you for a handful of days and you've given me more than any woman ever has."

I can't imagine how and I raise my eyebrow, hoping he'd explain, but he doesn't.

"So when did she enter your mind again?"

He thinks for a moment. "Not until we were in my car and heading for the airport."

I exhale and turn away from him. That's a mighty long time to forget you have a girlfriend when you're taking another woman away with you. Rocky relationship or not.

"Wait a minute," he says and I look towards him. "You think we're still together, don't you?"

"She answered your phone and called herself your girlfriend. You called her your girlfriend, too, not your ex. What am I supposed to think?"

"Did I say that?"

"Yes." I frown. "How long have you been apart?"

He shrugs. "Three, maybe four months."

"So, this is all pretty fresh in relationship terms." I nod slowly. "But you still saw her opening night of the play."

"She really worked hard for that role. I wanted to see."

I look down at his hand holding mine. "No wonder you bristle when I wisecrack about her. You're on the rebound and I made a lucky catch."

His brows come down in a dark angry line over narrowed eyelids and his jaw twitches from gritting his teeth. "God *damn* it, Evadne. Will you stop with the self-pity shit?" He lets go of my hand to rake his through his hair.

The venom of his outburst makes my throat constrict and Talley's warning about his temper being on permanent simmer comes back to haunt me. Suddenly, the color and condition of my fingernails become of interest. I start studying my manicure and he—he's not looking at me, because I don't feel it. I take a sidelong glance in his direction. He's lounging back, one arm along the back of the sofa, the other elbow braced on the armrest, his forefinger and thumb making a sturdy, backwards 'L' to support his head. Although he faces me, his eyes are averted towards the fireplace. His childlike petulance barely disguises the burning virility underneath. If anything, it enhances it.

"Why did you two break up?"

His gaze slowly slides in my direction, his violet irises partly hidden by half-closed lids, but still bright even in the dimmest light. When he sees me watching him, he shifts in his seat. He reaches for the wine bottle and tops off our glasses.

"We were miserable. Sorta like Charles and Diana. We looked good together but couldn't stand each other. Sarah wanted to keep up appearances." He chuckles. "She has plans to go to Hollywood or New York like all actors do. She was getting steady acting and voiceover gigs. I was getting offers for my designs, enough for me to quit my nine-to-five and go it alone. Sarah wanted to start living and looking like the rich and famous. It became an obsession. One night, I snapped."

"How?"

"I forced myself on her." He downs half of his glass of wine. "Made her satisfy me for a change. I guess you could say I got carried away."

I shiver involuntarily. It's not like I can say I know the man, but from the way he clenches his teeth and drums his fingers on the sofa, this confession is taking more nerve than I'm giving him credit for.

"I won't plead temporary insanity, because I don't believe in it." The rest of his wine makes it down the back of his throat. "I had had enough. Tired of pretending to be perfect. Tired of not being myself." He rests his gaze on me. "What I did to Sarah was wrong and I can never apologize to her enough for it. If you were anybody else, I wouldn't be telling you this." He tries to smile and his awkwardness touches my heart. "The last thing I want is to scare you away."

Is this what Talley meant when she asked if Jared had scared me yet? I can only look at him and try to absorb it all. He has this mysterious, dark, Byronic air about him, but this is more than I expected and that he's concerned about my reaction touches me. I take his wineglass and take his hand in mine.

"Did you hit her?"

"Oh, God no. Nothing like that. I just . . . let's say I decided it was time to get creative."

"I see. And what happened next?"

He looks at our hands and then at me. "She left. That night. I stayed at home for two days waiting for the police. But that would've been too scandalous for Sarah. Her image as a self-styled princess is more important to her. No, instead she wrote me a very long, very persona letter telling me to stay away. So, I did."

As long as he's being vulnerable, perhaps now's the time to match his confession with one of my own.

"Jared, Talley told me about your parents … or lack of."

Now it's his turn to look at me, stunned. He's motionless for what seems like minutes.

"You and Talley covered a lot of ground in a few hours."

But his annoyance doesn't deter me. "She also said that's probably why it's difficult for you to leave someone behind."

For the first time since I've known him, his eyes turn dull and cold, not with anger, but as if his fire has gone out because his secret is known. But I can't let his reaction get to me. "Maybe we should stop this."

From the expression on his face you would've thought I told him his best friend just died.

"Eva, don't . . . please."

I don't know what cleaved my heart more: the catch in his voice or his eyes. He looks at me with the eyes of a man who knows what it's like to be abandoned. It's easy for me to see him as a four-year-old child right now because, despite being in his early forties, his face still has a boyish charm and a freshness many women would kill for. But what gives his innocence away is the set of his jaw, as if steeling himself for a blow. And after years of disappointment and uncertainty, he has come to expect the worst. Either he's being sincere or he is the most convincing bullshit artist I have ever seen. His expression combines panic and anguish so pitiful it rips straight to my soul. I can't take it so I turn away.

"Eva, if Sarah—"

"Jared, this isn't about Sarah. I'm not Sarah. I'm not an ice princess. But I just don't think you're ready to let her go." I force myself to meet and hold his gaze. "You made it clear a few minutes ago that I better not talk trash about her. Why was she at your place, anyway?"

"It was her birthday. She'd been drinking."

He looks at me embarrassed and I nod knowingly.

"Did you give Sarah her present in bed?"

He sighs and runs his hand through his hair before replying.

"Eva, Sarah is the past. There is no comparing you with her. I don't want to be anything but honest from now on, because that is how you make me feel. I've hurt you and deceived you and all I can offer is my apology and my word never to do it again." He looks at me and the dim lighting softens one side of his face while keeping the other side dark, hard.

"She wants you back, doesn't she? Admit it."

"OK, she does," he says angrily. "Happy?"

I bite down hard on my lip. I don't know if I'm more disappointed or frustrated or annoyed. I've been second choice many times and have known guys who use women like toilet paper. And while I'm not entirely convinced that Jared's a compulsive dog, I take a few deep, calming breaths before I speak again.

"Jared, it doesn't matter how sincere you are or how I've changed your life. You say you need me, but if you still want Sarah, I can't—I won't compete with an old flame." I look up and see his intense gaze leveled on me. "Do you want her back?"

"Eva, I don't just want you for sex." He sounds insulted and sits up. "Has it ever occurred to you that my relationship with Sarah was purely physical? Despite her lack of enthusiasm and warmth, I only ever wanted her for one thing." He closes his eyes a moment and when he opens them, they shine with something that I can only imagine the source.

"I know we haven't been together very long, but from the moment I saw you in the movie theater, my years with Sarah seem wasted compared to the last week. I have fallen in love with you, Eva. Not in lust. I want you to be comfortable around me, to be yourself. Don't change to fit someone else's image, it doesn't work." He gives my hand a gentle squeeze. "Do you still want to leave me?"

The air in my throat compresses and I can't help but squeak as his hands tighten around mine briefly before loosening, his thumbs stroking my wrist bones.

There's a knock on the door. Our dinner has arrived. I watch the waiter come in and place everything on the table. Jared, however, keeps his eyes on me, waiting for my response.

I think I stopped breathing several minutes ago and have bitten into my lip hard enough to draw blood. I exhale slowly. We both want trust and honesty and, in return, we both expect to accept each other as we are. Is this really too much to ask?

"Jared," I say, struggling to find the words and sigh. "I'm not cut out for high drama. Promise me that I can trust you . . . please?"

He presses his lips in a thin, firm line and grips my wrists to the point of discomfort.

"Evadne, I promise you."

CHAPTER ELEVEN

"A FAMILY AFFAIR"

I can't fault Jared's menu choice for me because the sirloin was perfection. When I mention the art show, I'm surprised at his eagerness to attend and risk meeting my folks. By the time we get to the bookstore things are going full throttle. Judging by the number of people present, tonight is a certifiable success. The shop windows blaze with lights and behind the green lettering announcing *Preston's Place, est. 1975*, I see dozens of people mingling and dressed in fine after-five wear. Some hold little plates of food, some hold cups, while others are becoming adept at trying to manage both.

Well, this is it. For the second time in my life, I am about to introduce a man to my family, or to be precise, my parents. The first time was an unavoidable fluke back when I was in high school and I hope this time isn't the same.

Mom and Dad hold court at the front door, greeting people with Maia and Tess standing nearby wearing identical pinafore outfits and passing out programs.

I grin when I see them. My parents are stylin'. Dad wears a teal-colored suit cut to flatter his portly stature and Mom wears a flowing, ivory-colored lace dress with her long black hair arranged in a crown so her streak of gray hair stands out like a badge of honor. My parents see us at the same time and both fail to hide their dumbstruck expressions.

I have a date.

And he's white.

Their shock makes me wonder if I've been wrong all these years about my parents' tolerance. Oh, hell. Do I really know my parents at all? Just because they spent years at the epicenter of the civil rights movement doesn't mean they are card-carrying members of the Love-Knows-No-Color Club. But when Mom reaches for Jared's right arm and Dad for his left, completely pulling Jared away from me, I want to kick myself for my paranoia.

"You must be Evadne's friend," Mom gushes.

Then Dad cuts in. "It's nice to meet you——?"

"Jared. Jared Delaney."

"Jared Delaney." Mom smiles at me. "I like that."

Yeah, I bet she does. The name Evadne Delaney is going through her mind right now. This is why I never bring men around to meet the family and, once again, I'm assured that I should never trust Beverly and LaRue with secrets.

"Hi, Daddy. Hi, Mama." They ignore me. They're already showing Jared around. When I take a step to join them, Mom spins a pirouette to face me.

"Eva, you stay by the door. We'll be back."

Well I'll be damned.

For the next twenty minutes, I play official hostess with my nieces. I meet the regular patrons, the society crowd, and several of the young artists with their families and friends. Although my parents took Jared away, it's Theo and LaRue who bring him back. They're all laughing.

"Hey, Squirt! I was just giving Jared a quick tour, but here he is, unscathed."

My jaw drops at the sight of Theo. Usually he wears jeans and a shirt hinting of Africa, with his bushy Afro adding a few inches to his 6'3" frame. Now he stands in a navy-blue suit resembling my dad's—and totally bald! The light shines off his pale almond skin and reminds me of how my late grandfather looked. Noticing my astonishment, Theo grins.

"Do you like?"

"Well—yes! You look great! But it's obvious LaRue dressed you, though." I turn to my sister-in-law who sports a red halter dress with a light, fringed shawl. Her long hair is in an elegant French roll.

"Yes, but what about the 'do?" Theo asks, smoothing a hand over his head.

"It looks great. Makes you look years younger."

LaRue rolls her eyes. "Eva, the man saw a patch of gray hair yesterday and freaked."

"Yeah, well I dare them to come back."

We laugh and I look at Theo and Jared. "Good to see you and Jared are playing nice."

"Of course, sis. Jared here is pretty hep. Ain't 'cha, bro?"

"Oh, I'm a wigger from way back."

The boys laugh and give each other a pound. Will the wonders never cease? I guess I'm the only one concerned, but Denver is pretty conservative and despite our being in a place full of so-called liberals, I don't see many mixed couples.

As Theo and LaRue leave, she catches my eye and tips me the wink. I blush, but a tug at my hem quickly catches my attention. I look down to see Tess staring at Jared.

"Jared, I want you to meet my nieces, Princess Tess and Princess Maia."

"Your royal highnesses." He does an elegant bow from the waist, but as he raises his head, he stops and rubs his eyes. "Why, bless my soul, I'm seeing double!"

The girls giggle.

"Now, which is which and how can I tell?"

"I'm Maia." She gives a slight curtsey.

"And I'm Tess." She copies her big sister.

"Yes, but how do I tell you apart?"

"Practice," they chime.

This is their response to anyone who asks, but I rediscover its charm all over again because of Jared's hearty laugh. He reaches into his pocket as he kneels before them.

"Well, two beautiful young ladies deserve special treats."

With a slight of hand he produces twin quarters from behind their ears. The girls squeal with delight. Jared can now call the girls his.

"Are you going to be our new uncle?" Tess asks.

Jared looks up at me with a combination of amusement and astonishment.

"OK, you two. Go have a browse." Mom has returned to her post and I am eternally grateful. "Help yourselves to grilled shrimp quesadillas in the alcove."

I grab Jared by the hand and lead him away.

"Your nieces are cute."

"Yeah. Just adorable."

Instead of going to the alcove I lead him upstairs to the exhibit. The room is crowded but we manage. We take our time perusing various drawings, paintings, and sculptures.

"These kids are good." He nods in appreciation, which I see as high praise coming from someone of his accomplishment. "From what I can tell, you got a bunch of kids that with the right training and encouragement, they can go far."

I smile. "Well, there's my sister Bev and her husband Alex. She'll be glad to hear that." I wave to get their attention. She grabs Alex by the arm and drags him over to us. Her willowy frame works the devil out of her denim jumpsuit. Alex, who used to box in the army, is stocky and slightly shorter than Bev. His dark skin melds perfectly with his chocolate-colored suit. When he's not working as a computer analyst, he helps Bev by counseling and organizing physical activities for kids.

After introductions, I have Jared tell Bev what he just told me and her face lights up. She looks so appealing it's no wonder people are eager to help her just to see her smile.

"Jared, you have no idea how much that means to me." She grins. "These kids deserve every chance they can get to know there's more to life than gangs and guns." She turns to me and frowns. "You know, one of Alex's kids was shot last week."

"Oh no, Alex, which one?"

"Cubby," he says.

Clarence "Cubby" Morton is one of the boys Alex councils. Cubby's a chubby cutie pie and only ten years old. I played hoops with him at one of the group's barbecues last summer and he's a charmer. His mother works hard, but can't stop dating the wrong men. Hearing that he was shot brings tears to my eyes and Alex notices. He puts his hand on my arm.

"He's doing fine at Children's Hospital. Just at the wrong place at the wrong time."

"Yeah," Bev says with a frown. "His daddy came home." Then she turns serious. "His mom is dead, though."

"Are you sure he's alright? What's gonna happen to him?" I ask and feel Jared's arm go around my shoulder.

"Evadne, everything's fine," Alex soothes. "We'll take care of Cubby."

I take a deep breath and when I exhale it makes me shudder. Jared's grip tightens.

"Jared," Bev asks, "would you possibly be interested in giving a talk one day? Maybe holding a workshop?" She gives him a sweet smile. She's working it and Jared is hooked. He looks at me and grins.

"I don't see why not." He reaches into his back pocket for his wallet and gives my sister his card. "Give me a call next week and we'll set something up."

Beverly takes the card and shakes his hand to close the deal.

"On a lighter note, we've been able to make nine sales already."

"Make it ten." Jared points to a canvas of a painting done in pointillism of a woman's profile whose long black tresses turn into a raven in flight. You would've thought Beverly just won the lottery.

"Thank you, Jared. All the money goes to the after school program and towards a college fund for the kids."

The three of them continue to talk but I don't hear. I can't take my eyes off my date. Less than two hours ago he was telling me his darkest secrets and now he's charming my family. His chiseled but delicate profile, long neck, and thick auburn hair make him look like a dusk-colored angel. He's so stylish and put together, could it be that after all my years of associating with frogs I have finally met my prince?

Why am I so skeptical? Because this kind of thing only happens in books and movies where the heroine is a size four and an oil heiress, that's why. If this is a dream, I'll follow it to the end. But if it's a joke, I'll be sure to have the last laugh. I shake my head. No, Evadne. That is the wrong attitude to have. Just take it for what it is. You have finally gotten what you deserve.

Jared turns to me and I guess I have this simpering look on my face because he raises his eyebrows and chuckles. "What's wrong?"

"Nothing." I smile and wrap my arm around his.

Bev and Alex start to leave. "Hey, Eva," she says. "If you see the boys, tell them I need them to set up a few more chairs in here."

"Will do."

"Who are the boys?" Jared asks as we walk away.

"Their sons . . . also twins."

He shakes his head in disbelief then pulls me close to blow in my ear. "You must be very fertile."

"Simmer down, cowboy." Actually, I'm terrified of the prospect—and surprised he isn't. His left hand slips down to my hip and gives it a squeeze.

"You feel pretty ripe to me."

The huskiness of his voice makes me tremble and his taking a nip at my earlobe doesn't help calm my nerves. I moan. We go down the back stairs and immediately to our right is "Eva's Corner." Guests are browsing the aisles and suddenly, we come to—The Door.

"What's this?" he asks with mock innocence after reading the inscription. I purse my lips together and before I can think of something smart to say, he has the door open.

This will be my first time behind The Door since that fateful day in 1977 and a lot has changed. For one, I don't remember the room being so small. Berber carpet has replaced the shag and now nice wood bookshelves, like the ones in the main store, line the walls. The room is painted a dark, hunter-green with oak wainscoting and English landscape paintings hang from the walls rather than nudes on glow-in-the-dark velvet. The whole room resembles a formal Victorian library.

There's a lot more books and how-to guides along with the requisite titles of *Playboy*, *Penthouse*, and *Hustler*. We're the only ones in the room and Jared pulls me along as our eyes scan the shelves. Going around to the next row, I see my nephews gawking at a magazine.

The two rail-thin young men look like junior members of The Temptations with their twin, slate-gray suits, black shoes, white shirts, pinstripe ties, and close-cut Afros.

"A-*hem*!"

Delius and Darien jump nearly two feet and I have to purse my lips to keep from laughing, but that doesn't stop Jared.

"Auntie Evie!" Delius says first. His brother is too spooked to talk. Both of them register blushes on their pale skin.

"What are you doing in here?" I ask.

The boys look at each other. At six feet, they're taller than me and almost as tall as Jared. If they hadn't been raised right, they could've told me to fuck off. Since their answer isn't forthcoming, I reach for the magazine Darien clutches. His knuckles are red from their death grip, but he lets go without resistance. Apparently the boys were lucky enough to stumble upon a magazine that had been separated from its protective sleeve. That's when I discover it's not a magazine, but a high-gloss comic book.

"*The Life of Lucrezia?*" I read the title aloud. The cover shows a sultry blond lounging on a sofa in what looks like a living room. She wears a peignoir trimmed in pink boa that barely covers her nudity. Her nipples and the dark triangle of her sex are visible. Her legs are crossed and she wears fishnet stockings and high heel mules to match her gown. She's talking on a princess phone with this demure look on her face, twirling the cord around her fingers.

"What's this?"

"It's an adult comic, auntie," Darien mumbles.

"Oh, really? And how long have you two adults been reading this comic?"

They look at each other but don't answer. I begin flipping through the pages. What I see is fantastic. The drawings put me in mind of old *Archie* comics circa 1950 that I have in my own comic collection from when I was a child. The images are drawn with bright, primary colors in stylized detail.

But talk about explicit! I've never seen Archie and the Gang do the things I'm seeing in this comic. The panel I look at takes up both pages and shows a man and woman doing it doggie style in a dentist's chair.

The temperature in the room goes up about twenty degrees and I fan myself. The artist not only captures the physical composition of the act but the emotion as well. You can feel the impact of the man moving inside the woman's body from the strain and the bulging veins at his temple and in his neck. Sweat beads at his hairline and his face is beet-red. And as far as the woman is concerned, you can practically hear the pleasured moan spill out of her mouth. Her face is one of complete ecstasy as her porcelain white features blush with exertion, and her blond hair is a luxurious mass of melted gold about her shoulders.

I'm getting dizzy. Despite these past days with Jared, seeing actual images of sex is rare for me. I've only been to a few X-rated movies, and all I saw was a lot of woman showing off full-frontal nudity and silicone castles, but never the penises of the men. I can't even bring myself to flip through a *Playgirl*—though I'm dying of curiosity. But this is just too intense. I raise a hand to my forehead.

"Are you alright?" Jared's voice, full of concern, comes from behind me. I'd forgotten he was there. I nod stiffly but can't look away from the picture.

"Boys, your mother wants you upstairs. Now."

I only hear the feet of my nephews stumbling over each other as they get away. Jared moves beside me and takes the book. "Eva? Sugar, what is it?"

"It's . . . well look at it!"

He opens the book. "Yes? And?"

"I'm sorry. You must think I'm so prude." I smile weakly.

"Hardly. But what's wrong? Does it offend you?"

"No! Quite the opposite. It's made me incredibly horny."

I lean against the bookcase, pick up the nearest magazine, and fan myself. I smile. "We've come a long way from *Archie* and *Ritchie Rich*."

Jared chuckles and continues looking at the book. I start reading the titles of the other comics. Not all are the same bound quality like the one he holds; most of them are printed on newsprint.

I should tell Dad he needs to lock this room when no one's around, or have a buzzer so someone can control who gets back here before some rabid, politically-correct consumer with nothing better to do accuses my dad of corrupting youth. But I see two problems with this move. First, most of the books and magazines have covers that conceal any juicy bits. And second, it would mean telling my dad I was behind The Door—again.

I'll just casually lock the door when we leave. My nephews' secret is safe with me. And as long as they're not like their mother, so is mine.

"Gee, Evadne, if this is the sort of reaction I can expect after you read one of these you should get it."

"Are you crazy?" I look around to see if anyone can see us, let alone hear us. "I can't go up to the register with this. My dad would have a thousand fits."

"Give the man some credit, Eva."

"No way." I shake my head and cross my arms over my chest. "I ain't doing it. I'll go to another newsstand." Jared makes an expression of mock astonishment.

"What? And give money to the competition? Eva, I'm ashamed of you." He looks at me then at the book. "Do you want it?"

I smile . . . and he grins.

* * * *

Hanging around the perimeter at the front of the store, I wait as Jared pays for his painting—and the comic. I pick up a book and watch them over the spine as Dad rings up the sale. Then my stomach drops to the floor.

Dad picks up the comic, his eyebrows shoot up—and he and Jared start *chatting* over the damn thing! Finally, Dad slips it into the stereotypical plain brown bag.

Oh . . . my . . . hell. Now my parents are going to think I'm dating a pervert. Time for some damage control. I saunter over.

"Ready to go?"

"We're all done," Dad says. "Hey, Li'l Bit, Jared and I were just talking about—"

"Preston Cavell!"

Dad turns at the sound of his name. We do, too, and see an older man with salt-and-pepper hair with his hand high in salute.

"Jackson Paul!" Dad grins. "Negro, where you been?"

I take this opportunity to grab Jared and the brown bag and exit the store. The painting will be delivered in a few days. Back inside Jared's Chevelle, I breathe a sigh of relief, but he's been laughing his head off since we left the building.

"Will you cool it, Eva? Your dad seems perfectly comfortable selling porn to his daughter's date."

I hide my face in my hands and he laughs harder.

"Actually," he says as he starts the car, "your dad recommends this book. He can't keep it on the shelf."

"Bully for him."

More laughter from him, but I feel faint. This evening has been a drain on my emotions. When I open my eyes, I frown. We're not near my apartment at all.

"Where are we going?"

"To my place. I want to make it up to you." He looks at me. "In private."

* * * *

Jared lives in a two-storey Victorian in the Five Points area of downtown Denver. I'm surprised he lives in this much-maligned, predominately black part of town—and that he's lived here for over ten years. The area has a reputation that's not entirely warranted, because it's really a lovely and historically significant part of town. I may have grown up in the 'burbs, but I feel at home in Five Points.

His house is painted brick-red with black gingerbread trim. A giant maple stretches to the sky from the tiny front yard, obscuring most of the upstairs windows, but I can see the leaded glass and a half-moon weather vane on the steepled roof.

After parking in the carport, he comes around to the passenger side and lets me out. We pass through a wrought iron gate and he fumbles with his keys in front of the heavy cherry-wood door. It has a large, oval, stained glass pane in bright kaleidoscope colors in an abstract, broken-glass design. The streetlight is diffused through the branches of the maple, making things look stark and black and white.

When he releases my hand to put the key in the lock, I hug myself, suddenly nervous. I've never been on his turf before and now I'm about to walk into his lair, the place where he leaves his public persona behind and can be himself. I think of Sarah.

So what if Jared's good looks and seductive manner are unnerving and he has a temper that I wouldn't want to provoke on my worst enemy? He's not a sex fiend. The man I've fallen for is quite the opposite. If anyone should be nervous it's him, because I am ready to stake *my* claim on him.

He opens the door, flips a switch, and the contrast is so brilliant I have to squint until my eyes adjust. A crystal chandelier hangs above the entryway, illuminating wood floors that brighten the space with the muted warmth of polished pine. Before me is a grand staircase with a landing halfway up before it splits in two directions. I must be gaping.

"Does it pass inspection?"

I can only nod as I hear him close and lock the door. He turns out the light and the entryway immediately takes on an eerie, multicolored glow owing to the stained glass and the streetlight. My shoulders tense and the hairs on the back of my neck stand on end. He's behind me. The whole thought of being in the dark with this man excites and frightens me but also stirs my desire and my pussy muscles clench in expectation.

I smile when his hands come around my waist to rest on my upper thighs and gently pull up the thin silk of my dress to encounter my stocking tops and garter belt. He continues until my dress is over my head and he tosses it on his shoulder. His lips touch my right ear as he pulls me back to brush against his swollen cock. I sigh and relax into his embrace.

"Eva." His lips are warm against the side of my neck, trailing across my shoulder.

"Mmm?"

"Eva," he whispers again, this time it's his tongue that burns on my shoulder blade. He inhales my scent of lavender and heat and exhales an open-mouthed kiss. I groan as he cups my breasts firmly. I wiggle against him, signaling that I'm more than ready for what he has to give. I take one of his hands and begin pulling at his forefinger with my mouth. He sucks back a gasp through his teeth and his reaction gives me a jolt of power.

"Jared?"

"Yes, Eva?"

"How bad do you want me?"

"This bad." He wraps his arm around my waist and thrusts against me, and I feel the long, solid proof of his want.

"How bad?"

He does it again, harder this time. I grab his hand and lead him up the stairs. We get to the landing.

"Go to your left," he instructs and soon we are in his bedroom— a vast, almost empty space with a high-pitched ceiling and a giant rose window that throws a red and pink colored patchwork everywhere. In the dim light and the glow, I assume the plush carpet to be off-white and its thick pile is soft beneath my shoes. I see a giant carved mahogany bed waits for us in the center, piled with pale-colored pillows and a coverlet.

That's when I notice several full-length mirrors, one in each corner of the room. If Jared was any other man, I would be put off by the thought of a man with so many mirrors focused around the bed. But right now, I could care less.

I move away from him and crawl onto the bed, knowing what kind of presentation my ass, garter, and stockings make as I do so. I turn over and lie there on my back, resting on my elbows, and my legs crossed at the ankle. The bed is so lush and rich I sigh with contentment. He approaches.

"Touch yourself," he orders me, his voice deep with desire.

I can't see his face. He is silhouetted against what little light comes through the windows, but I get a thrill at the command. I start stroking my cleavage before caressing my belly. I let one hand go beneath my garter belt to touch between my legs. Then, with the other, I unsnap the front clasp of my bra, letting my breasts free. He sucks in his breath as I squeeze and pull at my own flesh. One advantage of having large breasts is that you can suck your own nipples, which I do. From his heavy breathing I can tell he likes that move. I sit up so I can remove the bra completely, bringing myself within a few inches of him, and take the combs out of my hair, letting its cool, sleek waves fall heavy past my shoulders.

He is taking off his clothes like a prizefighter about to enter the ring. I hear the *whoosh* his belt makes as he rips it through the belt loops and the sound of metal as he undoes other buttons and the zipper to his pants.

"Ooh, Jared, hurry," I mew, caressing and squeezing my breasts. When he stands naked before me, I trap his jutting cock in my cleavage and press my breasts together hard.

"*Jesus!*" he growls and begins thrusting into me. A drop of his essence lubricates my chest and I put my lips to the task, tasting his saltiness.

I force myself, and him, to go slow. For the first time, I'm able to deep-throat him and take in his long, full, thick cock, but he's not fully aroused yet. Nevertheless, I think we are both proud of my accomplishment as he lets out a few short pants. For several minutes I work him, taste him, and love every minute of it. When he extracts himself from my mouth, his penis is a large, wet, shiny rod gleaming in the dim light.

Turnabout is fair play and Jared wants his turn. Gently, he pushes me back on the bed and kneels between my legs, stroking them from their stocking tops to the tops of my ankle-strap heels and back again. I reach to touch his head and caress his hair, my fingers trailing through the thick auburn strands.

His eyes fix on mine as he goes down until his mouth reaches its target. My breath catches in my throat and I close my eyes as his tongue whips me into shape. He pulls me to the edge of the bed and drapes my legs over his shoulders. His mouth is like a warm velvet hand cupping my intimate center, caressing my ache as I clench around him. His tongue probes far, twisting and tasting while his hair rubs like satin between my thighs.

"Ooh, baby . . ." I sigh as I come.

He kisses and nibbles his way back up, over my hips, his tongue tickling my tattoos. He pays special tribute to J.E.T. on my right hip and I smile, stroking his head. Then he continues his journey to my navel, and then up the center of my belly to the space between my breasts. There he spends a few moments, gently pulling and sucking. Now, he's at my neck, the weakest part of my body in terms of my resistance, and I clutch at him. I can't wait any longer.

He raises his head and looks at me. "Ready?"

I nod. All it takes is for him to shift his hips and he finds my entrance. I moan as he engulfs me.

"Ah, yes, purr for me, kitten," he breathes, slowly thrusting deeper. "Take me in."

"Jared," I sigh, "love me . . ."

Those must have been the magic words, because he grabs my hands and pins them on either side of my head, his mouth crushing against mine and he proceeds to do so. He impales me hard and deep, moving slowly, deliberately, making certain I feel everything.

"Evadne," he breathes into my mouth. "I need you so much."

His words make my pussy lips swell with heat and passion and I transfer this to him by gripping his cock tighter, keeping him lodged deep. I don't mind his squeezing my hands so hard it hurts. I don't care if he turns me black and blue as long as I can feel his warmth and his love flow inside me. I rock my hips and he raises himself above me.

Still holding my hands in place, he starts slamming into me hard and fast, making my breasts quiver. The look in his eyes and the force he exerts tells me the movement of my ample bosom is an unexpected bonus. I throw my head back and offer my neck for him to bite, to suck, to worship. He does and I cry out with my second orgasm, clamping my legs around his waist.

"God damn it, Jared, fuck me!"

A loud, guttural roar is his reply as he nails me deeper into the mattress. I become a live wire beneath him, gyrating and writhing. He releases my hands so he can brace himself and I cup his face for a kiss. We try to smother each other with our hungry mouths, and when I break away, our breathing is harsh and fills the room along with the steady rocking sound of the bed.

"Eva," he bites out through gritted teeth, each thrust making me cry out. "I want more. Give me more!"

I pull at his hips, urging him deeper. Looking up at the cathedral ceiling, I can only imagine how we appear with his hulking body plunging into mine. The thought brings me to climax again and this time leaves me weak.

He pulls out of me and I moan in disappointment, but he touches my cheek reassuringly. Getting up, he leaves me lying in a lewd position and too feeble to do anything about it. He stands at the side of the bed with his cock still erect in front of him, but his face is again hidden by shadow. My eyes drift closed.

"You are so beautiful, Evadne."

He speaks so softly it's almost as if he's thinking out loud. I open my eyes. "Jared?"

"Shh. Be still."

He stands there, silently stroking himself. I lie there open and wait. He lifts my left leg and removes my shoe. Then he does the right foot. Placing a knee between my legs, he balances himself and undoes my garters and gently rolls my stockings down. He moves away.

"Turn over."

It takes me a moment but I obey and he unhooks my garter belt. When it falls loose, I arch, raising my rump in the air so I can slide the garment away. Jared moans and soon his weight is upon me, forcing me down. I turn my head and we kiss. He squeezes my breasts before letting one hand slip down between my legs. I arch against his erection and he groans. He reaches to push his cock down but lets his hand linger on my ass.

"Evadne," he says, his breath hot against my ear, "have you ever had it there?" He touches my asshole and I gasp.

"No." I bury my face in the mattress, not sure what his reaction will be. Sure enough, he's silent. His fingertip touches the entrance and presses, opening me ever so slightly. I suck in my breath and he stops.

"Will you let me?"

I raise my head from the pillow. "Yes."

He kisses my shoulder and strokes my bottom. I lay my head down and close my eyes. I feel him leave the bed. He returns a minute later and has me lie with a pillow under my hips, raising me up slightly. Then, starting at the base of my spine and working his way back up, he starts kissing and rubbing me once more.

"Loosen up, it's important. I'm not gonna hurt you, sugar."

He says that last bit with so much tenderness and care that if he wished to rip my heart out, I'd let him.

"I know you won't," I whisper.

He kisses my shoulder again and makes me stretch my arms out and starts massaging them. When I start breathing deeply, he goes to the next step: preparing the way. I hear him squeeze out some lubricant before feeling two, cold, slick fingers slide between my ass cheeks and press into me. I gasp.

"Do you want me to stop?" he asks quickly.

I sigh and push against him, making his fingers go deeper. "No . . . please . . ."

"We can't rush this, darlin.'"

He continues stroking inside me, his fingers gently moving up and down, in and out. Resuming his position between my legs, he simulates the action he'll soon be doing when his fingers are replaced with his cock. He removes his fingers and rolls to his side.

I look over to see him put on a condom and squeeze on more lubricant. Up and down I watch his fist pump and prime his shaft and I moan in anticipation. He turns his head to me and the pale light makes his face look ghostly, like an angel with earthly, carnal desires.

"Are you sure you want this?" His eyes radiate the light coming through the rose window, enlarging his pupils and making his gaze both bright and dark. I reach out to trace his high cheekbone to his full, luscious lips that reflect a smile back to me. He moves back on top of me. "Just relax ... and breathe deep."

When I feel the head of his cock touch my ass, I tense.

"Relax, Evie. Please, honey."

His cooing words and his nibbling at my neck dissolve anymore hesitation and I relax enough for him to push a half inch inside me. I suck in my breath.

"Sugardoll," he moans into my shoulder with so much tenderness and relief, I melt, letting him advance more. He reaches beneath me and begins stroking my pussy, his long fingers softly stroking my clit, causing me to grind against his fingers and push back against his cock.

It is slow going but worth it. I am in sweet agony feeling a combination of being ripped open and stuffed simultaneously. Some moments later, Jared gives a sudden thrust and we both cry out. He is completely lodged and I constrict around him. He embraces me and we lie still, both of us trembling.

"My God, Jared," I say, turning my face to him.

"Are you okay?" he whispers, his eyes full of worry as they search mine.

"Jared," I gasp. "This . . . is *wonderful.*"

And we stare at each other in utter amazement. He looks at me with so much longing, like he can't believe I'm letting him love me this way. I can't keep the tears back.

Then we move, neither one of us taking our eyes off the other as we rock along slowly. He lets me adjust to his size and the motion, stroking my hair, his hips gently pushing into me. He smiles.

"I'm gonna have to come up with a name for you and this lovely, hot ass of yours."

I smile, close my eyes and enjoy the ride. "How about Miss Hot Crossed Buns?"

He gives a throaty chuckle. "Nah. It has to be seductive . . . like you." He kisses my shoulder and raises his head suddenly. "Sister Friction. That's it. From now on, whenever I want to have your ass like this, I'm gonna call on Sister Friction."

I chuckle. "We really are a couple now."

"What do you mean?" He rocks gently against me, going in and out, pressing deeper and deeper.

"We're speaking in code." I sigh and my eyes roll back into my head. It doesn't take long for him to make me come again. When my eyes focus, I see the faraway look in his eyes telling me he's about to come too. A few more solid thrusts, his body tenses, then collapses. I ease him down to earth, my back cushioning him. He holds me tighter in his arms and sighs.

"Dear, sweet, Eva."

An aftershock trembles through him and then me. I reach up to stroke his face. He kisses my palm. I don't know why I feel compelled to do so now, but I must ask.

"Jared?"

"Mmm?"

"Is this what you did to Sarah?"

He is still for so long I don't know if he's asleep, if he heard me, or just too angry to respond. Finally, he answers.

"Yes."

It is not until I nuzzle my head against his that he relaxes and kisses my hand again. I hold on to him as tightly as he holds me.

I fall asleep on my stomach. Our sleep is heavy, like we've been drugged. I feel a tug in my hair and open my eyes. Jared's left arm and leg remain draped over me, the sheets tangled in a mass across the bed.

He is fast asleep, running his fingers through my hair. He looks innocent like a child, so pale and pink. I touch his chin with my forefinger and he sighs. His caress soothes me back to sleep.

* * * *

The next morning is rough. I have to urge Jared not only to get up and drive me home so I can change, but to keep him from begging me to call in sick.

"Don't go." His puppy dog eyes and kiss-bruised lips make it very, very difficult for me to resist but I do.

"Jared, I have never played hookie on my job. Besides, I have to go. I'm giving an exam today." I run my hand through my hair, trying to summon the energy to get out of bed as Jared's fingers trace a design on my back. Then I realize he's not drawing, but writing, and it's the same thing again and again.

L-O-V-E Y-O-U.

I turn to look at him over my shoulder, and sure enough, he's watching me, waiting for me to catch on. Normally, I think it wise to ignore confessions of love made during the height of passion, or even in the afterglow, but he's not playing, not after what we just went through. His message changes.

L-O-V-E M-E?

Still smiling, I nod and turn around so I can rest on top of him.

He gives me a kiss. "Good. Time for a quickie?"

I frown.

"Time for breakfast?"

I look at my watch. It's seven-thirty and my class is at ten. I smile.

"Right." He makes a big show of getting out of bed, stretching, and strutting his nakedness before me as he makes his way to the bathroom. He looks at me, holds out his hand, and I join him.

"No funny business. I can't be late."

"Madam, have no fear." He puts his hand over his heart. "I will protect your honor."

As it turns out, we do have time for a quickie.

* * * *

Now that it's daylight, I can get a better understanding of my surroundings. His house is huge and his is definitely the "master's" bedroom. It comprises half of the space on the second floor including the turret, which he created into a loft space where he has his office that includes an oak table, a few file cabinets, and one of his computers. The space can be closed off by a hanging curtain tapestry. Decorated in a masculine, Empire style, his room contains the majestic mahogany bed with matching side tables, an even larger wardrobe, and a blanket chest. Otherwise, it's minimalist in its furnishings.

The rest of the second floor has his studio, his assistant's office, and another, smaller bedroom. Each room has its own full bath and can function as a guestroom if needed. The house could be a bed-and-breakfast if he wanted.

The first floor has a professional caliber kitchen with walk-in butler's pantry, a sunroom conservatory, a formal library with hundreds of books, another guestroom, and one and a half bathrooms.

As he cooks breakfast, I wander about the place. The rest of his home is reminiscent of the arts and crafts period making his home seem airy and open compared to my cozy sultan's den. Plus, he's a better housekeeper than I am.

As to be expected, Jared has a lot of artwork but is also a collector. I'm drawn to his collection of tin toys and other toy collectibles. Did he have these when he was in foster care or is he trying to recreate a lost childhood?

His art collection consists mostly of work by other artists in practically every kind of media and a lot of animation memorabilia, but I think I've found my favorite piece. It hangs over the living room mantelpiece—a huge, 6'x3' canvas in pale pink and soft brown hues with little contrast. I step back, craning my head right then left, trying to figure it out.

"So, what do you think?"

I'm startled and look up to see him standing in the doorway, wiping his hands on a dishtowel, and watching me, grinning.

"Is that a collarbone?"

"Could be."

"It is, because I can make out the throat now. Ooh, yes, Jared, I like this."

"Thank you."

"You did it?"

"That's what the signature says," he says with a chuckle.

I step closer and catch a glimpse of his signature, a reddish squiggle that looked like J. A. Delaney, but I'm not certain. So that's why Talley wanted to know what I thought of his nudes. "They'll knock you on your ass," she had said—and she was right.

"Come on." He reaches out his hand. "Your waffles are getting cold."

CHAPTER TWELVE

"DRIVING ME MAD"

It's been twelve weeks, I'm dating a man with notoriety, and I am in complete awe.

Sometimes, when I'm at his place, I may be sitting in the window seat reading a book while he's in his office on the phone headset. One time, I actually heard him say: "Have your people call my people."

Jared has "people." Or, to be precise: his attorney, his accountant, and his personal assistant, Trey Harker.

Trey will talk to gallery owners about exhibits while Jared does his thing. I like Trey. He's a natural-born Goth if ever there was one and is always dressed in black. His cream-colored skin is flawless and accented by rosy, sensuous lips, which he's not afraid to gloss a light shade of pink, and his two-toned brown and blonde hair is stylishly sleeked back. Forget Tom Cruise—Trey should've been the Vampire Lestat. Piper, Trey's wife, is a gorgeous Goth, too, but is more like a prettier, younger Morticia.

But I'll never forget the time when Jared, clearly annoyed with a caller, said: "You call that a royalty? Well, I ain't saluting it."

I looked over to Trey who was writing something in a notebook. He must have sensed my gaze, because he raised his head and mouthed the words, *Contract negotiations.*

I nodded and looked back at Jared who was pacing with his arms crossed over his chest. Suddenly he stopped and spoke in a voice that was soft, polite, and menacing all at once. And although he was looking in my direction, he definitely wasn't seeing me. I could tell from the set of his jaw that his patience had breathed its last.

"I think you better regroup and call me when you're serious."

He tapped a button on the keypad attached to his belt. End of discussion. But the chill that went up and down my spine was both frightening and arousing, which disturbed me. I never thought I could be turned on by male dominance. I'm a modern woman after all, and it's hardly PC for me to admit that Jared's ability to take control makes me wet.

Jared then blinked and it was as if he'd woken up. I must have been staring because he seemed surprised I was there and quickly changed his demeanor.

"Hey there, Sugardrop," he said with a smile. "Come over here and give me a kiss."

* * * *

This evening, I'm snuggling in the crook of Jared's arm reading *The Life of Lucrezia* under the soft glow of the lamp beside the bed. We're at my place since my work schedule is more formal than his.

"I am really digging this. The artwork is amazing." I touch the thick, quality paper the comic is printed on and the light coming from my nightstand bounces off the page at an angle and seems to create a photo negative.

"Does this mean you're getting horny again?"

"You'd love that, wouldn't you?" I turn a page and he kisses the top of my head.

This little comic has added an aphrodisiac element to our relationship. I don't need the theater for my thrills now that I have Jared. Ever since he discovered that I'm not put off by anal sex, it has become a part of our repertoire. The first time, I was caught up only in the experience. Now, I've come to realize it's not just about feeling, but more importantly, it's about trust.

Our last encounter has me feeling a bit banged up and I need to rest even though the pictures start stirring my libido. Apparently, Jared is very familiar with this comic or "graphic novel," to be PC about it. My arts education has resumed and he has taken up the role of tutor.

From what he tells me, *The Life of Lucrezia* serial started less than a year ago and comes out every month allowing for longer issues covering more plot. The central character, Lucrezia Spence, works as an elementary school nurse and, needing extra cash, she starts a call girl service with a bunch of bored housewives. It's a risky proposition in the suburbs, but Lucrezia (alias Lucy) pimps her girls during the day to satisfy visiting executives.

"Lucy's Ladies," as they call themselves, take pride in their traditional, almost plain appearance so when they are out on business with these powerful men, they don't scream "trophy wife" or "prostitute." But it's behind closed doors when the drawings become so intense.

"There's something very erotic in a woman, old or young, who can still be a total slut in the bedroom," he whispers as his fingers toy with my hair. I smile.

In the issue we're looking at, Lucy's in a jam. One of her customers, Patrick Klein, is the school district's superintendent. This would be fine if Lucy hadn't allowed a photojournalist to see her picking up one of her ladies outside Patrick's home early one evening. Patrick's been using school money for excessive entertainment purposes and rumors of an investigation have reached the media.

So when Lucy is presented with the "Employee of the Year" award by Patrick, he realizes who she is as she comes forth to accept her honor. Cameras flash. They play it cool, but when a major daily paper puts the photos together—eyebrows are raised and foreheads furrow.

"Uh, huh," I say as we look at the last panel in the issue.

"You sound unimpressed."

"Well, I wouldn't say that. I love the noir style and dry sense of humor. Who writes this thing?" I turn to the cover. The creator only goes by the name Ali. "But . . . "

"But what?"

"I dunno. I have a problem with this Lucrezia chick."

"Really?"

"Yeah." I close the comic and move so I can straddle his waist. This produces a big grin from him. "From what you've told me and what we've read, surely you must've noticed."

He gives me a blank stare.

"She has no control," I say, throwing my hands in the air for emphasis. Meanwhile, I feel Jared coming back to life. I start rocking my hips in a riding motion and he moans, stroking my haunches. "She's a wimp. A twit. Dare I say, 'pussy?'"

"Damn, Eva, tell me how you really feel."

"I'm sorry, but she's a stereotypical blonde. Reminds me of the joke: what do blondes and turtles have in common? Once they're on their backs—they're screwed! How can she stay in business when she lets things happen to her but does nothing to try and stop it?"

"You're a teacher of literature. It's called 'complication of plot,' or something, isn't it? Besides, life's not predictable." He coaxes me up so he can sit me on top of his rock hard penis. I slide down slowly, both of us exhaling together, but I'm not ignorant of his grimace.

"I don't mean it that way. But she is getting sloppy in her dealings. She lets people railroad her," I say and grind myself down on him. He bucks his hips in response, making me gasp. "Soon she's gonna fuck it up and all hell's gonna break loose. End of story. If I were Lucrezia, I'd be a bit more—"

"Commanding?" he interrupts and thrusts up suddenly. My words catch in my throat, so it takes me a moment to reply. I look down at him.

"Proactive," I say with a smile, "and I'd have more self-control." I give him a wicked grin and match his rhythm. Then I open the comic, aimlessly scanning the pages as I ride my own personal stallion. "If I were running that service, I'd do it with both eyes open." I shrug. "I'd just like to see her stronger, harder. But after six issues, Lucrezia showing a spine would be tough for me to swallow."

"Well, Evadne, comics are meant to be fantasy." He grabs me by the waist, stopping my ride, and snatches the book out of my hands. He's scowling. I guess I am being overly critical of something he likes very much, but the English lit professor in me has taken over.

"That may be so, but readers are more sophisticated than they think. Besides," I say, giving my hips a twist, pleased with the sudden pressure on my clitoris the action provides, "wouldn't this 'Ali' person like to think that years from now, people could pick up a copy and be impressed with how well written it is and not just admire the artwork?" I shrug again. "Maybe that's too much to ask of a comic book—sorry, I meant to say graphic novel."

I put my hands on either side of his head, letting my breasts dangle scant inches from his mouth. He looks up at me, not knowing how to accept the gift I present him. Trying not to laugh I ask, "Or would you disagree?"

He throws the graphic novel across the room and pulls me down. "Enough theory," he growls. "Time for practical application."

* * * *

It's a Friday evening in early October and my weekend to stay at Jared's house. As I put my key in the lock, the door flies open making me jump. "What the fuck!"

"Sorry, babe." Jared gives me a quick peck on the nose. "But we don't have much time."

"Huh?"

He's dressed in a nice casual suit while I'm in a faded sundress I threw on. I was expecting a quiet weekend at home. I need some R&R before facing the troops again on Monday. He takes my bag and puts it on a chair by the door, then leads me out by the elbow.

"Come on."

"Jared, where are we going?" Now we're in his car.

"Evadne, I've screwed up royally and if we don't show up," he says, throwing the car into gear, "well, we're both dead."

"What are you—"

"Talley's in town promoting her new book at the Ulterior Motive Mystery Convention. She sent me an announcement inviting us three weeks ago and I forgot."

"Oh. Where is she?"

"The Brown Palace. Tonight is a combination reception and book signing."

"Damn it, Jared, I'm not dressed for that!"

"Hush, darlin'!" He pats my knee. "You look gorgeous. Absolutely edible."

He obviously hasn't looked at me. He's dressed for an elegant cocktail party in black slacks, black blazer, and a cream shirt, while I'm dressed for a tea party hosted by Sanford and Son. We soon arrive at the hotel and my eyes grow large at the number of cars and the outfits on the people coming out of them.

"Just how big is this reception, Jared?"

"Pretty big." He gives me a sheepish glance.

I glare at him, but when I'm helped from the car, I hold my head high despite several conspicuous looks at my attire. My skin heats with embarrassment. Jared comes around to join me and offers his arm and a smile. I take it but I'm too livid to look at him. Sensing my mood, he says nothing but pats my hand affectionately.

We navigate through the atrium lobby crammed with people and make our way to the Grand Ballroom. I've read Talley's latest suspense novel, *Jigsaw*, and it's gotten raves. Now she's here promoting it and the room is packed. Waiters try to make their way through the crowd with trays of hors d'oeuvres and wine. In one corner, I see a giant book display framed by a giant poster of Talley's book cover, but no Talley.

Cameras flash and I cringe. Jared and I are both homebodies by nature when we're not working. We prefer quiet days and nights together, or we drive out of town to spend time in some romantic hideaway. Hell, I've even done the camping thing with the man. But I'm out of my depth here.

"Do you see her?" I ask.

"Who?"

"Talley!"

"Oh. No. No, I don't."

"Well," I say through gritted teeth, "let's find her and give her our regards, shall we?"

He strokes my arm. "Relax, Evie."

I grimace. The last time Jared told me that, I got fucked up the ass. Literally.

A waiter comes by with a tray of champagne and I take a glass. I don't bother to ask Jared if he wants one and the undulating crowd pushes us farther into the room.

"Jared!"

We both look around, trying to discern in which direction the voice came from, and I flinch when a hand suddenly clamps down on my shoulder. It's hard, rough, and masculine, and I feel it through my dress. I turn to see the hand is attached to a tall, barrel-chested man in dark jeans and a dark plaid shirt. A black cowboy hat sits atop his head, covering most of his dark brown hair.

"I thought that was you. Sorry to barge in, little lady, but I had to say howdy to the man."

Little lady? Say howdy to the man? Who is this asshole? Jared, as if reading my mind, answers.

"Honey, I'd like you to meet Charles Arlen. Chas, this is my girlfriend, Evadne Cavell."

"Howdy, ma'am," he says, tugging at the brim of his hat and flashing me a charming smile. On any other occasion I would've responded in kind, but right now the best I can do is pull my lips back and expose my teeth in an artificial grin.

"Chas and I were roommates one summer at UT-Austin."

"It's a pleasure, ma'am. As usual, Jared, you picked yourself a good one." His eyes give me an inspection like I'm some prized heifer. He turns back to Jared.

"Say, man. I need your advice on some art purchases I plan to make next week in California." Chas puts his arm around me. I don't believe this guy!

Seeing my reaction, Jared speaks. "Chas owns a sheep ranch in Central Texas."

"Yet, unlike many others, Miss Cavell, I try to expose myself to more than sheep." He gives me a squeeze and I admit, for a split second, his unfortunate choice of words makes me smile.

"You must love your work."

Jared chokes on his champagne but Chas grins. "Are you interested in ranching, Miss Cavell? You should come during the lambing season. I'll hook you up with some of the best lamb chops in the hemisphere." He squeezes me again.

I reach for another glass of champagne and the action causes him to lose his grip on me, but he doesn't mind; he's already talking to Jared about something else. I take the opportunity to wander off, ostensibly looking for Talley, but really for a place to hide. Maybe if I see her, I can talk to her for a minute and then steal off to the ladies' room until Jared is ready to leave.

All the people, all the voices . . . I'm getting sick from all the money in the room. The jewelry some of the women wear could pay my rent for a year. And here I am thinking writers are poor.

I've been to book signings and book launches before, but when I pick up a flyer off one of the tables with convention promos, I pick up a high-gloss press release featuring the *Jigsaw* cover. This evening is a double celebration, because this is Talley's first book under her new contract with Tony Lobos and Carnie DeLuna's Howling Moon Publishing located in Arvada.

I didn't even know they were courting her! This is her seventh book and rumors are coming from Hollywood. This is a coup considering Tony and Carnie just branched out into book production two years ago.

I swear if Tony doesn't have his finger in everything. Talley too? Nah. That's not Tony's style. But between his charm and Talley's personality, there's no excuse for them not to hit it off—as far as business is concerned, anyway.

So this means Tony is lurking around here somewhere. Maybe he can help me beat a graceful retreat.

More people come in and more cameras flash from various places in the room. The Ulterior Motive is a specialty bookstore in town and a Mecca for mystery lovers throughout the West, not to mention a major rival of my dad's. Five years ago, the owners decided to host a mystery convention and it has grown to warrant the space and the glitz of The Brown Palace Hotel. This is the last night of the convention and the social event of the month—or at least the week. I get a plate of cheese and meat from another passing waiter and grab my third flute of champagne from yet another.

Jared is going to pay for this. Big time.

"There you are."

Speaking of the devil, Jared comes into view and steals a cube of cheese from my plate. He looks at me anxiously. "Babe, I know you're upset with me and I'll make it up to you."

I purse my lips together, unimpressed.

"Honey," he says, "I'm trying to find her as fast as I can."

"Really? Where's your friend?"

Jared snorts and studies my plate for another tidbit.

"He went to scam on the other side of the room. I swear, I could barely stand the man when I roomed with him, and that was nearly twenty years ago." He chuckles. "I didn't know he could read so I'm surprised he's here." He looks at me to see my bland expression, then puts his hands on my hips and pulls me close. I have to open my arms to keep from spilling the contents of my drink and plate on him. He nuzzles against my cheek.

"I don't know why you're so worried. You look fine."

"Jared, I don't appreciate—"

"Eva! Jared!"

To hear my name coupled with Jared's is a shock to me. At first, I thought it could be Talley, but realize it's a man's voice. I turn around and see Tony walking in our direction. And he has company.

"Woman, I thought I recognized the back of your head." Tony is all smiles as he plants a kiss on my mouth. "Where have you been hiding? The bedroom?" He winks at Jared.

I give a short laugh. "Jared, you remember Tony Lobos, don't you?"

"Yes, nice to see you, again," he says and shakes Tony's hand.

"Here, let me introduce the group." Tony steps aside. "These are my friends. Ivor Wozniak, Allison Speed, and Jared, you know Sarah Radcliff."

I have to laugh to keep from screaming. Tony and I have this silly, long-running competition as to who can make the other embarrassed in public without law enforcement getting involved. Tony is really pushing it this time.

"Jared," Sarah says first. Her voice is clipped but cordial. She wears a white sheath dress that flatters her lithe physique, and her pale coloring brings out her wide, almond-shaped, sapphire-blue eyes. It's those ice-blue eyes that run me up and down, freezing me to the spot. Her features are catlike—sleek, exotic, and expressive. Her pale blonde hair is either natural or a very good, very expensive dye job, and is piled on her head, held in place by seed pearl combs. She's several inches shorter than me and much more delicate. She looks exquisite, like a doll of fine bisque porcelain. A fairy princess. No, definitely a Snow Queen.

I glance up at Jared and you would've thought he had rigor mortis. He stands ramrod straight and barely moves his lips to speak.

"Hello, Sarah."

"Is this your new girlfriend?" Her gaze on me intensifies.

Oh. So now I'm a "this."

"Dr. Evadne Cavell, let me introduce Sarah Radcliff."

"Good evening, Sarah," I say, oozing with warmth. "It's nice to meet you at last."

I don't get upset, like some people do, if someone doesn't address me with my title in a social occasion. It depends on the crowd. But I notice how Jared made a point to use it this time. When she looks at my plate, then at my torso, I believe my waist expands a few inches, the dimples on either side of my elbows become more prominent, and my cheeks plump with chipmunk fullness. Doctor or not, some things just don't quite measure up.

"Living large these days, Jared?"

"Oh, yes, Sarah," I reply for him. "No more slim pickings for him."

Tony, who has shifted to stand behind Sarah, gestures as if to say, *Meow!*

"What is it that you do, Eeee . . . ?"

"Evadne. I teach at Bellingham College. And you are?"

Tony's mouth falls open but I ignore him.

"I'm an actress."

"Oh? Isn't that nice. Is there much work for actresses in Denver?" That one hit home and Sarah's delicate complexion reddens.

"Yes, there is."

"That's good. At least you're not a starving artist."

"You would know something about starving?"

"No." I look her straight in the eye and let her know I am done being polite. "I prefer to digest my food."

"Jared!" Tony breaks in. "You and Eva have been too selfish with your company. Come join us for dinner."

I chuckle and look away. I love Tony but I am going to kill him after I'm finished with Jared, who takes this moment to put a possessive arm around my waist, possibly more for Sarah's benefit than mine.

"That's mighty friendly of you, Tony, but we plan on having an early night." He lowers his head to kiss my temple and, to my chagrin, it does provoke a twinge of excitement in me. He gives me a slight tickle under my ribs and I smile despite my anger. Tony grins knowingly along with Trevor and Allison. Sarah is not amused.

"Well, you go, girl!" Tony gives me a playful shove on the shoulder. "Don't let him keep you up all night."

"Tony," I growl, but why? It's in his nature to shock.

"That's my name! I'll talk to you tomorrow, friend-girl. I'll be sure to call when you're awake—and at home."

"*Goodbye*, Tony."

"Ta-ta, tootsie!" He can be camp when he wants to so he gives a little finger wave. His long, lean, elegant figure is soon leading his party away like a queen bee and her faithful swarm. Sarah, however, lingers for a moment.

"By the way, Jared," she says coming close to touch the arm he has around my waist. "If you happen to find my little cloisonné hair combs, I'd be grateful if you could return them." She looks at me. "They were a birthday present," she explains. "I left them behind the last time I was over."

I feel Jared stiffening behind my back—and not in a good way.

"I'll be sure to do a search," he says.

"High and low," I add with a smile.

Sarah gives me a nasty little glare and then floats away. I think Jared can feel my rage through my clothes because my temperature has shot up fifty degrees. I give one of the ubiquitous waiters my plate and glass.

"Jared, you have two minutes to find Talley and then I'm outta here."

He doesn't even try to argue. Taking me by the elbow, he maneuvers us through the crowd. We finally reach our goal and spot Talley. She's appeared by her book display and stands out like a golden Amazon in a white, modified tuxedo sans jacket, but with a fitted, strapless shirt that shows off all her feminine attributes. Her hair is now completely platinum and slicked back in a chignon. She looks like a latter-day Marlene Dietrich—a queen in the realm of literary royalty.

Standing around her are some prominent citizens like Mavis Taylor-Goode, a coal heiress, and Titian Petruz, who is president of a coalition of local gallery owners. There are others but I have no clue of their significance.

"That's Gunner King," Jared informs and points to a tall, distinguished man standing next to Talley with silver-gray hair and a tan darker than my natural skin tone. "He owns Mountain Lakes Publishing. He published Talley's first book and has been trying to get between her legs ever since." Jared winks at me in an attempt to make me smile. It doesn't work.

"I'm surprised he's here since she's now with Tony's company."

"A lot of publishers are here. This is great PR."

Talley looks up to see us and grins. "Jared! Eva, you made it!" She barges her way through her admirers and comes to us. She gives Jared a quick hug and is about to do the same to me when she notices my attire.

"Hey, chèr, I know Denver is casual, but . . . "

That does it. I have been insulted enough for one night. It's bad enough to be underdressed for a social outing, but to endure, not one, but *two* of your boyfriend's ex-girlfriends? I don't think so. Tears of frustration born of rage sting the back of my eyes and I shoot an arsenal of daggers at Jared. He clears his throat.

"It's my fault, Talley. I forgot to tell Eva and sprung this all on her at the very last minute."

Talley's struck dumb and reads the expression on my face. "Oh, Jared, you didn't." She looks at me with all the sympathy in the world and gives me a warm hug. "You poor little thing."

I see more cameras flash and I just want to drop dead. Turning around, she blasts him.

"Jared Alistair Delaney, didn't your mama never tell you to give a woman enough time to dress for a function?"

"No, Talley. She didn't."

Even I know Talley made a mistake referring to his parentage, but she blows it off.

"No matter. You know now," she says and strokes my hair. "Come on, Little Eva, let me introduce you to the people." She leads me away and Jared brings up the rear, but I know he's pissed from the set of his mouth.

Despite my wanting to do otherwise, Talley keeps us there for nearly an hour. I make pleasant conversation with the social elite, score some points for being an academic if not a fashion plate, and leave Jared to do his own mingling.

I am wiped out. As I struggle to look interested as some blue-haired woman talks to me about varicose vein surgery, Jared comes to my side.

"Ready to go?"

I nod, then to the older woman, I say, "I'm sorry, but will you excuse me?"

"Certainly, my dear." She turns and picks up the conversation with Talley and another man as if I never existed.

The crowd has thinned considerably and Jared takes my hand, quickly leading the way. When we get outside, it's chilly from a light rain and I'm freezing in my sleeveless dress. Jared takes off his blazer and wraps it around my shoulders. I shiver, but when I inhale his Obsession cologne, it warms me.

"Are you okay?" he asks, his voice full of concern.

I just pull the blazer tighter around me and close my eyes, trembling from both the cold and pent-up emotions. The car finally arrives and Jared hurries me into it. After putting on the seat belt, I turn in my seat so my back is to him, my eyes still closed. He turns on the heater and I feel the car pull away.

We ride back to his house in silence and when he parks the car, I don't wait for him to open my door as he likes to do, but get out on my own and wait for him by the front door. Giving me a quick, worried glance, he puts the key in the lock.

I go straight to his bedroom, toss his blazer on the bed, go to the wardrobe where I have a robe and nightshirt stored, and get in bed. Meanwhile, he stands inside the bedroom door watching me with a frown on his lips, like he has something to frown about!

He hasn't been snubbed and insulted all evening.

CHAPTER THIRTEEN

"LOVE BIZARRE"

News that I'm dating a man with a reputation has followed me to work.

I try very hard to keep my private life separate from work, especially when I was going to the theater, and apart from Glynnis, no one knew about Jared.

That is until the Sunday edition of *The Rocky Mountain News* prints a photo from the Ulterior Motive Convention with the caption:

> Artist Jared Delaney and friend Evadne
> Cavell smile at a private joke with
> businessman and arts patron Tony Lobos.

This reminds me of my need to kill Tony.

He knows everyone associated with the local press. I don't usually pay attention to the entertainment or business news. I guess I have to now.

The snapshot caught the moment Jared tickled me. I admit, I do look good and smiling makes me look cute and bubbly in a pinup-girl sort of way. Jared is roguishly handsome with his head tilted and his hair falling over his right eye. Whoever took it must've used a long lens, because it's close up and I don't remember being blinded by the flash. But the fact that someone captured what was, in reality, a very awkward situation and preserved it on film means the snapshot permanently records a bittersweet memory. It didn't make the rest of my weekend with Jared go any better, either. In the end, I accepted his apologies and promises not to spring surprises on me in the future.

When I came into my office today, I found the page, the photo, and even the whole paper left on my desk. Some caring individual even put it up on the refrigerator in the faculty lounge.

"Our little celebrity," Glynnis teases when she sees me. "Does Jared have a brother? Older, younger, it doesn't matter."

Sitting at my desk having lunch, I have lots on my mind. The scandal concerning my former colleague, Professor Terrance Hyde, has reached new levels.

The student he got pregnant is suing him and the college. Meanwhile, Hyde is suing the college for breach of contract or some other kind of bullshit. This nonsense has been cooking for months on a low boil, but now the big cheese himself, Dean J. Paul Mathis, has just informed me that I might have to make a statement. Apparently, I am on both the college's and Hyde's list of possible character witnesses.

"Prayerfully, Evadne, neither one of us will have to call on you," Dean Mathis said when I was summoned to his office after my morning class. "I just wanted you to know and apologize for putting you in such a situation."

Prayerfully, he says. I roll my eyes and mull this over while nibbling on my ham sandwich.

"Hello, Eva."

I snap back to reality and see Neil Hollister standing before my desk; his lazy smile is charming but off-putting.

"Can I help you, Mr. Hollister?"

He hesitates a moment, not used to my change in attitude. Usually, I call my students by last name or tagged with "Mr." or "Ms.," but drop the formality and shift to first names when they take more than one of my classes. Neil falls into the latter category since he's not only my aide but has signed up for my Women in Modern Literature class this semester. But like I said, today, my thoughts are not within these four walls.

"You said to drop by during lunch and do some work."

"Oh, yes, I did. Help yourself."

Neil has been hanging tough ever since I lived up to my promise and treated him to a drink at the pub. I proved I could handle as much lager as he and then some. Now he seems more determined than ever to show me how manly he is. It's not that I doubt he's a man—more of a manchild, really—but he has his share of groupies to glam with.

I watch him from a distance as he sits at the desk on the other side of the office. I look down. My giant desk calendar is stained with meals past and my little doodles. A brass paperweight with the insignia of my alma mater, CU Boulder, does a lousy job weighing down a stack of papers. A desk lamp that belonged to my grandfather when he was a school principal sits in the middle of the far edge of the desk. It's an art deco piece with a brass clock and a pair of lounging hounds on either side of the clock face.

Amongst the usual desk clutter are photographs of my family. A hinged picture frame holds two pictures of Ana and me in our cap and gowns. The one on the left is us in high school and the one on the right is from college. We are in the exact same pose. There would have been three, but the only reason there isn't one of us from our postgraduate ceremony is because we went to different universities.

But there is a new addition to my little photo gallery and that's a shot of Jared and me. It was taken by Alex at the youth center when Jared gave his art workshop as promised. It was a very hot day in September and I wore an off-the-shoulder peasant top and low slung Capri pants. So low, in fact, you could see the head of the J.E.T. black cat poking up from my waistband. Jared wore an old T-shirt with the sleeves cut off. He had just finished playing basketball with some of the kids and stood behind me with his arms about my middle and his head on my shoulder. The J.E.T. black cat on his upper left bicep is in plain view. The way Jared's arms wrap around me gives my bosom a boost. Neil comes across with some files and I catch his eyes lingering a bit too long on that particular photo.

"I saw you and your boyfriend in the paper the other day."

"Yes." I grimace. "I'm afraid everyone has."

"So." He gestures towards the picture frame. "You and your boyfriend have matching tattoos?"

I make a noncommittal sound, throw away my sandwich bag, and give him a smile that maybe suggests more warmth than necessary, but anything to change the topic.

He squints at me. "Are you alright, teach? You seem tired."

"I'm fine. What's up?"

"I have an assignment and I need some help." He takes a seat on the edge of my desk. "But I think I have my topic."

"Good. What is it?" I cross my legs and lean forward, thankful I'm wearing slacks since Neil doesn't hide his attraction to my legs.

"Sexual Roles of Women in Early 20th Century Literature."

"That's pretty broad, Neil. Can you reel it in a bit?"

"Certainly. I was thinking of focusing on Colette," he says with a smile. "I'm intrigued by her portrayal of working, single women."

The boy has been doing his homework. He's trying to get a rise out of me. I have often said to my class that Colette is one of my favorite writers and I incorporated some of her work in my thesis on a topic not too different from the one he suggests.

"You know, Neil, I've done a lot of research along similar lines. Do you realize what that means?"

He looks me straight in the eye. "That you'll be riding me hard on this?"

The corner of my mouth twitches as I try not to smile, but I think my eyes give me away, because he grins and his brown eyes make a soft, sensual proposition.

"Those are your words, Neil, but the sentiment is correct."

"I look forward to it."

"That makes two of us."

His eyes widen once again, showing that if what I just said can rattle him, then he still has some cool points to earn. I am used to sparing with more experienced players. On the other hand, I'm willing to play this little game with him, for now.

A girl's gotta have her fun, doesn't she?

* * * *

"Damn, Eva. Do I need to put you under lock and key, or something?"

Jared lets me sample a spoonful of stew he made for our dinner and I laugh. He's at my place tonight because his house is getting its yearly pest treatment. Now that I'm back at work we tend to only have time for phone sex during the week but make up for it on the weekends.

"Oh, please. Neil Hollister is a wannabe stud muffin who thinks that just because his great-uncle is chancellor all he has to do is charm his way to a degree."

"You mean ya'll spoil him."

"No, we don't." He's pressed one of my buttons now. "Contrary to what you think, not everyone in higher education gets caught up in the politics."

"Just the ones with all the power."

"I'm gonna let that one slide. Neil has been known to insinuate his way close to certain profs—but not me." I stick my tongue out at him and go finish setting the table. "The sad thing is he's really very smart."

Jared brings the pot of stew and a plate of sliced crusty bread to the table and starts dishing it out. "It's your overt sexuality."

"Overt? Me?"

"The outfit you were wearing the day we met—you call that subtle? You can't hide it, Eva, especially not from me." He laughs and sits down. "You are far too sensuous. And your vibes are like a beacon to others." He fixes me with a mesmerizing stare. "You attract people."

His smooth Southern drawl drips thick with suggestion and my pulse starts to race.

"If that were true, I'd be leaving men in my wake."

"You cause a disturbance every time we go out. Take that night at DeGaulle's." He takes a bite of stew before saying, "There was the valet, then Baptiste, two guys in the lounge, a waiter, not to mention several glances from women as we made our way to the elevator."

He's actually ticking them on his fingers. Now it's my turn to laugh.

"Give me a break! I didn't see—"

"No, you didn't, because you refuse to look. You said, on the day we met, that I was very observant. You are like the sun, girl. You emit but you do not absorb," he says with a smile.

I shut up. Glynnis practically told me almost the exact same thing with regard to Terry Hyde. "You seem to have a keen interest in how many men look at me."

"Have you always been so guarded?" He continues like I haven't spoke, but I say nothing.

"I'll tell you what I think," he says with a twinkle in his eye. "I think you've been conditioned by your family, your work, your friends—everybody—to believe that you are untouchable." His voice softens, but he levels a gaze on me that goes deeper than my skin. "But you want to be touched. You need someone to touch you. Does that embarrass you?"

Truth is I am getting embarrassed. What can I say?

"It's my defence mechanism."

He nods. "And a very good one too. Freud would be impressed. Look, but don't touch. That's exactly how you were when we met at The DeLuxe."

"Yeah, but you ignored the sign."

"I did. Unlike many of these so-called men, I have balls."

This time we both laugh, but when we stop, he reaches out to stroke my arm.

"Evadne, you're the only woman I've met whose defence mechanism is tuned to perfection." He raises my hand and kisses it. "And I've known many women."

"You're so modest."

"Why should I be? How many men have *you* been with?"

Now there's a question. Apart from the orgy at Trisha Stevens's, my sexual experience with men has been pretty limited. That doesn't mean I'm naive about sex. I read. And I do have ideas that are not vanilla, not by a long shot.

"Eight."

Jared blinks. It was a rhetorical question, but he asked.

"I assume you've had more than eight women?"

". . . Yes."

I snicker and we busy ourselves with our food.

"Getting back to you and this Neil joker," he says, wiping his mouth. "You say he's smart. How smart?"

I purse my lips together. "Not that smart."

"I don't know, sugar. When I was in college, there were some professors I wouldn't have minded teaching them a thing or two after class."

I shake my head. "The college is in enough trouble because one faculty member couldn't keep it in his pants."

"Well, some student couldn't keep it in hers, either."

"Point taken." I raise my wineglass in salute.

We finish eating, put the dishes in the sink to soak, and then go to my room. I turn on the TV and we make ourselves comfortable by stripping down. Jared goes about the room lighting candles and incense.

We've developed a ritual on our weekends. For example, Friday night is "Book Night," where we take turns reading aloud to each other from the latest in *The Life of Lucrezia,* if there's a new issue, or some kind of erotic novel.

But this is Saturday Night. Movie Night.

Tonight's feature: *House of the Seven Orgasms.*

Jared is expanding my tastes. I've come to discover the different types of porno flicks from soft-core features to gonzo-style compilations of nothing but non-stop, hard-core sex for any taste imaginable. Judging by the title, tonight is a soft-core night.

I get into bed while he turns off the lights, letting the candles do their thing, and pops the DVD into the player. Giving me a wolfish grin, he takes a flying leap onto the bed and we snuggle, eagerly turning our eyes to the TV and waiting like two kids who just sneaked into an X-rated movie theater.

"I love their names." I giggle as the opening credits appear: Angel Pye, Coco Buerre, Jack Hoff, Dick Cummings, and Vas Deferens. "He must be German," I say and we laugh.

"I bet he and Dick are related."

Actually, the movie isn't half bad. As with all things, some of these flicks are more professional than others. Now that I am actually seeing some of the "classic" movies on DVD, I do have favorite actors and actresses. I like Veronica Hart, Jeanna Fine, and Ona Zee, so Jared does his best to find their videos. Ron Jeremy cracks me up because he'll fuck almost anything. And Sean Michaels . . . mmm, gotta love that ebony hunk of a man.

Generally, when we watch the feature films, we just snuggle, which usually leads to a round of leisurely lovemaking. But this movie has an orgy scene at the end so intense and nasty compared to the rest of the film, we had to create a scene of our own.

"Damn, girl," he breathes onto the side of my neck when we're through. "Where did you learn to do that?"

I laugh but say nothing.

"I've seen orgies, but this one." He gives a low whistle.

He lets me sit up and then rests against me. I stroke his head then let my hand slide down to tease his nipples. He sucks in his breath and I smile.

"Have you ever been in an orgy?" I ask him.

"No, damn it." He strokes my legs from under the blanket. "Have you?"

When I don't answer, he cranes his head to look up at me, his face showing his surprise.

"Evadne Louise Cavell, I am shocked!" Then he turns on his side to make himself more comfortable. "You better tell me all about it."

I press my lips together in a poor attempt to be modest, but he grabs me and tickles me into submission.

"Stop it, Jared! Quit!" I am weak and nearly pissing myself from laughing so hard, but that doesn't prevent him blowing a raspberry against my belly, making me squeal again. When I catch my breath, I sit up from the supine position he had me in.

"Let me just preface it with this," I say, pushing my hair off my face. "*Je ne regrettez rien.*"

Jared's lips curve in a little smile.

"This happened almost four years ago, and until I met you, my little sex machine," I say, patting his cheek, "it was the last time I'd been fucked within an inch of my life."

He grins at that admission.

"It all started with an invitation from Trisha Stevens. She was an assistant music professor and wanted to have a combination housewarming and New Year's Eve party . . ."

Years ago, when I still thought clubbing was fun, I just went to have a good time. I never fooled myself thinking I'd ever play with the hearts of men and I think that's what attracted Eddie to me.

Eddie Norton worked as a bouncer at Turbo's, the best nightclub in town at the time. He was a health and fitness Nazi, and the fact he gave me the time of day nearly flattered me out of my panties. I say nearly because I wasn't thin enough for him.

"Come on, Eva," he'd say. "Let's go to the gym and I'll help you tone up."

I was so happy that a man with his body and good looks wanted to spend time with me, I didn't mind his only wanting me as a workout buddy. Hell, I could use the exercise.

Eddie was extremely fit with a body that could grace the cover of any fitness magazine. His black hair and blue eyes created such a startling contrast I got aroused just looking at him. Plus, he was good for free admission to the club and all the drinks I could handle, which was—*is*—quite a lot. But I soon found out drinking wasn't good if I was going to "tighten and tone."

I'd go to the club, my friends would drink, and I would have water and "treat" myself to one Coke. Eddie would come by and check on me to make sure I was being good. He had me on an eating, drinking, and exercise regimen: no sweets, no meat, work out an hour a day, five times a week, alternating weight training with aerobics. After the gym, Eddie would take me to a movie or the park. But he would never buy me dinner or lunch or anything, only water or the occasional iced tea or lemonade. I went from a size 18 down to a size 12 in the three months I associated with him.

And although I was proud of the results, I felt like shit. I was tired, cranky, and my periods got all fucked up. But more importantly, I wasn't happy. No one gave me a second thought when I was heavier, but they are now? What was up with that shit? I was the *exact* same person—only smaller.

People noticed and started treating me differently. I was getting more longing looks and compliments. People were friendlier. Even my family changed. Instead of criticizing my clothes, my mom wanted to take me shopping with her—something she never wanted to do in the past because I needed to go to the "heavy stores," as she put it, and that was too inconvenient for her. So I became my own fashion consultant. I thought I did a good job, too, even though I never dressed in a way to draw attention away from Theo's athletic form or Beverly's and my mother's dancer's grace.

"All you needed was to lose weight," Mom said. ". ⌐
time."

But Dad was dubious. "I don't want my Li'l Bit to get too .

I never introduced them to Eddie. It wasn't like he wantᴄ
come around and meet the parents. Yet, he was my measuring tape and ⸳
still wasn't small enough.

"You're pretty now," he'd say, "but lose another five or ten
pounds and you'll be gorgeous!" Or, "Eva, you are so cute. I know you
don't think so, but you'd feel and look better if you'd exercise more and
ate less."

The few times he did handle me, he would squeeze me as if
determining the quality of fresh produce. Firm here, a little over ripe
there. Then he'd give me an earth-shattering kiss at the club in front of
my friends, a quick grope, and say, "Have you been a good girl by doing
all your sit-ups? I'm feeling a little pudge here."

Like a dumb-ass, I would giggle and say, "Yes," flattered by the
attention, but then go home and do sit-ups until I puked.

Finally, I thought I struck gold when Eddie accepted my
invitation to come with me to Trisha Stevens's New Year's Eve Party. It
would be our first official, non-workout date.

The party was a few weeks away and in the meantime, I was
under all kinds of strain. I had just endured the pressure of finals for the
first time at work and was on a "fitness" program that threatened to tear
me apart. Then, two days before the party, I had a revelation.

This was all a bunch of bullshit.

It came to me one night at the club and I saw Eddie for what he
was—a full-metal jackass. I had ignored the way he flirted with and ogled
every woman who came through the door that looked like she would
snap in half if caught in a strong wind—the ones with chests so flat they
made the walls jealous. Eddie was trying to make me look like a string
bean with a pulse.

I saw him hugging, patting, kissing, and gyrating against some of
those "broads," but ignored it because I had *all* his phone numbers. It
made me want to hang my head in shame.

But, I would get my revenge, and if there's one thing I can do
well, it's revenge.

When Eddie picked me up at Ana's home in Montbello looking
like a Russell Crowe wannabe, I noticed how he sized Ana up and down
appreciatively. She was and still is a size 4, but she ignored him because a)
she saw how he treated me before I figured it out and b) the overly
muscle-bound aren't her type. Then Eddie looked at me.

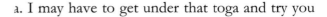

…and it's about
…le."
…to

a. I may have to get under that toga and try you

even a few days before, I would've felt flattered,
…vere too arrogant for me to take. All I wanted to
…o on a plate with his testicles on the side.
lived in a house in the Capital Hill area. That New
…he freezing weather, twenty guests showed up.
…ately dressed to the party as Trisha requested. The
ladies wore togas a… the men wore gladiator gear that Trisha reserved at
a local theatrical shop. At first, I thought it was a fluke that the men
outnumbered the women thirteen-to-seven, but Trisha explained that the
men were expected to have a gladiator's gusto.

Food, wine, and spirits flowed in our version of bacchanalian
worship. It wasn't long before guests started to feel at home, removed
their costumes, and strutted about naked before eleven o'clock. No one
cared. We all assumed it could be the last time we'd be able to act with
such abandon before being dumped in a nursing home by our kids.

Since Eddie flexed and posed for anyone who cared to look, it
was hard to tell we came there as a couple. I, however, made several new
friends. Everybody was nice, but I noticed while dancing that a few of
the guys danced closer than necessary and paid a lot of attention to the
way my toga clung to my chest. I wasn't wearing a bra—and it was a little
chilly in Trisha's house.

Time passed and soon it was next to impossible to pass a dark
corner without hearing giggling or heavy breathing over the sound of wet
kisses. At about 11:45, everyone had more than their share of alcohol and
Trisha imposed a lockdown to keep us off the streets.

"I don't know, Trish," said Brady Sherrer. "With this abundance
of feminine pulchritude near defenceless from excessive drink, we may
have suitable cause to re-enact the Rape of the Sabine Women." His
speech reflected his recently passing the bar exam.

There was a cheer from the men and giggles from the women.

Trisha, tall, raven-haired, and decked out as Minerva, shield and
helmet included, stepped out into the middle of the den and spoke.

"Nay! There shall be no rape on this holy night, centurion! But
I'm not adverse to virgin sacrifice." She tossed down her battle gear.
"Line up, virgins!"

Ana and I looked at each other. Obviously, she didn't mean us.
Trisha noticed our reticence.

"What is this? Lady Evadne, Lady Ana, you do not obey the
order of your goddess, Minerva?"

I made a point that night not to get too drunk, because I wanted to have a clear head and nerves of steel when I put Eddie in his place, but I had no clue how I would do it—until that moment. I approached the center of the room.

"O Goddess, I beseech thee, leave these poor young innocents alone!"

"The goddess, in her infinite wisdom, demands sacrifice!" a man called out.

I turned in their direction. The guests had formed two camps according to sex. On one side, the "maidens" huddled in various stages of undress, whereas the men looked like the aftermath of a fraternity party. A wicked smile formed on my lips.

"There is no need for sacrifice when one is willing." I reached up and untied the knot in my toga. It fell to my feet exposing my nude body. The whistles and catcalls hurt my ears. Someone even started singing "Brown Sugar."

Eddie busted through the ranks, his face dark with rage.

"Evadne, what the fuck are you doing?" He reached out to take me by the arm but I slid out of his way.

"Now, now, Claudius! No need to get upset. We're just having fun."

Eddie made a face, not comprehending the name I gave him, but others did.

"Ah!" Brady said. "If he's Claudius, that means you are—"

"Messalina," I said and curtsied. "At your service." More riotous approval.

"Yes! I, Messalina, do hereby propose a competition between me and this beautiful wench—the number one prostitute in all Rome." I ran up and took Ana by the arm.

"Hey," she pouted. "Who you calling a 'ho?"

I laughed. After years of her scolding me for being uptight and not rattling the cage, she damn well couldn't refuse me.

"Okay. I challenge this—Scarlet Woman—to best me in satisfying all you fine, strapping centurions!"

"Yeah, yeah, sure, sure," Eddie butted in. "If it's satisfaction you want—" He made another attempt to embrace me but I pushed him away.

"Please! Messalina only made love to Claudius out of duty! You will get none of me tonight, O Emperor."

The look in Eddie's eyes was colder than the blizzard outside and I gave as good as I got, crossing my arms over my chest, daring him to try me.

"Eva," he ground out through gritted teeth, "you are drunk."

I smiled patronizingly and patted his cheek. "You just keep telling yourself that, dear."

The locker room "oohs" from everyone didn't help. Eddie gave me the once-over, as if to say, *Good luck with that body, sister.* But I didn't care. He and his body-obsessed bullshit could take a walk and from that moment on, I orchestrated the festivities. I had the men arrange two couches parallel to each other in the den.

"Hey, I like this," Trish said. "I think I'll keep it this way."

She made everyone ante up any condoms they had and put them in a giant bowl on the coffee table. That, along with her private stash, provided more than enough for our Roman orgy. Our hostess then became a participant when I assigned her and the other four women the duty of getting the men's blood boiling before sending them over to Ana and me.

I'd be lying if I said all the men present were representative of Roman gods. If they represented anything it would be different races and body types. On the other hand, Eddie was fully prepared to ignore me and try his luck on Ana who brushed him off.

"Get in line," she ordered and lay on the opposite couch, where one man fanned her with a giant decorative fan while he received a blow job from one of the wenches.

As I watched men and women stripping off, jerking off, and blowing off, no one was paying attention to any so-called body "defects." I saw muscles so taught I thought they would rip to threads and mounds of dimpled, dough-like flesh so pale, all it needed was thirty minutes in an oven to make it that more tempting to bite into. Tan lines created stark demarcations as brown flesh turned white, whereas other bodies had all-over natural tans of honey-gold or melted dark chocolate. Breasts stood at attention while others lay against their owners' chests and penises unfurled obeying their masters' wish to join the party. I was getting hot.

"Hurry up!" I said. "'Tis nearly midnight. Time to get this ball rolling."

"My Lady Messalina," hailed Ana.

"Yes, my Scarlet Woman?"

"The stallions approach." With a languid gesture, Ana pointed to two men at the ends of our couches, standing proud in more ways than one.

I stretched and purred. "Very well, centurions. Proceed."

I hadn't had sex since breaking up with my last boyfriend a year before, so I kept my eyes closed, not out of fright, but to heighten the sensation as mouths came down on my skin. Some were moist like a soft sponge, teasing with their tongues; others were wet and overflowing, drenching me as they sucked my flesh before clamping down with hard pearls of teeth. Still other mouths were dry, rough, and hungry, their teeth nipping here and grinding there.

Hands addressed me in similar fashion. One pair would caress, another would cling. One man had manicured fingers, another needed his cuticles trimmed.

I had no idea about Ana, but I didn't let anyone kiss me. I had no stomach for the aftertaste of liquor, food, and cigarettes. I wanted them to be intimate with me from the neck down.

As the air became electrified with excitement, the flowery and spicy mix of perfume and cologne dissolved into the thick musk of sex. With regard to actual penetration, I have little recollection, except my body had to adjust more for some than for others. My eyes closed, and I wasn't interested in supporting or debunking stereotypes.

It amazed me that the men could still get it up after all the drinking we'd done. What did fascinate me were the sounds the men made, from low, powerful grunts to whistling "Dixie" through their teeth. One character, nibbling and breathing heavily against my ear as he reached his climax started reciting Shakespeare—Julius Caesar's final speech, to be exact.

"I am constant as the Northern star!"

I busted out laughing. I couldn't help it. When he rolled off me and onto the floor, he mumbled, "I was constant . . . constant . . ."

That performance garnered applause and made me feel better for my lack of composure. It was the only time I opened my eyes and from my vantage point, I couldn't see Eddie. But I did see people having sex one-on-one, two-on-one, three-on-one, and gender was not an issue. That got me wondering if any women sneaked in on me, because there were a few times when I thought the fingernails were a little too long or the skin a little too soft.

I had no idea what time it was when I stopped getting mauled with frequency. Opening my eyes again, I sat up and around me bodies were strewn with as much care as a bomb blast. Some slept and others masturbated half-heartedly.

Rome had fallen.

I looked over at Ana who was in a similar state. She was alone but eating grapes from a bowl. The Queen of the Prostitutes lay in repose, her dark hair glistening with sweat, and her long spiral tresses cascading limply over her shoulder and off the side of the couch.

"Hey, ho," I said and smiled.

She looked at me, mid-grape.

"Was it good for you?"

She shrugged, went back to her grapes, and I laughed. Stiff and sore, I picked my way over the debris of bodies and found the bathroom. I gave myself a thorough scrubbing with hot water, even washing my hair knowing I wouldn't be able to fix it properly until I got home. I bumped into Ana as I came out. "You see Eddie anywhere?"

"Oh, he left after we started."

"Bastard."

We laughed. Years later, we are still laughing.

"I gained all the weight back of course," I say, looking down at Jared, who is grinning up at me. "But I think you've helped me work some of it back off." I stroke his cheek.

"Wow. Talk about your dark horses."

I hit him playfully in the gut. "It's not something I brag about."

"You should." He's serious so I hit him again.

"No way, man. Fortunately, almost everyone involved has moved away. But," I giggle. "A year later, at another New Year's party, I did run into the few who are still around and we just started laughing. No one could get us to tell them why. It's a big inside joke, really."

Jared takes my hand and starts kissing it. His lips are like the softest, richest velvet on my skin. "How could anyone want to change you like that? Why did you let him?"

I sigh. "I thought it was what I wanted. It's hard 'living large,' as some blond chick once said." I give him a pointed glance. "All my life I've had to deal with going out and wondering: Will my hips fit in this seat? Will this shirt close over my boobs? What are those people looking at? And when I was thinner, I felt like a fish in a bowl with people being less than tactful with their staring. I'd much rather keep in the background."

He studies me but says nothing for a long while. Yes, I'm defensive, but after years of criticism at home and living in an image-obsessed society, it's hard not to be. My reference to Sarah probably tells him the whole incident still has me harboring a grudge.

"I'm sorry," he says. "I didn't know."

"Why should you be sorry? It's not your problem."

"Why is it yours? I think you're beautiful. You are beautiful."

I close my eyes to keep from rolling them.

"Jared, I don't want pity."

"Who's giving you pity? I don't get it. You say you want to be in the background, but at the theater, you wanted men to see you. You wanted to tempt them."

"That's different."

"How?"

"Because I'm the one in control." I scowl. "It's up to me when, where, and how I choose to be seen."

He shakes his head in amazement. "I've said it before and I'll say it again. You're a cocktease." He rolls onto his back. "Why are you so fucking concerned about how people see you?"

"I don't need eyes on me, judging me."

"Who's judging you?"

"Everyone! My work, my family."

"For crying out—Eva, will you grow up? You're thirty-five years old. Why do you worry what mommy and daddy think?"

This pisses me off.

"Jared, unlike you, my parents care about what I do. I have to live with my family."

Oops. But it's too late.

He lays motionless on his back, staring at the ceiling. I don't even see him breathe. Two or more minutes pass. I can't stand it. I reach out and touch the bed sheet close to his waist.

"Jared, I'm sorry."

"Don't be."

I frown. Easy for him to say. "I didn't mean to throw it at you like that. It's just that you hit a nerve."

"So you decided to hit one back?"

"No!" I'm about to show him how sorry I am when he looks at me with a rueful smile. I change my position so I'm lying next to him on my back, both of us with our feet resting against the headboard. Together we watch the flickering shadows from the candlelight on the ceiling. "Talk to me, Jared. You know my deep, dark secrets. Now it's your turn."

He moves his arm beneath my head and pulls me close.

"My earliest memory is of living in a trailer," he begins, "one of those silver bullet kinds, you know?"

I nod.

"The grass was brown, what grass was there anyway. And mud. Lots of mud. Couldn't tell you where exactly we were if I tried, but when they found my birth certificate, it says I was born in Dime Box." He laughs. "What a name, huh?"

I prop myself on my elbow and look at him. "Talley told me about your name."

At first, I thought he would get angry. How easy can it be to admit you were four years old and didn't know your own name? But he just keeps gazing up, his eyes as dark as the ceiling.

"That was the one smart thing either of them did—getting that birth certificate. By that time, I was living in a home in Weatherford, Texas. Started school there. It all started there. I was moved six times in five years."

I shake my head. I haven't moved that much in my life. "Were the homes bad?"

"No. No, not really. Let's just say I knew that it wasn't permanent, so I didn't make plans to stay very long."

"Did you get into trouble?"

"Not more than any other kid." He stretches and his body resembles an ivory statue in the candlelight. "But when you're a foster child, trouble is amplified." Settled once again, he strokes my arm.

"Talley said something about the . . . ?"

"The Petries?"

"Yes, that's it. Sorry. Couldn't remember." I glance away.

"Hey, don't worry about it. I really should have talked about them before now. If it wasn't for them, I probably would have ended up like my dad."

"What happened to him?"

He takes a deep breath. "Last I heard, he'd jumped bail on an attempted murder charge and was last seen in Juarez, Mexico. That was in 2002."

"And your mom?"

"Dead. Overdosed in '99."

Jesus Christ. I can understand his lack of feeling for his parents, but I can't imagine having that childhood. I stroke his hair off his forehead; his skin is warm.

"Tell me," I say, leaning my head to the side. "You go by Delaney, but the Petries adopted you. Why didn't you change your name?"

He sighs. "I choose to use Delaney as my way of showing my parents I survived despite them. That's the name I was given and it's part of me whether I like it or not. So, yes, Evadne," he says, turning on his side to look me in the eye, "I have to live with my family too."

CHAPTER FOURTEEN
∧
"BITCH GODDESS FROM HELL"

It is February and about four months after my orgy confession. Jared received word of a major assignment and has been busy for weeks. Whenever I ask what it is, he just winks at me and says it's something that will allow him to spoil me in the manner he wants me to get accustomed to. As if spur of the moment trips out of state, dinners in super-exclusive restaurants, and silver Elsa Peretti earrings from Tiffany & Co. for our six month anniversary weren't enough.

At least I got his car detailed (he loved that) and took him on a romantic weekend to The Broadmoor Hotel in Colorado Springs (leather restraints and toys—batteries included) for his Christmas present, even though I shared the benefits.

I miss him. Jared is full of surprises and I'm amazed how bold I've become over the months. Who needs an orgy when you have an imagination and a willing partner? We get very physical and I love it. But bruises, bites, and scratches aside, I miss the simple act of sleeping next to him. As a result, I've had to put my sex drive in reverse. Part of me is annoyed, but I'm sympathetic to his needs. He's been too busy to spend much time with me and has had to go out of town on business a few times. But mostly, he's cloistered himself off from the world.

"He's in the middle of a project, that's all," his assistant, Trey Harker, says one day when we go to lunch. "You've never dated an artist before, have you, Cookie?"

"No." I smile. It's amazing how the people in my life find it so easy to tag me with a pet name and Trey is no exception. He says he calls me "Cookie" because he thinks I'm sweet—plus I'm the first girlfriend of Jared's that he's been able to get along with.

"Creative people get more single-minded and focused when they're in the middle of something big." Trey looks at me a little too keenly, almost appraisingly. "And what he's doing now is big. Actually, Eva, you've distracted him for so long he's backlogged."

Well, hell. I didn't mean to make Jared's life a hassle.

"But what's he working on?" I ask. "He doesn't even talk about it. Or let me see it, for that matter."

"You know how artists are," Trey says and laughs.

"No, I don't."

"Oh . . . that's right. No matter, sweetie, don't let it bother you. I've yet to meet an artist who lets people see their unfinished work."

I press my lips together unsatisfied with his answer, but it will have to do. It's been weeks since Jared and I spent any real time together or had sex.

Our last date was a disaster. We were just going to dinner and a movie and had dinner first. Big mistake, because what we ate gave us food poisoning. Suffice it to say, there is one major hamburger chain that will never see the color of our money again.

It was terrible. Within a couple of hours of eating, we were at my place taking turns worshipping the Porcelain God. The second time I emerged from the bathroom I found Jared raging on the phone to the manager of the restaurant. His voice started out deceivingly and dangerously calm before erupting like Vesuvius. It was scary, but I found it hard to keep from laughing. He may have been sick, with his red eyes and heavy sweating, but, for a moment, I felt sorry for the person on the receiving end of his wrath. Yet it gave me a thrill to see Jared in full force. I love seeing a man being a man and taking care of business. He is usually so calm and reassuring, especially during my rants and raves. This image was only slightly marred when he hung up the phone abruptly and nearly knocked me down on his way to the bathroom.

Jared was in no condition to drive home, so he stayed. For three days we holed up in my apartment too weak for anything but cuddling and spooning. My mom and sister checked on us each day and Trey took care of Jared's house. When he was fit to go home, he gave me a rain check for a night of "wild, passionate monkey-sex."

I'm still waiting.

* * * *

Things start looking up when Jared calls me to say he's going to New Mexico for the week, but when he gets back on Sunday:

"I intend to cash my rain check."

I'm in a good mood all week, even on Monday, and although I planned to prepare for Jared's return at his place, I accept an invite to my parent's house for Sunday dinner.

My parents live in Park Hill not far from the golf course. They've seen the neighborhood boom, bust, and boom again. Although they can afford a home much larger than their 1940s bungalow, they have no plans to move from the house we all grew up in. Especially not since the property values have risen. If they hadn't converted the basement into extra living space years ago, it may have forced them to move, because family dinners like these, with the grandkids included, wouldn't be possible.

Along with her talent for dancing and teaching, Mom likes to show off her ability to cook enough for an army. Tonight is no exception with lasagne (with homemade pasta); home-grown veggies of green beans, cucumbers, onions, corn, and tomatoes; and crusty bread. My parents added a conservatory to the formal dining room and that's where we all sit. If Jared had been present, we would've made a baker's dozen for dinner because Bev and Alex have taken Cubby, who's completely recovered from his gunshot wound, into their home and may now adopt him. We plow into dessert of marble cake topped with homemade vanilla ice cream.

"I've been meaning to ask you about that purchase Jared made the night of the art show," Dad says. "Did he like it?"

"Oh, yes. He has it hanging up in the guest room."

Dad shakes his head. "I meant the other purchase. The magazine."

I was about to take another mouthful of cake when my belly bottoms out.

"Sorry?" I blink, feigning ignorance.

"Jared bought a magazine called *The Life of Lucrezia*. Didn't he show it to you?"

Pressing my lips together, I quickly cast a glance in the direction of my nephews. They were bent over their dessert bowls when Darien looks over and nudges his brother with an elbow. They are laughing! Silently, but laughing nonetheless. Delius raises his head to see me glaring at them and he brings it to the attention of his twin.

"Uh, Mom, can we be excused?" he asks.

LaRue looks at their plates as if expecting to see food left behind.

"Take your dishes into the kitchen and wash them for Nana."

"Yes, ma'am." Delius wipes his mouth with a napkin and he, Darien, and Cubby leave the room.

"You girls go too," Beverly says. "You won't be happy until you get to do what the boys do."

The girls get their plates and hightail it after their cousins.

When they're gone, I reply, "I may remember seeing it. Why?"

Dad shrugs. My dad is a big man, so even a "subtle" gesture like a shrug is significant.

"A bit racy, isn't it?"

"Wait a minute!" Beverly laughs. "What's going on? Has Eva's been caught behind the Green Door again?"

Theo, LaRue, and Alex all start going, "Oooh!"

"Shut up!"

"Evadne," Mom snaps. "Keep your voice down. Your father is just asking a simple question. Why do you have to overreact?"

"Because you are asking about my private life. Jared and I have been dating for over six months and you're coming up with this now? How the hell do you think I'm supposed to feel?"

"Watch your mouth, young lady," Dad says, putting his fork down. "Remember who you're talking to."

My face gets warm as the memories of a thousand scoldings come to mind as well as my anger. When I speak again, I try to keep calm. "I am not a child. Do not talk to me like I am."

"I don't care for your tone," my mom says and tries to stare me down. I'm in no mood to play, so I just roll my eyes and poke at my cake, which has turned into a soggy mush underneath melted ice cream.

"I don't mean to pry into your private life, Li'l Bit," Dad says as if to prevent war breaking out between me and my mother. "But I'm not sure if I'm comfortable at the thought of—"

"Dad! Stop. Please. Don't worry about it." I put my spoon down. I have been embarrassed in front of my siblings and in-laws like some infant. Thank God my nieces and nephews weren't here; otherwise, I'd never maintain what little authority I have over them. I stand up.

"Think I'll go home now. Thanks for dinner."

Mom clicks her tongue in annoyance. "Don't go away sulking like a spoiled brat, Evadne."

"I'm not sulking." I toss my napkin on my chair. "I'm just fed up."

* * * *

I am so fucking sick of this. Why is it that people with nothing better to do sit around and decide how I should live my life? Perhaps because I've let them do it for so long. This has got to stop. Now. Tonight. And I'm in just the mood to do it.

I get to Jared's house at nine o'clock and remember how I'm supposed to be waiting for him in the bedroom, ready for him to return. I'm sitting on the edge of the bed, in the dark, when the phone on the nightstand rings.

"Hello?"

"It's me."

"Hello me. Where are you?"

"Outside parking the car."

And sure enough, I hear his car pull up into the drive. The night is so still and quiet I can hear the *ding, ding* of the car door as he gets out.

"Don't forget your car keys," I say and he laughs.

"Are you ready for me, precious?"

"Oh yes."

He hangs up. I hear the car's trunk open, him taking out his luggage, and closing the trunk again. A minute later, there's the sound of a key in the front door lock and the soft creak of door hinges. He's on the stairs now and his footsteps are solid, almost trudging. He's tired but not too tired for sex. He is never too tired for sex. A moment later, I see his silhouette filling the doorway. He flips on the light.

He wears black jeans, a black tee, and a red and black flannel shirt that carries the scent of ozone from the storm brewing outside. His lips freeze in a surprised smile. My smile is frozen, too. Mine's a bit more twisted than Jared's but a smile nonetheless. He drops his suitcase.

"I was expecting you naked."

"Nope. I'm not naked."

"I can see that." He chuckles. "Need help?

I shake my head and he looks at me questioningly.

"Strip and lie face up on the bed," I say.

His eyes lock on mine as he kicks off his sneakers and removes his socks. He unbuckles his belt and undoes his jeans, but I notice he has to maneuver carefully when pushing them down over his crotch. When he removes his jockey shorts, his cock springs forward and looks even larger now that we started shaving our pubic hair to facilitate some of the sex toys we've been experimenting with lately.

Next to come off is his shirt, which he tosses onto a nearby chair. I take a moment to appraise him in all his glory—the defined muscles of his chest, legs, and arms, and the way his body seems to exude an aura of its own in the soft light. Jared has the smoothest, clearest skin I've ever seen on a grown man. I remember the hundreds of times my hands have caressed that skin and felt it slowly change from cool, to warm, to hot and slick as we made love. Tonight, I am going to make that skin burn.

"Get on the bed," I tell him. "And I suggest you make yourself comfortable. You're in for a long night."

His long legs carry him to his destination in a few strides. Lying supine, his head on the pillows, his gaze softens but another part of his anatomy is getting harder. I open the blanket chest at the foot of the bed and beneath the comforters and quilts I uncover what Jared calls "bedroom hardware." Ignoring the handcuffs and other restraints, I pull out a small collection of items and glance at him from over the lid of the chest.

"I'm not going to restrain you, Jared, because it's very simple." I close the lid of the chest and rest the objects on top. "You are not to move or touch me unless I tell you to. If you do, I'll go home."

The footboard of the bed keeps the toys out of his sight, but I take one item with me and sit beside him on the bed. He opens his mouth to speak, but I stop him with a steady gaze and lean across his chest, my left hand bracing me.

"You are not allowed to speak unless I say so, and when you do, you will address me with the utmost respect." I tweak his nipple with my free hand. His eyelids spread wide for a moment.

"Now." I sit back. "What do you say to that?"

"Yes . . . Messalina."

We look at each other. For a man so big physically, whose presence can be intimidating and his anger downright frightening, Jared looks at me with complete trust and longing. I struggle to keep my gaze cool, but the honesty in his eyes throws me a curve. Here is a man who's been neglected, abused, alone. And now, he's putting himself at my mercy. I place my hand around his throat and feel his racing pulse before caressing his long, graceful neck. My hand continues across his chest and over his nipples. I break our gaze to watch my fingertips take in the ridges of his abdominal muscles. Jared may not have a six-pack, but he's muscularly defined just the same. I swirl my index finger around his navel, knowing how it tickles him, and he suppresses a chuckle with a sigh. Not allowing myself to smile, I glance up at him. He's watching me.

My God, how his eyes sparkle. Where does it come from, this inner fire of his? Is it from surviving his childhood and becoming a success, or simply because he's a good, loving man?

I can't allow for distraction so I turn my head away and let my hand continue its journey down. I caress his cock, feeling it pulsate and get harder. I pick up an item taken from the chest and slip a bolo-style cock ring around his shaft and over his balls, then adjust the ring to accommodate all of him. This will keep him under control for now.

My forefinger gently taps the head of his cock, as if testing the ripeness of a different kind of passion fruit, and I am rewarded with a little drop of juice. I use my finger to bring a sample to my mouth to suck and nod approvingly.

He has been holding his breath and releases a long, ragged sigh. Sensing he's about to speak, I shoot him a disapproving glance and he sucks in a breath through his teeth. I stand up and begin to strip. His eyes follow as I undo my wrap around skirt and expose black bikini panties. Bending down, I undo my ankle-strap heels and then remove my blouse. I keep on my black push-up bra knowing he likes the presentation it makes.

"Turn over." The sound of my voice startles both of us because it's deeper and huskier than I've ever sounded before. Jared's back presents as beautifully as his front—smooth skin, defined muscles—and a few faded scars where my fingernails have marked him in the past.

"Close your eyes and keep them closed until I say otherwise." I bend over to see that he complies and whisper in his ear, "I'd hold on to the headboard, if I were you."

I see a slight tremble in him as he grips the wood so tightly it makes a soft groan of complaint. His knuckles slowly turn white. I give his shoulders a quick massage.

"Relax. Don't tense up on me now."

Jared exhales again and relaxes into the mattress. I start massaging his body from his wrists, down his arms, then his back, finally arriving at the two perfect mounds of his buttocks where I linger for a while. I continue down his legs to his feet before coming back to his bottom. I give him a hard slap across the ass and he bucks up. I do it again, and then again. His ass is now a peach with a rosy blush.

I move away from the bed and go to the bathroom to turn on the faucet and dampen a few towels with warm water. I see him turn his head in my direction.

"Keep those eyes closed. I'm watching you, Jared. Don't think for a moment you're fooling me." My tone is sharper than my emotions, but by his grimace, he doesn't know that. Nevertheless, I'm so eager, I want him inside me now, but this is an exercise in control for both of us.

Having returned to the bed, I give him a rubdown with the towels, relaxing him even more. I even run a towel in a playful, shoeshine fashion between his ass cheeks and finish by "polishing" each bun. I flick his rump with the wet towel, causing him to flinch and suck in his breath. I do it several more times until I see the nice, rosy glow return to his cheeks.

"Good. I think you're ready now." I walk to the foot of the bed and pick up the rest of my equipment. Placing a slim dildo inside a harness, I strap it around my waist. The toy is smaller than what I'm used to, but considering what I'm about to do, I'm going to be just as considerate as he was with me by going slow. I squirt a generous amount of lubricant into my hand and slather it onto the dildo.

Since he introduced me to anal sex, I've become more open and confident with exploring my sexual desires, and he's been generous of every one, from bondage to nipple clamps. Finally, about a month ago, he acquiesced to my even touching his little rose-hole. Since then, he's been more relaxed, letting me play and linger in this area.

Tonight, I will do more than linger. I will dwell. I am going to possess him until he knows who is Mistress. When I straddle his legs and squeeze a large dollop of lube between his ass cheeks, my intentions become clear and he raises his head.

"I hope you're not planning to talk, Jared. In fact, you just moved without permission." I start to get off the bed and he moans loudly as if in agony.

"Are you trying to tell me something?"

Even though his face is hidden, he nods.

"What do you want?"

He raises his head, looks at me, and my heart stops. He looks so sad. I wonder if this is how he looked when moving from home to home. I straighten my spine, hoping to appear more resolute than I really am, but after all, part of me is trying to come out of a sexual shell. Then I realize he's waiting for my permission.

"Speak."

When he does, his voice is soft, breathless.

"Please, don't leave me, Eva . . . Messalina."

He sees me in my regalia and his jaw tightens before he buries his face into the pillows and increases his grip on the headboard. I resume my position on my mount, allowing my toy phallus to slide up and down between his ass and up to the base of his back. I do this several times until his body shivers and I have to clench my thighs around him to restrain him.

"Whoa there, big fella." I stretch myself on top of him and remove his hands from where they're gripped, so I can place my head on his shoulder. "I need you to relax, babe."

In a sure way to achieve this, I nibble his ear and reach under him to rub his nipples while slinking my body up and down. Jared's heart thunders in his chest, his skin is very warm, and he's starting to sweat. I kiss the side of his neck and then his shoulder, letting my lips caress and suck. I do this for several moments as I continue rubbing against him and the action causes the dildo to stimulate me as well.

When I hear him exhale and deflate into the mattress once again, I take advantage of the situation. The tip of the phallus slides forward with little resistance before he tenses and I have to brace myself, using my weight to keep him from squeezing me out. It's a balancing act, but I don't advance and I don't withdraw.

"Now, now, lover," I murmur and kiss his ear. "Don't be shy."

In reply, I get to advance another inch, and then another. Finally, I give a gentle nudge until completely lodged.

Jared releases his pent up breath again and starts trembling all over. His body turns gelatinous as his nervous system responds to the intruder inside him. I clamp my legs and arms around him, hugging him tightly, pressing my breasts hard against his back.

"Shh, Jared." I kiss his shoulder. "It's all right. I'm not going to hurt you."

Once the words are spoken, we realize that's the exact same thing he said to me the first time. I kiss his neck and stroke the hair from his forehead, waiting for him to adjust to the sensation. But I'm aroused, too. I give a tentative thrust and he groans. I do it again and continue kissing the back of his neck and shoulders as I slowly, gently stroke into him. I reach under his waist and can't help but gasp. He is diamond hard. Oh, fuck—the cock cage! I know Jared is stoic when it comes to pain, but Jesus Christ, he must be in agony!

"Jared, how are you feeling?" Although concerned, I keep my voice stern.

"I'm fine, Messalina," he whispers and leans into the hand caressing his head. I pet him a little, but I swear his cock's about to burst. But not yet. A little more won't hurt. He can't see me grin, but I can feel my orgasm as it trembles through me and the harness—and through the dildo inside him.

Now I'm satisfied. Riding victoriously astride my stallion, I signal my approval with one good, solid thrust. I loosen the cock cage and he cries out, his body going rigid as he comes in torrents across the sheets and collapses onto the bed. I slowly extract myself from him and stand up. My legs are weak and I stumble but quickly recover. We are both drenched in sweat. His skin is so red he looks sunburned with a full-body blush.

"Look at me, Jared."

He turns to face me where I stand with my feet planted shoulder-width apart, emphasizing my artificial enhancements, and my fists on my hips. His eyes are dilated and his lips are set in a thin line.

My hair hangs limp in my eyes, so I pull out the hairpins and fluff my hair about my neck to cool myself a bit. One of my bra straps falls off my shoulder it's so limp from sweat. I unclasp the harness and shimmy out of it. Jared, in response, flexes his muscles starting with his arms, then clenches his buttocks and legs, and finally flexes his feet.

I stoop to pick up one of the damp towels and find it cool instead of warm. He stares as I run the towel over my neck, chest, down my arms and belly, and then between my thighs.

"I'm done—for now."

I toss the towel at him. It lands on his face.

"Your turn to sleep on the wet spot," I say and walk around to my side of the bed and lie down with my back to him. I close my eyes but feel him move and turn over. The bed jostles as he lifts his large frame and I hear him walk to the bathroom.

I must have dozed off, because the next thing I know, my eyelids pop open when I'm grabbed, dragged to the center of the bed, and rolled onto my back. Jared moves between my legs. He has taken a shower and is still damp; his hair is slicked back, giving off a dark chestnut sheen and his expression pins me to the spot. If I didn't know better, I'd say he looks ready for battle. My eyes drift down and I see it.

Jared is now wearing the harness and totes an artificial rod that the catalog calls "The Punisher." He's slicked both himself and the dildo with lubricant.

I swallow hard. Usually, Jared would simply use a dildo to get me ready for him. Despite all our fun and experimenting in the bedroom, I have yet to be double penetrated, but the look in Jared's eyes says that is about to change. He anchors my legs over his haunches, positions himself at each of my entrances, and cradles my bottom in his hands. Then he stops. Our gazes lock with a palpable intensity. He's giving me a chance to protest. Instead, I tilt my hips up to give him better access and clutch the bed sheets.

He moves forward and you would have thought I had been electrocuted. A primal scream escapes my lips as my most private spaces are simultaneously filled and stretched, causing me to spasm with an immediate, bone-rattling orgasm. I release the sheets and wrap my arms and legs around him, pulling him onto me. His strong arms tighten around me while giving him traction to move deeper. My body reacts the same way his did when I took him, but I'm not stoical about it. Tears spill from my eyes and my chest constricts as he squeezes a sob out of me.

His kiss smothers my cries while creating a chain reaction, and we climax together. I shudder with yet another aftershock and it takes several minutes before we are able to look at each other. When we do, it's evident in our faces.

We are a perfect fit.

CHAPTER FIFTEEN

"THE LIFE OF LUCREZIA"

"Eva!"

I look up and see Harold Seigel, the 18th century literature professor, heading my way. His usual happy countenance shows concern. "Are you OK? You look a little off color, if you don't mind my saying." He smiles knowing I'm not so touchy to be offended by his choice of words.

"I'm fine. Just a little sore and tired. What's up?"

His gives me a questioning glance, then asks, "What time is your last class?"

"Two o'clock."

"Great. Can you meet me in the lounge at three-thirty?"

"Sure. What's going on?"

"You'll see, but you're gonna want to be in on this." Harold's medium-sized frame is quickly swallowed by the student body filling the hall to near capacity, leaving me feeling both curious and suspicious.

* * * *

My suspicions are well-founded. My colleagues want to hold an open debate about faculty/student "relations" since these lines, never clearly defined to begin with, got blurred even further during the tenure of the last Chancellor. However, with his retirement and the increase of more conservative colleagues, like my dean, J. Paul Mathis—plus the Hyde affair—we have a full-blown crisis on our hands, at least as far as public relations are concerned.

"It'll be a panel discussion," says Harold. "One side argues for stricter rules of conduct; the other side defends a person's right to choose their nookie partner. The administration won't be able to participate because of the lawsuit, though I'm sure a representative will be present. This is strictly to get the rank and file to discuss the issue in the open.

After all, this is a college. The exchange of views and ideas should be encouraged."

I sigh. Yeah, right. But my cynicism bothers me. I'm starting to sound like a pessimistic lifer.

Harold continues, "There will be a total of twelve participants, three faculty and three students on each side, all from different backgrounds. Professor Alicia Beecham, from Comparative Religions is going to head the pro-restriction side."

"We want you to head our side, Eva." Kent Melbourne, a linguistics professor, blurts out. He's another guy popular with the students.

My eyes open wide. It's nice to know your peers like you enough to ask you to take the lead, but this is different. I shake my head.

"I don't see how. If we're trying to get people on our side, first, I'm hardly the most popular or senior faculty member. In fact, I'm the youngest in our division. Second, I was Hyde's protégé. And third, I may be called as a character witness."

"But that's what makes you perfect for the cause, Evadne," Howard says. "Unless you are subpoenaed or under a gag order, you can still participate. Besides, we're not discussing the case but talking in generalities."

Kent smiles. "We even came up with a name to call ourselves."

"Oh, good lord, what?"

"The Cunning Linguists."

* * * *

Tuesday has yet to start and already I get a glimpse of the foolishness yet to come by way of a memo in my office mailbox. Two more students have come forward to confess their relationships with Terrence Hyde.

The tabloids are having a field day. More than once I see TV unit trucks prowling around. They haven't been on campus yet because we are a private institution. Nevertheless, the strain on everyone is getting worse.

For weeks, memos have been coming out practically every other day and one-on-one conferences between faculty and the bigwigs in administration have become common, creating an atmosphere of hypersensitive, politically-correct paranoia. For many of my colleagues, The Cunning Linguists and myself included, the steps taken by our bosses have become a bit ridiculous.

But when I hear one joke too many about "Horny Hyde," it doesn't help my attitude. Over lunch, Glynnis and I talk about the latest proclamation from on high.

"They are trying to prevent a witch hunt while setting the stage for one," I bitch. "It's been nearly a year. They need to hurry up and put an end to this. I mean really. What's this crap about keeping our office doors open if we have a student in there?"

"Well, you know what happens behind closed doors, Eva."

"Quiet? Privacy?"

"Yes, but it's also easier for people to do what they shouldn't."

I laugh, but she frowns.

"I should think you'd be more appreciative of the new guidelines."

"Why me?"

She looks over the top of her glasses at me. "You mean apart from your participation in The Great Sex Debate, being Terrence Hyde's protégé, and that you've had a bit of notoriety in the press lately?" She takes a bite of her sandwich. "Also . . . you have a puppy."

Puppy is the term we use for students who follow us from class to class wanting our undivided attention. It's reserved for students brown-nosing (or tonguing) and those who have crushes on their professor. I chuckle.

"I wouldn't call Neil my puppy, but so what if he is? I've never had one before."

But Glynnis doesn't see the humor; instead she just nods.

"That's what I thought the first few times it happened to me. Evadne," she says, taking her sandwich out of its wrapper, "they always have ulterior motives. How long have you been teaching at college level?"

I shrug. "About five years."

"You're still young."

"Damn! I hate when people say that. Does that mean I'm stupid too?"

"No. It's just that, in our profession, it's easy to get caught up in the unbridled hormones around us."

"Hyde has taught for over twenty years. Sounds like he's been a lech for all of them."

"Yes, but he's a man."

"I had no idea you were so sexist, Glyn. Wasn't it you who once said I should 'get fucked?' Those were your exact words."

"I'm not sexist, just practical." She gives me the eye. "My suggestion served you well."

I look away. The last thing I need is anyone speculating about my sex life at work.

"Is something wrong?" she asks.

"No."

"Hmm, well I'm just saying, don't go looking for love in all the wrong places."

I start laughing, not minding the looks we get from others in the cafeteria. "Can we please stop playing *Name That Tune*? I'd like to finish my lunch."

* * * *

The Life of Lucrezia Spence is turning me into a slacker and with Jared so busy, it's the one thing I have to take my mind off matters. I've even got Ana and Tony reading it and loaned them my previous issues until they get their own subscriptions.

If I'm not rereading the latest issue, I'm hanging out in *The Life of Lucrezia* chat rooms and listservs under the name "BlackCat" in honor of my last tattoo. I've made some interesting friends online, like RazorBrn and TriXXX, and I bet I'm the senior citizen in a group of cyber-kids. Either they are very reckless or full of shit—I suspect a bit of both.

The official *The Life of Lucrezia* website, authorized by the writer and creator, Ali, and with a webmaster named RudeBoy, is my favorite *LoL* website. It doesn't matter when I sign on, RazorBrn and TriXXX always seem to be in the chatroom—and they're not even moderators.

One of the most popular threads is about Lucy being under surveillance. One of the school's second graders, Carrie Dover, is the child of single parent and police detective Jack Dover. Jack is a young, sexy hotshot rising through the ranks. He knew instantly what was implied when the papers ran the photos of Lucy receiving the Employee of the Year Award from Superintendent Patrick Klein and the one taken outside his house. Apart from a few voices of discontent from local bible-thumpers, the incident blew over. But Jack refuses to let go and when he finds evidence implicating the district attorney and a justice of appeals, Jack is ordered to back off by Police Chief Adam Lawson.

blkcat:	things are getting spicy
RzrBrn:	yes finally
triXXX:	o come on razor give the man a break
RzrBrn:	who said ali's a man?

triXXX:	of course he's a man. this is a man's fantasy
RzrBrn:	i dunno could be a bull dyke
lickitty:	thx razor 4 b n so sensitive
RzrBrn:	i don't mean you lickitty. i'd cut off my dick to be with a hot babe like you :-* nice to see you could join our threesome :-)
blkcat:	hate to admit. would love for LoL to come out weekly
triXXX:	embarrassed?
blkcat:	no. addicted:-)
lickitty:	ain't no shame blackie. if i had tits like lucy i'd want to see more of em 2
RzrBrn:	hmmm, blackcat and lickitty. r u a couple?
lickitty:	a couple of what?
blkcat:	does that turn you on razor? ;-)
triXXX:	he's jerking off at the thought
lickitty:	well, maybe if he's a good boy, blackcat and I will get a pvt room. what u say blackie?
blkcat:	;-D

I glance at my desk clock.

blkcat:	must go 2 class now
RzrBrn:	aw that SUX!!!
lickitty:	why don't u ditch?
triXXX:	yeah. tell the prof to go fuck him/herself
blkcat:	sorry can't. besides, this prof is really pretty cool :-)

I laugh as I log off and put the computer to sleep. A sigh escapes me when I realize I've wasted another break getting my Lucy fix instead of creating my midterm exam.

Oh well. If I can't see Jared, it'll give me something to do this weekend.

I grab my purse and briefcase and exit the office. Making my way through the throng, I catch glimpse of a brightly colored flyer on top of a stack of notebooks before realizing it's not a flyer, but the cover of the latest issue of *The Life of Lucrezia*. I'm surprised that, through all the bustle in the hall, I'm able to single it out. Perhaps I've become sensitized. I smile to myself. At least there's one other person in our cloistered community who's not adverse to a little creative smut.

I'm just being mean. The students on our campus are no different than elsewhere, but the "Hyde Affair" has stirred up dormant issues about sex and academia, and the lines of demarcation are rising up and creating factions on campus. I laugh out loud at the thought of *The Life of Lucrezia* becoming a sort of banner for sexual freedom.

Let the revolution begin.

* * * *

It's been less than twenty-four hours since I last chatted in the *LoL* chatroom and I've found a feature article in a popular e-zine called *Redd Ink,* which focuses on things on the verge of making a splash, for better or worse.

Reporter Creighton Day has written a piece about the growing appeal of what he calls "dark animation," or animation dwelling on sinister and adult issues. Day lists several popular action, goth, and manga titles, but his article is really about "a pulp fiction throwback in modern graphic novel style mixing exquisite and technically detailed drawing with sexually charged writing."

I devour the rest of Day's article:

> Under the title of *The Life of Lucrezia*, "Ali," as the mastermind of the serial goes by, has created an anachronistic world full of explicit sex and mob-style violence that would make Dick Tracy spew. But not intrepid police detective Jack Dover, one of the newest faces to enter the town of Sugarville, "where the sweetness can rot you to the core" as the cynical Dover puts it. He's been transferred to the town from the capital, under protest, for reasons unknown to us and already he's stumbled on a potential scandal to shake all the sugar out of Sugarville.
>
> It took some doing, but I was able to catch up with Ali while he was on vacation and staying at the swank Hotel Monaco in Denver. I offered to meet him there or at The Brown Palace. Not that I was staying there, mind you, but mostly to show I wasn't some hack. He

declined to interview in person and, considering how I had to get past his staff, I asked if it had anything to do with the subject matter. Did he have to keep his identity secret?

"Lucrezia is the star, not me," he said.

So, we chatted over the phone for nearly an hour.

The interview shows "Ali" to be a funny but modest man (so much for RazorBrn's theory to the contrary), and that he has a girlfriend.

"She didn't care for the story at first, but I think she's coming around," Ali said. I asked if any of the heart-stopping sex scenes were literally drawn from personal experience and what his girlfriend thought. But he just laughed and said, "Let's just say we are both happy mixing art with life." Of course Ali wouldn't divulge the name of his muse, only that she is "the ink in my well and my inspiration."

I ask if she's the model for Lucrezia.

"No," Ali confesses. "She is a character in her own right."

I smile. How sweet. Lucky bitch. Must be nice to be a muse.

It makes me feel better that I'm not the only female who was slow to warm up to the story, and for similar reasons. When I first started lurking in the various *LoL* chatrooms, there was a collection of people—mostly women, or at least people claiming to be women—who were disappointed that the storyline seemed a bit simplistic and contrived. Sure, the sex was top quality, but Lucy and the whole Sugarville gang deserved more.

Apparently Ali took these comments to heart and the story has become more complex and intriguing. In the January issue, it was announced that *Lucy* will change to a biweekly.

I logoff the Internet and bring up my notes for the upcoming debate next week. I think I have more than enough ammo to prove my point, but right now, I'm struggling with my own convictions.

How can I argue for sexual freedom and openness when I cringe at the thought of my own family seeing me as a sexually active woman? Freedom, openness, *and* a right to privacy. Is it really possible?

"Knock, knock. How you doin', teach?"

I look up and see Neil's head peeking around my door.

"I just thought you might be nervous about tonight, that's all."

"Me? Nervous?" I pick up a pen and pretend to write a list. "Neil, I talk in front of people every day. Many of them are hostile or have a grudge against me."

He scoops his work into his strong right hand and places the wire basket back on the counter. "Yes, but you're not talking about their private love life."

"Neil, tonight's debate isn't about anyone's love life. It's about using your freedom of choice."

His laugh makes me raise my head.

"You don't have to convince me, teach. I'm on your side." He steps closer to my desk. "Don't worry. I'll be there to cheer you on."

"I didn't doubt it for a second." I smile. "Now get to work. We got one hundred freshmen who need their exam copied."

He snaps straight to attention, salutes, and exits the office.

* * * *

Jared and I wait at the stoplight to cross the street and we see about thirty people heading to the student union.

"It's gonna be packed." He sings, trying to get a rise out of me and smiles.

"You're enjoying this, aren't you?"

He puts on a face of mock innocence. "How many men get the chance to see the woman they love debate a person's right to have sex to a crowd of strangers? Are you kidding? I am *loving* this." He tugs me into his arms for a kiss and gives me a squeeze about my waist.

"Hello, teach!"

My eyes pop open and I step away so fast Jared loses his balance. I look past him and see Neil approaching. He's dressed like a baby yuppie in Dockers, shirt, and dark blazer. He fills out his clothes well and his honey-colored hair is brushed to a shine. I'm surprised he doesn't have a date with him.

"Jared, I'd like you to meet Neil Hollister."

Before he turns to face Neil I catch the gleam in Jared's eyes and it makes me nervous.

"Neil!" Jared reaches out a hand. Neil takes it and I see his cheeks flinch as Jared squeezes. "Nice to meet you at last. Eva speaks of you so often, I'm jealous. I hope you're keeping her out of trouble. There's only room for one scandal at Bellingham."

I grit my teeth and Neil looks at me with a mixture of surprise and something else. Satisfaction? I sense he is doing a quick appraisal of Jared and assessing my taste in men. And what's this nonsense about my going on as if I talk about Neil constantly when I've only mentioned him on occasion?

"So, Neil," he continues. "You're here to give your ol' prof some moral support?"

"Yes, sir. Dr. Cavell is my favorite." He looks at me. "I got her back."

I turn away. I knew Neil was fond of me, but his favorite? The kid is a Political Science major and aiming for pre-law. Looking up, I see the light is now green and cross the street. I glance over my shoulder and see the two men are talking, and taking their time. I give a whistle. They look up and Jared waves me on.

"We'll catch up!"

I smile weakly and walk away. My man and my infatuated "puppy" are making friends.

My life is now complete.

* * * *

It doesn't take long for the debate to get heated. When Professor Alicia Beecham mentions how the ancient Greeks had a system of mentoring that sexually "abused" young men, I have to call in a point of order.

"It seems that my colleague on the other side of the aisle is confusing the issue with information I'm not sure she understands."

There are a few audible gasps and wide-eyed stares from both sides of the stage and the audience, but I don't care. The woman is talking bullshit.

"How am I misinformed, Dr. Cavell?"

"We can sit here today, thousands of years later, with our 21st century morals and debate whether or not the ancient Greeks sexually 'abused' their young, but it doesn't negate the fact that they used sex as an effective form of teaching."

"Are you saying that all students should have sex with their professors?" Beecham frowns.

"I find the taste of other people's words in my mouth quite bitter, professor."

More "oohs" and "ahhs" from the audience, but I go on.

"If a faculty member and student choose to have a relationship, it's not my business."

"Does the same go for mentoring, Dr. Cavell?"

This question is asked by Professor G. E. D. Smith, a man so self-righteous he makes Mother Teresa look like a drunken whore. But the scary thing is that he's the head of department for Politics—and another man associated with Neil.

I turn and look at my colleague, Professor Harold Seigel, in disbelief and he looks at me with the same, as does Dr. Kent Melbourne, the third faculty member on our side of the panel.

Unless I'm mistaken, Professor Smith has made a thinly veiled insinuation that my relationship with Terrence Hyde was something far more intimate.

"Perhaps I am not following your argument, Dr. Cavell," he continues. "Did the ancient Greeks have more morals than we do today? Were their methods of teaching and mentoring more appropriate?"

"Professor, I am not going to try and compare our modern methods to theirs. What I will say is that, as consenting adults, we don't need every aspect of our lives given a stamp of approval by those who feel morally superior."

The professor and I proceed to have a mini showdown as we glare at each other from across the stage until the moderator, Dr. Lawley Gillis, steps in.

"Thank you, everyone, for your comments. Let's open the floor for questions."

After a few questions about college regulations and consent, the topic swings into that of mentoring and student assistants. I'm asked if student assistants are regarded in a differential way.

"No, they're not. At least they shouldn't be."

Then, to my horror, Jared stands up.

"But you're biased, aren't you, Dr. Cavell? Don't you have a student assistant? What is your relationship with him—or her?"

My eyes bug out for a moment, and if they could, they'd shoot lasers and disintegrate him on the spot. I try to keep my smile serene, but I get the feeling I look like a demented cat about to strike. Neil takes this opportunity to stand and it's all I can do to keep from banging my head on the table.

"I'm Dr. Cavell's assistant and I am more than pleased to work under her. Not once has she complained about my service."

Of course this gets laughs and Neil takes a bow, but I think I'm the only one who notices Professor G. E. D. Smith looking first at Neil and then at me. His churlish expression turns even more sour, if that's possible.

And so it begins. People start voicing their feelings about favoritism between professors and their assistants, and the fact that the girl Terry Hyde got pregnant was his assistant is raised by a reporter from the student paper.

It's not like we can comment, but I remain quiet for the rest of the discussion, knowing that I succeeded in ruffling the feathers of a few esteemed senior members of faculty and don't feel like digging myself in deeper.

Yet, in the end, everything comes to an amicable conclusion. I'm not saying we solved anything, but we succeed in creating a very lively dialogue amongst the campus population.

We get back to Jared's place and I am dragging my ass. Jared, on the other hand, has barely stopped laughing.

"Aw, babydoll. You were perfect."

I spin around and point a finger at him. "You and Neil did not help." Despite my anger, he laughs harder.

"I think there's something to be said for stricter rules between faculty and students," he says as we enter the house. "I got a vested interest in this. That assistant, Neil, is a nice-looking fellow." He gives me a sidelong glance. "And he has a massive crush on you."

CHAPTER SIXTEEN

⋏

TRUTH AND CONSEQUENCES

It's now March. Three weeks since the article in *Redd Ink* and the first of the biweekly issues of *LoL* is out. In issue #13, ironically enough, Lucrezia Spence's double life is about to be exposed by Jack Dover. I've been waiting for my lunch break, so I can lock myself in my office and read it. Now, a visibly scared Lucrezia makes a call to her benefactor:

> "Unless Mark Starr can prevent his
> wife Astrid from going to the cops,
> Charity Escorts is through!"

The remaining panels are bordered by a phone cord, framing the action as Lucrezia speaks to a person sitting on a high-backed chair obscured by shadows.

> "I can't get Chief Lawson to help,"
> Lucrezia continues. "His ass is in
> too deep."

> "I wish you'd approached me
> sooner, Lucrezia," the mystery
> person replies. "Now, I may have
> to use tactics that I'd rather not."

> "I'm sorry . . ."

Whomever Lucy is speaking to must have some awesome power, because the drawing of Lucrezia captures her fear so well it's hard for me not to feel sorry for the silly woman.

"When you asked me to help smooth the way for your expansion of Charity Escorts, you said everything was under control. What happened?"

"Things took longer than was estimated."

"So it's my fault?"

"No! No, no, I don't mean it like that."

"Then what do you mean, Lucy?"

The frames get lighter, revealing more detail. The mystery man sits in what could be described as a study with tall, mullioned windows, Empire furniture, and bookshelves full of leather-bound volumes.

"Just help me . . . please?"

"I'll help you, Lucrezia, but I warn you. Be careful. I would hate for anything to happen to the business
. . . Or to you."

The phone cord framing the panel has turned into a rope with a noose at the end. I smile. Ali's sense of humor shines again.

"I have always tried to never let you down."

Lucrezia looks paler with each passing frame, if that's possible. Her angelic face is dripping with sweat.

"And I am grateful. Lucrezia, I go into every endeavor with both eyes open. Remember that."

The darkness now falls in a solid diagonal across the frame, exposing the mystery person as having nice shapely legs and wearing a tight, dark-blue dress. A very revealing neckline exposes a chest that threatens to break free of its confinement and the black silhouette of a cat's face on the right breast. I grin from ear-to-ear. The mastermind behind all this is another woman! The last frame shows Lucrezia visibly relieved and slumping down in a chair.

"I will remember. Thank you, Messalina."

I'll be damned.

I drop the book onto my desk, not caring that my salad is beneath it. Calmly, I pick up the phone. "Hello, Trey. Is Jared around?" When Trey replies, I swear he sounds like I caught him doing something he shouldn't.

"Oh! Hello, Cookie. Let me see if I can find him." Trey puts me on hold but he's barely gone before he's back.

"I'm sorry, sweetie, but he's on a conference call. I don't know how long he'll be."

"That's fine. But tell him I want to talk to him ASAP."

My tone is sharp and I hang up before Trey can respond.. Resting my head in my hands, I suddenly feel a monster headache coming on. I may have threatened to kill him before, but right now, if Jared Delaney were near me, he would have good reason to fear for his safety. I take a few "calming" breaths but it hardly helps.

OK, he may be too busy to talk right now. But I know who isn't.

lickitty:	messalina! a woman after my own heart!
RzrBrn:	get in line, toots
triXXX:	let's hear it for the ladies!!! woo hoo!!!
Damocles:	well, she talks tuff but does she have the balls to really do anything
blkcat:	not balls. ovaries.
Damocles:	whatever
blkcat:	newbie?
Damocles:	i've been lurking for a while
blkcat:	nice to meet you anyway
Damocles:	feeling's mutual. i enjoy reading your comments
lickitty:	hey lovebirds, get a room!!
blkcat:	only if you make it a threesome, lick
lickitty:	nah. too many dangly bits. no offense, damocles
Damocles:	none taken:-)

Well, apart from the skeptical comment from the newest member of the group, the thirty other people that log on within the hour rave about the "woman behind the woman" as Lickitty puts it.

triXXX: i cant wait to see her face
caberet: if lucy's anything to go by, this Messalina chick will rock. hey, did anyone read the latest redd ink?

Several people speak up in the affirmative.

GQMan: ali must have a goddess for a girlfriend
RzrBrn: lucky bastard
Damocles: unless he's a lying bastard
lickitty: damn, damocles, u r a happy piece of work!
Damocles: nah, just dubious. don't mind me
triXXX: nothing wrong with that. after all, this is a MAN'S fantasy. right razor?
RzrBrn: ha ha
blkcat: i wonder if messalina will live up to her name
GQMan: what do you mean?
blkcat: look it up

I log off from the chatroom. What kind of professor would I be if I didn't make them work for it? If I get my way, this comic book Messalina is going to crash and burn like her ancient predecessor. And the sooner the better.

Neil Hollister comes whistling into my office to start his shift, looking as chipper and charming as ever. I put on a smile and clear off my desk, shoving the comic in a drawer.

"What's up, teach?"

"Hi, Neil." I watch him as he retrieves the work I left for him in his basket.

He looks at the contents of his "IN" basket. His short hair emphasizes the graceful curve of his neck and his smallish ears. His fingers are long and sturdy. Some afternoons on my way to the parking lot, I've seen him playing basketball at the courts with his friends and I've noticed the way his fingers clutch the ball. They reminded me of the way

Jared's did that day at the art center. I try not to think of fingers these days because then I start to remember my days at The DeLuxe.

Neil lifts a piece of mail with those fingers, the sunlight reflects off a fingernail, and I sigh. He looks up.

"Is there something wrong?"

"Oh, no." I think of a lie to cover myself. "I'm just wondering if I've given you too much. That's a lot of filing. Not much fun."

He smiles. "I'd do anything for you, you know that." He winks and continues looking through the basket. His assertion of fidelity does nothing to curb my anger at men in all their forms.

I've just been betrayed by one of their own, the one I thought was the best.

* * * *

Jared Alistair Delaney.

Ali.

That bastard.

I'm so mad, sweat seeps through my clothes despite the chill in the air. It all makes sense: Jared's defensiveness at my initial criticism, his wanting to discuss the story line with me, the similarities in some of the sex scenes, and now, the new character—Messalina—complete with a black cat tattoo.

And here I am thinking, like a jackass, that it's all just a happy coincidence. Jesus Christ! If it ever comes out that Jared's the creator of *The Life of Lucrezia* and that Messalina is—

"That goddamn bastard."

I went to a bar for a drink, thinking it would calm me down before confronting Jared. It didn't work. I now have three vodka martinis inside me as my car screeches to a halt in front of his house. I park on the street. His car is in the drive, but Trey's ride is nowhere to be seen. Then again, it's after six o'clock.

Using my key, I enter the house and don't bother searching for him, but go straight to his bedroom. Sure enough, he's sitting at his desk in the loft, but he's gazing out the window watching the world outside get darker and darker. Judging by his look, he's miles away. I make my stand at the foot of the bed, hands on hips.

"Who the hell do you think you are?"

He closes his eyes and leans back in his seat. Does he think he can fall asleep on me? Finally, he opens his eyes and comes down out of the loft. As he nears, I notice how tired he looks, as if he hasn't slept in days. His eyes are red and puffy and he has stubble on his chin from not shaving. Even his clothes are wrinkled.

"If you calm down, I can explain."

"Explain what? How you played me for a fool? 'Oh, Jared! Isn't the latest *Lucy* so wonderful?' Or that you used me as a model without my knowing? Or how now everyone will know whose body they're ogling?"

"Come on, Evadne. You're overreacting. Who's going to know it's you?"

"I figured it out."

"Yeah, but how many people who read this know my middle name?" He is trying to keep his tone level, but even I can detect the anger.

For a long minute we glare at each other. Me with my arms crossed over my chest. Jared with his dark violet eyes cutting into me, not with heat, but with an iciness that makes the flesh on my arms tingle. I may be attacking his baby, but he's attacking my privacy.

"There are other things. The black cat tattoo is a giveaway."

He laughs. "Is it really? Who have you been flashing your naked hip to, Eva? Neil? The tattoo Messalina has on her right breast is a different size and style. Besides, her face hasn't been completely revealed yet."

I shake my head in disbelief. "Why did you do it?"

He sighs and runs both hands through his hair, making it stand on end. "Eva, I don't have some big conspiracy planned to humiliate you." He looks at me. "It just . . . happened."

I say nothing, leaving him room to elaborate, which he does.

"Remember in Dallas when I said I wanted—needed—to do something with you? Well," he says with a shrug, "this is it. Thanks to you, I've gotten over a severe case of creativity block that was affecting my commissioned work and making me want to chuck it in altogether. I had originally created *Lucy* to give me an outlet and to have some fun, but I was running out of steam. What started as fun just turned into another chore as it slowly became more popular. Now, I have been able to create a story line that'll last for months."

I'm speechless, incredulous, and continue staring at him, frozen to the spot. By the way he's looking at me and grinding his teeth, my lack of response is pissing him off.

"Come here, woman."

Before I can move, he grabs my hand and drags me across the hall. His long fingers clamp hard around my wrist and I try to ignore the pain. We get to his studio and he opens the closet door. Pulling down a box that used to hold copier paper, he drops it at my feet and it hits the floor with a heavy thud.

"See this?" He releases my hand and I wiggle my fingers to restore the circulation in them. "This, my love, is fan mail. There's over five hundred letters in this box alone. I'm paying Trey overtime to handle it all because we answer every one."

"That's very admirable of you."

He scowls at my sarcasm and I scowl back.

"How long were you planning to keep this from me? Were you ever going to tell me?"

"Evadne." He lowers his head and shakes it wearily. "Why are you so upset? I mean—this is a flattering portrayal of you."

I press my lips together. "Flattering? Here I am thinking you're such a sensitive man, but you're just like Eddie Norton, trying to turn me into something I'm not. I could be outed as a sex hound by my students, my friends—my family. And I'm supposed to fall at your feet and feel *flattered?*"

Now it's Jared's turn to look confused.

"Sex hound?"

"Jared, the things we do to each other when we make love are private. At least I always thought they were."

"But Eva, these scenes are fantasy. Sure, some of it is drawn from life, but—"

"I don't care." He frowns at my interruption. "This is libel. This has the potential to ruin my reputation."

He stares at me in disbelief. "Are you threatening to sue me, Evadne? Because you wouldn't have a case."

I can count on one hand the times that I have been struck dumb. This makes number four. I turn my back, too angry to look at him. I am actually shaking and I hear him take a step closer until I feel his presence. It's at times like this when Jared's dark side moves closer to the surface that makes me more than a little nervous.

"For an assistant professor, you can be pretty dense. But go ahead and try. You may be sexy, but you're not the head of a sex conglomerate. The way I portray you as Messalina is fantasy. My fantasy. It's you, but then again, it isn't." He leans forward and the warmth of his breath touches my ear.

"Messalina is Evadne Cavell unleashed and uninhibited," he says, stroking my left elbow with his finger. "We've known each other for nearly a year, and yet you still hold out on me."

"Are you saying I'm not good enough for you? I don't satisfy you?" My hands squeeze into fists until my fingernails pierce my skin.

"I didn't say that."

"You feel the need to construct me?"

"Deconstruct, actually." There is a smile in his voice and it enrages me.

"Really? Deconstruct this." I haul around and slap him. For the longest moment, he stares at me in shock. Then he starts to blink. Slowly. Each time he opens his amethyst eyes they harden with violet fury. His chest heaves up and down like a breathing mountain, a volcano waiting to erupt. Even his hands clench and unclench into fists, but I don't care. Let him get mad. And let him try to hit me. My lips curl up in an empty smile and I tilt my head up, daring him to do something.

"Come on, Jared. You owed me that."

He remains still, grinding his teeth.

"You have lied to me for the last time Jared Alistair Delaney." I step aside. "Get out."

I may be kicking the man out of his own home, but right now, he needs to get the fuck out of my face.

And to my surprise, he does. He turns on his heel and clomps down the stairs. For such a heavy oak door, it creates a terrible reverb when he slams it shut hard enough for the stained glass to shatter. Less than a minute later, I hear the sound of tires burning rubber as he tears out of the driveway and speeds away down the street.

CHAPTER SEVENTEEN

"OUR STORY SO FAR"

Trey calls me on Monday at four o'clock in the afternoon just as I'm preparing to leave for the day. To say that my day has been shit is a gross understatement. Usually I can prevent any of my outside issues from creeping into the school with a smile and a cheery word. Today there is no smile and the only words out of my mouth are those necessary to get the point across.

"Hey, girlie. Will you come over here and do something about this man?"

I sigh. "What are you talking about, Trey?"

"He is completely insane! I'm just coming in the door because I had a fucking doctor's appointment and they felt it necessary to keep me waiting for nearly two hours, as if my time ain't precious. Then I get here and you'd think we'd been hit by a tornado. I'm talking 'bout shit *everywhere*. The stained glass on the door is *gone*—completely shattered. On the floor."

I close my eyes and swallow. My head starts to throb and I feel sick to my stomach.

"Paper's everywhere," Trey continues. "Some of his prized Rookwood pottery is nothing but rubble on the floor. And there's a hole in the wall of the foyer that, if I didn't know better, looks like someone put their fist through it."

I lower my head in my hand and cringe at the thought. "Where is he now?"

"Locked in his studio. I'm thinking I should call the police. I asked if I should but he said no. What do you think? He won't come out of his studio so I'm hoping you'll talk sense to him."

"Trey . . . I can't help you."

"Huh?"

If I weren't being serious, I'd laugh at the way he sounded. He can be such a drama queen I sometimes wonder if he and Tony are related. "I'm saying that Jared's behavior is no longer my concern. But it sounds to me like he needs anger management." There's silence on the line and I do believe it's sinking in.

"You mean Jared did all this?

"That would be my assumption."

"But why?"

"I know what's been going on. What Jared's been doing. And you." It's a struggle for me to keep my tone even and cool.

More silence and I suppress a sob by biting my lip. I rummage my desk for a tissue to spare using my sleeve. All day I've been able to wear a stony mask of indifference; one simple question, and now I'm about to become a blubbering mess.

"Evie? Cookie, are you listening to me?"

I don't know what he's just said, but I make a sound of acknowledgement.

"What are you doing now?"

"I'm about to go home."

"See you in ten minutes."

He hangs up before I can protest. The fact that both he and Jared can be at my apartment inside of ten minutes used to amuse me, now I find it unsettling. I'm not certain I want company right now, least of all from a man I have issues with.

No, I have issues with Jared, not Trey—not exactly. I will say this: Trey is a loyal employee if he can keep a secret like this for so long. I get up to make my second attempt to leave the office, wipe my cheeks, and put my sunglasses on. The lenses are opaque so no one can see my eyes, but the blotchy wet skin on my face may give me away.

I'm barely home two minutes when my buzzer rings. I release the door downstairs and wait for him to arrive. Soon he's standing there looking mighty sheepish and holding a big bouquet of blood-red, long-stemmed roses. How he managed to get the flowers and get to my apartment in a matter of minutes will remain a mystery.

"Friends?"

I take the flowers and sniff them. After a moment, I let him in. He follows me into the living area and I get my favorite vase from the china cabinet. He stands inside the room looking lost, as if he's never been here before.

"Take a seat," I offer and he sits in the middle of the couch, watching me. I sit in a chair near the balcony doors. I get a strong sense of déjà vu, then realize we're going through the exact motions Jared and I went through when he returned from Dallas, but he didn't bring me flowers. I wonder how far Trey and I will go as we play "kiss and make up."

"He broke his hand, you know."

I grimace and, for a second, I'm sad, then guilty—then pissed. What an idiot. Did I tell him to drive his fist through a wall? Better the wall than me, I suppose.

"Right or left?" I ask.

"Left."

"That's good. He can still work." Trey doesn't miss my point.

"Evadne, I apologize."

"And he's a goddamn fool to have destroyed his Rookwood—fit of anger or not."

We look at each other. Trey's big, blue, very expressive eyes helps him to be the smoothest player when he wants to be, but we know each other too well. After what he's told me about his run-ins with Jared's women in the past and about his open marriage with his wife, Piper, I don't doubt he can read women. I stand up.

"Care for a drink because I'm having one." I go to the wet bar and pour a double whiskey.

"I'll have the same."

"Straight?"

"Rocks."

I give him the glass. He clasps both hands around it and leans forward resting his forearms on top of his legs, head bowed, and sighs. Returning to my seat, I feel a volley is near, but decide to keep the ball in my court. I want some answers first.

"Tell me, Trey, did you know he slept with Sarah when he returned from his trip to Dallas with me?"

Slowly, he raises his eyes to look me in the face.

"Yes. But, be fair. How was I to know about you?"

"True." I nod.

"Fuck, I mean, Jared and Sarah are always breaking up and regrouping. They've done it twice since I started working for him—why not three?" He jiggles the ice in his glass. "But something about this last time told me it would be the *last* time."

"What was that?"

"Jared made Sarah give back the keys to his house." Trey finished his drink. "He left them on my desk and told me to keep them as a spare set."

I laugh and get up. Going through my purse, I pull out a set of keys and toss them to him.

"That's the same set, isn't it?" I raise my eyebrow at him.

He looks the keys over and then back at me. "Right down to the Broncos key chain."

"Well, there you go. A spare set for the next spare woman to come along."

"Cookie, you really do need to give yourself more credit. When Jared returned from Dallas, I could see a change in him—and you know he's not the most demonstrative man with his feelings. Shit, he can teach Tom Cruise a thing or two about reticence, but . . ." He shakes his head. "It didn't take a genius to see something happened to him, you know?

"That day, I let myself in through the kitchen door, as usual. Sarah was standing there in an evening dress, looking a fright with her hair and make-up a mess and fixing a cup of coffee. I glared at her, she glared at me. 'Going to work, I see,' I said to her."

Despite my peevishness, I bite back a smile.

"But, unlike Sarah, she said nothing and just left through the back way. I went upstairs and found Jared at work. I asked him about his trip and he looked up at me with this big—*grin*—on his face! I swear, Eva, I'd never seen the man grin before. Surely it didn't come from fucking Sarah." He looks at me. "And I was right."

I sit down and listen to Trey tell me how Jared revealed his idea to rejuvenate *The Life of Lucrezia*.

"He was serious, Evadne, and the more he talked, the more his drive and enthusiasm came through. Then I met you," he says and smiles. "And I knew he was on the right track."

I sit looking at Trey, not knowing what to think.

"Evie, I can't say sorry enough for not telling you what we were doing. Jared will have to speak for himself, but what I do know is that he didn't want to lose you over this."

"Well, ain't that a bitch? Costing him a small fortune, am I?"

Trey sighs and finishes his drink. "Eva, can I ask you something?"

"Sure."

"What bothers you more: the fact that Jared's been using you for his inspiration or that he's sharing your image as art?"

I mull it over. "Good question, Trey." Now it's my turn to finish my drink. "Our entire relationship has been based on lies. He slept with Sarah after seeing my card and before telling me it was 'over' between them. That's some way to break up, if you ask me. Then Jared looked me straight in the eye and said he would never hurt or deceive me."

"But Evadne, can't you see past that? You've inspired Jared to turn out some of his best work ever. And Sarah?" He snorts. "Sarah's a waste of a heartbeat. Don't throw Jared away over this."

"Is that what you think I'm doing? Throwing him away?"

When Trey nods, I'm surprised.

"Now, this is just my simple mind making an opinion, but Eva, if you decide to end it and sue him for damages, I'd say you were acting out on principle." He puts his glass down on the table. "But if you end it with him because you're still mad about the Sarah fling, well . . . that sounds more like pride to me."

I have a hard time keeping from staring at him agape.

"Would you care to explain that? I mean, who's screwing whom here? I don't need his money. What if I don't want my sex life open for the world to see?"

Trey laughs. "This from the same woman who played 'thumble fumble' with strangers in a dark theater. A kind of exhibitionism that has done you well, I may add."

I turn my back on him and go out onto the balcony. It doesn't take long for him to follow me. "Talley once told me that Jared expects honesty, but he's lied to me, deceived me. Why should I forgive him?"

Trey gives me a friendly kiss on the back of the shoulder. "Would it help you to know that he's beating himself up over this?"

"I thought you said he could speak for himself?"

"I did . . . I just wanted you to hear it from someone who can actually see it."

* * * *

Time heals all wounds. Time marches on.

What a crock of shit. When you hurt, time stops. It actually goes backwards, over and over, until the time span covered becomes raw. I can't help but relive the last year of my life over and over again, each time from a different angle, and every time through the eyes of a fool.

In less than a month, news starts floating around the theatre scene that one of Denver's leading ladies has reunited with "her" man.

On the other hand, the talk on the *LoL* boards has been how things are aiming towards a big sexual showdown between Messalina and Detective Jack Dover. This is easy to understand, because the last issue of *LoL* is grittier than ever before.

Messalina and her henchwomen, Sister Friction and Jane Bondage, have become a virtual triumvirate of hardcore sexual power.

Lucrezia now sees how the once quaint idea of a bedroom-community bordello is serious business with lives at stake, especially when Sister Friction "accidentally" eliminates an investigative reporter under the apparent instructions of Messalina.

Meanwhile, in the real world, I discover just how far-reaching the Denver theatre community is, Tony notwithstanding, and for the first time since my arrival at the college, I dread the theatre department's annual showcase on campus where many local professionals participate and give workshops. Several of my students are involved and invite me to see them perform. But I'm running into people I've met through Tony.

Despite my trying to avoid the theatre school or any other place where the actors and crew tend to hang out, I still see a few recognizable faces. Thankfully, the showcase only lasts two weeks and I'm on the verge of making it through this ordeal with no one grilling me about my association with Jared or Sarah.

It has been a hectic day. The morning was lost to various meetings and I barely have time to pick up a burger from Wendy's. Breakfast is a distant memory and I get a double cheeseburger before heading off to sit in the quad. It's a sunny day, with only a slight, crisp nip in the wind coming from the north, but pleasant enough to sit outside in a light sweater. Setting my briefcase down, I pull my burger out of the bag and place it on my lap.

"You're Evadne Cavell, right?"

Looking in the direction of the voice, I have to squint because of the sun. "Yes?"

"I thought I recognized you. I'm Della Grey."

She says her name as if I'm supposed to know it. My lack of recognition doesn't go down well, but the fact that I have to look up to her seems to fit with Della Grey's opinion of herself.

"Sarah Radcliff pointed you out to me at the Aurora Fox some time ago."

"Oh, I see." I make an *ah-ha* type movement with my head. So, I've been pointed at, have I? "You're Sarah's friend?"

Della's shape barely conceals the sun from my eyes, but I can still see the smirk on her pouty lips. Despite the chill in the air, Della wears a light dress that billows around her small, delicate body. I find it amazing how some people tend to make friends with people they resemble. Della and Sarah have the same build, but Della is dark while Sarah is fair.

"Yes. I'm her best friend. And you're Jared's ex." She takes pleasure saying that as her voice oozes with artificial sweetener.

"Yes. Yes I am." I grin happily. "I'm surprised you know about that."

"Oh, darling, everybody knows about that." She gives a casual flip of her black hair.

"Really? Slow news day in the theatre world?"

The ice from Della's gaze bounces off my sweater. I cross my legs, feigning interest in our conversation. "And how is good ol' Sarah these days?"

"She's doing very well, Evadne. Since she and Jared got back together things have just been perfect." She purrs. "Mmm-hmm, she's on a great assignment through her new agent, and pretty soon," she says, twisting a raven curl around a slender finger tipped with frosty pink polish, "you and everyone else will see a lot more of her."

"Goody."

She frowns but it's quickly replaced when her lips curl in a devilish smile.

"All things considered, with the history she and Jared share, I expect wedding bells before too long. You know how it is when people who've been apart realize what a mistake they've made and then get back together." This time she doesn't try to hide her contempt when she looks at me. "They tend not to make the same mistake twice."

"Oh, honey." I laugh. "If I made mistakes, I'd agree with you."

Her eyebrows shoot up, surprised by my reaction. I lift my cooling hamburger and take a bite.

"I'm sorry. I didn't mean to disturb your lunch."

"Yeah, well, life's full of little inconveniences."

"A big girl like you needs to keep up her strength." She turns and goes back in the direction of the rock from whence she came.

Despite my wanting to ignore her childish jab about my size, the hunger for my now-cold hamburger fades.

* * * *

After Trey's initial visit the day after Jared and I broke up, Trey and I still manage to have lunch together every Wednesday. Not because I'm interested in hearing about Jared, though. I would be happy not to discuss him at all if it weren't for the fact that Trey and I share other friends by way of Tony and Talley. It's purely a means to keep up with the gossip.

"Cookie, you should've heard it," he says as he scoops into his strawberry shortcake. "That Talley can burn up a phone line. No need to pick up the extension to eavesdrop with her booming voice." He glances at me before taking a bite. "They were talking about you."

"Why?" I frown.

"She called to ask Jared, and I quote, 'What kind of 24-karat jackass do you think you are, Jared Alistair Delaney?'"

I shake my head in disbelief.

"It's true. And guess what he did."

"What?"

"He hung up on her."

"No . . . way."

"Yes way. I couldn't believe it myself. You do not hang up on Talley Monroe. Not ten minutes later, the doorbell rang and I tell you, I was afraid to open it and see her all the way from Texas ready to draw blood. But it was the delivery guy."

"Lucky."

"Right." He takes another bite of his dessert. "What about you? I won't hold it against you that, thanks to *you*," he says, pointing his spoon at me, "Sarah's in my field of vision again."

My stomach clenches and I try to sound casual. "Does she stay over a lot?"

"Not at all. Nor does he stay with her. It's just that she's always *around*." He shivers as if he's covered with ants, "Hovering like a gargoyle waiting for the next big rain so she can piss it on you from above."

I laugh. "Is it really true about the commercial?"

He rolls his eyes dramatically. "Jesus God, it's true. I'm glad I'm not a woman."

Trey confirmed to me earlier that Della's eluding to Sarah's good fortune was true and soon Sarah Radcliff will star in a national tampon campaign. I nearly lost my appetite. Nearly.

"Then again," Trey continues, "the thought of using her mug to plug my bleeding twat—if I had one—appeals to my vengeful nature."

I nearly do a spit-take as I laugh with a full mouth of ice cream and get a brain freeze.

"Well," I finally say, "I'm glad with my rags." And I toast him with a scoop of hot fudge sundae. This gets us laughing so hard I develop a cramp in my side and when I tell him, it just makes us laugh harder. Finally we both recover.

"How's work going?"

"Everyone's still in knots." I put down my spoon. "But it's been quiet. The case seems to have stalled over the last few months. I don't know if it's a blessing or a curse."

"And what about your student?"

"If you mean Neil Hollister, he's still around."

"Is he a blessing or a curse?"

"Let's just say he's my gargoyle. Whether he'll rain blessings or shit from above remains to be seen."

"I tell you, Cookie. That little boy made Jared awfully nervous."

"Why? As you say, he's a boy. Jared's a man. No contest."

I decide to keep to myself how that last week I went to the matinee at The DeLuxe Theater and saw Neil Hollister come in as I waited in the upstairs lobby. It was the first time since getting involved with Jared that I'd set foot in the place and I actually wanted to see the movie. I ducked out before Neil saw me, went straight home, and joined a DVD club.

Trey shakes his head. "Well from what I've heard, Jared doesn't trust him. Just you be careful."

CHAPTER EIGHTEEN

∧

"MESSALINA"

It's here.

Two months since my split from Jared, and almost one year to the day since we met, the issue everyone's been waiting for—the one causing so much speculation that *LoL* chatrooms, blogs, and bulletin boards are multiplying daily—has arrived. People are already calling it "The Sex Issue."

Why all the suspense? Because in *The Life of Lucrezia* issue #17 the wait is over. Messalina and Jack Dover are to consummate their lust for each other.

I open my mailbox and see the familiar magazine in the brown wrapper protected by a plastic sleeve, even though I had let my subscription run out.

They are sent.

And it's not like I can simply toss it aside and pretend it doesn't exist. That would be like I stopped using my left arm because I was mad at it. No, *The Life of Lucrezia* is a part of me, like it or not. Taking it with the rest of my mail, I head back to the elevators.

I must look ill, because I hear Hank the security guard ask, "Are you OK, Little Eva?"

"I'm fine." I smile. "Guess I'm just thinking too hard."

We laugh and one of the elevators opens. I step inside and punch the button. On my slow assent, I think about whom else I know that will get this issue and know its significance?

Ana, Tony, Talley. Obviously.

Dad. But he doesn't know it's me. Does he? After that blowout over Sunday dinner about Jared simply buying the book, I suspect Dad's been paying more attention to it.

"Shit."

The twins! Oh, hell! I can only hope they haven't read or even touched this magazine since Jared and I busted them at the bookstore.

We never spoke of it, but they are kids and if they want something, they'll find a way. On the bright side, they won't know it's me.

Neil. He suspects something, I know it, and this issue could be the one that confirms everything.

"Fuck."

Sarah? I don't doubt she'd pass up an opportunity to see me humiliated.

"Bitch!"

The elevator doors open just as I say the word and all its venom gets directed at my neighbor, little old Mrs. Parkhurst. Her green eyes, magnified by coke-bottle specs, get even bigger with surprise.

"Oh! Mrs. Parkhurst, I am so sorry. I was thinking of someone else." I help the old woman into the elevator.

"Well," she says, "I hope she's housebroken."

I smile. "Frankly, ma'am, I doubt it."

Indicating the ground floor with my finger, she nods. I press the button and rush down the hall. I need to read this thing quick and figure out how much damage control it'll require. Once inside, I go to my chair in the den and make myself comfortable, because I know I'm in for a shock. I fluff the cushions, put my feet up, and place one chenille throw about my shoulders and the other over my legs. Tossing the other mail aside, I tear open the plastic and slowly rip the brown paper sleeve. The first thing I notice is how this issue's cover is totally different from its colorful, sexually teasing predecessors.

Usually, *The Life of Lucrezia* comes in a plastic wrapper with a belly band to shield any overly-provocative images. This time, with the exception of the upper left-hand corner stating the issue number and cover price, the cover is totally black with only a white, gothic "M" in the center.

The back is also completely black except for white space containing the barcode.

There is no way anyone without a clue is going to guess what's in between these covers. But the sheer simplicity of the cover is enough to make it stand out on any magazine rack.

I take a deep breath, swallow my pride, and open the book.

What I see inside is magnificent, sublime. There is no dialogue. The time for talking between Messalina and Jack Dover is past. This issue is all about action and Jared has laid it bare with cinematographic perfection.

It starts with Messalina standing in the doorway, hands on hips, feet planted. Her tall, hourglass body fills the doorway, blocking any means for Jack to escape, even if he wanted to.

Jack is sitting on the edge of her desk, calmly smoking a cigarette, which he flicks aside and they meet in the center of the room, each prepared for a battle.

It's all over from there. From that panel on, there is nothing but wild, unbridled sex presented in the most erotic, sensuous drawings I have ever seen and the color scheme changes to suggest pleasure and pain—red, purple, black, blue.

Jared has captured some of our most intimate moments and has recreated them for the world to see in vivid detail: a Jared and Evadne "greatest hits" retrospective. The straining muscles, the yielding flesh, the sheen of perspiration on skin, it's all here.

And Jack and Messalina are an energetic pair. They start in the office on her desk, but their passion is so intense they move from the desk to the floor, out the door, into the hall, and beyond, but the progression is natural, seamless.

My eyes cannot look away from the images on the pages before me; they absorb the heat Messalina and Jack produce and transfer it into my body. No one can doubt the force and power in their lovemaking. It's like the first image I ever saw of Jared's graphic work in the bookstore. He has conveyed the same emotion—and cranked it up.

You can feel it when Jack plunges into Messalina or when her nails cut into his skin. Jared's decision to use no dialogue or scripting of any kind makes the images more forceful. You don't need bubbles with "Oh!" "Sigh!" "SLURP!" when it is all in their faces. This is body language in the extreme and the things Messalina and Jack's bodies are saying is lewd.

Regardless of my tutelage in porno flicks, I am struck dumb by what I see. Sure, it's titillating, but it is also beautiful. Jared and I never videotaped our lovemaking—not to my knowledge, anyway—but as I see it playing out before me, I find it hard to believe that it all came from his memory.

The mirrors. I remember being unnerved at the thought of all the mirrors in Jared's bedroom but by the time we split, their presence seemed totally natural. They have served their purpose well. I take what I see on these pages before me as genuine.

But it's more than Jared's memory I'm seeing. The way he has composed this issue has given me the most insight into his feelings about the time we spent in each other's arms. The detail he puts into drawing the oral sex, the vaginal sex, the anal sex, the way Jack gropes Messalina's flesh or grits his teeth.

A drop of sweat falls into my eye making me gasp. It's a perfect reaction to the next panel of me—Messalina rather—moaning out of ecstasy. He captured what I have never seen: my face during orgasm. I didn't know how blissed out I looked. I know I felt that way, but I never realized my expression was so soft, so enraptured.

Damn. I'm *beautiful* when I come!

Of course, Messalina doesn't have my face, but the way she moves her mouth or expresses with her eyes, I see myself. And Jack doesn't resemble Jared, but from the way Jack talks or reacts, I can look see Jared.

He has really outdone himself. This one sex scene is an extended game of cat and mouse. Jack and Messalina fight and change position between master and servant at least three times until the last page where they are hammering away at each other with him on top. In one panel, there's a close-up of his eyes and, in the next, one of her eyes. Suddenly, Jack grabs her by the waist and they turn over. Messalina now straddles him between her strong, exquisite thighs.

Finally, it happens. Silhouetted against a background that's a firework explosion of color, Jack comes inside Messalina. The last frame is of her riding him to glory, head thrown back, hands gripping his as he holds her down by the hips.

With amazing accuracy, Jared has captured the moment during my last night with him in Dallas. He has immortalized the one moment in my life I thought was totally private, that I thought was mine alone, because no one else in the world would place as much significance on it as I would.

The night I went to Nirvana . . . Jared went too.

I drop the comic onto my lap. I can't hold it any longer. I am drenched. The chenille throws were thrown aside long ago. I'm sweating, aroused, and can feel heat and dampness between my legs. But I am also crying, trembling.

The phone rings, startling me out of my seat. It rings again.

Fuck, I can't deal with anyone right now. One more ring and the answering machine does its job.

"Hello? Eva? It's Ana. Pick up friend-girl." Her voice is soothing, sympathetic.

Silence.

"C'mon, Evie, pick up." She's sharper now.

My mind races until I finally pick up the receiver.

"I knew you'd be home." She says.

"I can't talk right now."

"Sure you can. You just did."

"Ana—"

"Evadne." Ana's tone is no-nonsense. She isn't going to let me wallow in self-pity. I blow my nose.

"What do you want?"

"To ask you what I should think."

"Huh?"

"What do you want me to think, Evadne? Is Jared a complete and utter bastard or a mother-fucking *genius*? Personally, I choose the latter, but you're my best friend and I love you and I got your back."

Her words remind me just why we've been friends for so long, but I am too drained to be in a rage. I'm not even sure what I'm raging against and sigh. "Think what you want, Ana-Marie."

"Well, what's your opinion?"

"Shocked. Mortified."

"But why?"

"Because it's me, Ana!" I can't believe she can be so slow. "It's us! Jared has taken our love life and exposed it to the world."

"Eva," she argues, "he's been doing that for months with the rest of the comic."

"That's different."

"How?"

"Because those acts between other characters can't be traced back directly to us."

"But you don't deny the experiences are genuine? You and Jared do—did—those things. Whenever someone has sex in *The Life of Lucrezia*, it's really a recreation of what you and Jared have done."

"It's still different, Ana."

"How?"

I roll my eyes. We're repeating ourselves. "This is personal, Ana. I feel so exposed."

"Why should you? There's only six people who know the connection—and we ain't tellin'."

I tell her about the possibility of my dad, nephews, Sarah, and Neil knowing.

"Personally, Evie, I sincerely doubt your dad and nephews know. This isn't the type of thing your dad goes for and the twins have probably progressed to stealing a peek at *Shaved Snatches* or *Horny Whores* by now."

I smile at her made-up titles.

"And Sarah," she adds, "she's just bitter."

"And Neil?" I prompt. "He's been trying like hell to get me in a compromising position. I can't think why. There is some kind of frat-house game I've heard about, but I don't see how I could be a target."

"Yes," Ana drawls and I hear her throw something into a hot skillet and the loud sizzling that follows. "He does pose a minor problem."

I chuckle despite myself.

"Seriously, Eva. You don't sound like the same chick that emasculated Eddie Norton. Where's your fight, girlfriend? This Neil kid can and will be eliminated."

This time I do bust out laughing. "Listen to you, Ana. You sound like a hood rat."

"Hey, I got some street in me. You do too."

"Ana, we're about as street as Clare Huxtable."

"What-*ever*," she says in her best snotty teenager voice. "You don't need street cred in order to scrap. And Clare Huxtable did become a partner in the law firm, remember?"

I don't say a word. My head is starting to ache.

"Think about it, Evie. Neil is a little schoolboy who's looking to be taught a lesson. You're the professor, so teach him. You know where I am if you need me."

* * * *

"M"

She is pure sex. Messalina is a voluptuous vixen with the business acumen of Warren Buffet and the sexual appetite of the Marquis de Sade. And she's in stores now—in the raw. So, come on.

. . . You know you want to.

Three days later and not only does the journalist for *Redd Ink* rave about the latest issue of *The Life of Lucrezia*, bringing up its popularity in the underground and its slow, but inevitable, crossover into the mainstream, but there are also rumors that it may be banned in some states. He goes on to list locations where people can get it.

Like Preston's Place in LoDo.

I put down the magazine.

Lucrezia is no more.

Long live Messalina.

CHAPTER NINETEEN

^

"A WOMAN SCORNED"

Messalina: Devourer of Men issue #1 hits the streets as a serial in its own right, in a way *Lucrezia* never did, and I am starting to see hints of it all around me.

The signs are subtle: a young man wearing a black button with a white, gothic "M" in the center, or a young woman wearing the same in the form of a baseball cap.

But last week, when I saw a woman standing in line at the deli by the campus wearing a T-shirt with the "M" on front and the new catchphrase: . . . *you know you want to*, on the back, I thought I would drop dead.

It's all very clever the way Jared (by way of Trey) is marketing his latest creation and developing a type of beacon for those in the know to seek out each other. Perhaps even more disturbing is what I see in *Messalina*. It's definitely a darker, more violent story line than the quaint idea of suburban bordellos in *Lucrezia*.

Jared and I have been apart for a few months and the issues are still sent to my address, but I don't need a Freudian to tell me the pages are a representation of Jared's state of mind. When you compare the two series, *Lucrezia* is drawn in a style similar to the old *Archie* comics, whereas *Messalina* has a noir feel reminiscent of classic DC Comics. This is appropriate considering *Messalina* is turning out to be more of a detective comic than erotic fun like *Lucrezia*.

But I have other things on my mind, such as my family and my future at Bellingham College.

During my years at the college, I've been living under the radar. Given my untenured position, I haven't gained the status to strike out at the establishment by making provocative statements, such as the ones I made at the debate. Since then, I've felt like I've been under surveillance by the powers that be.

It's lovely when you're teaching a class and someone higher up the food chain comes in halfway through your lecture, all smiles, and takes a seat in the back as an "unnoticed" observer.

And I consider myself lucky that, over the last few months, I've been called into my head of department's office on four separate occasions to be asked how I'm doing, or if I've heard anything or needed to talk to someone about the Hyde case, especially since I've been mentor-less while on the verge of being offered tenure.

Nevertheless, these gestures of support have done nothing but make me skeptical and rattle my nerves. I'm thinking a long vacation may be in order—away from Bellingham, away from Colorado, away from everybody.

* * * *

My office isn't too big or small. It has windows and, apart from the summer months during some of the mini-courses, I have the office to myself. So when a large envelope with the word OSCAR written across it in black marker appears on my desk . . . my heart stops.

Sitting down, I open the envelope. Several photographs and paper clippings of various sizes fall out. I don't even have to look at them to know that I'm in a world of shit.

I get my eyes to work and this is what I see: Jared and me kissing on his doorstep; Jared leaving my apartment building; the newspaper clipping of me, Jared, and Tony; and a clipping from the campus paper about the debate with my name highlighted along with the quotes.

But that is nothing compared to the next series of photos of me bent over the arm of Jared's couch with him fucking me from behind. It's an excellent photo taken from between a gap in the curtains allowing anyone with a high-power lens on their camera to have at it. The tattoo on my hip is clearly visible, but there is something else about the photo that turns my mouth into cotton.

Quickly, I get up to close and lock the door to my office, then I go about closing the blinds, never mind that I'm on the second floor and my office windows open out onto the quad. Whoever took these snapshots is spying from afar and an open window is all it takes.

With the blinds closed and the clouds coming in from the west giving credence to the forecast for rain, my office is dark enough for me to turn on my grandfather's desk lamp.

After slipping all but one of the photos back into the envelope, I undo the latches of my briefcase and open it. Inside the last compartment, behind a half dozen student essays and articles waiting to be copied as part of my lecture notes, I find my copy of the "Sex" issue. I pull it out, open it to the page in question, and place it next to the photograph.

The way the scene in the book is illustrated, with the background in shadow, it is easy for the casual reader to overlook the décor. I'm not a casual reader, but I definitely have not been observant. Like everyone else, I was too busy looking at the action.

It never occurred to me when I saw it the first time, or the hundreds of times since, that it was all here in full color. On top of the bookcase in Messalina's office sit several pieces of pottery. The shadows make it impossible to see detail, but their shapes are distinctive and they are the exact same shapes in the exact same order as the row of pottery sitting on the mantelpiece in Jared's living room.

Next, I notice the floor lamp in the corner of the drawing that throws a small circle of light in the comic book is the same lamp standing in the corner of Jared's living room.

Like the image I saw when catching my nephews with the magazine all those months ago, instead of a dentist and his patient doing it doggy-style in the dentist's chair, there can be no doubt that this is Jared and me—Jack and Messalina—screwing each other like it's going out of style.

We are the centerfold.

"I am such a *fucking moron*."

I turn to the first page of the issue and instead of engrossing myself with the bodies before me, I analyze each and every object in every frame. The mystery photographer would not know that the bronze in Messalina's study can be found in Jared's hallway, or that the painting hanging in her bedroom is a miniature of Jared's own creation located in his spare bedroom. But I do.

And I had missed it all.

Stupid, silly me with the advanced degree missed all the little details where the Devil lies pointing at me, mocking me.

"God damn." I rub my forehead, then my eyes. The birth of a migraine is starting at the base of my neck and will reach my temples within the hour. I start packing everything away and when I pick up the envelope. All the snaps fall out and scatter across my desk, including a white piece of paper.

Pressing my lips together, I turn the slip over and read:

Dear Evadne,

I am sure you would like the memory card to go with your photos so I suggest you be in your office at this time tomorrow.

My initial curiosity has now changed to survival instinct.

* * * *

Over the next twenty-four hours, I try to think of my battle plan only to discover I don't have one.

I consider calling Ana, Tony, even Trey, but decide there is very little they can do but give me a pep rally. Glynnis? No. Not because I think she'd gloat, but because she warned me several times and I ignored her.

I could try to contact my "mentor," Terrence Hyde, and get his opinion as to what it's like being in the center of a sex scandal.

Fuck that. If Terrence Hyde kept his pants on, he could have been here to prevent this.

Oh, who am I kidding? This is my own personal fuck-up and I'm going to have to handle it myself. Sitting in my dark apartment, I watch the rain and come to realize that this is what happens when you listen to everybody else and to your own excuses for so long.

I was the good girl, the baby. I used to tell myself that the reason I didn't have a man was because there was something wrong with me. I was fat and everyone made sure I knew it—from my mother, to people like Sarah, to every piece and type of media in the world.

I told myself to "protect my body and exploit my mind" while doing just the opposite with my schizoid reasoning and picking up men in a theater, while ignoring good advice from Glynnis, Ana, Talley.

And Jared.

I'm just as image conscious as everyone else, and look where it's gotten me. I'm still alone, still fat, and still unhappy. The only time I felt happy and satisfied was when I allowed myself to ignore what people would think. Like the time in Dallas. And, if I admit it, during the debate, because I was sticking my neck out to I stand by what I said.

I'm a grown woman still letting people treat me like a child. I've said it before, but this time I mean it. Starting tomorrow, I have to take charge—and responsibility—for my actions. Regardless of Jared's covert way of exposing me, Neil Hollister has forced my hand.

All night I sit, watching the rain, watching the sun rise.

Thinking of my next move.

* * * *

When I arrive at work, I can't believe how calm I am. Perhaps it is the lack of sleep, but I'm feeling apathetic yet serene.

At exactly three-thirty, I enter my office, open the blinds all the way, and turn on my desk lamp. Now anyone who wants to can see that I am in and ready for any visitors who wish to see me.

So when Neil Hollister walks in and closes the door, instead of my heart missing a beat at the unmasking of my blackmailer, I have the strong urge to stifle a yawn.

"Hello, Hollister."

"Hello, Evadne." He smiles warmly and sits in the chair at the side of my desk. The way his body occupies the chair's curved structure is so smooth it's as if Neil's true, slimy composition has revealed itself, allowing him to move with a fluidity I have never seen before.

"I see you got my present yesterday," Neil speaks in a whisper the way doctors do when trying to sound compassionate as they deliver bad news.

"Yes, Hollister. I received your present. I'm surprised it was for me, though."

"Oh, yes." He smiles and leans back into the chair. "You most certainly deserve the top prize, because you, my dear, Evadne," he says, looking at me from top to bottom, "are the big one."

I want to reach out and claw the smirk from his face, but instead I say, "First of all, I would like to thank the Academy, if I knew who they were. But what did I do to deserve such an honor?"

"Oh, for no specific reason except that I've always fancied you." He looks at me and his brown eyes, which used to have a cute, puppy-like quality, are now hard as his gaze tries to penetrate my own.

"You see, the other fellows wanted to call you Miss Black Achievement, but I didn't think that award carried as much status."

I bite the inside of my mouth at the slight. "What 'others?' You mean you're not the only one behind this?"

"No. My associates and I have had you in our sights for quite some time."

For the first time, I feel uncomfortable. "What are you saying? You all fancy me?" This time when Neil laughs I want to cringe.

"I'm afraid not, Evadne. You're not the boys' type. They prefer their meat white and lean, while I," he says and grins, showing a perfect set of teeth, "I'm more open-minded."

"What do you want, Neil?"

"Well, it's not just me who wants something, but my associates too."

"Spill it. Now."

He sucks in his breath and reaches for my hand. I don't pull away.

"I wouldn't suggest adopting that tone, Evadne. Especially when we have your reputation to consider."

I grit my teeth and take a deep breath before saying, "Neil, you and your 'associates' have gone a long way to get me here. Now would be a good time to tell me why."

"OK." He lets go of my hand and leans back in his seat. "We want you to change our grades to what they should be."

"I beg your pardon?"

"Over the last twelve months, you have given me and a few of the lads grades that, if they stand, will prevent us from transferring to our chosen graduate schools. All we ask is that you admit your error and give us our proper grades."

Admit my error? My look of disbelief prompts him to continue.

"There are five of us." He holds up his hands. "I know, I know, it's going to look bad for you to go in and say that you fucked up the grades of five graduating seniors. But let's face it," he says and his smile takes on the charm of a rattlesnake, "the chance of me calling you 'Professor Cavell' is as likely as me calling a black man 'sir.'"

I am stunned. Never had I guessed he harbored such thoughts, but then again, I gave him more credit than he deserved for a long time. Once again, I've let myself be played.

"And to think you used to threaten that we would live to regret our GPA." He has a hearty chuckle. "You see, Evadne, I've known for a while that you were involved with this *Messalina* thing. I knew you were the 'black cat' on the bulletin board. One only has to look at the photo on your desk to put that together." He indicates to the empty space where the photo of me and Jared once occupied.

"Mind you, I only stumbled upon the comic book by accident when one of the guys brought it to the frat house. When I saw Messalina's tattoo, it reminded me of another one I'd seen elsewhere." He shakes his head. "I'm just disappointed that you didn't figure out my alias too."

I frown, not comprehending.

"Geez," he says, rolling his eyes with annoyance. "Call yourself a teacher? I'll give you a hint. Remember that day in class when you, yet again, got off topic and asked us to name our favorite corny movie? You said *The Rocky Horror Picture Show*. I filed that information away for future use and it served me well."

Yes, I remember the day. The little prick. Accusing me of being "off topic." I always ask that question when I'm lecturing on stereotypes in media. Seems we have both missed our share of clues.

So Neil Hollister is 'Damocles' on the *LoL* bulletin board and has been hanging a sword over my head. Mostly he lurked, but when he did pop up, he always seemed to try to take digs at me, and a few others, but me more often than not. When we didn't rise to his bait, he would fade back into the shadows.

"Anyway," he says. "I'm going to need you to fill out one of those grade forms you keep in your desk and turn it in to the registrar tomorrow so our grades can be recalculated."

Neil gets up, walks around my desk, and reaches for my lower desk drawer. I stop him.

"I can't use those grade slips. They're obsolete. I'll have to get the current ones from the registry tomorrow."

As if on cue, my antique wall clock chimes four o'clock. All administrative offices are now closed for the day. Saved by the bell.

"No worries." He makes is way back to the other side of my desk. "I will meet you here tomorrow at the same time. You'll fill out the correct forms—in front of me—and we'll go to registry together."

I nod. "And what about your end of the bargain? How can I trust that you won't duplicate these photographs?"

"Evadne," he says, once again reaching to squeeze my hand, "you have my word."

I stare at him blankly and he chuckles and goes to his seat to pick up his backpack. "Once you turn in those grades, I'll give you the memory card containing all the photos."

"Just out of curiosity, how many photos do you have of me?"

Neil makes a face as if trying to think before leveling his dark brown eyes on me. For such a complete bastard, he still has the looks to make some hearts flutter.

"Five hundred and fifty."

My stomach clenches as if I've been punched in the gut. They must have been watching me—us—for months. With that said, Neil walks out of my office whistling "The Sword of Damocles."

I give myself a minute to calm down. My little interview with Neil, although expected, has left me rattled. But this is nothing compared to what I have to do next. I pick up the phone. I need to do this now. My nervous breakdown will have to wait.

"Hi, Mom. Is Dad around? I need to talk to both of you."

* * * *

"Modeling?"

My mother's voice is full of disbelief, much to my chagrin, when I tell her and my dad how I've "modeled" for some of Jared's drawings. I'm sure she's thinking how could someone with my build be a model? It's not a lie, strictly speaking. I am the model for Messalina and the sex scenes are reminiscent of what I've done with Jared; it's just that I didn't know it at the time.

"Eva," my dad begins, but he doesn't sound skeptical, only disappointed. "Why?"

We are sitting in the dining room, in the same seats where I was taken to task so many weeks earlier. Dad sits at the head of the table on my right and Mom is at her station on the opposite end to my left. Both of them are staring me down in the same way they did when I was a child. Today, I'm determined to put a stop to it.

"Because Jared, in his way, has helped me feel better about myself."

"How can posing nude make you feel better?"

"How can having people constantly comment about my weight make me fell better? Gee, Mom, let me guess."

"Eva, I only say—"

"What I already know. Thanks, Mom. I get the message."

And for the first time in my life, my mother is speechless. Perhaps even hurt judging by the look in her eyes. I turn to my dad who just looks confused and ask.

"Tell me. Do you both even like Jared?"

"Of course we do, Eva." Dad reaches for my hand. "We just worry, that's all."

"Stop worrying." I laugh, even though it's forced. "I'm thirty-six years old now. What I do is my business and my responsibility." I try to smile, but my lips seem to stretch too tight. "And that goes for any consequences too." I look at my mom who nods. Whether she's conceding defeat or a draw remains to be seen.

When I leave my parents' house, I drive away a few blocks before pulling over and letting my emotions wash all over me. I've just stated to my parents that I'm a sexual being and an adult prepared to handle my own affairs but sit on the side of the road crying like a big girl. When I'm done, I'm empty and weak. I need food, drink . . . and company.

* * * *

The atmosphere at the circular booth we occupy is like a war room; we sit, staring into our drinks, waiting for our food, and decide our next maneuver.

"I say we string the little shit up by his pubes," Ana says before downing her lemon drop.

Tony looks at me with big, sympathetic brown eyes.

"Is this that bastard kid you failed?" he asks.

"I didn't fail him. I gave him a C. It should've been a D."

"Why didn't you give it to him?"

"Because I felt sorry for him," I reply, ignoring Ana's sarcastic gagging. "He did put in an effort towards the end, so I gave him a little boost."

Tony shakes his head. "Kids like him don't need a boost, chica. Society gives them one already."

We sit in silence. It's just past five o'clock and the downtown crowd is starting to come in looking for pub grub inside of this ersatz English tavern. The weather outside has turned as predicted, and despite my situation and my need for company at the moment, I feel our war council won't last too long.

Trey, the final member of our group, arrives as does our food. I had taken the liberty of ordering stuffed artichokes for him. He removes his woolly overcoat and the sleet is visible on top of his collar and shoulders. He moves in next to Ana.

"Hello, all. What have I missed?"

"The next round," Tony informs and hails the waiter so Trey can order.

Over the next few minutes, I fill Trey in and he sits, staring at me, his face registering both anger and pain. When I finish he takes a deep breath.

"Fuck."

"That sums it," I say with a weak smile.

After several minutes of silence and everyone sinking deeper into their drinks, Tony speaks. "Evadne, if I were to come to the campus tomorrow, would you be able to point out this little *pendejo* to me?"

"Sure. You're not planning on murder are you?" I try to laugh.

"No." He smiles. "But I am thinking about life insurance."

CHAPTER TWENTY

"DEVOURER OF MEN"

My days at Bellingham College are numbered.

As promised, I wait for Neil to arrive at the office and fill in the grade forms for him and his four "associates." They're all over-privileged bastards just like their ringleader and none of them deserve even the slightest little break like the one I gave Hollister in my moment of misplaced altruism.

It's a quarter to four and we walk across the quad towards the registrar's office. Once inside, I see my friend Marlena Mondragon behind the counter.

"Hi, Marlena," I say with a smile. "I'm afraid I have some corrections for you." With Neil's presence at my side, I can sympathize with people who are forced to do something at gunpoint.

"Not a problem. It happens to the best of them." Marlena takes the forms and gives them a quick glance. She whistles, opens her mouth to say something, and then realizes Neil is standing there.

"Evadne?"

"Yes, Lena?" Beads of sweat form on my forehead.

"You have five corrections here."

"Unfortunately, yes."

"OK, chiquita. I'll handle this for you and get it done ASAP."

"Thanks. I appreciate it."

Neil and I smile at her and she smiles back, albeit confused.

Once outside the registrar's office, we turn in the direction of the parking lot. I turn to him and hold out my hand.

"Oh, yes," he says and chuckles, "mustn't forget my part of the bargain, must we?"

He digs into his front jeans pocket and produces a tiny chip.

"Here you go, princess. All five hundred-plus snaps of you doing all sorts of things." He winks and I swallow the wave of nausea rising to the back of my throat.

"How about a drink to celebrate the closing of our transaction?"

I should be surprised at his offer, but considering his arrogant nature and what we've just done, I'm not. I look down at my feet.

"Aw, come on, Evadne! No hard feelings, eh . . . prof?"

I force myself to join in his hearty laughter this time.

"I thought you said you'd never call me professor."

He shrugs. "Evadne, my dear, you may never become a full professor, but being an assistant isn't so bad now, is it?"

Neil offers me his arm. Defeated, I take it.

"Shall we go over to the pub?" he asks.

I shake my head. "Actually, I'm thinking in the direction of downtown. I'm in the mood for someplace quieter than the pub. More like a hotel."

At the word "hotel," I swear I could see Neil's cock twitch in his trousers.

"You're on."

And with that, Neil Hollister follows me to the place where I will cement my undoing.

* * * *

On Thursday of the following week, I sit in my office grading papers when Neil Hollister storms in, and once again, I am ready for him.

"Ah, Hollister. Close the door. Have a seat."

Neil does, but stops short when he notices I'm not alone.

"This is my friend and associate, Gator Ferguson. Gator, meet Neil Hollister."

Gator Ferguson is six feet of solid packed muscle with a shaved head, trimmed beard, and no neck—the type of man who goes sleeveless and rides his Hog year-round. He pulls out a chair, positions it directly in front of my desk, and motions for Neil to obey. He complies and Gator maintains his position behind the chair, arms folded across his tank chest.

"Wait a minute," I say, looking at Gator. "I'm sorry, but you and Neil have met before, right?"

"Yeah." Gator chuckles, his voice thick from a thousand smoked Marlboros. "We got to be real friendly the other night."

My desk clock chimes three-thirty and I smile.

"Speaking of meetings, we really have got to stop meeting like this, Hollister, but I'm glad to see you got my present."

Neil's face is a mask and his eyes burn a black fire, but his skin is pale and flushed. I lean forward, loosely lace my fingers together in front of me, and look Neil Hollister dead on.

"As you can see from the series of photographs and the DVD you received earlier, I have decided it would be in my best interest *not* to take you at your word—valuable though it may be. I needed to take some measures with regard to my privacy." I flash him a cold smile. "Call it insurance."

Neil starts chewing his lower lip.

"You, Peaches, and Gloria all had a good time in that motel, didn't you?"

Gator's hearty laugh makes me want to clear my throat.

"So you see, Neil, if I ever catch wind that you or any of your 'associates' are showing any of my photographs you've stored in any way, shape, or altered form," I lean in closer for the kill. "Not only will your uncle, your mama, and your daddy receive a copy of your sex video . . . I'm gonna start peddling your ass on the Internet."

Still smiling, Gator gets on one knee and moves in so close I'm sure his breath heats Neil's already flaming cheek.

"Let me add to what the little lady is trying to say, you fucking limp-dicked cum stain. And that is: don't mess in grown folks' business, boy. I know who you are, where you live, and what power you think you have, and it don't mean shit to me and my running crew. I'll wipe your ass out."

Neil is breathing hard through his nostrils and his mouth is set in a thin line. His skin is turning dusky pink and I perceive dampness around his hairline.

"Damn, Neil. When you told me you were 'open-minded,' I didn't know just how open you meant." Both Gator and I enjoy a good laugh out of this.

"You're kinkier than me, boy." Gator leans over and says into Neil's ear. "And I'm the type of sick fuck who would kill your mama and rape your dog." He gives Neil a hard, but playful, slug in the arm. Neil flinches at the touch and I wonder if he's shit himself.

I'm busting a gut from laughing. "Hey, Gator, from what I spotted in the video, I see Gloria has had her surgery but Peaches is still waiting for his, right?"

Neil's involuntary shiver makes me laugh harder.

"You're not going to tell anyone about our little meeting, are you, Neil?" Gator asks.

And for the first time, Neil moves voluntarily to shake his head.

"As far as you're concerned, Dr. Cavell here has given you and your pals your grades and you're gonna leave her alone." Gator stands up. "Now go and tell your little pussy friends that if I find out any of you *haven't* left her alone," he says, swinging around get square into Neil's face, "you won't live to regret it."

Neil rises to his feet, looks at me, and tries hard to stare me down, but my gaze is harder than granite.

"Who you eyeballin', boy?" Gator shoves at Neil's shoulder. "You stupid enough to be making threats?"

Neil ducks his head and raises his hands in surrender and makes for the door. Gator beats him there and puts his hand on the doorknob.

"Remember, cum-stain, my crew is everywhere. There is no hiding. Dr. Cavell is under our protection, you got that?" He opens the door. "Now fuck off."

Neil is out of our sight within seconds. Gator closes the door, turns to me, and smiles.

"Will that do, prof?"

I stand up and go and hug the big muscle-man. "That'll do fine, Gator. And, by way of reward, tell the girls that I got you all booked at The Marriott for the Southern Decadence weekend in New Orleans."

Gator gives me a squeeze.

"Aw, heck, Evie. You don't have to do that. Not that we're ungrateful, mind, but when Tony told me what that fuckwit was doing to you, the girls and I were more than happy to stick it to the Man for fun. And I'll tell you this," he says, leaning down to whisper in my ear. "It ain't like any of us got his cherry."

I break out into a genuine ear-to-ear grin for the first time in months. And here I am thinking there is nothing left that could shock me. Minutes after Gator's departure, my phone rings. It's Marlena Mondragon.

"Hi, Evie. I'm glad I caught you before going home."

"Hey, Lena, what 'cha know good?"

"Well, it's about those grades you gave me."

"Yes?"

"I just wanted to tell you that apart from the changes made to Neil Hollister, the grades you have for the others are the same as what we already have recorded. So, all the grades should be D, correct?"

"That's right, Lena. Those are the grades they deserve."

CHAPTER TWENTY-ONE

"PAR-TAY"

Tony Lobos, along with his cousin and housemate, Carnie DeLuna, aka The Howling Wolf cousins, know how to have a good time and now is the time of year when they throw their annual "Cinco de Mayo Costume Carnivale."

This mutha of all parties usually starts around 6pm on the day and lasts until: a) noon the next day, b) until the police come, or c) both.

Tony and Carnie use the party to say thank you to the community, and to all those who've worked in their two restaurants and publishing company (read: business expense)—and to all the family members that accept Tony's bisexuality and Carnie's lesbianism.

One of the big pleasures is getting the official invitation from them. Those who are so privileged wait eagerly to see how they will beat last year's creation. This year is no different and they top themselves by burning the invite on a CD full of pictures from last year's bash and a retrospective of things that happened during the prior twelve months.

Personally, I cannot wait. Twelve to eighteen hours of solid boozing is just the ticket I need to congratulate myself on surviving the last few months.

The first part of the party is to be held in the ballroom at The Westin Tabor Center with food, drink, and dancing. Then, for the second part of the party, about thirty of us will go back to the cousins' home, where Carnie will bless us with one of her famous breakfasts, full of homemade Latin goodness, and room to crash on the floor afterwards.

At seven o'clock, my door buzzer tells me that Ana and Frankie have arrived in the limo to take us to the party, because in a few hours, none of us will be in condition to drive. I step out of the apartment building, sporting a short, red PVC dress with a corset top and accented with buckles from cleavage to hem. Black patent leather thigh-high boots and a short, black PVC jacket complete the ensemble. When Ana and Frankie see me step out looking like Lady Latex, their mouths drop open.

For once, I had no reservations about my choice of clothing. After being portrayed as a sex goddess in the comic world, I may as well attempt it in the real one.

"Wow, Eva," Frankie says. He's dressed like Sinatra and eyeing me with a smile as the driver helps me inside. "You look ready to party."

"Not 'party,' Frankie," I correct, "but par-*tay!*"

"Say it, sistah!"

Catwoman Ana gives me a high-five and I see that the Benedettos have already started on the complimentary champagne. I motion to Frankie and he pours me a glass.

For the next five hours, I lose myself among Tony and Carnie's three hundred closest friends truly enjoying myself. The booze and the food are top-notch and I find I don't have to worry about the cash bar, because when I try to buy friends drinks, they refuse.

The gang's all here: me, Ana, Frankie, Talley, Trey, and his wife, Piper. I even saw Jared, but almost didn't recognize him dressed as a bomber pilot. That means Sarah is lurking somewhere. I see other people I met while dating Jared, but it doesn't faze me. Whenever I catch a glimpse of him from across the room talking to someone, I keep on stepping.

"Woman, you are gorgeous!" Talley shouts out over the music. She's decked out as a prison warden and her latest girlfriend, Kristina, is her prisoner.

"Totally edible," Trey adds and kisses my neck. He surprised everyone who knows him by wearing all white and dressing like a televangelist.

Tony and Carnie are floating around in their capacity as host and hostess: Tony is dressed as Elvis during his '68 comeback, and Carnie, *quel surprise*, is Mother Nature. Press photographers help create a strobe-light effect with their flash pictures. The clock strikes two o'clock and the main party ends and the private party at the house is about to begin. I am surrounded by three new male friends, wait staff from Te Amo Café and DeGaulle's, which closed in time so employees could attend the festivities. Suddenly, arms take hold of me and spin me around. Lips find mine and my three new friends take turns kissing me goodnight. But when I feel a hand slip up under my dress, I laugh and twist away. Just like my DeLuxe Theater days, I'm out to flirt and entice, nothing more.

"Not tonight, hun. I'm in full flow." I wink.

The look on my would-be paramour's face is priceless and I laugh. The easiest way to make a strong man cringe is to refer to anything menstrual.

$$* * * *$$

It's 3 a.m. by the time we reach Tony and Carnie's place. There are at least forty of us still partying strong, but at least we're not the only house on the street with guests. I can't say how many drinks I've had or what I've eaten tonight. Right now, I'm running on pure adrenaline to put my recent past behind me.

The sunroom leading to the backyard has been designated as the dance floor. Carnie's girlfriend, Marisol Cruz, is a club DJ and has taken control of the music. But as things start to wind down, Tony and his famous karaoke machine get hooked up and a list of brave souls develops. I'm in the kitchen, getting a drink of water of all things, and chatting with a couple who know Tony from high school when he comes in and grabs my arm.

"Come on, Eva, it's time for Los Locos."

"Oh, my God, Tony, you've got to be kidding me."

"No, girl! Come on!"

Tony leads me to the sunroom and the little makeshift stage. Ana is already waiting and pulls me up. I start laughing because she's just as tipsy as I am, if not more so. Marisol has kindly hooked up two extra microphones and after giving Ana and me ours, she heads to the front of the stage.

"Ladies and gentlemen, I present to you—Los Locos!"

She hands the mike to Tony and steps off the stage, starting the karaoke machine as she passes. When the first few bars of Blue Swede's "Hooked on a Feeling" start, people stop what they're doing to see their host, looking like a tired, fried lounge lizard, with two tipsy backup singers.

Ana, Tony, and I then put on a mighty fine show as we reprised an act we did in college for a student talent contest. We didn't win, but we made it to the semi-finals. It was the mix of Tony's sultry, Latin looks, Ana's dark and petite cuteness, and me with all my bouncy curves that was the secret of our success. When we did this originally, I was self-conscious about myself, but when I finally decided to relax and let things happen, we had a good time and got some fans. Now, over ten years later, I think my curves are one of my best assets and I'm finally owning up to them.

Our effect tonight is no different as Ana and I relive our comic roles as the "Ooga-Shaka Girls." Back then, Tony dressed in a borrowed, silver-lamé suit while Ana and I dressed as cavewomen and worked a pair of maracas each. This time, we look only slightly better.

We are jammin' and I think everyone left in the house has come out to see. They're laughing and clapping to the beat. Meanwhile, Ana pulls faces at me during our routine, making me laugh and nearly fall out of what little rhythm I have left. Tony croons and flirts with a woman standing in front. I turn away from Ana to focus and that's when I see Jared staring straight at me.

He's a good twenty feet away, but he may as well be standing in front of me, his gaze is so strong. If he's been looking at me all this time, I can't believe I haven't felt it before now. Then again, I've been trying to keep mingling all night. Always smiling, always moving.

But I'm tired. I can't keep up this pace and this carefree façade going forever, and my mind and body knows it. This sudden encounter with Jared's stare is more than enough to disrupt my false sense of control.

And the man is presenting a mighty fine picture in his bomber jacket. His lips are upturned in a slight smile, but I wouldn't call it happy—perhaps wistful would better describe it.

I analyze all this in about a second, but it's enough to throw me off for a few beats before I pick up and place my attention elsewhere.

We finally end our routine to a riotous ovation and take our bows. Since everyone has filled the conservatory, it's a few minutes before we can get off the stage, but I'm reluctant to go. My unwillingness increases when the crowd disperses enough for me to leave, but Jared still holds his position by the entrance, blocking my exit.

With a handful of people still in the room, I can no longer pretend that I can't see him or need to duck past him. Those options evaporate completely when he steps forward and offers his hand to help me off the stage. His grasp is warm and firm reminding me how I've missed that strength over these past months. When my feet touch the floor, I wobble but his hand remains steady. I clear my throat, but when I say, "Thank you," my voice sounds squeaky and exhausted.

"Are you OK?"

"I'm fine." I look up at him. "How've you been?"

When he smiles, this time there is warmth in his indigo eyes.

"You look like shit."

I glare at him and open my mouth to say something, but then again, so does Jared. He hadn't said a word.

We turn in unison to see Sarah approaching, clicking towards us on her stilettos. I'm still a head taller than her. Earlier in the evening, I had grudgingly admired how she worked her World War II nurse's costume. She still looks fresh and I wonder if she's had anything to eat or drink all night, but when she gets closer, I can smell the gin.

"Really, Evadne, you should pull yourself together."

"I beg your pardon?"

"Evadne," she begins, folding her arms over her chest and taking the tone of someone about to give a lecture to a child, "I think it time someone educated you on the facts."

I adopt the "Oh, really?" stance that I do when I'm about to go apoplectic on someone's ass. I believe Jared senses this too.

"That's enough, Sarah."

"I don't think so, Jared. It's time someone told this woman it's bad enough that, through *you*," she says, flashing her steely blue eyes on him, "the world now has images of what this thing could look like while rutting like some fat slug."

"*What?*" I couldn't keep my voice from sounding like fingernails running down a chalkboard. "Listen, bitch, I've had enough of you talking about my size."

"Oh, please." Sarah scoffs. "How can one not?"

I am vaguely aware of others coming into the room, because they keep their distance.

"Sarah," I say, "your problem is that you're shallow. Your tiny view of people is proportionate with the rest of you. This is not about size, this is about substance."

"You certainly have that, my dear. All night you've been trying to strut your stuff like some pork sausage in a bright red casing."

I put my hand on my hip and lean in. "Little girl, I'm not gonna tell you again. Knock it off about my weight."

"Sarah," Jared says. "Leave it alone."

"Why are you defending her?" This time it's Sarah's turn to screech. "Look at you. Holding hands."

Jared and I both look down not realizing this was the case.

"Why do you keep *hurting* me so?" she whines, making my skin crawl.

I stare at her heart-shaped face and quivering, apple-red lips. Her icy blue eyes have melted and brim with tears and her pale, powdery complexion contributes to her waif-like appearance. If I didn't know the monster that lies beneath, I might actually feel sympathy for the wretched woman-child.

"Jared," Sarah says, squaring her shoulders, her voice suddenly showing no trace of frailty, "you are not going to embarrass me again with this—this thing!"

"Sarah," he replies through barely moving lips, "you are only embarrassing yourself."

"Maybe I am." She gives a short but hysterical laugh. "I am embarrassing myself by being seen with a trailer-trash bastard like you."

I shall call what happens next as "The Slap Heard 'Round the Room" because Sarah does a roundhouse that connects with Jared so hard, the resulting welt starts forming before her hand leaves his face. The people in the room all take in their breath and I'm amazed we don't get sucked into the vacuum it creates. Then, to my surprise, Sarah pivots, faces me, and builds up to give me the backhanded version. The next thing I know, my cheek gets in the way of her palm and I feel the heat and sting of her slap.

Now I may talk tough but I am not a violent person. I make Sarah the exception and haul off and punch the bitch square in the jaw.

Perhaps it's the alcohol still flowing in my system that makes me giggle as Sarah does a pirouette, arms outstretched, like some kind of ballet princess, and falls face down on the floor, looking like a crumpled mass of white tissue.

"Hey!" Carnie's voice booms from the entryway. "What the hell is going on in here?"

* * * *

I walk out into the backyard and to the farthest, darkest corner away from the house and the party lights. We've been lucky with the weather this week and it hasn't rained; nevertheless, I am starting to get cold in my outfit, but I'm not about to go inside.

Tony and Carnie have the luxury of big, mature trees that must be at least eighty years old and next to one particular tree is a wrought iron bench. I take a seat and close my eyes. Leaning forward, I reach up to cover my face and a sharp pain shoots through my right hand.

"God damn it." I sigh and shake my hand. It's stinging and I think the ring on my finger cut me where my fist connected with Sarah's face. I try to remove the ring, but the digit is already swollen. When I put it in my mouth I can taste blood.

"Fuck."

I can't believe I actually fought over some man. Well, not just any man, to be fair. But he's not my man anymore, so why should I care if someone insults him?

Because I still love him, that's why.

As I try to work the ring off, I hear footsteps approach. Looking up, I see movement in the shadows and ease back into the seat. The figure stops in front of me.

"Are you okay?" Jared asks.

"I'm fine." I try to look around him. "How's *she* doing?"

"Carnie got an ice pack for her."

He sits beside me and drapes his arm behind me on the seat. For a long while, we say nothing and look at the action going on behind the kitchen curtains. People are milling about, probably waiting for round two. I'm just waiting for the inevitable.

"I don't think the cops will come out for this," he says, as if reading my mind. "At least six people can say she took a swing first. But if you're talking lawsuit," he says, clicking his tongue, "it's hard to tell with Sarah."

I turn to look at him. "What are you doing out here, Jared? Trying to cheer me up?"

He gives a noncommittal shrug. "Just checking on you."

"Well, I'm fine. You can return to your date now." I return focus to my hand. Perhaps I should ice my knuckles.

"Trey's been telling me about your lunch dates . . . and what you've been dealing with at work."

I say nothing.

"And Tony tells me you're thinking of leaving Colorado."

I keep silent and massage my finger.

"Don't go."

Sighing, I lean forward to rest my arms on my legs. "Jared I am tired."

"I can imagine. I'm sorry."

"Aw, Jesus, what the hell for?" I scowl. I've had enough apologies for one evening.

"For everything," he replies softly.

Then I feel the wool lining of a bomber jacket, warm with body heat and smelling of Obsession for Men, going around my shoulders. My longing for him stabs my heart and I bite my lip. His hand lingers on the small of my back. I look up at the sky for a moment, taking in the darkness and actually seeing a few stars. I smile to myself, at the sky.

"Jared, for a long time, I've been unsatisfied with my life and didn't know why. Then I admitted that I was letting people define me so I wouldn't have to." When I laugh, it's full of relief and when I see his concerned look, I rein it in. Sitting back, I look up at the stars again.

"From now on, I'm going to be the sex goddess I keep telling myself I am. I've never admitted it to anyone, but I love sex. I *am* a sexual being!" I start laughing because I sound so corny. "And I'm not going to be ashamed of my appearance, either." I turn to face him. He sits there, mouth slightly agape, his expression perplexed.

"You may have forced the issue, but life is short . . . Thanks for the kick in the ass."

He remains frozen as if I just admitted I was pregnant by an alien.

"Besides," I say with a shrug. "I've been a bad girl since the last time you saw me." I smile and that's when I notice the slightly flared nostrils, and the deep, steady breathing. My smile turns into a grin. He's getting turned on.

"Yes," he drawls. "I've heard how you put Neil in his place. I'm impressed." He adjusts his position and uncrosses his legs. "Not that I ever doubted your ability to be bad. If anything, I admire your creativity."

It wasn't hard. Changing Hollister's grades and having the forms already filled out and stashed in an envelope in my purse was easy. It's not like Hollister is a rocket scientist. It was Tony who contacted Gator and the Girls, but what they did to Neil was all down to me. I took the pictures and video, and I had fun doing it.

"Evadne, please . . . don't go."

"Why should I stay?"

"There's your career, for a start."

I laugh. "You should know that my 'career' may no longer be an issue."

"Maybe there'll be a reason for it not to be." He sits up so he can touch my face.

"Care to explain?"

"Sure. I have years of making up to do and would like you with me while I do it."

This statement of intent earns my full attention and I turn towards him. In the dim light, I can make out his lips and their fullness reminds me of their softness. I can also see and feel his eyes on me.

"Jared, are you—"

He nods as his long fingers start smoothing my jaw and massaging the back of my head and neck. Closing my eyes, I lean into his caress and feel him move in close. I am about to experience a luxury I have come to miss.

The kiss is a short peck that soon deepens and he pulls me onto his lap. His jacket falls to the ground, but it's no longer needed as I'm engulfed in a warm bear hug. My hands go around his neck, beckoning him even closer.

"Jared? Are you out here?"

Carnie DeLuna's voice calling from the back door makes us freeze. I don't know about Jared, but I'm praying she doesn't turn on the patio light and illuminate the situation. Our mouths part with a sigh.

"Yeah, Carnie. What 'cha need?"

"It's Sarah. She's asking for you."

"I'll be there in a minute."

I hear Carnie return indoors and I try to stand, but Jared holds me fast. I take one of his hands and kiss his palm. He moans and brings me in for another kiss, but despite our desire, we keep it restrained. This is not the time to get carried away. I stand up.

"Cool it, Jared. This evening has become too much like high school already. Go and take your date home. I'll wait for you."

He gives me an embarrassed glance and I smile. He gets up, still holding my hands, raises them to his lips and kisses all my knuckles. I wince when he gets to my right ring finger.

"One more question," he says, looking at me while taking my right hand, and then kisses my sore knuckle again. "Why'd you do it?"

I free one of my hands so I can stroke his cheek.

"Because I knew you couldn't."

* * * *

By the time I return indoors, Jared and Sarah have made their exit. The remaining guests are mellowing out and starting to eat breakfast, but I feel some may have lingered just to get one last glimpse of the ruffian in question.

"Damn, girl," Ana says and pops an aspirin. "I haven't seen that right hook since you clocked Teri Vaughn in the eleventh grade." She pops another aspirin and winks at me. "We saw you out there. I hope Jared knows what kind of hood rat he's getting."

"Good thing I civilized her," Tony says and grins.

CHAPTER TWENTY-TWO

"THE EVER AFTER"

So, there you have it.

It's five months since the party, we are in Curacao and after making love for the *nth* time, I am ready to pass out, but Jared, although tired, is ready for something more active and strenuous—like a stroll on the beach. As I lie on my back, arm stretched above my head, Jared slides down to kiss my stomach and my navel.

"See you in nine months."

"Ha! You think so, do you?"

He looked up at me with a wolfish grin.

"Oh yes."

Smug bastard. He must've known something because it doesn't take long before I am sick as a dog. A big dog.

And I am carrying twins.

At least I don't have the need to purchase a certain feminine product promoted by a certain bitch for the next several months. The engagement ring Jared gave me is a sizeable amethyst surrounded by diamonds.

"The eyes of Jared are upon you," Talley sang when she saw it.

"Exactly," he said. "There's no way I'm letting her out of my sight again."

It not like I have anything to do apart from preparing for the arrival of the twins.

The photos I took of Hollister cavorting with Gator and the Girls came out better than I ever imagined, so I have decided to develop my hidden talents as a photographer. I'm starting by making a scrapbook for the kids with captions like: Where Mommy and Daddy first met, Daddy at work, and Where Mommy used to work."

Before classes started in the autumn, I wasn't surprised when I was called up before Dean J. Paul Mathis and other senior faculty to discuss the situation concerning Neil Hollister's grades.

Was I aware that this would mean the Chancellor's nephew would finish considerably lower in his class than expected?

Yes, I was aware, but there was no need for concern. I had made an error in my calculations and felt it important for the correction to be made. It was my responsibility to uphold academic integrity and the student's responsibility to make the effort. Neil Hollister did not make the effort until it was too late. Also, I resented the implication that his class ranking was my fault or a reflection of my teaching ability. If they wanted to dilute that honesty and keep the incorrect grade, that was their choice.

This was not the response the forces at Bellingham College expected. They were hoping I would beg for mercy and forgiveness, but they were not in a position to argue. After paying a huge out-of-court settlement to the pregnant student and Terrence Hyde, if news got out that they were giving grief to Hyde's "protégé," they would never get the whole sorry affair behind them. They offered me tenure. I declined.

People may criticize me for walking away from a career in education, especially when being offered permanent employment and a freedom of expression not afforded in other careers. To those people I say: yeah, whatever. My life, my choice.

I have cheerfully given up concern about what people assume to be "me" and have started being true to myself. Fortunately for me, I have friends—and family—who support me and, with Jared's help, I am expressing myself in an artistic manner.

"You have a good eye, sugar," he said one day as I hung up my prints in the darkroom he built for me out in the backyard.

I'm enjoying witnessing how Jared and Trey take *Messalina* to another level. Production and promotion for the series is now being handled by Howling Moon, leaving Jared with more time to create. He's also been a panelist at comic book conventions and when he does a gallery show, he includes some never-before-seen artwork from both comics.

I usually go on these tours or conventions with him, and no longer feel uncomfortable when people look at me after he proclaims my involvement with his work. In fact, some of the loose-flowing dresses I've found in various Goth shops that Piper recommended make excellent maternity wear and the evidence of my fertility has won many admiring, sometimes longing, glances.

Yes, I'm feeling much more at ease in my skin these days.

The old Evadne Cavell is dead.

Long live Messalina.

ABOUT THE AUTHOR

Zetta Brown wrote her first novel at the age of 10. She is the author of several short stories and a regional first-place winner for The National Society of Arts & Letters (NSAL) Award for Short Fiction in 1998. Her work has been published in literary journals produced by Tarrant County College in Hurst, Texas, Mary Hardin-Baylor University and Southern Methodist University. In 1999 and 2000, her stories were adapted for performance in *Letters Live!* at the Craft of Writing conference in Denton, Texas. Currently, Zetta lives in Scotland with her husband, author and publisher Jim Brown. She is currently working on her next novel, "Malice."

Visit her website at www.zettabrown.com

MESSALINA – THE SOUNDTRACK

I'm inspired by music. I think it was Brian Wilson of The Beach Boys who once said, "Music is the soundtrack of life." I couldn't agree more.

As I wrote this story, certain songs seemed to fit the mood I was trying to create within a chapter leading me to create the "soundtrack" of Eva and Jared's life.

I've listed the songs and the artist for each chapter. Some chapters were inspired by more than one song. If you want to get an idea of my taste in music and perhaps a deeper understanding of Eva and Jared, I encourage you to find and listen to a recording of the following tracks *:

	Chapter	Song	Artist
1	Dark Places	*"Y Viva Suspenders"* *"Breaking Down"*	Judge Dredd Randy Crawford
2	TGI Thursday	*"Fever"*	Peggy Lee
3	The First Date	*"I Touch Myself"*	The Divynls
4	Flight	*"Please Don't Go"*	K.C. & The Sunshine Band
5	Climax	*"In the Warm Room"*	Kate Bush
6	The Next Day	*"Brass in Pocket"*	The Pretenders
7	Wild Night	*"Wild Night"*	Van Morrison
8	Dish	*"Everybody Plays the Fool"*	The Main Ingredient
9	Aftermath	*"Say It's Not Too Late"*	Matt Bianco
10	Meant to Be	*"Meant to Be"*	Squirrel Nut Zippers
11	A Family Affair	*"Family Affair"*	Sly and the Family Stone
12	Driving Me Mad	*"Driving Me Mad"* [1]	The Hotknives
13	Love Bizarre	*"Love Bizarre"*	Shelia E
14	Bitch Goddess from Hell	*"More"*	Sisters of Mercy
15	The Life of Lucrezia	*"Back to the Underground"* [2]	Agent 99
16	Truth and Consequences	*"Tempted"*	Squeeze
17	Our Story So Far	*"The Bitterest Pill"*	The Jam
18	Messalina	*"Body and Soul"*	Sisters of Mercy
19	A Woman Scorned	*"I Want You"*	Elvis Costello
20	Devourer of Men	*"Jane Bondage"* [3]	Skapa
21	Par-Tay	*"Why Should I Love You"*	Kate Bush
22	The Ever After	*"The Real End"* *"Coffee & Cream"* [4]	Rickie Lee Jones Idle Hands Collective

And here are a few extras that helped to keep me motivated:

"Samson & Delilah" – Bad Manners
"Right Side of a Good Thing" – The Fleshtones
"Right Here" – The Go-Betweens
"Temple of Love '92" – Sisters of Mercy
"The Sensual World" – Kate Bush
"Baby, You're Mine" – Basia

* Some of the groups listed above have disbanded and the only way you'll find these songs may be off of a compilation. I've included the names of the CDs where I got the songs here, but even these discs may be hard to find. These can (usually) be found on Amazon.com except where noted. Good luck!

1   *Ska Heroes* (Amazon UK)
2   *Ska Down Her Way* (Vol. 1)
3   *Skank Down Under*
4   *Moonshot! A Moon Ska Records Compendium*

Future Perfect
A Collection of Fantastic Erotica
By Helen E. H. Madden

What if you made love to a woman at the end of the universe, only to discover she was devastating black hole? What if the archangel Gabriel fell in love with the Virgin Mary and never delivered the Annunciation? What if a female dominant saw the future . . . every time she had an orgasm? For years, speculative fiction has asked the question "What if . . .?" Now the tales of *Future Perfect* go one step beyond and speculate on the possibilities of the erotic.

From the distant future to a biblical past and everything in between, *Future Perfect* examines the role of sex in a fantastic world. The stories range from hard science fiction to urban fantasy, but through it all runs a thread of explicit sexuality that embraces a wide range of orientations and relationships. Whether presented as the force of cosmic creation or the deceitful lure of Satan, *Future Perfect* takes sex beyond the limits of the everyday to show it as the impetus for change on a universal scale.

So open the cover and leave the mundane behind. A world of "What if . . ." is waiting for you.

Future Perfect – A Collection of Fantastic Erotica is available worldwide in paperback and digital (ebook) formats, direct from www.logical-lust.com, or from Amazon, Barnes & Noble, and all good retailers!

Bittersweet

Stories of tainted desire
by Amber Hipple

Not all sex is romance or fun. Sometimes there's desperation. Explore the deeper, darker aspects of love and want in "Bittersweet", Amber Hipple's intensely emotive debut collection of tainted erotica. Be moved by the cycle of wanting to be wanted and the pain of wanting too much. "Bittersweet" is a lesson in reality; it's what love and desire can be. Expect no "happy ever after" in these stories, but expect to be left wanting more.

Jim Brown, owner of Logical-Lust, says; *"Amber Hipple has come up with something quite out of the ordinary in 'Bittersweet'. Gone is the sugary-sweet romanticism and the happy-ever-after, to be replaced by the profound emotions and outpourings that are real in love and sex. You'll find your heart being wrenched apart by the yearnings and the despair of the characters, yet still be stirred and aroused by the sheer passion in the erotica she produces."*

BITTERSWEET by Amber Hipple, is released in both digital (ebook) and print formats, and will be available worldwide through **www.logical-lust.com**, Amazon, Barnes and Noble, and all good online retailers.

Crimson Succubus: The Demon Chronicles

By Carmine

"A few years back, I began receiving emailed submissions to the erotic literary ezine *Sauce*Box* from a writer known to me only as '*Carmine*'. These submissions were short pieces ('flash-fiction', if you will) detailing yet another 'Tale of the Crimson Succubus'. Each was a stand-alone jewel, horrible, cruel, fantastically, outrageously, graphically sexual, but also somehow (dare I say it . . . forgive me, Carmine) charming. I liked them very much and published every one that was sent.

"Now I find that some these short tales along with longer pieces concerning the 'adventures' of the Crimson Succubus, and a third section concerning a mythical nymph Mytoessa who also becomes involved with the succubus have been collected together in one place—a delightfully, tastefully disgusting book, **Tales of the Crimson Succubus, The Demon Chronicles** by Carmine.

"This person, Carmine, is one sick puppy, but one with adorable eyes and floppy ears. The tales involve much blood- and semen-letting, murder, torture, deception and pain, but at the same time, I often want to laugh and wish that the creatures would appear for real, in front of me, so that I could see with my own eyes and even touch (very, very carefully, mind you) these monsters formed from the primordial slime of all of our great cultural myths.

"And of course, like all myths, these tales speak to our deepest fears, and hopes and fantasies . . . perhaps to archetypes from times before even the written word, times long forgotten in consciousness but remembered in the collective genetic code. I don't know. Whatever. They're a great read, an exciting read and one that will tickle your nightmares and daydreams long after you've put this book down."

Guillermo Bosch, Editor: *Sauce*Box*, Ezine of Literary Erotica
Author of **Rain** and **The Passion of Muhammad Shakir**

Swing!

Adventures in Swinging by Today's Top Erotica Writers

Edited by Jolie du Pré

SWING! is a stunning anthology of swinging adventure stories from some of the world's top erotica writers, compiled and edited by Jolie Du Pré.

Being edited by Jolie Du Pré, you can expect some hot, sizzling sex stories, both well written and highly creative. We don't pull any punches when we say we expect **SWING!** to be one of *the* top erotica releases of 2009!

ABOUT THE EDITOR

Jolie Du Pré is an author of erotica and erotic romance. Her stories have appeared on numerous Web sites, in e-books and in print. Jolie is also the editor of **Iridescence: Sensuous Shades of Lesbian Erotica**, published by Alyson Books, and is the founder of GLBT Promo, a promotional group for GLBT erotica and erotic romance.

SWING! is published in paperback and digital (ebook) formats. Get your copy direct from www.logical-lust.com, or from Amazon and other worldwide online retailers!

Breinigsville, PA USA
26 November 2009
228156BV00002B/123/P